THE VIEW NORTH FROM
LIBERAL CEMETERY

JOEL WAPNICK

WAPITI PRESS

ISBN-13: 978-0-9938662-0-3

For Varley O'Connor

Heading the gruesome-ways-to-die list is decapitation. Next comes burning, concomitant with the value-added agony of asphyxiation from dense black smoke. A dozen years ago a woman, the seat she was strapped in, and a nearby chunk of fuselage were propelled through clouds, courtesy of a spot of Semtex. That ranks third in my book. In fourth place must be drawing and quartering. Drowning effected by gaping ragged shark gashes, heart-piercing half-foot stainless steel bolts fired from crossbows, crumbling bones rattling in resonance to the frequency of excruciation provided by billions of cancer cells—I could fill a dozen pages with such gems, but surely no gateway to the Great Unknown horrifies like dying in one's sleep.

My contention has nothing to do with misplaced machismo. The notion of facing one's own death like a man, of striving toward alertness with just seconds remaining before being voided into eternity, holds no appeal. I prefer it because the alternative is worse. Most people consider sleep-death the only good death. From the outside it's the gentle path, the painless option. Drug some poor clod into obliviousness and watch him sleep, still as a bedpost save for the slow rise and fall of his chest. He's going to die before the next sunrise, but from the outside he looks peaceful, goddamn it. That's worth something, right?

Wrong. When the current in a man's brain goes limp he loses the possibility of escape. He cannot wake. Time distorts, as if funneled into a black hole. The passage of hours as measured by bedside death-watch family and friends equates to an infinity distended to the exactest calculation of pi for the victim.

Charming. So this is how I get a leg up on my New Year's Resolution, by scribbling out irrelevant bullshit? Focus, Carl. Hone in on the problem. Nail this:

I will determine how to spend my remaining time.

The proposition is quest rather than goal. It prepares for change, and differs from run-of-the-mill resolutions because *why?* is at its core. Consider the following statement:

I will go on a diet.

How ill-suited it is for withstanding temptation. Even a more goal-oriented variant such as *I will drop twenty pounds in the new year* fails, because denial works well in the abstract but not when Spaghetti Bolognese tops the menu. To resist the meatballs, one must place the *why?* front and center. Easy, nothing to it really. Temptation doesn't tempt me in the slightest, as long as I can keep my personal Prime Axiom at bay:

Life amounts to nothing.

Fuck. Why can't I sleep?

7:17 P.M. Tuesday, January 1st

Ah, the joys of winter life in Montreal. It is blizzarding once again. They forecast the storm two days ago, and from the way the Manoir

Westmount mother hens have been clucking since, you'd think the apocalypse was at hand. Blame the Weather Station: "A winter storm warning is in effect. Expect heavy snow, high winds, whiteouts, and severe drifting. Stay home; you can go bowling some other day." I shouldn't complain, because the hens ask fewer questions in bad weather. The Nosiness Index declines a little. Not that the men are any better, just that there are fewer of them.

It had already started snowing when I headed out after lunch for my afternoon walk. The Incredible Hunk, a.k.a. Ralph Hendrickson, blocked my way. He's the only burly geezer in the place, the Manoir's Henry VIII complete with mop toupee crown. Unfortunately, his bulk does not compensate for deficiencies in other realms.

"You going out in that mess?"

"Hmm. Let's see." Quick double-check: "Boots, coat, scarf, gloves, tuque, not to mention boxers, socks, pants, shirt, and sweater. It would seem that I am."

"Where to?"

"Mount Tremblant. Hank's going to pick me up. He's got a Harley, and the plan calls for me to wait in front of the Y." I pointed my cane in the general direction. Don't need the thing, just carry it around for style points. "The weather looks promising for some great downhill, eh?"

Ralph looked puzzled, so I added, "You know Hank? He's Hell's Angels, Westmount branch. Got me into this joint. Don't worry, he handles his bike fine."

I smiled, thought Ralph got it when he smiled back. No such luck: "Yeah, well, give him my best."

"Sure thing. Oh and by the way, you might want to tape an arrow to the underside of your toupee."

"What for?"

"You wore it backwards twice, at lunch yesterday and also on Saturday morning while you were waiting by the door for the family. Or you had it on right those times but wrong every other time I've had occasion to observe."

"Really?"

"Yup. Do it. That way you'll know whether you're coming or going. The women around here, they appreciate men who know forward from reverse. That's their main requirement, in fact. So tape it in, but remember to go private before checking out the arrow."

"Okay."

Amazing, no umbrage taken. What a shlemiel. He would have been surprised to see me at dinner had he been able to recall our conversation.

Now that I'm a resident, I'm supposed to putter. *Everyone* in this place putters. They're busy bees buzzing about in slow motion. Not me. I almost flunked my admissions interview because I didn't convince the committee I would be good at puttering. Truth be told, they had reason for concern. Within three days of moving in I had initiated my custom of spending afternoons sitting outside alone, often without props of book or cell. I took a liking to a particular bench on the Manoir grass, despite its existential resemblance to the residents—wobbles a bit and needs a paint job. I'll spend time on it even in winter, provided the temperature doesn't plunge to double digits on the minus side of the Celsius scale. The residents favor the big terrace behind the Manoir, and then only in warm weather. Pathetic. Scant sunlight shines back there, and the view encompasses little more than a greenhouse's rump and two squat houses. I prefer watching people stroll by out front, and I enjoy the big oaks, maples, and blue spruces, even though they partly block my view.

At 2:45 P.M. on the afternoon of Wednesday, last September 24th, Madame Olive Forget interrupted one of my reveries. I had been taking in the breeze, sunshine, and local color per my usual unsmiling manner. An observer might have deduced that I was doing nothing. *Doing nothing.* I like that phrase. It's an oxymoron, akin to *being dead.*

"Yoo-hoo!" Madame Forget waddled over and sat down next to me. She wore a dark gray skirted suit, ironed to a crisp. A silver schnauzer pin adorned her left lapel, and the usual pearl necklace encircled her neck. Her white hair was done up short and tight, nary a strand hanging loose. I, on the other hand, was attired in frayed black shorts, worn out tennis shoes, and a ratty "Fighting Terrorism Since 1492" t-shirt. A faded black-and-white photo of nine unsmiling old-time Indians brandishing rifles was centered above the aforementioned inscription.

Madame Forget is ten years younger than me, lives in the Manoir, and is an assistant to the manager. Her semi-official self-appointed title is Social Director, which means that she serves as empathic busybody for the diminished. She talks slowly and loudly, uses a circumscribed vocabulary, and employs a despicable pet phrase: "Do you understand?" Most residents walk the other way when she enters a room, but a few flock to her like children gathering around their kindergarten teacher in anticipation of story time.

"Hello, Dr. Anderson! How are you today?" Spoken at a tempo one click above a snail's pace, with an emphasis on the *are.*

"Fine, thank you."

"That's *good.* Enjoying the beautiful weather?"

"Actually I'm contemplating whether the inevitability of death renders life meaningful or meaningless. There are good arguments on both sides."

Her smile dimmed. "You could spend a lot of time with that one."

"As a matter of fact, I've been thinking of starting up a thanatos appreciation workshop. Some of our residents need cheering up, and such an activity might be just the ticket."

"Thanatos?"

"Death. You know, that thing that bites us all at the end. What do you think?"

"Hmm. May I be frank?"

"Frank? As in telling me exactly what you think of my idea? Why not?"

"It's not your idea that's problematic, Doctor Anderson, it's you. For your own good, you should be made aware of the effect you're having on the other residents."

"Effect? I'm having an effect on people? Not that I care, but please do fill me in."

"'Not that I care.' That's precisely your problem. You spend afternoons sitting out here by yourself, and when we do have the honor of encountering you in the elevator, a hallway, or at meals, nine times out of ten your facial expression says 'get lost.' Choose to be a hermit and a misanthrope if you like, but don't be surprised if the others regard you as aloof, arrogant, and a pain in the ass."

"It's that bad, is it? I've managed to alienate everyone in the joint, and in record time, no less?"

"Close to everyone. I'm the one exception. I like you, which is why I've taken the time to stop by."

What luck.

"You know, you really don't need to act that way. If you were to make even the slightest of overtures, you could change everything."

"The slightest of overtures, eh? Pray tell, exactly how might I effect such a transformation?"

"Smile every now and then. If you encounter someone in the hallway, say 'Good afternoon' and wish him or her a fine day instead of blanking out like some adolescent kid afflicted with Asperger syndrome. It's easy! Just be a little bit social, for goodness sake. You might even enjoy taking part in some of our group activities. And please, never inject death into the conversation. We don't want to hear about it, nor about illness or anything else upsetting."

Before I could respond, the "Russian Sabre Dance" exploded from within Madame Forget's handbag. The timing was perfect enough to have been preplanned, though I'm probably being a bit paranoid here.

"Excuse me." She walked a few feet up the lawn, extracted her phone, and spoke the following:

"Oh the sweet dear, but really, he should have waited until I came back... Yes, I'll be right there, don't worry about a thing, okay?" She turned toward me, waved goodbye, and walked toward the Manoir entrance with phone still glued flush to her right ear.

I envy those wizened guys in old westerns. They spent their golden years dozing off in front-porch rockers, their only multitask comprised of sleeping, chewing on blades of grass, swigging whiskey, burping, and pondering the universe. How satisfying it must have been to polish off one's life so cleanly. But here at the great big Manoir on the ground, we keep busy. Prevailing theory holds that busyness is therapeutic. Without busyness filling up time, we would wind down like depleted Duracell Energizer bunnies. Keep moving, don't stop. And so, heeding advice from those who follow rather than precede us, we nurse our insomnias and move along with the sunrise to survive yet one more day. We march off to medical and dental appointments, take group shopping expeditions, help out charities, sit around yakking, interfere in our children's lives, attend Manoir committee meetings, and divert ourselves with cards, Scrabble, pool, cribbage, mahjongg, Monopoly, and that summertime pastime named after us, shuffleboard (shuffle/bored). We're vibrant or avoidant, take your pick.

Students from high schools, CEGEPs, and universities perform concerts and plays on the premises. Sometimes they keep us company for the hell of it, other times for our supposed betterment. A thin sandy-haired girl stops by twice a week to administer what she calls music therapy. She's in training, and we serve as her guinea pigs. I term this practice reverse-engineered volunteerism. Heh. She sings and plays her guitar at the same time, and oh does the music creak. Watching her belt out French Canadian pop songs from the '50s, Sinatra, some Beatles for the youngsters depresses the hell out of me. How is it possible to pack so much phony enthusiasm into one slight body? I last spoke with her nineteen days and five hours ago, asked her to tell me why she sings such crap. Her response: to help *les vieilles* dredge up memories and awaken long dormant feelings, thereby making the present more meaningful through evocation of "the reality of the past," as she so stylishly phrased it. *Les vieilles*, eh? I replied that such logic demanded she bring in her boyfriend for a demonstration fuck. She smiled like she had a tic up her ass, told me she didn't have a boyfriend, and left the room.

True enough: I capitulated to my children and now reside at the Manoir. The move took place some time ago, back on September 2nd to be precise. Helen and Michael didn't have to argue strenuously in the end, because I don't give a damn where I live. Nothing compels me to live in a big house, and nothing forces me to remain here either. I have a condition of emotional imbalance, an infirmity of affect. I cope with it in a manner analogous to coaxing reluctant catsup out of a bottle—by squeezing it gently on a sideways angle rather than by enlisting some member from one of the helping professions to stand me on my head while he smacks the soles of my feet. Viewed philosophically, think of it as an acceptance of fate in small doses.

They ganged up on me one week after my dog died. He expired on Sunday, April 22nd, in the middle of his afternoon walk. We had been enjoying an ideal stroll on a perfect day. He—Herman by name, a French bulldog—he had been in a prolific mood, having marked the bases of two trees and a bush. To top it off, he plopped his sole defecation onto underbrush deep in the woods, so far off the beaten path that I did not have to bend down and clean it up. Yes a perfect walk it was, right up to but not including its denouement.

We spent Herman's last three minutes still, me standing unsuspectingly on the sidewalk bordering the east side of Cedar Crescent, he sitting with his tongue hanging out on a strip of grass belonging to the St. Joseph Oratory. Under a clear sky and warm sun we listened to "Le Coucou," as rendered on the Oratory's big carillon bells. The performance lumbered on and on, inharmonic as vinegar, as if the evoked cuckoo bird was a limping grimacing colossus striding the earth. Herman looked up at me with the sweetest of French bulldog smiles. But then he coughed twice, lay on his side, and died. Just like that.

What a companion. He was the best of listeners, always hung in no matter what I ranted about. He would lie next to me on the couch and I'd scratch him behind the ears, or he'd mount a mini ottoman across from me, an overstuffed thing that at one time was yellow. When I ran out of words we would gaze into each other's scrunched up faces. I got the better of the deal. Regarding looks, I am nothing much. But he was the noblest, the handsomest, the most magnificent of French bulldogs. Find me a beautiful woman with a French bulldog's personality and QED, I accept the existence of God. Find me a woman who both looks like a bulldog and has a bulldog's personality and QED, I accept the existence of Satan.

Upon Herman's death, the population of creatures bigger than bugs inhabiting my house was finally, permanently, whittled down to one. In the early '80s it had been six: my wife Renata, Helen and Michael, Clover and Darius the Great (our pets—a dumb Bengalese cat and a brilliant Chihuahua, respectively), and myself. But Renata died, followed in short order by the two pets. Helen moved out twenty years ago, and when Michael left eight years after I decided to up the old homestead's population to two instead of hanging myself à la *And Then There Were None*. I drove to the Gatineau, chose Herman from a litter of four. Best pal I ever had.

My house was big—two storeys, four bedrooms. Nevertheless, taking care of it entailed little effort. Every other Tuesday Amparo dropped in. She vacuumed, changed the sheets, ran the wash, cleaned up the kitchen and bathrooms, and returned stray items to their proper places. Right after an Amparo visit my house looked downright manicured, like the cemetery lawn on the far side of Côte-des-Neiges Road when the workers aren't striking. And like me, the house was well maintained. The roof had been replaced three years earlier, plumbing and electrical systems were solid. Summer of 2002 I had the whole thing painted, inside and out. It still looked good on the morning of my departure five years later. Getting around wasn't a problem. I move well, don't really need the cane, so the stairs were no obstacle. I'd dial up food from National once a week, cook when the spirit moved me. Why seek a solution when there's no problem?

Nevertheless, my children harangued the hell out of me. They claimed I would fare better in an apartment, or even in a seniors residence. I asked them why they thought I would be happier coexisting with a hundred querulous and broken down old people. "I'm free," I told them. "I can close the blinds, get naked, and scream my head off. Why should I surrender the option?"

Helen asserted that being with others "like you," as she put it, would stimulate me: "You would flourish." What am I, a fucking flower? Michael chimed in with the health factor: "Aloneness is a risk factor for elders." He claimed that if I were to stay put in my house like a stone in a rock garden, I'd end up as crazy as Howard Hughes or Norma Desmond.

Bullshit. Did they think me so clueless that I wouldn't see through to their self-interestedness? Let someone else take care of dear old Dad, just install him in a place where he won't fritter away our inheritance. And as for the perils of isolation, more bullshit. One man's isolation is another's solitude. Helen persisted, bless her snap-shut lawyerly mind. She put me on a couple of waiting lists. "No big deal," she said. "It's good to have the option, because you might feel differently about it later."

I'm grumbling over spilt milk, and without consequence. I've moved, and that's that. Besides, I've come around a little. Contemplation of the aftertax dollars netted from the sale of my house, succinctly expressed by a four with five zeroes trailing after it, warms me better than a cup of cocoa. Plus I appreciate living next to the library. I can escape to it whenever I want, and without having to breathe in frigid air. I wouldn't mind being buried in the vicinity, say in twenty years or so. Just dig a hole near one of the pines opposite the entrance to this place, dress me up pretty, dump me on my back, and close the lid tight. All I ask is to be allowed escape every now and then. Yes, if on occasion I might slip my skull and flit through the coffin's side entrance....

My *joie de vivre* would take the form of a non-corporeal see-through baby blue butterfly, immortal and well nigh invisible. Let me flutter through steel-gray pipes connecting my coffin to subterranean corridors snaking underneath the Manoir, Victoria Hall, and the greenhouse. My destination lies just beyond: Westmount Library. Up from the basement I float, up again to the main floor's hallway, where I execute a few laps up and down its length before entering the Findlay Room. That's the big one left of the circulation desk. I admire its high yellow slatted ceiling and those windows with the best of names burnt into them—Locke, Galileo, Gutenberg, Virgil, Shakespeare, Socrates, Gainsborough. I absorb light glowing from the brass lamps, their bulbs shielded by glassy green shades, and I feel pleasure as I take in the big oak chairs and their plush green coverings.

I scout the room, then alight on the woman of my choice. From my vantage point atop one of her shoulders, I read along. We learn about gardening techniques, terrorism warnings, evidences of global warming, relationships, whatever. Or perhaps I curl up on a pretty girl's navy blue cardigan and browse some young-adult novel with her. Then again, maybe I choose not to read at all, just to watch as she tackles her trigonometry homework.

Through giveaways and throwaways, I've reduced my earthly possessions to a manageable magnitude. I've sprinkled them throughout this vast three-hundred-square-foot estate I now call home. Some residents try shoehorning housefuls into their rooms, but the cluttered look does not suit me. I'm going out simple. Desk overlooking Sherbrooke Street, flush against the far wall. Bed tucked in the near right corner, an ensemble of soft beige reading chair, small table, and reading lamp twelve feet to its left. Underlying everything, my prized possession—an ornate green, blue, and white Kashmiri rug made of silk. A couple of Japanese prints hang on the bedside wall, a foot past and three above my nocturnal toes. One depicts a sad woman in a boat, the other a warrior mounted on his steed. Both characters are bathed in moonlight. Other than a filing cabinet, various photographic, literary, and sonic memorabilia, and a few small electronic devices, that's it. My books wouldn't have come close to fitting, so I donated them to the library. I was promised that the esoteric ones, those related mainly to my professorial work, would be catalogued and added to the shelves, as would anything else "worthwhile," as the girl at the desk put it—worthwhile but not yet owned by the library. They plan to recycle my chick-lit collection.

I will avoid a second downsizing and skip straight to the final one should I pass out of this world in the same manner as did Herman. But if I slowly waste away, my increasing dysfunctionality will require another move. The totality of my earthly possessions will become circumscribed by the lengths, widths, and depths of a couple of dresser drawers. A consolation: such a way station prepares one for the Final Downsize. Alas, an irrational belief, given that the dead do not suffer claustrophobia. Humans have a tough time imagining nothingness, however, which explains why cremation has yet to go out of style. Given even the remotest possibility of waking at a time after one has been lowered six feet under the ground—of finding one's forehead flush against the casket's dome and one's arms and legs constricted by its sides—why not avoid the problem completely? Exit quick and easy. Burn to a crisp in a jiff. No fuss, no muss, no concerns about being closed in, crushed, worms crawling up your nose and out your ass.

It's 8:42, too early to go to bed. I often take an after-dinner walk, but tonight they'd find my corpse frozen stiff under some drift. I would not be remembered as the Captain Robert F. Scott of Westmount. More likely, the *Examiner* would print a small write-up on page nine: "Stupid Old Fart Freezes to Death." I can be sensitive about my dignity, so discretion trumps valor for now.

Is there anything as satisfying as watching a snowstorm from the comfort of an upholstered chair in an abundantly heated room? The snow descends flatwise, and the traffic light lording over Sherbrooke and Arlington stiffens hard against bracings, its faded green, yellow, and red beams no match for the wind-whipped whiteness enveloping it.

4:30 P.M. Thursday, January 3rd

An idea for a scholarly paper materialized unbidden this morning, which, mildly putting it, is a rarity these days. Though my academic career spanned almost forty-five years, the nineteen months intervening since its termination have made that world distant, as if it concluded shortly after it began. Sometimes I feel as though it never existed.

Despite giving up the academic ghost a full sixteen years beyond what McGill regards as the normal retirement age, when the time came I was more than ready. I had seen too many of my emeritus colleagues, most younger than me, wandering through halls like zombies searching for ideas to munch on, ideas that fluttered just beyond their grasps. Better to go out intact and on top. Once committed, I never looked back. I acted like Caesar crossing the

Rubicon, minus half the bravado. I actually uttered his *Alea iacta est* in response to the toast proposed by my dean at the Great Retirement Reception of 2006. Everyone cheered, despite not knowing what the fuck *Alea iacta est* meant.

Four of us bit the dust that day, surrounded by a jolly fellowship of colleagues, administrators, support staff, and friends. Consistent with recent tradition and designed to both limit expenses and inconvenience as few people as possible, the event was held immediately after the last Faculty Council of the year. We feasted on cheese, grapes, strawberries, and miniature pastries, drank grocery-store wine from plastic cups, and were gifted with nifty crystal paperweights and coffee-table books about McGill. Whoopee.

Academia requires competition between young and old, both people and ideas. Every retirement signifies capitulation and opportunity, and *renewal* will forever remain a stylish academic buzzword. When I was a young turk, I secretly loathed the phalanx of eldest professors puttering about the Faculty. I considered them lazy snoozers who earned a tenth of their keep, and I vowed never to become one of them. I would remain the Peter Pan of the Faculty of Religious Studies. In academia, however, you don't have to stop publishing to find yourself irrelevant. Keep churning out your research and before you know it, boom, you're a relic anyway—out of touch with younger scholars, department chairmen, deans, university publicity mills, and central administrators who rake in three times your salary because they are nine times savvier than you when it comes to determining strategic academic priorities. *Strategic*—now there's a bullshit word for the ages. The verbiage filling up all those official blue papers and white papers and green papers boils down to who gets the money and who doesn't.

Here's my advice for you up-and-comers: pick a hot topic like the brain or the environment, involve professors beyond the borders of your country, work at the intersection of your discipline and someone else's, and make friends with colleagues serving on granting agencies. Be a cross-everything scholar. Show how the Old Testament influenced organizational underpinnings of the United States Golf Association's *Rules of Golf.* Demonstrate the similarities between decision-making processes on TV reality shows like *Big Brother* and *American Idol* and those exercised by biblical luminaries such as Solomon, David, and God. You'll be set for life, or until someone discovers that the emperor once again needs a change of wardrobe.

I could stretch my morning's idea into an essay. Unlike my published research, however, I'd be plucking it out of my backside rather than rummaging through libraries and archives all over Europe and the Middle East. My genius back then was not so much in digging up source materials as in making connections between different versions of sacred texts, then tracing them backward to a smaller number of streams. At conferences I wowed audiences by reciting from memory extended parallel passages in Greek, Hebrew, and Aramaic. Look Ma, no hands. Moreover, I was as meticulous as they come. I illustrated my presentations with timelines, color maps of the Holy Land, graphs, charts, and even animations in my later years. I combined the mystical with the precise, substance with form. Created quite the stir, but that was then, no longer now.

My paper's title would be "Divine Authority as Reflected in Star Trek's Principle of the Prime Directive." The Prime Directive consists of the following: when encountering an alien civilization, do not mess with its technological development. Don't give those aliens fancy weapons. In fact, don't provide them with anything of a technological nature, not even a dildo. Adulterating their culture and fucking their women, assuming creatures resembling women roam their planet, sure, go right ahead. Everything else is verboten.

My essay would link the Prime Directive to conceptions of divine intervention. Back in Old Testament days, God was a fearsome meddler. Biblical grandfathers and grandmothers, fathers and mothers, sons and daughters all experienced interruptions from above on a regular basis. These days, however, the faithful hang around for decades waiting for the Messiah to return. Give those folks a nice round number or a numerologically derived date from scribblings in obscure apocrypha and they're good to go. They anticipate for naught, however, because a policy change regarding divine intervention has been in effect for the last several thousand years. Our present-day God is a bashful god. He has become circumspect, his miracles impossible to come by. I'm talking unmistakable larger-than-life Cecil B. DeMille miracles, not made up fake ones like cripples discarding their crutches, or the discovery of multiple undershirts around the world blotched with stains depicting the Virgin Mary gazing heavenward. Think parting of the Red Sea, Jesus gliding on water barefoot and without a motorboat, fiery talking bushes, angels swooping down from heaven to halt filicides in the nick of time—real miracles, nowadays rarer than hen's teeth.

I'm not going to write that paper—too much work, too small an audience, far too little compulsion. But if I did, I'd pretty it up to look more like science than speculation. I'd graph it all out: miracles per hundred years measured on the ordinate, chronology from biblical times to the present running rightward along the abscissa. I'd derive a formula, a mathematical measure of best fit, to describe the downward curving line. McGill public relations would have a field day. They'd sic a *Gazette* reporter on me, and the resultant article would include a sidebar predicting the exact moment of the next miracle, as determined from my abracadabra calculations. I could be famous again if I were willing to make an ass of myself.

10:46 A.M. Saturday, January 5th
I write from the Starbucks near the corner of Sherbrooke and Claremont, a twenty-minute walk from the Manoir. I've become a recent regular, and in accordance with my status I make sure to dress up a little. Heaven

prevent me from being mistaken for one of the homeless-guy regulars.

I got lucky, and am occupying one of the two window tables. After shoving a half-crumpled *Gazette* to the side, I placed an extra-hot skimmed milk cappuccino and a life-extending non-trans-fat cranberry-orange muffin on the table. The muffin required imagination, as it neither tasted nor smelled of cranberry or orange. Between bites one and two I glanced at the newspaper, which was lit up white-yellow in the winter sunlight and open to the obituaries page.

As a rule, I make it a rule to avoid reading obituaries. They are monotonous and repetitive. Well worn phrases cycle through them: *passed away peacefully, courageous* (or *valiant*) *struggle* (or *battle*), *sadly missed, with dignity* (or *with courage*; or *with dignity and courage*), *leaves to mourn*. My interest was piqued only after I spotted two abasements of the English language:

(1) She was an avid bingo player, a recreational tennis player, and a talented knitter. They won't be the same without her.

(2) But in a short four years, Gilbert was struck with Alzheimer's disease.

Comedy is hard, dying is harder. Decent writing? Impossible.

On the obituaries page, every entry begins the same way: somebody died. Not one item varies from this formula. We do not learn how Millicent Carambola almost kicked off from a bout of pneumonia but is now recovering nicely at the General. Nor do we read about some guy expiring and then springing back to life, like that newspaper boss in *The Shipping News*.

Every morning, legions of devoted obituary readers spook breakfast tables and coffee shops throughout Montreal. These death readers, to call them by their proper name, look for ages and causes. How exactly did Jack Schmertzberg die, and was it at an age advanced enough to have gotten good value? They know the code words: *Suddenly* signifies death by heart attack. *Suddenly at home* means exactly that, whereas stand-alone *suddenly* connotes something else—the guy checked out while fucking, drinking, running, or yelling at someone. The *after a long and brave struggle* ploy is euphemism for death by cancer. A necessary fiction, I suppose. No friend or family member wants to read something like, "After a painful and futile-from-the-get-go struggle, Mabel Hawley succumbed and is now dead." As for those unapproved and out-and-out revolting ways of dying—messy suicides, asphyxiations during sex, accidental shootings, farm machinery mishaps—they are never recounted, not even on slow news days.

The probability of stumbling across a feel-good story among the obits is as low as returning to my room to find a black-haired nymphet bearing a likeness to Goya's "Maja" reclining nude on my bed. Nevertheless, I took the plunge. Who knows why. Maybe I was feeling a little too chipper and needed to balance. Mind-numbing predictability notwithstanding, the experience was similar to eating potato chips: I could not stop myself. But then I came across the next-to-last entry, never made it to the last one:

Villeneuve, Marcie (nee Smith). March 17, 1927—January 3, 2008. Beloved wife of the late Guillaume Villeneuve. She will be sadly missed by her six children and nineteen grandchildren, as well as by her brother James, nephews, nieces, and friends. Condolences to be received at Notre-Dame-de-Grace Church, 5333 Notre-Dame-de-Grace Ave., on Monday January 7, from 10:30 A.M., followed by the service at 11:30 A.M.

A Marcie Smith, but not *my* Marcie Smith. The birth year is off by two, and the Marcie I knew was an only child.

5:47 A.M. *Sunday, January 6th*

I should have gone to my desk immediately and written it out. Afterward I would have slept long and deep, destined to awaken three hours from now fresh as a daisy and cleansed of nocturnal horror. Instead I toughed it through the wee hours. Stupid stubborn me. I finally threw in the insomnomaniacal towel twenty minutes ago—got out of bed, put on my robe and slippers, exited the room, and tiptoed down to the alcove where they keep the decaffeinated tea bags, silent heating kettle, and fridge. Not that I needed to tiptoe, what with loud coughs emanating from behind a couple of doors along the way.

The Attila the Hun of nightmares paid me a visit three hours and one cup of chamomile ago. It began innocuously enough: Summertime. I'm wet, wearing a bathing suit, stretched out on a long, flat, hard slab of rock eight feet above a swimming hole. Pines, maples, oaks, and beeches surround me. Above, a few birds circle lazily.

The sun dries me off, so I slide into the shade to keep from burning up. I'm aware that I went swimming with my brother, but I can't remember his name. I peer over the rock's edge and lo and behold, there he floats facedown, his body bobbing a couple of feet offshore. I spot a gash at the peak of the back of his head. A mixture of blood and brain matter, diffuse gray stuff, flows from it, creating an expanding oval around its central point.

Now I am with him, up to my knees in crimson water. I drag him to the beach, kneel down and examine his face. My brother's light blue doll's eyes are stuck in the open position. I try closing them by pressing my fingers hard into his sockets. No success. Purple discolorations spread under both eyes, around his nose, and down through his cheeks. I'm scarring his face and I can't stop myself.

Though my brother's lips don't move, I hear a woman's faint

shriek from within his body. It's weak, as if it originated from the bottom of a hundred-foot mine shaft. I turn away and look upward. A young woman—one of the library workers to be precise, noticed her for the first time four days ago—she stands on the rock where I had been just a moment ago. Her hair is long, straight, and reddish-brown, and her light blue eyes and facial features mirror those of my brother. She wears a white gown, embroidered also in white, but because of the lack of color contrast I cannot make out the design.

She looks at me for a few seconds, expressionless. Then she emaciates, morphing from beauty to gauntness. She becomes wrinkled, stooped, her hair a brilliant white, her skin dark and blotchy. She sickens past ghastliness—eyes, nose, mouth, and skin now translucent, inadequately obscuring her skeleton. Finally she fades to lightness until nothing remains.

The good news is that I don't have a brother. I never had a brother.

11:17 P.M. Thursday, January 10th

I assault problems with logic, always have and always will. When the big decisions pend, sober reflection wins out over intuition, hunches, impulsivity, and every other form of irrationality. I don't deny that the impulse to go with one's gut has appeal. Gut-going can be impossible to resist because it's appeal is closer to that of the viscous surface of a caramel macchiato than to the liquid most closely approximating the purity of logic, water. Nevertheless, anyone who permits his life to be led by his emotions is an idiot.

I purchased a pad of legal-size paper from the stationers stationed at Westmount Stationery this morning. As soon as I returned to my room I placed the pad on my desk and wrote, at the top of its topmost page and in bright green ink:

Options for the Remainder

From the central point in the heading, halfway between the *for* and the *the*, I ruled three lines downward. They radiated left, center, and right, and I labeled their terminations Hedonism, Volunteerism, and Exploration, respectively. Selfishness, selflessness, and cluelessness, the entire universe of possibilities accounted for by three words.

Under Hedonism I scribbled: Bahamas, filet mignon, gambling, massage, red wine, women, and dark chocolate. An appealing list, though some of its items are expensive, life-shortening, and occasionally beyond my capacity to appreciate.

I wrote nothing below Volunteerism. I have no interest in ferrying sandwiches and movies on plastic disks to bedridden hospital patients, reading to blind children, or plucking candy wrappers and condoms off the grounds of some park. Maybe later, when my abilities shrink, but for now the altruistic route equates to surrender. Take a good look at the semi-decrepit mossbacks out there shelving library books, helping kids cross streets, and serving food to indigents. Submerged in their brains is the following thought: *I might as well do something useful.* I'm not yet that pathetic.

The Exploration option required exploration, so I created two branches below it. I dispensed with the one I had labeled World and instead contemplated the other, the inward-looking one: Self-knowledge. Because self-knowledge is a compound fracture, its branch required an additional fork one level below: to the left, Nature of My Being; to the right, Facts of My Life.

Nature of my being? I am eighty-two years old yet don't fit in, never have. Plop me down anywhere and I'm an anomaly. "Now there's a man who's comfortable in his own skin." Whatever the fuck that means, it's not me.

To top this admission off with a metaphorical poisoned maraschino cherry, I doubt the totality of my accomplishments.

Consider Tibetan monks and the sand mandalas they create—those intricate glories of form, color, and design, constructed over months and destroyed after completion. *Anicca*, that's what they call it, the lesson of impermanence. My books, articles, all those lectures and paper presentations—might as well pulverize them as well. They lounge unread and unheard in libraries, on the Internet, and engraved on DVDs and hard disks throughout the world of ideas and hypotheses, their permanence both assured and irrelevant.

Enough. Everyone and everything vanishes, and there's nothing to be done about it. My more pressing concern is with the Facts of My Life branch. I'm missing my first six years. Granted, blanking out on the first three or four is to be expected, but for the *tabula rasa* to extend a full six years beyond emergence from the womb? Such a state is inconceivable for a person of my abilities. I retain no memories of my first day at kindergarten, nor of fright from darkness, night terrors, and physical examinations. I'm lacking the good stuff as well—no glowing memories of motherly affection, no recollections of being taken care of, cocooned, played with, protected no matter what.

Many years later, Ma explained it to me. At the age of two years and eight months I came down with a case of encephalitis lethargica. Weakened by a cold, the wrong mosquito zinged me in the neck. I was hell on wheels for a couple of weeks, then descended into a monthlong coma, which was followed by a long recovery. Ma described my recuperation as "starting over, like you were reborn." I had been a bright-eyed brilliant kid, delighting my parents with utterances such as "when the time is right," "not now but eventually," and "tomorrow brings a brighter day," all spoken before I had reached the one-year mark. Upon emergence from my coma, however, it became obvious to Ma and Pa that I had been robbed of my precocity. I wasn't equal to the dullest of normal little kids because I was unable to recall anything, save one notable exception:

I asked Ma: "What about the crack?"

"What do you mean?"

"My head. I remember it smashing into something. The back of my head, wasn't it?"

"Yes. You fell backwards and hit your head again a wall. That's how we knew you were seriously ill."

"And the scream?"

"What scream?"

"I remember being yelled at."

"By who?"

"Someone angry. I couldn't understand the words."

"There was no yelling except from me right after you fell. It was either that or the disease played tricks on your brain, that's all."

Before moving here I hadn't felt a need to consider my beginnings. There is something about living in this place, however, that whispers, "Time's up." It's causing me to think too much, just like Wilma Coate did in the last year of her life. She lived four houses down. Our dogs introduced us one summer sunset back in 2003. Sugar, her dachshund, and my Herman would wag their tails furiously whenever they spotted each other. Wilma and I often would pause to give them a chance to jump around a bit before getting down to their more serious task of ass sniffing.

Like her pet, Wilma was built low off the ground. She was a jolly woman with pink cheeks and short white hair, a three-way cross between Kris Kringle, Cinderella's Fairy Godmother, and Yoda. Our conversations revolved around the dogs, weather, restaurants, and movies—putter-putter stuff, pleasant enough though of no import. In her last year, however, Wilma distilled her concerns down to one, which invaded and took over her consciousness: the death of her daughter Jeanette in childbirth sixty-two years earlier. Jeanette had been a twin, and the surviving boy amounted to "so much lint in the wind." Wilma died one year, one month, and three days ago, a suicide or the victim of an accidental overdose.

What's the moral of this story? Every story has a moral, doesn't it? Maybe it's this:

The unexamined life is not worth dying for.

Taking this dictum to heart, I shall:

(1) uncover the circumstances of my early years. Given that I was able to spend my life successfully researching the origins of an ancient book, surely I can uncover the far simpler mystery of me.

(2) recount the significant events of my adolescence. I need to get the story on paper because writing it out may reveal clues extending further back in time. Plus I'll enjoy the exercise. Strange that I never related the adventure to anyone, given that I'm proud of what I did. I guess I didn't want to let the cat out of the bag for fear I'd be asked to tell the story over and over again. I know people like that. They can't keep straight whom they've told and whom they haven't told. More than likely, they've told everyone.

(3) acquaint myself with that librarian—not because she had a bit part in my dream, but on account of.... Oh I don't know. She's a librarian, she doesn't creak, and she seems friendly enough. That makes three strikes in her favor, so why not?

Yep, everything I do runs by logic, no question about it.

8:10 P.M. Monday, January 14th

Her appearance this morning varied a touch from last week's nightmare. She had been a specter then, but today it was impossible to deny her physicality. Though not beautiful in the classic Angelina sense, she possesses a lushness best described by the word most responsible for giving onomatopoeia its good name: voluptuosity. She wavers oh-so-slightly on the zaftig side, and her smile comes freely, genuinely, and without the slightest hint of a shadow snicker. She radiates openness.

This librarian bears a few features previously unnoticed by me:

a two-inch tattoo of a red rose located below her left collarbone, an oval bloodstone pendant dangling from a spiky silver necklace, and two small silver ringlets, one firmly hooked to her left nostril and the other fluttering from heat convection off her right eyebrow. She wore white in my nightmare, whereas this morning she sat at the circulation desk dressed head to toe in silver and black: unbuttoned black cardigan with black v-neck t-shirt underneath, silver belt polished to a high sheen, black jeans, black high boots studded with silver buckles. Meet Shelley Randell, your typical neighborhood goth librarian.

I caught a moment when she had no customers, introduced myself as a resident of the Manoir, and asked for a recommendation, fiction only. I prefaced my request by informing her that as my time on Earth exceeded eighty years, and as only God knew how much longer my eyes would hold out, I would no longer tolerate frittering away my remaining moments reading trivial stuff. I intended to die with great literature fresh in my consciousness. Could she therefore suggest something suffused with significance? I added that I wouldn't mind if her choice included some sex and violence, though the violent bits would have to be integral to the story.

I've befriended more than a few librarians in my time. Counter to stereotype, they are not wishy-washy, not even the ones looking prim and proper. Many acquire a specialty or two in which they are well versed. Fortunately for me, Shelley knew novels. She suggested many of the classics, and after each I replied, "Read it." I was not truthful, just wanted to extend the conversation and impress her a bit. She looked doubtful when I told her I had read every word of Proust. I did plow through a hundred pages of *Swann's Way* on a summer evening back when I was sixty, following which I put the book down, walked to a depanneur, and bought a box of cookies.

After a few minutes of this little game she said, "I have just the ticket, mister. Follow me." She led me to a deserted reading room across the hallway, dropped to the floor and emptied the contents of her bag. Last object out was a chunky paperback. She hurriedly threw her possessions back in, excepting the book.

"I suppose my stuff wouldn't look proper in a Gucci. But that's okay because you didn't see anything, right?"

Wrong. Once I acquire an image, it's forever: "You mean the pair of beaded necklaces, three pieces of crumpled up paper, four packs of condoms—assorted brands no less, faded Harry Potter wallet, two mini Kleenex packages, six vials of pills, one unopened bottle of Naya water, and lipstick? Nope. Saw none of it."

"Now just how in hell did you do that?"

"Do what?"

"Remember everything."

"It's a circus trick. So you wear lipstick sometimes? You don't have any on now. Actually you don't look like a lipstick kind of girl to me."

"It's not lipstick. Tell me how you did that."

"What's not lipstick?"

"Shh. You can't tell anyone. It's pepper spray."

"Pepper spray in a bright pink lipstick container? No kidding!"

"Quiet! It's not legal here. I could get arrested."

"You're warning me not to make a pass at you, right?"

She guffawed. Oh man, what a sound—not as bad as a donkey braying and laughing in quick alternation, but a close second. She snatched the book from the floor, rose, and thrust it at my midsection. I raised my hands just in time to avoid being punched by it.

"Ta-da! *Metamorphogenesis*."

"Catchy title."

"Catchy title and great book!"

The book's cover included drawings of a rabbit, a red-tailed hawk, a lion, and a naked blonde woman in profile. That's right, naked comes before blonde, alphabetical order notwithstanding. Got to have the naked blonde woman in profile, along with a New York Times review one-liner: "Not to be missed." Perhaps the publisher added the "Not?" Unfortunately, I couldn't find a "Soon to be made into a major motion picture" sticker.

"What's it about?"

"Evolution and the connectedness of life forms. It begins with a three-page description of a bacterium, prokaryote, the simplest organism there is. Three whole pages filled with magnificent mind-blowing imagery! Over the millennia this prokaryote morphs its way up the evolutionary ladder. She's a she throughout, and she differs from every other living thing on the planet by retaining consciousness through death. The author is Lyle Meblenny, and he would have been better known had he not jumped off the Golden Gate Bridge when he was twenty-three. That was, umm… forty-two years ago."

"Well I'll be damned. For the longest time I had believed, taking into consideration the zillions of novelists who have scribbled over the centuries plus those currently breathing, that every conceivable plotline had been taken. Clearly I was wrong."

"Oh come on, give it a try! The prokaryote part is amazing. Meblenny describes how it has sex with itself, then splits in half. Talk about blending sex, violence, and betrayal."

I asked Shelley if the book was in the Westmount Library collection. She didn't know, and it doesn't matter. I am destined to read her copy.

12:04 A.M. Thursday, January 17th

Humans are nothing more than oddly shaped animate pinballs. We get slapped on our asses at birth and sent on our merry ways, traveling a path of least resistance until we crash into, or graze by, someone or something. We get deflected. People like to believe they are the masters of their own destinies, but such thinking is flat out delusional. Marcie was my first big deflection.

At 11:15 A.M. on Wednesday, November 20th, 1940, I entered

the Liberal High School library. Other than the boy's gymnasium and the auditorium, the library was the largest room in the school. A double-door archway entrance contributed to its grandness, and the sixteen windows on your right as you walked in, arranged in four two-by-two squares and all well above eye level, made it the brightest room in the school. One thousand seven hundred books occupied oak bookcases lining its walls, and fourteen rectangular tables, each with four standard-issue wooden chairs assigned to it, took up every inch of floor space. The library often was crammed with students because it doubled as study hall. On this particular November morning, however, only one person other than myself was present—Harley Smitts, a scrawny and bespectacled ninth-grader who was known as something of a math genius. He was lost in some book, oblivious in the extreme to my arrival.

My teacher, the jovial and corpulent Miss Audrey Bove, had asked for a volunteer to go to the library and pick up a replacement copy of *Macbeth* (We used to joke about Miss Bove's name: if she's A. Bove, who's B. Lowe?). Someone had excised the opening witches' scene from her copy. Things like that happen in Kansas.

I immediately raised my hand because Elvis Rushel, the kid who sat behind me, had been ramming his desk into my chair whenever Miss Bove angled her backside fullface toward us. Teachers should never write at the blackboard while rotating their bodies one hundred and eighty degrees away from their students. Fortunately, Miss Bove chose me and off I went, with the intention of delaying my return as long as possible.

Macbeth was waiting for me on Miss Mahan's desk. I opened it, found the witches' scene intact and unblemished. Back down it went. *Maybe it's Miss Mahan's personal copy. I'll look for another one.* I turned around, noticed that a door directly behind the librarian's desk was ajar. Time to investigate, in the best interests of the library. Who knows, maybe I'd prevent some lexokleptomaniac from swiping a bushelful of books.

I entered a three-dimensional trapezoid. Just past its threshold you could walk ten feet to the right or to the left, but the back of the room was twelve feet wide at most. Two of the walls, those at the back and to the left upon entering, were angled slantwise, seventy or eighty degrees up rather than the usual ninety, and the floor was covered by alternating gray and white linoleum tiles, many of which had been bent out of shape by unknown forces.

In contrast to the library's spaciousness, lightness, and openness, this storeroom smelled of must and dust. Its bookshelves were made of metallic black wire mesh. Clumps of dirt, sticky from annually compounded accretions, clung to their bases. Fluorescent light bulbs recently had been installed throughout the school. Elsewhere they hummed softly, but in this ugly little space they buzzed like a thousand cicadas. I switched them off, then noticed the storeroom's only natural source of light—a small oval window set in the wall at the far right end of the room. It seemed out of place, like a large white eye occupying north center of someone's chest, where the solar plexus ought to be.

I ambled slower than slow down each of three narrow aisles. My eyes skittered over letterings on dozens of book spines, taking in colors and fonts but neither words nor meanings. Had another copy of *Macbeth* been lounging on a shelf a foot in front of my nose, I would have missed it.

And then I spotted it. Truth be told, *it* couldn't have missed. Sunlight, compact and intense, streamed through the window and lit it up, nothing else. It was positioned at the end of the third shelf from the bottom, on the extreme right side of the front row of shelves—a thin book with gold gilt lettering embossed on a faded green cloth background. Its title glowed front and center, projecting into the air like a tease sticking out her tongue: *Memory: How to Develop, Train and Use It*. I stole it. Not that it would have been missed, for according to the due date tag it had last been read in the year of my birth.

Memory was authored by William Walker Atkinson. Years later I would learn that Atkinson had been a prolific crackpot who flourished for some thirty years, beginning in the 1890's. Sometimes he wrote under the name of Yogi Ramacharaka. The story goes that because Atkinson admired the real yogi so much, he decided to add to the man's legacy by writing books in his name. More likely, the yogi was a figment of Atkinson's imagination.

Back then I did not know that Atkinson was an advocate of mentalism, occultism, reincarnation, personal magnetism, and telepathy. I was a farm boy from Kansas. My reality was parents, teachers, friends, enemies, dogs, cats, chickens, buildings, furniture, wheat fields, sky, and earth, plus a few odds and ends such as string, thumb tacks, books, paintings, and songs. I did not believe in entities I could not see, touch, hear, taste, or smell, but Atkinson was consumed by them. Had I known that about him back then, I would have concluded that his book had to be as cracked up as he was. I would have left the library storeroom empty-handed, and nothing would have turned out as it did.

8:30 P.M. Sunday, January 20th

In that fall of 1940 I was an uncomfortable fifteen-year-old who could count his friends on his thumbs. Left thumb was Nelson, a thin nervous kid with stringy black hair, slumped posture, an inability to look anyone straight in the eye, and a bad case of acne. Nelson's face in flareup mode looked like a raspberry pie blanched by a summer afternoon's Kansas sun. Back then, kids thought acne was something you could catch. The belief contributed little to enhance Nelson's popularity, nor did his Great War fixation, which especially unnerved the girls. Though usually a quiet kid, Nelson could, and would at the slightest provocation, volunteer the essential facts for every major encounter, straight from the Battle of Liege through to the Battle of

Sharqat: beginning and ending dates, ebb and flow, who won, what was won, and how many died and were injured on each side. Nelson's father was caught in crossfire on June 6, 1918, during the Battle of Belleau Wood. A bullet pierced his gut, and he spent his remaining nine years in off-and-on agony because some bozo medic botched the job.

My right-thumb friend Jimmy was a head shorter than Nelson and me, sported bright red hair, and looked like a miniature zeppelin. He was no jolly roly-poly kid, however. His *modus operandi* for surviving school, cultivated over a decade's accumulation of fat-boy taunts and occasional beatings, was to strike back with his tongue and his pen. The former option brought him added grief, but the latter one provided enough solace to get him through.

Jimmy loved reading. He was drawn to those genres in which revenge is exacted decisively and without ambiguity: war stories, crime and mystery novels, science fiction. He also devoured tons of travel books, which provided him with an additional escapist outlet and an extensive collection of motley facts with which to amaze Nelson and me ("What enclosed body of water is larger than Germany?").

Jimmy wrote science fiction stories, and he often read them to us newly minted, on the way to school. He was quite a sight on those mornings—a short red fireball plodding down the middle of the road, shirt untucked, jacket open, pages held in both hands and at arm's length. Nelson and I shared the burden of lugging his stuff, which was fine with us because Jimmy's stories were entertaining. They always included attacks from malevolent and seemingly invincible aliens. The best minds and the most powerful armies and weapons prove useless against superior alien technology. But then a teenager, despised by his classmates for being too smart, too sarcastic, too short, and sometimes even too fond of food, saves the day by applying brilliance, insight, and logic to the desperate circumstance. In Jimmy's stories, characters bearing resemblances to his real-life tormentors met disgusting ends. Aliens ground them into powders and fed them to giant tarantulas, or forced them to chew and swallow dozens of slices of white bread, vomit the mess up, and ingest it again in its infinitely more repulsive form.

Nelson and Jimmy were unhappy and disliked, but at least they possessed identities. Not me. I was stupid and unpopular in an ordinary way. My mental capacity had come under attack early. Miss James, my second-grade teacher, told me I was borderline. I had no idea what she meant, but from the accordion of wrinkles that lined her face whenever she frowned, and which showed up in full force when she broke this news to me, I intuited that borderline was not good. The other side of the border was dirty and squalid. That's what we were told about Mexico. Thus the other side of me, the one I was so close to because I teetered right on its edge, had to be very bad indeed.

I was ordinary Kansas dirt, and so I yearned to accomplish something, anything, that would set me apart. I wanted admiration and I wanted popularity, particularly with the girls. As I walked back to Miss Bove's class on that November morning with an unadulterated copy of *Macbeth* in one hand and the Atkinson book hidden under my shirt, the idea struck and stuck: I would become a master memorizer. I would astound everyone in the school, and in the state as well, by memorizing the entire Bible. Bang. Snap decision, like a tropical rainstorm.

Instead of hanging out after school with my two buddies that day, I slipped away and walked a couple of miles down an out-of-the-way dirt road leading to McGrady's. Back then, wheat fields in winter looked like the other side of the moon. The McGrady field was pockmarked with blotches of white soil and decayed stalks, residue from burnt stubble. Elsewhere, the field's hard bumpy terrain ran the dead-color spectrum from light gray to dark brown. I chose the setting because its unsightliness and obscurity lowered to zero the probability of someone stumbling upon me while I was acquiring Atkinson's secrets. Also, I savored the idea of initiating my journey at the nadir. I would not merely conquer the world; I would progress from abject nothingness all the way to the summit. What better manifestation of nothingness could there possibly be than this ugly field?

I sat under a sycamore fifteen feet off the road and began reading. The first two chapters were filled with quotations from famous and not-so-famous personages concerning the importance of memory. I blew through them quickly. It was the third chapter that gripped me, the one titled "Celebrated Cases of Memory." Atkinson wrote of generals who could identify on sight each of the thousands of soldiers under their commands. He recounted instances of child prodigies possessed with vast literary memories, and of pandits, rabbis, preachers, and Mohammedans who mastered their respective scriptures. I was most taken with the exploits of two individuals, however. They became my heroes, and in succeeding days I conjured up their greatest triumphs, as filtered through my own world view. To wit:

Clark was known for reciting all of Shakespeare, and for memorizing the *Iliad* in the original Greek. I envisioned him, an intellectual Superman, as resembling the then recently invented Clark Kent—tall with a full head of dark hair, bespectacled yet handsome, mild-mannered, clean-cut, intelligent, well spoken, and more than a little on the bland side—the kind of guy that today I would pay money to avoid having a conversation with.

Clark attends the theater. He waits amidst a sold-out Broadway audience for *Hamlet* to begin. After a lengthy delay, the stage manager mounts the stage and announces that both the actor who plays Hamlet and his understudy have come down with the creeping crud. The manager describes their symptoms in excruciating detail and with a misplaced dramatic emphasis often found in third-rate thespians, then states that unless a replacement Hamlet materializes within ten minutes, the performance will be cancelled.

Grumbles ripple through the audience. Then Clark's friend

Marv, who looks a lot like Jimmy, declares, "My friend can do this! He knows all of Shakespeare by heart. I've actually heard him recite *Hamlet*, and let me tell you, he's one hell of an actor."

Marv's outburst appalls Clark, who tries to convince everyone that he is an accountant, not an actor. A woman, dressed in an off-the-shoulder black satin dress and looking like Lois Lane's sexy older sister, approaches him. Clark rises from his seat. The woman places a gloved hand on his shoulder, leans in, and whispers something. Clark's face turns dark pink. "Well, er, okay. I'll give it a try." He performs brilliantly. After, he gets the girl, many times over.

The Dutchman's signature exploit stupefied me. He could read a newspaper and recite all of its text from memory immediately afterward, beginning with the last word on the paper's final page and finishing with the first word on its front page. He was so fast and accurate that it seemed as if he were reading right off the pages.

Never mind that the real Dutchman was probably an idiot savant who spent his adult life in an Amsterdam insane asylum. My Dutchman lived on the French Riviera, in Cannes or Monte Carlo. We learned about Cannes from Jimmy. He told us that Cannes must be a great town because "It's Kansas without the asses."

In my youthful imagination, the Dutchman was to be found on the beach during the day and in the swankest of nightclubs and casinos throughout the evening. He is thin, handsome, dashing, and elegant, a cross between Error Flynn and David Niven. The Dutchman's aristocratic bearing, even in his speedo, as well as his clever banter, charm, and impeccable manners, make him irresistible to women and the envy of men. There he is by the water's edge, looking dapper in his straw hat and sunglasses. He stretches out on a fluffy white towel while a blonde and a brunette attend to him. The Dutchman closes his eyes and recites the day's newspaper backwards and in French, occasionally pausing to utter some impossibly brilliant *bon mot*. Every now and then the brunette strokes his hair and interrupts the recitation with extended deep-mouth kisses. The blonde presses her body against his as she massages his thighs with her long, thin fingers. They find their way under his speedo....

Ahem. Back to McGrady's field, late afternoon of November 20th, 1940—a bitter day, made worse by contrast with two golden Indian Summer days preceding it. I read so hard that I hadn't noticed the darkening sky. Rather than move when the rain came, I sat cross-legged under the sycamore. I protected myself from the downpour by removing my arms from my coat's sleeves and pulling said coat over my head. Said head plus elbows served as support points for a tetrahedronal chamber encompassing the space extending from my lap to my forehead. Hunched within this space, I might have resembled a Talmudic student poring over scriptures in the dim light of a candlelit attic. Or perhaps I was becoming less of a student and more of a mystic, like one of those solitary superannuated beer-guzzling Quebecois ice fishermen who spend hours seated on benches in huts over frozen lakes while waiting for messages from God—messages disguised as yanks on the other end of a fishline punched through the ice, drifting aimlessly in frigid darkness.

I read to the end of the sixth chapter. Here Atkinson addressed attention, the concept at the heart of his book. He wrote of "voluntary attention" and "determination to use the will." I wanted the great secrets, but they weren't to be had. Chapter VI concluded with this statement:

The great Art of Memory is Attention.

I knew that. Everybody knows that! How many times had my teachers demanded of me the same thing?

"Carl, stop your daydreaming and pay attention."

Drenched and stiff after spending two hours in a moonscape of a wheat field, I wanted, I craved, I deserved the top-secret knowledge my heroes had applied so expertly back in Chapter III. Instead, Atkinson offered up exactly one disheartening platitude. I tossed his book into the field, where it lay faceup in the dirt, rapidly absorbing rainwater. I backed up against the sycamore and watched as *Memory*'s pages flapped back and forth in the wind. *Soon you will be unreadable*, I thought. *You will die.* At that moment I understood that it and I shared something—forlornness. I felt sorry for a dumb, inanimate, lifeless object.

I picked the book up, gave it another look. Displaced from its place of honor in the library storeroom, it no longer had pretensions. It was merely a thin volume with a plain green cover. If a book can be said to possess a persona, this book's persona was that of an intelligent and quiet spinster, pleasant enough but no great beauty. Heck, she hadn't been out on a date in fifteen years. On the other hand, she never fired a gun at anyone. Earlier, she had been sitting silently in her warm dry spot, minding nobody's business. Now she was cold, wet, dirty, and in danger of disintegration, courtesy of my intervention. I guess I didn't have it in me to commit bookicide. I reasoned that just as a child should not be blamed for having stubby fingers, a broad nose, or bulging eyes, a book should not take the rap for the print branded on its pages. I was angry with the author, not the book.

The rain tapered to a drizzle on the walk home, so I took *Memory* out and opened to a random page—page ninety-three as luck would have it, five pages in from the beginning of the chapter titled "Training the Eye." It is on this page that Atkinson cites a passage from Rudyard Kipling's novel, *Kim*. The Irish boy Kimball O'Hara competes against an Indian boy in a memory game. The Indian boy recalls jewels on a tray flawlessly, and in such detail that Kim is amazed. Later, he asks his teacher how his opponent had become so proficient:

By doing it many times over, until it is done perfectly, for it is worth doing.

"...until it is done perfectly." Not until it is learned well, but until it is fried to perfection. Maybe I could be perfect. Of course I could.

At lunch the following day I let Nelson and Jimmy in on my master plan to memorize the Bible and become rich, famous, and desired by women. To say that my assertions were met with a tidal wave of skepticism would be hitting the nail right on the head.

"Well burst my britches," Jimmy said. "That's bound to get you girls. Oh wait, I have a vision... Here it is... I can see it now. Yeah, picture this, genius boy. You strut into school with your magic brain and Melissa comes right up to you, your heads just inches apart, and she says [at this point Jimmy switched to a grating falsetto], 'Oh Carl, I need some Leviticus now. Be a good boy and show me your Leviticus.' [falsetto off] The two of you stop dead still in the hallway and stare into each other's eyes, transfixed. Then you recite, 'And the Lord called unto Moses, and spake unto him,' followed by whatever the fuck's in the next fifty verses. Sweet Melissa stands still as a mannequin, fixated on those lips from which emanate your every word, and you continue with your recitation, oblivious to kids behind her giving you the finger. Oh divine Melissa! She gazes longingly at you, and you intone your stuff while staring into her big blue eyes and at those luscious red lips, and you peek at her tits every now and then, like every three seconds, and when you finish she exclaims, yes exclaims: [two-word *falsettissimo*] 'My hero,' and she demonstrates her rapturous admiration for your super-duper memory by deep-kissing you, her tongue avidly exploring the mysteries of your adolescent Kansan throat. No doubt about *that*."

Nelson was more plain-spoken but just as skeptical. If his compelling recitations of Great War battles didn't grab a girl's attention, nothing could. He claimed that a fellow needed all four of the following qualities to make it with the girls: tallness, darkness, handsomeness, and stupidness, so I was one-fourth of the way there. Then he called me "freak-boy." My friend—imagine that!

I walked home alone from school that day, repeatedly muttering the following mantra to myself: "The attainment of perfection brooks no deterrence." Later that afternoon I finished off *Memory*. Atkinson's chapter on memorizing words came near the end. Although its content was most pertinent to my intentions, I initiated my quest with "Training the Eye." The appeal was irresistible:

> ...you will also be able to perceive and remember thousands of little details of interest, in everything, that heretofore have escaped your notice. The principle is very simple, but the results that may be obtained by practice are wonderful.

I expropriated a battered porcelain plate that had languished for years on the top shelf of our kitchen cupboard. I memorized its two hairline fractures resembling the Missouri and Mississippi River system, a yellow-brown stain near the rim, and a couple of blotchy discolorations close to the plate's center. These imperfections provided a background—an unbalanced but unchanging grid over which items placed on the plate's surface could be oriented.

Without skipping a day, I spent the rest of November, December, January, and half of February in training. I would sit on my bedroom floor with the plate positioned in front of me. My collection of objects included marbles, dice, pebbles, leaves, jumping jacks, miniature blocks and the like. I'd grab a few of them and lay them on the plate. I added a wrinkle to the Atkinson formula by feeling them up with my eyes still shut, positioning them relative to each other, then imagining the entirety of the plate as it appeared with the objects upon it. Only after doing so would I open my eyes. What a pleasure such looking was! I lingered over the dozens of surfaces, colors, and angles. I enjoyed the blendings of greens, yellows and reds in a leaf, the diagonal wood-grain curvature in my blocks, the mysterious methods employed by marbles and dice to greet each other. Then I would turn away. With my eyes open but focused on nothing, I acquired the image. Yes, that's precisely what it was: acquisition.

I began with a few objects, but increased their numbers from week to week. By February I could acquire anything. The plate might have six marbles on it, say three cats-eyes of different colors—pink and white, green and black, blue and yellow—plus three solids, maybe orange, aquamarine, and gray. Add five or six yellow and green leaves of different shapes and sizes and a few pairs of dice: white spots on a black background, black on green, red on white. Day after day I captured dozens of such scenes, down to the numbers of spots showing on the tops and sides of each die. By late January I had became fast, oh so fast! A ten-second look and it was mine, all of it, the image reduced to a set of vectors and patterns branching and swaying together and apart from each other, like a map of an interstate highway system on the periphery of a heavily populated city.

4:12 P.M. Wednesday, January 23rd

As of this morning, *Metamorphogenesis* had languished undisturbed on the far right-hand corner of my desk for eight days, twenty-two hours, and four minutes. Ugh. Why the hell should I be interested in the inner lives of microscopic life forms? The one excellent reason: friendship cultivation. I had stopped by the circulation desk three times since my initial encounter with Shelley: Wednesday morning and Friday afternoon of last week, yesterday before lunch. I kept the visits brief and pleasant, nothing too demanding. Growing a friendship, especially one between two people of opposite sexes and varying ages, requires tact, particularly with reference to details of timing. Not that I'm interested in her romantically, because I'm not insane; nevertheless, a friendship could be satisfying for both of us.

But how to cement it?

I believe there is something to be learnt from the behaviorists and their work with so called "schedules of reinforcement." They thought they had discovered the keys to predicting and controlling all human behavior, but the universe played a trick on them. That's what universes do when you get too cocky. It turned out that behaviorism's only finding worth shit is that uncertainty is powerful. If one visits a new friend on a set schedule, say every Monday, Wednesday, and Friday at 10:00 A.M., the visitee might consider such constancy manipulative and preplanned—part of a campaign rather than a more improvisatory "thought I'd drop in as I'm in the neighborhood" kind of thing. Women like spontaneity. Too much regularity on the part of a suitor creeps them out. Obviously I can't let Shelley read any of this, even after we've become friends.

Given the context, whither *Metamorphogenesis*? Ah yes, that brilliant work of a fevered literary genius who snuffed out his own life before attaining full flower. I navigated through its first ninety pages before lunch. Meblenny possessed a perverse talent for endowing the microbial world with nauseating imagery. He described the massive rush of ten million cytoplasms spilling from their burst cell membranes as "impure brown torrents lumpy with sewage from rent strands of DNA and RNA, drifting aimlessly through life's dark fluid." Nuclei got ripped apart, as if "slashed by the sharp silver scimitars of Saladin's fanatical foot soldiers." An illogical time displacement for sure, but that's what happens when artistic freedom bursts from the stable for a riderless gallop.

I cannot in good conscience detail the abominable viciousness with which the author portrayed asexual congress. His descriptions were so violent that, by comparison, most published narratives of sadomasochistic goings-on (not that I have any particular expertise in that oeuvre) seem as innocent as doofus cocker spaniel puppies play-flopping all over each other. I was rather taken with one particular passage, however, in which the protagonist, little more than a cell body herself, waxes poetic while drifting through the "caramel warmth" of a protoplasmic sea at rest, her essence

> bathed by the silver wavelets,
> they flow through me
> at one with all living things
> the universe a chrysalis of the animate.
> I rejoice here, and everywhere!

I had promised Shelley that I'd have *Metamorphogenesis* polished off by the end of last weekend. The book weighs in at 504 pages. Suicide is preferable to wading through the remaining 414. Incipient friendships do not benefit from rigid constructionist demonstrations of honesty, however.

"Hi there."

I caught her off guard, reading a book while on call at the circulation desk. Surprise looks good on a good looking woman, especially if it's midwinter and all she's wearing is a purple tank top, green jeans, and assorted hand, wrist, and face jewelry. I wish my thermostat was calibrated like hers.

"Aha! Yet again comes the man with the golden memory. Have you finished my book yet?"

"Umm, not exactly. I'm up to page 160 or so." A minor exaggeration in the larger scheme of things.

"And how do you like it so far?"

"I'm spellbound."

"Excellent! Now keep going. You promised me you'd have it read by now, but it's a savory book, eh? Each of Lyle's sentences need to be appreciated, like sips of fine wine. No monster swigs allowed."

"Exactly."

I never lied to my students. If they read or wrote crap, I told them straightaway. With this librarian, however, I'll be gauging things just a little bit differently.

9:24 A.M. Tuesday, January 29th

On the evening of Friday, February 14th, 1941, I began memorizing the Bible. The precipitating event was my personal Saint Valentine's Day massacre.

Miss Audrey Bove had been employed as an elementary school teacher from the mists of time to September, 1939, and one of the customs she imported from that previous life was the exchange of valentines. Instead of delving deep into the intricacies of *Little Women*, we spent the second half of our February 13th English period constructing the cards. Miss Bove required each of us to make at least two. No, she was not an early advocate of polyamory. She just wanted to increase the likelihood that every student would receive a card, so feelings would not get hurt. Her deal was niceness. She was the sweetness-and-light teacher of Liberal High School. If only everyone acted nicely to one another, the world would be, in her words, such a wondrous place. Truly, "wondrous" was a favorite word of hers. But really, multiple valentines? If Joyce Clyde Hall had fancied the idea back in the nineteen aughts, his "Be One of My Valentines" card line would have cost him his shirt. Hallmark would have been stillborn.

I addressed a card to Melissa, the girl I secretly lusted after. Pale face, clear complexion, an inch taller than me. Okay, make that two. Rich blonde hair, soft blue eyes, the symmetry of her visage rendered ever so slightly askew by the jagged profile of her lower front teeth and a couple of missing eyelashes. That buoyant bustline, the curves of which corresponded to gentle fluctuations in the space-time continuum so perfectly that one might have apprehended infinity not as a frightening concept, but as an intimation of warmness and pleasure. I scribbled "to Betty" on the second card, then crossed her out and wrote "to Susan" in its place. We didn't have names like Madison back then, and all three of our Ashleys were boys. I filled out that second card with another half dozen names, crossed them all out, and wrote at the bottom, in large block letters: SPOILED BALLOT. Slipped it in the pile when no one was looking.

Jimmy received three valentines. Despite Miss Bove's good intentions, neither Nelson nor I received any. One other student matched us in futility: Marcie Smith. Marcie was rail-thin and quieter than a dead mouse. Her dirty blonde hair was in fact dirty and blonde, and was always uncombed. She was slow, in fact so bad at stringing words of a sentence together that her ascent to tenth grade seemed a minor miracle. Nobody had much contact with her, the girls because she held no interest for them and the boys because they were afraid other boys would taunt them with inquiries such as "How's your retard girlfriend?" Nevertheless, the three of us liked her. Like us, she was an isolate, therefore a kindred spirit. Also like us, and unlike most kids who went home for lunch, she was a walker. I lived on a farm two miles east of the big city. Jimmy and Nelson lived a mile further out, and Marcie had to walk in from the southwest. Her home was located just a few feet north of the Oklahoma state line—a full four miles from Liberal High School.

Most days, Marcie ate lunch with us. None of us could tell if she appreciated our company or if she was being polite, as her predominant facial expression approximated a washed out Mona Lisa half-smile. We charmed her with our jokes, and she smiled. She smiled as we were telling them, and she smiled when we sprung the punch lines. She smiled when she ate jello. Had we sung "Ninety-Nine Bottles of Beer on the Wall," she would have smiled each time a bottle fell.

Every Friday Marcie would scrape out a half-crushed vanilla-iced cupcake from the bottom of her lunchbox and give it to one of us. Jimmy was the chief beneficiary. One Thursday, though, he went to the bakery and bought three of them. I don't know how he found the self-control to forgo eating them overnight. Maybe he bought nine.

We planned it on the walk to school. When Marcie offered up her cupcake toward the end of lunchtime, out came ours, accompanied by the three of us singing the newest song in Kansas—"Eat your Own Damn Cupcake," four lines with the same lyrics and sung à la "Happy Birthday to You." We held our cupcakes aloft and rollicked. Marcie smiled—no big surprise there—then we finished off the song and gobbled up our desserts. Come to think of it, that description is inaccurate. True, Jimmy devoured his in the time it would have taken an Airedale—mumph galumph and gone. Nelson and I required a couple of minutes. But Marcie, oh how she savored that cupcake! She floated it on her fingertips as if it were the Hope Diamond, then, very slowly, brought it to her mouth. Eyes closed, she extended her tongue and gently swirled it around and through ridges of icing. On subsequent Fridays we insisted that she keep, and eat, her precious cupcake. While we watched.

I guess you could say there was something about Marcie. If only she didn't look half-vacant, and if only she washed her hair and brushed it properly, and if only there wasn't the occasional piece of egg or smearage of jam ground into the fabric of her sweater. If only.

Zero valentines. Even Reginald Massetrim, a shrimp with buck teeth and fierce body odor three days out of five, received one. Marcus Tern, an oaf who used to bully Jimmy and was as dumb as a tree trunk, got eight. Why not? He met all four of Nelson's criteria.

That afternoon I decided enough was enough. True, the unanimous opinion of our gang of three was that the girls in our class were intellectual lightweights. Nevertheless, they were *girls*. If only I could impress just one of them. I would have settled even for Fiona Jackendorff, who wore dungy coveralls to school everyday and was big-boned all over. Okay, maybe not. Nevertheless, I so needed to win a girl's heart, to say nothing of her body, and I was going to do it through brain power. Yes, the time had come to leave the little pebbles, marbles, and dice behind. It was time to grow up and memorize the Bible.

First I had to find one. Bibles are as ubiquitous as wheat in Kansas, but none survived in my house. We used to own one with a brown leather cover. It was a sharp looking volume, and it lolled about undisturbed deep in an upstairs closet. I destroyed it one rainy day when I was seven. I tore out all of Genesis and most of Exodus, and drew stick figures of soldiers, cannons, and airplanes throughout the rest of the Old Testament. The New Testament was not spared either. Jesus may have walked on water, but I milk-soddened the pages describing that miracle and many others. When my abridgements were discovered I received a pretty bad spanking.

My replacement Bible came from Jason Sherman. Jason was one of only six or seven Jewish kids attending Liberal High School back then. His family had moved in the previous summer, and Ma was a member of the Welcome Wagon triumvirate that visited the Sherman home. Everything proceeded swimmingly until Mrs. Snodgrass offered Rachel Sherman a pristine copy of the New Testament, embossed with a large golden cross on the front cover. Mrs. Sherman refused the book in the nicest possible way. "I was brought up never to look a gift horse in the mouth," she said, "but in this case I must respectfully decline both the peek and the gift." In order to ensure no lingering hard feelings, Mrs. Snodgrass returned the following day with an apology and a brand new Old Testament. There's nothing like neighbors chipping in for a Bible to make a newcomer feel welcome, eh? I figured Jason might have access to an extra one, and I was right. He accepted my offer of fifty cents for it, and said "Don't let it warp your mind" as he placed it in my hands.

The Old Testament was not written with the bromide,

"Brevity is the source of wit" as a guiding principle. No one admonished its authors for not adhering to the wisdom prescribed by Occam concerning his beloved razor. On my first day of ownership, I took the thing home and tossed it on my bed, where it produced a small indentation. What a hell of a doorstop it would have made. One thousand, one hundred and thirty-five pages, two columns per page, small type—ponderous enough to keep most any door open, or shut.

In his chapter "How to Remember Words, etc.," Atkinson urged his readers to adopt the following plodding approach:

> This natural system of memorizing is based upon the principle...by which every child learns its alphabet and its multiplication table....[It] consists of the learning of one line at a time, and reviewing that line; then learning a second line and reviewing that; and then reviewing the two lines together; and so on, each addition being reviewed in connection with those that went before.

It took me fifteen days to get through one column using Atkinson's system. At 1,135 pages, a column memorized every half-month would result in complete memorization after only 1,135 months, assuming no forgetting. That's ninety-four years and seven months, give or take a few days. If I were to memorize a page a day, it would take me three years to finish. Perfection to a crisp notwithstanding, three years was too long. The Dutchman could have rattled off "day fifth a, morning was there and evening was there And" all the way back to "earth and the heaven the created God beginning the In" without breaking a sweat. What was he doing right?

I persevered for over a month and memorized all of two and a half pages. There had to be a better way. Then one day Miss Bove foisted another relic from her elementary-level teaching repertoire upon us: papier-mâché masks. Those foul smelling newspaper strips provided the imaginative spark. God: if you exist, please bless Miss Bove's bones.

At 8:30 P.M. on Sunday, March 23rd, 1941, the moon was full and the sky cloudless. Ma and Pa had been snoring away for half an hour. As usual, they sounded like a pennywhistle dueling with a foghorn.

I removed the porcelain dish from under my bed and covered it with a small green hand towel. After fishing out a pair of scissors from my desk drawer, I carried *Scriptures* to the windowsill and opened to a random page—page 748, toward the end of the second verse of Nahum, as it turned out—then inserted a scissor blade deep into the valley where the page met the spine. I sliced the newly detached page in half, cutting slowly and carefully so as to avoid severing words. Fortunately, the publisher had the good sense to coincide the vertical dividing lines on opposite sides of each page.

After positioning the left column of page 748 over the plate and covering its corners with dice, I gazed. In the following minutes I came to see that text is camouflage of tracery. Before, I had read words. Now I absorbed lines, circles, crescents, and right angles—symbols racing across and down the page, the mass of them taken together miraculously in harmony with their meanings. I then turned away, stared deep into nothingness, and captured it all.

I tiptoed downstairs, slid my heavy coat over my pajamas, slipped my boots over my feet without lacing them up, and walked twenty-five paces into the snow-covered field back of my house. Turning to the moon, I whispered my recitation:

> The lion did tear in pieces enough for his whelps,
> And strangled for his lionesses,
> And filled his caves with prey,
> And his dens with ravin.

I recalled all twenty-eight lines perfectly. A few minutes later I went to bed, feeling, for one of only two times in my life, unadulterated jubilation.

I told no one, not even Ma and Pa. As soon as they were asleep I would scissor out eight or ten columns, each of which would take a turn on the green cloth. After I finished for the night, I would take the strips outside and burn them one at a time. Watching a flame as it crawled from one edge of a strip to its opposite edge gave me great pleasure. And so on the Atkinson Diet, Jason Sherman's copy of *The Holy Scriptures* wasted away over the spring, summer, fall, and winter. By mid-January of 1942 it was all gone.

10:15 A.M. Saturday, February 2nd

I would have finished my task sooner had I not spent time thinking about content. Back then I knew nothing of how the Bible was written. I believed its author to be none other than the same guy who issued the Ten Commandments—God Almighty himself, for who else would have known what happened before there was life? The idea of scribes being injected with the divine vision never crossed my mind. I thus wondered, given that *The Holy Scriptures* was the Word of God, why it was penned in the third person. Imagine the power, the directness, the crushing authority of these words:

In the beginning I created the heaven and the earth.

to say nothing of its magisterial drum-rolling segue:

And I said: Let there be light.

The difficulty factor piqued my curiosity. Given that universe creation is something of a tall order, was it accomplished easily? Perhaps God snapped his fingers and boom, instant Big Bang, the whole nine yards. Or maybe he struggled with inner demons for a few dozen eons before undertaking the task. Did he overcome a crisis of confidence? Might he have been afflicted with Creator's Block? If conjuring up the universe was hard work, would he have admitted it? Or was his attitude no different from quite a number of expert woman cooks I have known, who, after presenting a magnificent meal consisting of, say, lobster bisque followed by an exquisite spinach and mandarin orange salad, succulent rack of lamb roasted to perfection, green beans and mashed potatoes on the side, baked Alaska and a fine cappuccino to finish up, smile demurely and murmur, "Oh really, it was nothing."

On only the second line of the first page of *Scriptures*, I spotted a semicolon. That puzzled me. Did they really have semicolons back then? Colons, of course: you need them for grand pronouncements and for enumerating who begot whom. Semicolons, however, require a sophistication that I would have thought postdated biblical times; moreover, they lead to long statements and bad writing, and I hate to think of God as the original promoter of labyrinthine constructions, for to identify him as the source of extended, dense, obtuse sentences that veer off in all directions, as a balloon zigzags right, left, up, and down while air molecules are expelled from its orifice at velocities approaching the speed of sound on a windy day—to think of him that way does not make for a pretty picture. God was a to-the-point guy, assured and assuredly.

Then there was Adam to consider. I didn't need to know how old he was. Chronologically he was age zero at the moment God created him, though he might have been eleven, or twenty-seven, or fifty-two as the world turns. Nor was I curious about Adam's weight, height, or hair color. What puzzled me was his personality. He was the first man, but he had no skills and was a wimp to boot. God told Adam what to do and what not to do, and Adam obeyed. Then Eve came along and Adam said, "Yes dear," thereby screwing things up royally for everyone who followed.

I found timing in *Scriptures* messed up. By eating fruit from the Tree of Knowledge, Adam and Eve learned of good and evil. Such entities could not have existed way back then. "In the beginning…" Nothing exists before a beginning. Or if evil had been part of a preexisting condition subsisting in some remote dark corner prior to Creation, Genesis should have commenced with "Somewhere near the beginning…." Such an opening would have been intolerable, even worse than "It was a dark and silent void."

My fifteen-year-old mind concluded that good and evil must have sprouted from saliva secreted during the First Bite. Knowledge always creates evil, regardless of whatever else it entails.

And the man knew Eve his wife; and she conceived and bore Cain.
And Cain knew his wife; and she conceived, and bore Enoch.

Even a cursory reading of the Bible reveals that there was a lot of knowing going on back then. "Know" was the original four-letter word. Maybe the Tree of Knowledge was about sexual awakening. To know you is to fuck you. Or is it the other way around? Is there a difference?

Adam and Eve's diet concerned me. I wanted to know if they were vegetarians. *Scriptures* states that God gave Adam the privilege of naming beasts, fowl, and fishes. It claims that animals became subservient to man (true enough, except for mosquitoes, black flies, and certain microbes). Nevertheless, there is no record of Adam and Eve abusing their positions as heads of the food chain. They did not eat steak, filet of sole, roast turkey, or even escargots. They ate from trees, thus were not killers.

The first death cited in the Bible was not that of Abel, but of Abel's unfortunate little lamb. Abel was the first killer, and God certainly was pleased with the deed. Nevertheless, not even in my adolescence did I imagine God devouring the little baa-baa. An eating God is one who drinks, shits, pees, and takes out the garbage. An eating God is an undignified God.

Sheep placement thus became an issue for me. God could have made dead sheep on his own, and he could have kept making them until the cows came home. He could have fashioned them perfectly white and perfectly plump and perfectly dead. Abel's sacrifice was therefore useless from a practical point of view. It was worse than useless, because it created a problem where none before existed: what's to be done with the body?

Before Cain killed Abel, human death was a theoretical proposition. God told Adam and Eve: "Eat from my Tree of Knowledge and you die." The serpent parried, "Don't believe it for a second." The serpent had greater credibility because Adam and Eve could not conceive of death. Later, after Cain bludgeoned Abel, he acquired for himself and for all who followed the terrible realization that strikes most of us when we are four or five.

8:22 P.M. Monday, February 4th

Shelley entered the library this morning accompanied by a guy who looked like he recently emerged from a wormhole connected straight back to the 1970's: thin, tie-dyed t-shirt, bushy moustache, long straight silky hair, insincere smile, hands permanently stuffed in jeans pockets, sandals. Yes, sandals in winter, though with socks on his feet. The two of them walked to a secluded aisle off to the side of the circulation desk. He gallantly helped her out of her coat and then kissed her goodbye while simultaneously cupping her left breast.

I stopped by a few minutes later.

"Well hello stranger!"

That smile again, warmer than sunshine.

"Hi." I handed *Metamorphogenesis* back to her.

"You finished it?"

"Yup."

"And? What do you think?"

"Total magic. Thanks for suggesting it."

"Oh I am so happy! I've lent the book out to four people so far, and you're the only one who truly got it."

"Really?"

"Uh-huh. My boyfriend hated it. Said it was stupid. Stupid, dumb, ridiculous, and implausible. He wouldn't read past thirty pages."

No comment from me. Never savage the boyfriend.

"So, what was your favorite part?"

Putting me on the spot. Never fear, I was prepared. "When she becomes a landlubber."

"Oh yes! She had no concept of the sun before that moment, nor of wind, sound, or solid ground. Can you imagine?"

"I am Ichthyostega, Empress of the Hard World. I share my domain with no one. I reign alone, I am its sovereign ruler, and thus I shall remain until time's end."

"What? You—you memorized it?"

"Pretty funny, given that Ichthyostega was little more than an inchworm. Not the whole thing, just a few sections. No big deal."

"Holy shit!"

"Now there's an oxymoron for you."

"Seriously, how did you do that?"

"Like I told you before, it's a circus trick. Anyone can do it."

"I can't."

"Sure you can. It's just a matter of seeing things the right way, plus a little practice."

"There's a wrong way?"

"Definitely. If you analyze things too closely, that's the wrong way."

"So the right way is kind of like letting go and not trying too hard?"

"That comes after. First comes the 'holy shit' part, when you go oxymoronic."

"You're losing me. Oh, I'd better get to work."

A line of seven customers had materialized behind me, so I didn't get a chance to explain. Energy and matter, life and death, nature and artifice, Abbott and Costello—you can't have one without the other. For me, the same applies to geometric forms and words. Good writing is nothing more than the artful arrangement of graphemic arabesques. I'm surprised more people don't know this.

5:09 P.M. Thursday, February 14th

A freshly washed black Ford, slick and shiny, cruises a country road. Viewed from a distance the car glides silently, its blackness cutting glare from fields covered with fresh snow. Two boys occupy the front seat. The girl behind them sits with hands folded as she awaits her destination.

Jake Stiles and Phil Jensen drove Marcie Smith to McGrady's field. Two days later they bragged to a few of their so-called friends, so-called because they had no real friends: "She's a fucking nympho. Once we revved her up, there was no stopping her." They left nothing to the imagination regarding methodologies employed for repeatedly relieving themselves on and inside her. Within a couple of days, everyone knew.

The boys weren't concerned with consequences. Marcie was sixteen, above the age of consent. Her family was poor and theirs were well off. True, there were indications of coercion. A policeman had taken photos at the hospital. None of Marcie's bruises and swellings would remain visible by the time of a trial, however. More importantly, there were no eyewitnesses; it was a simple case of believability. Not that the boys calculated it out. No, they acted on impulse, pure and simple and evil. They spotted Marcie shivering in her threadbare burlap coat as she walked home from school, and snap!—raping her sounded like a grand idea.

Jimmy raised the topic over lunch, on the day before Marcie returned to school. Despite a potato chunk occupying most of his buccal cavity, he managed to complete the following short sentence:

"Things will be different with her."

Nelson looked up from his comic book. Jimmy raised a hand in response, signaling that his next utterance was imminent. It succeeded a burp, which in turn followed hard on the heels of an emphatic swallow.

"Everyone ignores her except us. But if there's a trial, heaven help her." He noticed puzzlement on both of our faces and shook his head.

"You bums don't know anything. It goes like this...." He knocked back another mouthful of potato before continuing. Potatoes figured prominently in his diet that day.

"Goes like what?" asked Nelson.

"The lawyers will make her out like a whore. They'll convince everyone, excepting us, that she got into the car to seduce them, with the aim of getting one of them hooked."

Seduce—a new word for me, but I didn't have to ask what it meant.

"Anyway, it's going to be bad. Bad, bad, very bad, trial or no trial. If there is one, the jury will find those guys innocent. She's the one who'll really be on trial, and found guilty too, in the minds of people. And after, who knows? She could end up being targeted by all kinds of slime balls. But if there's no trial, she's in danger whenever she's out alone."

"You learned this stuff from crime books?" asked Nelson.

Jimmy nodded as he finished off the penultimate potato, then motioned for us to come a little closer.

"My pop has this book. It's got a blonde on the cover, she's wearing a red dress, cut down so her tits are almost showing. She looks sad *and* like she needs a fuck. Totally unforgettable! It's called *No Orchids for Miss Blandish,* and Pop hides it on the highest shelf in the clothes closet, underneath some old blankets." Despite Jimmy's relish in telling the story, he barely spoke above a whisper.

"There's all kinds of bad stuff in it. The villains kidnap Miss Blandish and one of them rapes her, but it's her father who does her in. Better dead than deflowered, that's what he tells her. So she takes daddy's advice to heart and kills herself."

"You read the whole thing?" I asked.

"Yep."

Down to defeat went the final potato. Jimmy then devoured a substantial piece of chocolate cake while Nelson and I stared at him in amazement.

Gershwin boards a train. The other passengers read newspapers, gossip, or sleep. Only Gershwin listens to the rhythms of the rails. In an instant he's snagged it: *Rhapsody in Blue.* A scribe contemplates the meaning of a recent crucifixion as he gazes out over the Sea of Galilee. He watches his son skimming stones over the water. Miracle of miracles, before you know it the scribe has received the divine vision of Christ walking on water, performing that miracle as casually as one might stroll along a park path on a sunny day. Just so: a Kansan boy observes his friend struggle to utilize his mouth simultaneously for two purposes, and bingo, the idea almost knocks him off his feet. He knows what it takes to save a girl.

1:22 P.M. Tuesday, February 26th

The snowstorm finally ended this morning. Thirty-two centimeters, that's what the pretty lady on the Weather Channel declared. It's a substantial dump, but not heavy enough to keep me off the streets, especially as the City of Westmount's crack snow removal team is on the case. The workers—they call themselves snow removal engineers around here, everyone else says blue collars—they gun around in double-treaded zippies looking like half a miniature tank, minus the weaponry but plus a small plow mounted underneath an oversized windshield. In the daytime it's easy to spot their demonic grins, demented unibrowed Albanians to a man. They vroom about with eyes wide open and terrorize anyone who gets in their way. That's what you get when you hire men passionate about their calling: clean sidewalks. Plus the occasional octogenarian on his ass in a drift.

I had just crossed to the north side of Sherbrooke Street, on my way into town after breakfast, when I spotted Shelley on the south side, walking in the opposite direction. She no longer retains even a shadow of zaftig, and that worries me. I fear she will fade away and die, just as she did in my nightmare. I know, crazy thinking, totally insane. Nevertheless I can't shake the thought. I sense fragility in her, but for no reason I can ascertain.

Last month's nightmare visited me again last night, but this time around I caught it before it attained *in flagrante destructo* status. While still in its grip, I tamped it down. I spotted my dead brother in the water and thought: *Oh it's you again. Go to Hell. You're a phantom, you never lived, let alone died. I know that and you know that, so fuck off.* I woke up immediately, though more shaken by the experience than triumphant over my ability to short-circuit it.

I'm inclined to examine the escapades of my nocturnal brain rationally. My best guess is that this one stems from some connection between my past history and my current residency, which, after all, is likely to be my terminal home. The nightmare's violence motif bears close resemblance to my all-time worst dream, which struck me when I was seven years old. In that one I beat up some kid, then reached into his throat and pulled out his vocal chords. I held them tight in my right hand, saw they were as brittle as uncooked spaghetti. Do untroubled children have such dreams? Or is there a connection between my inability to recall anything from my first half-dozen years and some event or series of events that were so transcendent in their awfulness that they needed to be blocked from my consciousness and made as inaccessible as if they had been vaulted in lead and placed at the center of the earth's core?

4:22 P.M. Monday, March 3rd

Pure logic breeds passivity and contempt. No one can live by it. This truth does not stem from difficulty in basing one's actions on the scarcity of rock-solid assumptions. There *are* absolutes. No one can doubt that raping a girl is evil. Taking this statement as a given, one must conclude that the perpetrators of such crimes should be stamped out.

"Not so fast," says the man of logic. "Is rape so vile a crime that it requires action whenever circumstances make the option viable? What if the perpetrators had victimized a girl who wasn't a little slow on the mental side, or was someone you despised, or was a girl you never met? Had they sodomized a boy would you still step forward? And what exactly are your motives? Are you acting for the public good, personal gain, revenge, a combination of the three, or some other reason hidden from view, perhaps even from yourself?"

I considered these arguments on the evening following Jimmy's potato lecture. To manage the problem better, I wrote YES at the top of one piece of paper and NO at the top of another. Down the left-hand sides of each I listed three categories, spaced every two inches or so: me, Marcie, Ma and Pa. I marked up the pages with imagined consequences, then read through my notes, scouring all the plusses and minuses. On the NO page I underlined my bottom-line rationale for inaction: Perjury conviction—jail time.

Marcie returned to school the following morning. Her left eye was blackened, and a purplish bruise spanned her neck and right shoulder. She did not smile that day, nor for many days after. I sensed that she felt shame. In retrospect, I deny taking action because

I couldn't bear seeing her so distressed. No, there was definitely an element of pride in the whole venture. All behaviors of apparent self-sacrifice are motivated by it.

9:59 P.M. Wednesday, March 12th

I don't want to write about Jake Stiles and Phil Jensen. I'd prefer to have them unremembered with a completeness so thorough that it approaches to within a hundredth of a degree of absolute zero. I wish not to recall Jake's half-inch crewcut and the angularities of his chin, jaw, and forehead. I don't want to remember that he was so gaunt his face looked like a jeering skull. He was a net negative, the square root of minus one. I would extirpate the relevant memory cells from my brain if I could.

I'd like to think of Jake as dimensionless—a stick figure with two dots for eyes, a straight line for a mouth, no ears, no elbow joints, no knees. The same with Phil. I don't want any trace of his loppy gait contaminating my neurons, nor of his raspy voice, and especially not of the slicked down cowlick that hung from his forehead like an oversized periodontal curette. Surely I can dispense with engrams depicting the two of them in proximity. They were an agglomeration of misaligned siamese twin parts, one head eight inches higher off the ground than the other, their bodies slowly oscillating between sharp thinness and dumpy sycophantic portliness. They were nullities apart, evilness together.

The plains have always evoked extremes in a few select beings, always will. Observe a wheat field on a calm spring day and what do you feel? Tranquility, most likely. Now listen hard. Hear the menace of a tone three octaves below middle C—a tone emanating one mile, ten miles, a thousand miles under the soil, a tone that is the root cause of all aberrational phenomena that burst, every now and then, across this landscape: conflagrations of dust and dirt, torrential thunderstorms, tornadoes, Starkweathers, all indifferent at best and reveling in pain, suffering, and the death of innocents at worst.

Jake's father gave him a pistol for his seventeenth birthday. Jake was so proud of the damned thing, and so moronically stupid about his pride in it that he showed it off to a couple of dozen kids the following morning. Nelson noticed the activity as soon as he entered the playground, and he ran over to tell us about it. Jimmy stayed back—there may have been history behind his reticence—but Nelson and I had a look. Jake had the gun resting on his open palms, as if it were a jewel-encrusted crucifix or a Faberge egg instead of a thin, spindly, metallic blue-black Mauser C-96. Its handle was made of wood, and a purple "9," representing nine millimeters, was carved in it. "As harmless as a toy," Stiles Sr. informed the flabbergasted Liberal High principal a few days later. Harmless because Mr. Stiles had not provided Jake with bullets.

So Jake descended from at least one bizarre parent. Who knows, maybe his father was a violent alcoholic and beat the shit out of him whenever he went on a bender. Or perhaps one of Jake's uncles molested him when he was too young to defend himself. None of that matters. When it comes to inflicting irreparable harm on another human being, extenuating circumstances are irrelevant.

4:00 P.M. Thursday, March 13th

On the afternoon Marcie was assaulted in the backseat of a car parked alongside a deserted wheat field, I was playing cards with my two friends at Nelson's house. That reality needed to be buried were I to stake my claim as eyewitness to the crime.

"I need a negative alibi."

I popped the request on the day after Marcie returned to school. The three of us were walking home at a slower pace than usual because an hour of handball had tuckered us out. Jimmy was huffing and puffing hard. It is curious that despite being out of shape, he was nearly invincible in handball.

Jimmy stopped dead in the middle of the road, put his hands on his hips, stared hard at me for a few seconds, and said, "No. Definitely not."

Nelson asked, "A what? What's a negative alibi?"

"Carl here wants us to deny, should we be interrogated by the powers that be, that we were in his august company at a certain time on a particular day. Let me guess. Would that be, oh, let's see—a week ago Thursday, sometime after school?"

"Fucking mind reader."

I was stunned that he figured it out on the spot, but I shouldn't have been surprised at all. All he had to do was put two and two together. I had tried to keep each *two* secret, but any kid with Jimmy's psychic tentacles would have uncovered them as easily as sweeping pine needles off a shellacked hardwood floor. The first *two* related to my rapidly developing retentive abilities. I had been circumspect ever since Nelson labeled me "freak-boy." Nevertheless, evidence of my progress leaked out from time to time. Just as air molecules, upon being disturbed by a moving bow or a vibrating reed, oscillate from extremes of compression to rarefaction and back, I either coveted the daydreamy joy that accompanies ownership of a secret weapon or I showed it off.

There were times when I could not resist the latter option. One instance particularly startled Nelson and Jimmy. A week after the event, I recounted the first twelve poker hands from an afternoon session at my house, including the sequence of faceup cards, amounts bet, raised, and reraised, who the dealer was for each hand, who won the hand, and the correct succession of variants. We used to make up our own, such as eight-card draw with fours and sevens wild, and my favorite, five-card prime, in which aces, deuces, threes, fives, sevens, jacks and kings could be substituted for each other. I even recollected a few incidentals for my friends' edification, such as what we were doing when Nelson started and stopped chewing on a yellow chip.

Chip chewing was one of his more disgusting idiosyncrasies. He thought it looked sharp, and there was nothing Jimmy nor I could do to convince him of the truth, which was that sticking a chip between one's front teeth and lathering it up with saliva contributed to the drooling idiot persona.

The other *two* revolved around certain kindnesses I had gotten into the habit of showing toward Marcie. In spare minutes toward the end of many lunch hours I would help her solve an algebra problem or two, or I might fix up a few lines from one of her English compositions. She sat to my right in both math and English, and Jimmy sat two rows behind us. He must have noticed. Crude though he had been concerning my attraction to Melissa, he never accused me of falling for a slow girl. Jimmy was fast approaching the land of obesity, which in the microcosm of high school life and in the infinitely larger macrocosm beyond it conferred upon him a status similar to the one the world laid upon kids like Marcie.

"Why?" said Nelson. "I still don't get it."

"Carl here wants to play knight in shining armor and avenge Marcie's rape. Isn't that right, Carl?"

"Just grant me the alibi, okay?"

"No, not okay. Not okay at all, and you know why? Because you can't pull it off. They'll catch you lying, or even worse, Marcie will say something contradictory and both of you will wind up in jail. And when you get there, well..." Jimmy held his arms out as if he were holding a keg of beer.

"Well what?"

"They'll send you to Leavenworth. You'll be locked up for years with hundreds of big savage homos who will beat you up and fuck your ass over and over again. You will be the weakest, you will occupy the bottom of the totem pole, and no one, no warden, no guard, certainly no prisoner, will lift a finger to stop it. By the time you get out—if you get out, because people get knifed to death in prison—your ass will be sore for five more years." Nelson punctuated Jimmy's rant with hyenic *yeahs* every few seconds.

I didn't put up a fight because Jimmy's intensity intimidated me. His vehemence in fact affected me so much that for the next two days I did nothing. On the third day, however, I decided to speak to the county attorney. *It will be all right,* I kept saying to myself. *It will be all right, and I have to do it.*

"They'll catch you lying." Jimmy's argument flowed from this assumption. All I had to do was make sure I wasn't caught. Fortunately, I didn't have to make up the story out of thin air. I was aided by two unsuspecting allies: Jake and Phil. Thanks to second-hand information that had been floating around the school, and that had originated from the perpetrators' imbecilic willingness to incriminate themselves, I learned what I needed to know about the rape's attendant details without having to interview the rapists. The scenario I constructed was therefore a three-boy effort. All I had to do was fabricate a few items concerning Marcie's behavior and Jake and Phil's brutality—items that would not stray far from the truth.

As for Nelson and Jimmy, I felt rock-solid certain that they would not let me down. Precisely *because* Jimmy vented so hard and Nelson enthusiastically backed him up, they would be loyal. Call it the irony of friendship—fight, then unite. To this day, I don't know if the police ever got around to questioning them.

9:45 P.M. Thursday, March 13th

It took me an anxious quarter of an hour, in freezing weather and against a strong headwind, to run to the courthouse from school. I arrived so out of breath that I began hyperventilating upon entering its overheated and disinfected entryway. I felt as if my lungs were about to rip themselves out of my chest. My response was to panic. I ran outside and around to the back of the building, where I scooped up fresh snow with my bare hands. I rubbed the snow into my scalp, down my neck, and over my face. After resting my forehead for a few seconds against the courthouse's redbrick wall, I closed my eyes and muttered, "Relax goddammit you fucking idiot relax." I repeated the mantra a hundred times, gradually slowing it down. And there you have it, the Carl Anderson remedy for terminating panic attacks. Nail it to your refrigerator door, because you never know.

I approached the courthouse a second time. This time I hustled through the entryway, climbed two sets of creaky stairs, and made it to an office door at the top floor's westernmost end. I stood there for fifteen seconds, finally knocked.

"Enter."

A woman, twenty-five or thirty years old, did not rise from her desk. She had long dark hair and wore a starched white blouse that accentuated her femality. I didn't know the word *sultry* back then, but that adjective summed her up pretty well. In a dime-store detective novel she would have been the private eye's full-time secretary and part-time lover. Or she would have been his part-time secretary and full-time lover. Come to think of it, is there a difference between a part-time and a full-time lover?

The sign on her desk read *Irene Morgan*. "Sit down. I'll be with you soon."

I never saw anyone type so fast. Her eyes fixated on some document, and her upper body moved incessantly and unpredictably, as if she were simultaneously dancing to the beats of a tango and a tarantella. Five minutes passed before she paused, said, "Now tell me who you are and why you're here."

"Carl Anderson, ma'am. I go to Liberal High, and I need to speak to Mr. Townsend. Mr. John Townsend." As if there might have been more than one Townsend floating about the office.

"And why might that be?"

"I have information about what happened to Marcie Smith?"

Yes, the question mark is appropriate. I was asking Miss

Morgan if she was familiar with the incident, and I was addressing
the question to myself, as in *What the fuck am I doing here?*

Miss Morgan tugged downward on her blouse and stared at
me. I tried staring back, but my eyes fell a little short.

"Go on. I'm listening."

"I'm sorry, but I'll only talk to Mr. Townsend."

"Mr. Townsend is in a meeting. I can't interrupt him. Talk to
me or I'll take you to a policeman."

"I don't want a policeman, just Mr. Townsend."

Miss Morgan approached me, then turned and lowered herself
onto the chair to my right with the feminine flourish—slow descent,
upper body angled forward, barely perceptible wiggle of the
backside upon touchdown as if blessing the chair, smoothing out the
dress, right leg crossing over left.

"Okay, have it your way. It may be a while, though, because
his meeting started just before you arrived. Coincidence." For the
first time, I noticed muffled voices behind Townsend's office door.

Miss Morgan recrossed her legs, tapped my right forearm with
her left middle finger, and gave me a half-smile.

"You sure you don't want to talk to me? Might save some
time." Spoken slow and soft.

What is it with women? They pry information from me so
easily, always have. Or rather, what is it about me that lets them do
it? Maybe it's the futility of it all. Women are clever and devious, at
least the clever and devious ones are. I put up token resistance then
gave up everything, the whole story, the entire series of fabrications.
Miss Morgan asked many questions along the way, all of which were
incisive. She probably learned interrogation techniques from her
boss. Either that or interrogation skills are part and parcel of a clever
and devious woman's arsenal. It took only twelve minutes to run
through it all.

"Maybe I should interrupt Mr. Townsend's meeting. It's

relevant." But before she could do so, two men and a woman emerged from the inner office. One of the men was ten inches shorter than the other. He stood out like half a birthday cake slotted between two candles, what with his double-breasted black silk suit, white shirt, dark brown string tie, and diamond stickpin sparkling off his lapel. Gold chain too, connected to what had to be a pocket watch hidden deep in his left pants pocket. The man's abundant straight black hair, gray at the sides, had been brushed back tight, forming an incipient ponytail at its rearmost point. Everything about him was firm and decisive, from the expression on his face to his gait and even to his considerable pot belly. He and the woman shook the tall man's hand, said goodbye, and left.

After I had repeated my story to Mr. Townsend, he rose from his chair, opened his office door, and approached his secretary. He placed a hand on her left shoulder, bent down a little, and said, ever so sweetly, "Reenie, honey, we've changed my minds about this. Don't send that letter. Write up another one and tell Porfiteza that we're rejecting the deal. Word it as you see fit and then show it to me when you've finished, okay? Oh, and be diplomatic. He's going to be steamed as it is."

Townsend stepped back in his office and closed the door. "I need to ask you a few more questions, boy. First, are you leveling with me? Because if you aren't, there will be hell to pay and you will be doing the paying."

"Yes sir. What I told you was what happened. I saw it all."

"Okay, good. Second question: are you and Marcie friends?"

"Yeah. Sometimes she eats lunch with me and my friends."

"What about more than that?"

"More? Oh, no. You know she's a little slow, right?"

"Lots of boys get caught up with slow girls."

"Not me."

"You know why I'm asking, don't you?"

"To see if I have a reason?"

"Exactly. Which brings me to Jacob Stiles and Philip Jensen. You have any history with them? Any bad blood?"

"No sir. I don't know them at all." A half-lie, because it was impossible to attend Liberal High School and not know about Jake.

"Excellent. Now there's just one more item, the police deposition. I'll have Miss Morgan walk you over. It won't take long."

"Sir?"

"Yes?"

"I'm not going to do it if Marcie is forced to testify."

"Why?"

"I'm afraid for her."

"What's to be afraid of? No one's going to hurt her."

"She hates arguing. At school she shrinks into herself whenever anyone raises a voice. I'm afraid she'd be crushed."

I knew that Jake and Phil's lawyer, Mr. Porfiteza I assumed, would have no problem getting Marcie to agree to almost anything. Marcie was agreeable by nature, and a woman's agreeability, so highly prized by the vast majority of men on every continent, is a liability in a rape trial. Agreeable women consent.

"Okay, kid, have it your way. Marcie Smith doesn't testify. But you know what that means, don't you?"

"What?"

"Think about it."

"About what?"

"About being the sole eyewitness, because you can bet your bottom dollar that Mr. Porfiteza will not allow his two soon-to-be dressed-for-church model citizen young defendants to be cross-examined."

I returned home two hours late. Ma asked where I had been.

"Played some poker over at Jimmy's."

Pa looked up from his easy chair. "Next time be back before

dark."

"Sure thing. We got a little carried away, but I'll make sure it doesn't happen again." Two lies and one significant omission, an untruth trifecta accomplished with just two brief utterances.

Silence. Ma set the table and Pa returned to examining his worn out copy of the 1938 *Sears Farm Equipment Catalogue*. We excelled at conversational efficiency back then. No words spilled, no messes to clean up.

Although my parents were quiet people, my mother conveyed a greater seriousness than did my father, whose conversational topics were limited to crops and the weather. Pa, being round both of face and of torso, approximated a grown-up and charmless Charley Brown in coveralls. Ma was his opposite—thin, short, and compact. She had acquired that weather-beaten worn out look commonly found in photos of women from the Depression and Dust Bowl years. The remnants of dirt, hardship, and pain had been permanently sandblasted under her skin. There had been a sister, born a year after me, who didn't make it past her first birthday.

I was confronted by two angry parents when I returned from school a few days later. The mailman delivered a letter addressed to me that morning, and its return address was that of the county attorney's office. Pa opened it without giving my right to privacy the slightest consideration.

"Looks like you have some explaining to do," he said. "Did you really think we wouldn't find out? Why the heck didn't you tell us?" That's right, Pa was a heck man. No hell for him.

"I didn't think you'd approve."

"You're damned right," thundered Ma. No darn for her on this particular occasion.

The letter was a notice commanding me to testify in an upcoming trial, and it ruined my supper. Ma had made spaghetti that night, my favorite, and the effort it took to keep lying was taxing enough to drain my tongue's taste buds of sensation.

"Don't do this," said Ma. "Nothing good can come from it."

"Have to, already spoke with Mr. Townsend. He's the county attorney. And according to Jimmy, Marcie could be in a bad way if there's no conviction."

"Jimmy?" Ma's face tightened. "That fat misfit boy is your source for how the world turns?"

"He's my friend. And besides, he's right."

"No he isn't! He is absolutely wrong, which is not surprising because he's a kid. He has no idea. *You* have no idea!"

"No idea of what?"

"Of the consequences. Rule number one around these parts is you never, *never* mess with folks who are better off than you."

"But what about Marcie? I can't leave her defenseless."

"You can and you will. You have to! Your family comes first."

As vehement as Jimmy had been in denying my negative alibi, he came nowhere close to the apoplectic level Ma was now approaching. Never before had I seen her this way.

"Amanda, calm down," said Pa. He had been studying the letter while Ma and I battled it out. "It's too late. They'll force him to testify."

Ma stomped up the stairs, which in retrospect was pretty funny, a tiny person stomping so forcefully. She slammed her bedroom door shut.

"See what you did!" Pa went up after her, and I then made it a perfect three for three by marching up to my room.

Through two shut doors I heard Ma say, "But what if he finds out?" Having been under attack that evening, I paid no heed to her question. But now I wonder: if the *he* in Ma's sentence was me, what were my parents hiding? And if the *he* wasn't me, to whom was Ma referring?

8:32 A.M., *Saturday, March 15th*

Sometimes doing nothing is the better option. A man drives along a high-traffic avenue. He spots a stray dog scratching itself on the sidewalk and realizes it's roadkill if it wanders into the street. He stops his car, gets out, takes hold of the dog's collar, and checks its tags. The dog's owner observes these actions from his living room window and concludes that the stranger is about to steal his pet. He grabs his rifle, bursts out the front door, aims at the man, and fires. He shoots his dog dead on the spot.

I met with Mr. Townsend a week and a day before the trial was to begin. We reviewed my deposition, then went through a "trial run" at his office desk, in which he role-played both himself and Mr. Porfiteza.

"Good. You described what happened clearly, responded consistently to my questions, and added no embellishments. If you stick to the same story next week and don't let Porfiteza rattle you, everything will turn out as it should."

"Sure thing."

"Sure thing? Don't fool yourself. Porfiteza will do most anything to get his clients off, and that includes threatening, shouting, and making fun of prosecution witnesses. Count on him giving you a rougher ride than I just did."

"How long will I have to endure him?"

"You'll be up there a while."

"Why? You asked me a lot of questions just now but we finished pretty quickly."

"Different frames of reference, Carl. You're thinking, all I have to do is say what I saw, but Porfiteza will be operating at the level of the gut: wear him down, make him crack. Just stay alert, be careful, and avoid being baited into saying something stupid, okay?"

"Yeah."

"Oh, one more thing," spoken offhandedly, as if the words that followed carried slight import: "Marcie will be testifying. She's looking forward to it, in fact."

"What?"

"It's a necessity, son. In Kansas, you can't win a rape case if the woman doesn't show up. And anyway, she's dying to do it. She really wants to nail those boys."

"Dying to do it? Just how stupid do you think I am? She'll get killed!"

"I understand your concern, truly I do, but look at it from my perspective. I *must* put Marcie up. No Marcie, no conviction. No trial, even."

"But she can't defend herself! You know that."

"Granted, Porfiteza will have little trouble, but I don't expect him to harangue her. Heaping abuse on the poor thing would not be in the best interest of his clients. He'll be civil about it. She'll screw up her answers, and the whole ordeal will be over in less than fifteen minutes. After, you'll set the record straight. Right?" He struck the desk with his fist and smiled at me. "Anyway, it's too late for you to go missing. The judge will hold you in contempt."

"Fuck the judge and fuck his goddamn contempt and fuck you too! Do you really think I give a damn about any of that shit? Either she doesn't testify or I don't testify, one or the other. *Let* them send me off to jail somewhere. See if I give a flying fuck!"

An uneasy silence ensued, during which I glared at Townsend while he just sat there and stared at his shoelaces. I was about leave when finally he looked at me and said something:

"Son, I'm going to take the liberty of assuming, despite the antipathy you currently harbor toward my person, that we remain united in our desire to see Mr. Jacob Stiles and Mr. Philip Jensen removed from society. So instead of reprimanding you for what in my opinion are unjustified multiple applications of profanity, I suggest that you calm down and allow me to provide, free of charge, a lesson in how the law operates *vis-à-vis* the matter of rape cases conducted in the great state of Kansas. Afterward, decide for yourself to go forward or not. Just keep in mind that Marcie *will* be testifying, whether or not you choose to protect her."

"But why can't Jake and Phil be locked up based on what I say?"

"Because a defendant has the right to confront his accuser."

"Really? Why didn't you tell me that before?"

Townsend extracted some change from his pockets. He placed a penny and two quarters on the desk, the penny to my right and the quarters to my left. Pointing to the penny, he said, "The woman. Worth as much as the two bundles of wheat. And over here," he said, motioning toward the two quarters, "lookie what we found. George Washington! That's right, the I-cannot-tell-a-lie cherry tree guy. *Two* George Washingtons in fact."

He picked up the penny with his left hand and the quarters with his right. "Here's how it unfolds, Carl. The woman accuses the man, and the man denies it. He says it never happened, or claims she wanted it to happen."

He held the penny in front of me. "She said." Then he brought the two quarters to within a foot of my face. "Versus 'he said,' or, in the present instance, 'they said.' Not close to a fair fight. But what's the girl to do? Nothing? Let the scumbags go free so they can keep on raping with impunity?"

"Why didn't you tell me all this when I first came to see you?"

"Sometimes truth is with the man, because as the saying goes, Hell hath no fury like a woman scorned. But most of the time it's the man who's lying. Fact is, rape is an everyday event, and convicting a rapist is akin to swatting a fly. There are too many other flies, and the screen door has too many holes. It's impossible to imprison all the rapists in Kansas, Carl, totally impossible. No matter how hard I and my fellow county attorneys toil, our great state will never be a rape-free paradise. Nevertheless, I get paid pretty good, so I do what I can. And just between you and me, I savor it. Nothing, absolutely nothing, gives me a bigger charge than hearing the judge announce 'ten to fifteen.'"

"Answer my question!"

"In a minute. Let me finish up first. It's important."

"Okay, but then I want an answer."

"You'll have it. Now let's draw the battle lines. The defense team's goals are straightforward enough: cast aspersions on the woman's reputation and truthfulness, then make it a he-said versus she-said proposition. Convictions are hard to come by because the defense needs to make just one of those two conditions stick. Accomplish either, then let the ubiquitous phrase, 'reasonable doubt,' the rabbit hole in our legal system, work its magic. All you need are twelve gullible citizens. See what I'm getting at?"

"That to convict, Marcie needs my help. Without it, Jake and Phil go unpunished. That's pretty clear."

"It's more complicated than that. Your testimony is necessary, but it isn't sufficient. It's equally important for Marcie to be brave. Take a moment to appreciate her for it. Sure, Porfiteza will refrain from the histrionics, but only because he won't need them. His questions will be damning, and I expect Marcie will find the experience a very uncomfortable one. Frankly, I'll be shocked if she leaves the witness stand feeling anything but deep and painful humiliation."

"Which is exactly why I don't want her to testify!"

"I understand, truly I do. Before you came to my office I wasn't planning to prosecute. I figured it would have been cruel to put Miss Smith through the ordeal of a trial, knowing full well that I would have had no chance of convicting her attackers. Despite the existence of the police photo and the knowledge that Marcie was dumped by the boys in a wheat field, I would have lost. And you know why? Because Porfiteza would have discredited Marcie so thoroughly that I wouldn't have gotten a shot at cross-examining Messrs. Stiles and Jensen. There would have been no need for Porfiteza to put them on the witness stand. Everything changes with your testimony, though, because you're so fucking believable! It's as if a movie camera had been placed on location and recorded everything."

"But what about Marcie? How's she going to get over this?"

"She'll recover when we win. Winning is vindication, it's everything! With you up there, we've got a great chance. If you are as good next week as you were today, Jake and Phil will be forced to testify. And if you are great I expect Mr. Porfiteza to do what any competent lawyer does in such a situation. He'll cut his losses and cop a plea."

"Jake and Phil go to jail?"

"At a minimum they'll have criminal records. They might be incarcerated, but I can't guarantee it."

"Why not?"

"First convictions. The criminal code goes easy on the first offender, especially if he accepts a plea bargain, thereby admitting guilt. It works like this, son: if you're a Kansas male, you're not colored, and the girl is over sixteen years of age, you're allowed one free rape. Usually it doesn't get reported, so you get away with it, no questions asked. Or you get your wrists slapped, because who knows, maybe it was just one of those gosh-I-didn't-know-what-I-was-doing-until-I-did-it kind of things, you know? Or maybe it never would have happened if the accused hadn't guzzled nine beers beforehand. I could reel off three dozen excuses I've come across over the years. So many slimes professing not to know what they were doing, as if the act of assaulting a woman, sometimes with a knife at her throat or a gun to her head, ripping her clothes off, and forcing a dick somewhere inside her amounted to an oversight, like absentmindedly walking into a doorpost or spilling a cup of coffee."

Townsend never did answer my question, and I didn't press

him on it again because there was nothing to be done about it. I had
to take care of Marcie. Despite tricking me into testifying, I ended up
appreciating both Townsend's determination to prosecute the case as
hard as possible and his cynicism with how the world turns. But as
for forgiving that son of a bitch for what he put Marcie through, and
for the deceit he leveled on me, never.

9:00 P.M. Saturday, March 15th

The trial commenced on the morning of Wednesday, May 13th, 1942.
In attendance were twelve jury members, prosecution and defense
entourages, two defendants prettied up in old-man tweed suits, one
septuagenarian white male judge, one female court reporter, a giant
of a bailiff, two policemen, a reporter from the *Southwest Daily Times*,
various witnesses including Marcie and me, and sixty spectators
seated in pews imported long ago from some church that went belly
up. A packed house.

"Your Honor, the state calls Marcie Smith."

So many years ago, yet I see her exactly as she appeared that
morning. She wears a freshly ironed white cotton dress-skirt combo,
and for once her hair, adorned with a pink ribbon tied in a bow, has
been combed neatly. Her pale complexion seems lighter than usual,
and her straight pure white teeth captivate. She sits still, a China doll
nervously displaying her everyday smile—a shade above neutral,
like sunlight filtered through layers of cirri.

Mr. Townsend began with a few innocuous questions: "How old
are you?" "What school do you attend?" "What grade are you in?"
Marcie rubbed her left thumb against her second and third fingers
repetitively as she answered them.

"Miss Smith, would you please tell the Court what happened
to you on January Eighth of this year?"

She looked around the courtroom. It wasn't hard to guess what
she was thinking: *So many people, all staring at me.*

"Just take your time, tell the truth, and everything will be fine."

"I walked home. It was cold. The car stops and they ask if I want a ride."

"Who were they?"

Marcie pointed to the boys. "Them."

Townsend walked to the defense table and stood behind Jake and Phil. "These two?"

"Yes."

"Did you take the ride?"

"Yes."

"And why did you do that?"

"It was cold. Very."

"All right, good. What happened after?"

"They don't take me home. We went someplace and they stop the car." Marcie spoke in her usual soft voice, audible as a bell even in the back of the courtroom where Ma and I were sitting.

"I know this is difficult, but please continue."

"The tall one says for me to take off my coat."

"Did you do so?"

"No."

"And then what happened?"

"He tells me he wants to look at it, then he returns it. He said he gives me a Chunky Bar. So I did."

"You removed your coat?"

"Yes. It was cold. No Chunky Bar."

"And?"

"He says I get my coat back if I'm nice. If I'm not, he makes me leave the car, but not with my coat. So I run away and fall. Then he— he hit me. I was down and he hit me."

"Which one hit you?"

"Him." Marcie pointed at Jake. "He hit me. He hit me."

Townsend introduced the police photo into evidence, then

showed it to Marcie. "Is this what he did to you?"

"Your Honor!" Porfiteza jumped from his chair, but the judge, Orrin Carnoway by name, ordered him to sit back down.

"Overruled. Miss Smith, please answer the question."

"Yes. All gone now."

"What's gone now?" asked Townsend.

"Looking bad. And hurt. All gone."

"Miss Smith, it may be difficult for you to talk about what happened next, but it's very important that we know."

"I was cold, and it hurt. Down there. And my head. And the people came, the nice people in the car, they took me away. To the hospital."

"That was it? You remember nothing else?"

"No."

"Nothing at all?"

"No."

Townsend asked a few more questions, some of which required Marcie to reiterate what she had already said. The others dealt with her experiences in the hospital and after she was released from it. Mr. Porfiteza then requested a twenty-minute recess. He told Judge Carnoway that in light of Marcie's testimony, he needed to confer with his clients before beginning his cross-examination.

That extra twist must have thrown him. Violation exacted upon an unconscious victim—well now, that wouldn't exactly sit well with the jurors, would it? Such behavior amounts to only twenty-eight degrees of separation from necrophilia: body versus room temperature. It's an act so far removed from normality as to deprive the accused of any empathy boost. Where's the fantasy, the subconscious upside, without a struggle? Porfiteza left the courtroom with a frown on his face and his two clients in tow.

I scanned the courtroom. Miss Bove had risen from her place in the middle of the pew two rows in front of us. She was wearing a formal green taffeta dress, suitable for a wedding. Mr. McGrady and the farmhand who discovered Marcie by the side of the road sat one row in front of her. Jimmy and Nelson also sat together, in the last-row pew far to my left. I had expected neither them nor Miss Bove to attend because it was a school day.

Also sticking in my memory was a solitary figure, a tall thin man with white hair and a tanned leathery face. He sat at the extreme left end of the front-row pew, wore a tan V-neck sweater vest covering a buttoned up long-sleeved dress shirt—anomalous attire, compared to the typical short-sleeved and undershirted Liberal adult male. Shortly after Ma and I arrived at the courthouse I noticed him looking at me with an intensity that unnerved me, especially as I had never seen him before. I surmised that Ma had sat us at the back of the courtroom and to the extreme right in order to be as far away from him as possible, but when I questioned her later, she said, "What white-haired man? I never saw no man with white hair."

Mr. Porfiteza began his cross-examination by approaching Marcie slowly, smiling like a benevolent grandfather. But of course. Let the jury know you're no bully. You're a sensitive, caring, empathic defense attorney, reluctantly charged with the unfortunate necessity of having to destroy a hapless girl's reputation in order to prevent an injustice.

"Miss Smith, before the afternoon of January Eighth of this year did you know Jacob Stiles and Philip Jensen?"

"No."

"But you saw them at school every now and then?"

"Yes." Marcie resumed rubbing her left thumb against her fingers.

"You never talked with them?"

"No."

"And why is that?"

"They are a year ahead. Not in my classes."

"So they are almost strangers to you?"

"Yes."

Porfiteza backed up a few paces and fixated on the jury for a few seconds. "Almost strangers," he repeated.

A short pause, then: "Miss Smith, didn't your parents tell you not to take rides from strangers?"

"Yes."

"So why did you get in the car?"

"It was cold. And I know them from school."

"But not well. Not at all well, correct?"

"Not well."

"Do you think the defendants are good looking?"

Townsend objected, and the objection was sustained. But Marcie had no idea what "objection sustained" meant and answered the question anyway: "The tall one. But he hit me."

Porfiteza launched a series of irrelevant questions, all of which went unchallenged by Townsend: Was Marcie attracted to the boys in her class? Would she like to have a boyfriend, like the other girls? Did she ever think about getting married someday, and would she want children? Marcie answered "Yes" to them all.

"I know it was cold that day, Miss Smith, but you've walked home on cold days before, correct?"

"Yes."

"So when Mr. Stiles and Mr. Jensen offered you the ride, weren't you at least a little bit excited by the possibility of being with them? And might you have felt flattered that they would even give you a lift?"

"Yes." She looked down at the floor, didn't look up again until after leaving the witness stand.

"Is it possible that the bruises shown in the photo could have resulted from your fall? Or did you actually see Mr. Stiles punch you in the face?"

"He grabbed me. I tried, but his punches."

"His punches?"

"Yes. He hit me."

"Are you sure about that? Maybe he was simply reaching out to stop you from falling."

No response.

"And is it not also possible that you weren't unconscious, but you don't want to talk about what happened afterward? That maybe you don't feel so good about that part?"

Again, no response.

"Miss Smith? Won't you say something?"

Nope.

Turning to Judge Carnoway, Porfiteza said, "Your Honor, I have no more questions for this witness."

Sometimes it is better to leave bad enough alone. Townsend's redirect began and ended with the following question: "Miss Smith, just to clarify: when I was questioning you before, you stated that you remembered nothing between the moment Mr. Stiles hit you and when Mr. McGrady discovered you by the road. That's correct, isn't it?"

Once again, no response.

"Miss Smith?"

"I've heard enough," said the judge. "Miss Smith, you're excused. Bailiff, please accompany Miss Smith back to her seat."

The bailiff, a tall heavyset man with a head completely devoid of hair, took Marcie's hand. She never looked up as he escorted her to the back of the courtroom.

2:21 P.M. Wednesday, March 19th

"Your Honor, the State calls Carl Anderson."

I rose, spotted Marcie's family across the courtroom. Her parents were standing in the aisle, but she was sitting with her arms folded, still staring into the floor. Her father tried taking her hand, but she was having none of it. By the time I turned around after reaching the witness stand, all three of them were seated and looking my way.

"Not yet," said the court reporter. "Get up and come here." I had sat down before being sworn in.

She grabbed my right hand and placed it firmly on the Bible she was holding. "Leave it there." Whoa, what a bitch. She was shorter than me by ten inches, weighed about ninety-two pounds, and her eyes glittered with anger.

"Yes ma'am."

"Mr. Carl Anderson, do you solemnly swear or affirm that you will tell the truth, the whole truth, and nothing but the truth, so help you God?" Spoken slowly, every syllable accented and enunciated with the precision of a stapling gun.

More lies were to follow, but this one was the whopper, the one that once committed would permit succeeding lies to roll off my tongue as smoothly as the Mississippi flows down to the Gulf:

"I do."

"Save that for when you get married. Try again."

"Yes?"

The court reporter smiled, finally. "Good. Now have a seat." She sat at the table directly to my right, took out her stenographer's pad, and looked expectantly at Mr. Townsend.

My left thigh started shaking even before Townsend had spoken a word. He tried to acclimate me as he had done with Marcie, by beginning with a few easy questions. I could barely answer them. All those people staring at me... I felt lost, psychically out to sea. Then I noticed the white-haired man honing in on me once again. Right then I decided I would answer to him, and only to him. He was a stranger, after all, therefore a person of no consequence.

"Mr. Anderson, please tell the court about the events you witnessed on the afternoon of January 8th, 1942."

"I was up in the sycamore tree by Mr. McGrady's field, about fifteen feet off the ground."

"On one of the coldest days of the year you were sitting on a tree branch?"

"More like in a nook, but yes. I have a pretty heavy coat."

"Wouldn't you have been more comfortable inside your family's nice warm house?"

"No sir. Cold doesn't bother me, not with my coat on, and I've been partial to that particular tree ever since I first saw it."

"Why?"

"It's my secret place. No one bothers me there. I had been reading the Book of Job, specifically the part where Job scrapes at his boils. That's when the car drove past and stopped about a hundred feet up the road. It was black."

Although Townsend had known what I was going to say, he feigned a pretty good Holy Cow look. Mr. Porfiteza looked up from his jottings and smiled.

"You were reading the Book of Job?"

"Yes sir."

"Most high school students don't study the good book in their spare time, son. Wouldn't you agree that's a bit unusual?"

"Mr. Townsend, sir, I memorized the Old Testament last year. I don't tell people about it because they might think I'm strange." Intense laughter, multiple guffaws throughout the courtroom. Ma remained grim as granite.

Judge Carnoway rapped his gavel three times and everyone shut up.

"Mr. Anderson," said Townsend, "how does memorizing the Bible put you up a tree in the middle of nowhere, and on a cold January afternoon, no less?"

"It's a bit of a story."

"Let's hear it."

The judge interrupted: "Keep it short, boy. What you say is relevant, because it reflects on your credibility, but it doesn't deal directly with this case. So tell us about your memorization stunt, but make it fast."

"Yes sir. I took a book out of the school library back in November of 1940, when I was in tenth grade. It was all about memorization. I first read it in Mr. McGrady's field, the same one where Marcie was attacked."

Porfiteza instantly objected, obliging me to change "attacked" to "found."

"I sat up against the tree that first time. Ever since, I've had a liking for the spot. I've returned there many times, but when the snow came I couldn't sit on the ground anymore, so I climbed up and dusted off a nook. The first time it felt hard, but no more. I've gotten used to it. Now I like it even better than the ground, because I get a nice view."

"Okay, very good," said Townsend, "but now let's return to the incident in question. Please tell the court exactly what you saw from your tree lookout."

"After the car stopped, nothing happened for a few minutes. Then the right rear passenger door opened. Marcie got out and started running up the road, and without her coat on. Boy was I surprised to see her."

"She ran up the road in the direction away from you?"

"Yes. Jake took off after her. He tackled her and they both fell in the snow. Marcie kicked him hard and screamed. I never heard her scream before. But Jake, he managed to get on top of her. He pinned her down, banged her head against the ground a couple of times, then grabbed her hard around the throat and punched her three times, twice to the head and once to the stomach. I think he knocked her out, because she didn't make a sound after that. Phil joined Jake, and the two of them kind of dragged Marcie back to the car. They managed to push her inside, onto the backseat."

"Could you tell if Miss Smith was conscious?"

"I don't think she was. She was limp when they were carrying her back to the car."

"Mr. Anderson, why didn't you try to help her, or at least run away and get assistance?"

"I was scared. I started to climb down from the tree, but Jake pulled out a gun from the car, so I froze."

Ah yes, the gun. A nice touch, if I say so myself. I can't take full credit, as it was well known that despite school rules, Jake stored the precious thing in the glove compartment of his car, along with a box of bullets he had managed to acquire.

"Really, a gun? Did Jake threaten Marcie with it?"

"No sir. I didn't see him do anything like that, and Marcie wasn't conscious, at least she didn't look like she was, so she wouldn't have heard him or seen the gun."

"Then why do you think Jake took this gun out from his car?"

Porfiteza objected on the grounds that Townsend was asking me to hypothesize about a motivation of which I had no knowledge. Sustained.

"Please tell the court what happened next."

"Phil and Jake got in the car and started it up. I thought they were going to drive off, but after five minutes or so, Jake cut the engine and both of them got out again. Jake opened the left rear door and went in while Phil stood behind the car, holding the gun. He kept it in his jacket, except for a couple of times when he took it out to have a look."

Other than Porfiteza's rasping pencil, the courtroom was silent. Townsend offered me a glass of water. I took a couple of sips and continued:

"They took turns, one of them in the backseat with Marcie, the other standing guard behind the car. Jake three times, Phil twice."

"Could you see exactly what was going on? I mean in the backseat."

"No sir. I was too far away."

"What happened after they finished with Miss Smith?"

"They dragged her into the field, about twenty feet from the road, covered her face with her coat, and drove off."

"Carl—Mister Anderson—why in God's name didn't you try to prevent this from happening?"

"I thought they'd shoot me. And if they shot me, they might shoot Marcie too."

"But after they left why didn't you go help Miss Smith?"

"I did. I was able to get her coat on her and move her a few feet closer to the side of the road. Then I saw headlights coming from the direction Jake and Phil had driven. I ran off because I was afraid it was them again. And if it was someone else, I could get blamed."

"What happened next?"

"I hid behind my tree. If the car had kept moving I would have returned to Marcie. Fortunately, though, it stopped. Two men got out, and while they were looking after her I ran off."

Townsend finished up by asking me a few questions concerning my behavior over the days following the attack. Judge Carnoway then asked Mr. Porfiteza if he wanted a recess before beginning his cross examination.

"No, your Honor. I would like to get right to it."

Porfiteza stood up, straight as an arrow. A short portly arrow.

"Mr. Anderson, before we begin let me remind you that you are under oath. Even though you are only seventeen, if you are found guilty of perjury—that's what we call lying in court under oath—you could go to prison for quite some time. Are you aware of that?"

"Yes sir, I am."

Porfiteza hitched up his pants and approached me until he was only two feet away. Despite the close distance, his next question was spoken more loudly than the previous one.

"Mind if I call you Carl?"

The thought of responding, "Not if you don't mind me calling you Antonio" crossed my mind, but I rejected the option. I knew that acting cocky would have pleased Porfiteza no end. So instead I said, "No sir."

"Good. Now then Carl, I'm having a wee problem believing that a red blooded Kansas boy like you would spend his spare time reading the Bible up a tree in the middle of nowhere, and on an ice-cold winter's day to boot. Enlighten me."

"It was like I told Mr. Townsend."

"I know. But I'd appreciate it if you would provide a few more details. You testified that you were reading the Bible, and in fact that you had been memorizing it."

"Yes sir."

"Look at these fine God-fearing folk, Carl," Porfiteza said as he extended his right arm in the direction of the spectators. "Most of them go to church regularly. But have any of them memorized the Bible? I'd bet the farm not."

Porfiteza addressed the spectators while sweeping both of his arms up to the heavens: "Those of you who have memorized even a single page of the Bible, any page, any version—please stand up!"

Total silence, utter lack of movement.

"Aha! Of all the people in attendance today, not one of them has managed even a thousandth of your accomplishment. Your supposed accomplishment, that is."

Porfiteza picked up the Bible from the court reporter's table and walked to the jury box. He looked at the forelady, a matronly type who reminded me of a character from a Marx Brothers film.

"So—you know everything in this book, correct?"

"No sir, only the Old Testament."

"What, you don't believe in Jesus?"

"Yes sir, I do, and I hope to memorize the New Testament after I finish high school. But for now I'm focusing on my schoolwork."

Porfiteza held the Bible in his right hand and repeatedly

rapped it against his left as if it were a nightstick. "Let's see just how well you really know the Old Testament." But before he had a chance to test me, Townsend interrupted.

"Your Honor, I object most emphatically. Mr. Anderson's expertise concerning the Old Testament is irrelevant to this trial, and counsel for the defense is way out of line in demanding that the witness demonstrate his memorization skills. In no way would Mr. Anderson's failure to do so invalidate his testimony concerning what happened to Marcie Smith on the afternoon of January 8th."

Some prosecutor. I was about to seal the deal, yet the dumb-ass was trying to stop me. I shouldn't have been surprised, given that Porfiteza's initiative was a novelty Townsend hadn't thought to confront me with during our practice session. He ranted on for another minute, then Judge Carnoway asked Porfiteza to respond.

"Your Honor, the witness purports to be telling the truth concerning circumstances surrounding the alleged crime of which the defendants are accused. Furthermore, he claims possession of a memory that is beyond belief. Surely the truthfulness of testimony regarding his own memory has to be relevant to this trial, as it reflects on his believability as an eye witness."

Townsend and Porfiteza sparred for another couple of minutes, one like a baby throwing a tantrum, the other like a cat quietly stalking its prey.

"Objection overruled." Whew.

Porfiteza leafed through the Bible until he found the passage he was looking for.

"Mr. Anderson, please recite the verse following this one: 'And thou shalt not glean thy vineyard, neither shalt thou gather the grapes of thy vineyard; thou shalt leave them for the poor and for the stranger: I am the Lord your God.'"

I looked past Porfiteza, right at the white-haired man: "'Ye shall not steal; neither shall ye deal falsely, nor lie one to another.'"

How apropos, those last five words. I turned back to Porfiteza, added, "And sir, you said 'the grapes.' In Leviticus 19:10, 'every grape' is written. At least it is in my version."

Even though Ma was seated at the back of the courtroom, I was able to see her flicker a smile.

"Very good, Mr. Anderson. Or a lucky guess. Shall we try another, say a little deeper in?"

"Won't matter."

"My, aren't we full of ourselves today."

It took him a few seconds to find the passage he was looking for: "Here we go. Where is this one from? 'The remnant of Israel shall not do iniquity.'"

Ah, the fucker knows his Old Testament! That was my thought right before reciting:

Nor speak lies,

Neither shall a deceitful tongue be found in their mouth;

For they shall feed and lie down,

And none shall make them afraid.

"Umm, that would be Zephaniah 3:13." Good old Zeph, one of my favorites—gloom and doom right from the start, what with the *Dies Irae* batting leadoff.

What a look on Porfiteza's face! He should have given up, but instead he plowed ahead three more times, citing selections from Numbers, Judges, and Proverbs. They all dealt with lying, and I nailed each and every one of them. He was about to test me a sixth time when Judge Carnoway interrupted.

"I've heard enough. The jury shall consider Mr. Anderson's memorization of the Old Testament to be flawless, for whatever that's worth. Now let's get on with it."

Porfiteza questioned me on the specifics of my story: how far up the road Marcie ran before Jake tackled her, how many times she kicked him, exactly where on Marcie's face Jake allegedly punched her (I told him I was too far away to tell, and that his blows were partly obscured by his own body), and so on. He inquired about clothing worn by all three. Not a problem. He also asked about the car, which was easy to describe. I added that its license plate was yellow on maroon and dated 1941, and that I caught its number, 84-123, right after it passed me. Porfiteza brought up the gun. Even though I could have described it easily, I replied that I did not get a good look. He asked if it might have been a toy, and I said yes. Then came a crucial question:

"Can you say conclusively that you actually *saw* Mr. Stiles and Mr. Jensen sexually assault Miss Smith?"

"No sir. I was too far away."

Porfiteza repeated the question for emphasis, which irritated me so much that I elaborated upon, rather than reiterated, my response:

"Each time Mr. Stiles or Mr. Jensen got out of the backseat, sir, each of the five times, well, whoever it was, Jake or Phil, he had to pull up his pants and buckle up. That is, umm, Jake buckled, but Phil didn't because he wasn't wearing a belt." Not a golden moment for the defense, although Porfiteza cleverly crafted some wiggle room:

"Even though Miss Smith appeared unconscious upon her return to the car, you can't say for sure that she remained in that state after being moved into the backseat, correct?"

"I guess so."

"Not only that—according to your own testimony, several minutes elapsed before Mr. Stiles opened the back door to join Miss Smith. Remember, you said that nothing happened for a while, and then the car idled for a few more minutes. Seems to me that this passage of time would have made it more likely for Miss Smith to have regained consciousness, no?"

"Maybe."

"In fact Miss Smith might even have woken up and engaged consensually with the two defendants, correct?" An unexpected blunder. Porfiteza should have saved the comment for his summation rather than take a chance I would challenge it.

"Consensually?"

"Voluntarily."

"Oh. And then she would have resumed being unconscious afterward, when they dragged her into the snow?"

Porfiteza successfully got my last comment struck from the record, but it didn't matter. Jury members don't blot out stuff like that. He then asked a slew of questions concerning my own behavior. He particularly wanted to know why I waited almost three weeks before approaching the authorities.

"I was scared. And I didn't think I would be believed."

Porfiteza requested a recess, claiming that he needed to confer with his clients before questioning me further. Request granted.

As I was walking to the back of the courtroom, I saw something that I have cherished ever since. Marcie smiled at me. It wasn't her usual half-smile. It was big and it was as beautiful as the bloom on a perfectly shaped rose. It lasted three seconds, and yes, that interval comprised the second of the two perfect moments in my life.

2:24 P.M. *Tuesday, March 25th*

The afternoon session began with Mr. Porfiteza asking for, and obtaining, a meeting with Judge Carnoway and Mr. Townsend. The three jurisprudential giants returned to the courtroom a quarter of an hour later, at which time the court reporter recalled me to the witness stand. She reminded me that I was still under oath, and that consequences would be severe were I to lie. As it turned out, not one untruth came forth from my mouth that afternoon.

"Mr. Anderson, close your eyes."

Porfiteza said these words as soon as I sat down. I looked at Judge Carnoway for confirmation, which came fast: "Do it right now, son." Porfiteza slipped a blindfold over my head, which did the trick; I opened my eyes and all was black.

"Carl, you need to know why Judge Carnoway has given me permission to blindfold you. This morning you amazed us all with evidence of your memorization skills. An outstanding feat, my boy. You have a remarkable memory, truly you do. However, you claim that your memory is infallible, correct? Infallible, as in incapable of error?"

"Yes sir."

"Son, that's taking it too far. Understand that I'm not accusing you of dishonesty. To the contrary, I think you're a fine young man. Yes, a very fine young man indeed, whom God has blessed with an excellent brain. I know you're sincere in believing that what you reported this morning was the truth. However, you *could* be wrong. None of us is infallible, none of us! In your heart of hearts you must know this. To err is human, and that applies to you as firmly as to does to everyone else. It's certainly no fault to own up to it, to admit that maybe, just maybe, you have doubts. And should you harbor even the slightest uncertainty concerning your testimony, understand that you could be committing a grave mistake. You would be condemning two innocent boys to fates they don't deserve."

I tried to look worried during Porfiteza's little speech. I frowned. I gulped a couple of times. I altered my sitting position and oriented my head downward, even though I couldn't see the floor or anything else. In truth, I was relieved. Why would Porfiteza blindfold me, unless after meeting with Jake and Phil he figured that *they* were the liars? Putting the boys on the stand in an attempt to rebut me would be risky, because in a hypothetical battle for the hearts and minds of members of the jury, *they-said* likely would prove less credible than *he-said*. Porfiteza's best chance for getting his clients acquitted thus required the adoption of an alternate strategy, one that challenged me not so much on the specific details of my story as on the infallibility of my memory. If he could show that I was in error concerning my own capabilities, then why couldn't I also be in error about my testimony? In addition, Porfiteza would have the "pride goeth before destruction, and a haughty spirit before a fall" factor working for him. What dull-normal member of the jury wouldn't have liked to kick some oddball kid down a peg or two?

"Sir, If your clients go to jail based on my testimony, they will in truth have deserved their punishment. I am sure of that."

"Very well then, Mr. Anderson, let's get started. I'll begin with something easy. The court reporter—you know, the woman who swore you in this morning and who spoke to you again just a minute ago, right before you sat down—what does she look like, and what is she wearing?"

Townsend objected before I could answer. He knew he would be tilting at a juridical windmill, but spoke up anyway:

"Your Honor, I hereby register my objection for the court record. For all the cows in Kansas, what possible purpose does this exercise serve save to unnecessarily retain Mr. Anderson on the witness stand, thereby retarding the wheels of justice's proper speed? What criterion of performance on this irrelevant procedure would need to be demonstrated by Mr. Anderson to satisfy the court? And why require of this particular witness a task that every other man or woman ever to testify inside a Kansas courtroom has never been forced to endure?"

"Mr. Porfiteza, would you care to respond?" said the judge.

"Most definitely, your Honor. We are dealing with a special case here. Mr. Anderson claims possession of an infallible memory. Perfect beyond anyone else's memory! If he is to be believed, when he exits the courtroom later today he shall retain in that head of his a complete record of the day's proceedings down to its most minute details, and that record will not degrade with time. It shall remain in its pristine and unmodified form for as long as he lives. Now really, who can believe such nonsense? Your Honor, it is likely that Mr. Anderson is mistaken about his abilities. It is not inconceivable that what he thinks he has seen is, in reality, little more than imagined filler—a series of fabricated visions, if you will—visions designed to satisfy the need for fancying himself a genius. Evidence of *any* inadequacy in his abilities would therefore render his testimony from this morning suspect. Highly suspect, I should think."

Judge Carnoway of course sided with Mr. Porfiteza: "Mr. Townsend, I understand your concerns. Nevertheless, no one here needs to rush out and catch a train. Let's hear what Mr. Anderson has to say. Mr. Anderson?"

For the next few seconds I said nothing. I had been distracted by Porfiteza's phrase, "he shall retain in that head of his a complete record of the day's proceedings."

"Mr. Anderson, did you hear me?"

"Oh. Oh yes sir."

"Then please begin."

"Sir, if I may—I'd first like to say something that could clarify how my memory works. Would that be all right? It might help Mr. Porfiteza understand me better." Despite Townsend's admonition against embellishment, I decided to improvise. At certain times in a life, it behooves the soul to venture beyond boundaries set by the Townsends of this world.

Porfiteza couldn't wait for Carnoway's reply: "By all means! Let's hear it!"

"Agreed," said Carnoway.

"Well, umm, it's like this. I have no problem giving you what you asked for. The court reporter is short and thin, has brown eyes and curly hair. She's wearing a gray dress, the bottom part of which is pleated. The top part has three largish white square buttons right up its front, and she's wearing a flag pin over her heart. But you should know that I don't see objects and people as separate, disconnected, and on their own. For me, everything works together. My memory isn't like a photo, or even a hundred photos. It's a story, and when my mind tells me the story, I absorb all of it at once."

"Tell us more, son. I'd really like to understand you better." Porfiteza probably thought, *the more such gibberish, the better.*

"Mr. Porfiteza, would you do me a favor?"

"Anything you like."

"Please walk to the courtroom entrance, then turn around and face me."

A few seconds later: "At your service, Mr. Anderson."

"Thank you. Now I would appreciate it if you would move forward very slowly. Please take a step every ten seconds or so."

"Yes sir!" I suspect Porfiteza saluted, because a few spectators laughed.

"Oh and one more thing. Please everyone, don't say anything. I'd like to provide a narration, if that's okay."

"Go ahead," said Judge Carnoway.

"You are my eyes, Mr. Porfiteza, and through them I take in the entirety of this great courtroom: the five pews on each side of the aisle just in front of me, the wooden railing bisecting the courtroom just beyond them, the two big tables for prosecution and defense, the jury box, witness stand, court reporter's station, and, way in the back, the judge's great bench up on high. My parents took me to pray in a big Wichita church once, at Easter back when I was eight. This courtroom reminds me of that church, with its grand ceiling and majestic pulpit, like where Judge Carnoway sits. So much ceremony and grandeur!"

So far I had said nothing remarkable. Anyone could have recited something similar after having looked around the courtroom for a few seconds.

"Mr. Porfiteza. Where are you right now?"

"Even with the middle row."

"Aha. If you look to your right, you'll find six individuals, four women and two men. From the center aisle where you're standing out to the wall, they are ordered woman-man-woman, woman-woman-man, and they have what I see as multiple points of connection. Notice, for example, how three of the women have white dresses on, the fourth wears a blue and white print, but the men differ, they wear brown and dark green shirts. White-green-blue, white-white-brown—a lovely pattern. Bald with green, moustache with brown. I could give you approximate ages and shapes if you like. But the important thing is seeing them grouped together, as a whole."

In response to Porfiteza's request, I described the seven people seated in the front row pew to his left, from the extreme end inward: first my white-haired man, then an elderly lady sitting to his right and wearing a gingham print blouse patterned with red, white, and pink squares. She had straight brown hair, and her cane rested on the bench a few inches to her left. To her right sat another woman looking very much like Miss Bove squared, but instead of noting the vastity of her endomorphic body type I simply reported that she was dressed in light colors, beige and white.

After depicting the remaining four people similarly, I provided physical descriptions of five jurors, selected at random by Mr. Porfiteza and made known to me by their positions in the jury box. I told Mr. Porfiteza that the jury box paneling looked as if it had been recently sanded, and that many of the brown leather chair backings had been worn away. I noted a small red stain high on Mr. Porfiteza's white shirt, probably a relic from his morning's shave, and I pointed out that there were two piles of papers and a brown briefcase on the table for the defense, though only a lone page graced the county attorney's table. I added that the stained-glass window above the courtroom's entrance was fractured in its lower right corner, and that a sizable crack in the floor by a wall near the jury box looked like it needed to be patched.

Porfiteza refused to give up. "What color are the pants of the juror sitting furthest from you, in the first row?"

Trick question: "Sir, that juror is a woman, and she is wearing a blue dress."

"Tell me about the floor."

"It's all wood except for up front; there's a little marble just to my right, in front of Judge Carnoway's bench."

"The right wall of this courtroom upon entering—anything unusual about it?"

"Photos. There are six of them, all of old men. The first has a very long beard, and all six of them wear—oh, they're judges!"

Porfiteza paused for most of a minute, which prompted Carnaway to ask him if he had any further questions.

"Yes, your Honor, I have one more. Or rather, I need to ask a different type of question. Recall of people's appearances, that's selective recall of Mr. Anderson's own choosing. It's impressive, but perhaps not so germane to this trial. More important is the recall of action sequences. The essence of Mr. Anderson's testimony depends on such recall."

"Mr. Anderson!" Porfiteza's voice boomed. "Take off your blindfold and repeat Marcie Smith's testimony from this morning."

Porfiteza got Judge Carnoway's permission to have the court reporter read back her transcriptions right after I recited either a question or Marcie's response. After I had gone through the first two minutes of her testimony perfectly, Porfiteza jumped around: the middle of his cross examination was followed by the closing portion of Townsend's questioning. It made no difference. I even provided a few additional touches, such as the locations where Townsend and Porfiteza had been standing when they asked particular questions. I also described Marcie's appearance and dress, pointed out her nervous thumb rubbing habit.

Porfiteza tried to salvage something from the debacle by

getting me to reiterate my uncertainty concerning Marcie's state of consciousness during the time she was engaging in "matters of an intimate nature," as he put it. There was no redirect from Townsend, and so my one and only experience as a trial witness came to an end.

The trial concluded the following day. Jake and Phil never testified, which must have been a great disappointment for Mr. Townsend. The boys instead pled guilty to one of those lesser charges you always hear about on the news, and were given five-year suspended sentences. Within two weeks both had enrolled in the army, and before an additional eighteen months had elapsed neither could be counted among the living. Phil died suddenly on a remote Italian road, shot in the head by a sniper during a nighttime convoy. Jake, however, concluded his life uniquely and in a manner deserving honorable mention on the gruesome-ways-to-die list. While napping in his barracks, he tossed and turned the wrong way. His beloved Mauser C-96, painstakingly hidden on his person or in his duffel bag for more than a year, and stored in his right pants pocket on the occasion of his nap, discharged. The bullet shattered Jake's thigh bone, and septicemia set in. He expired within the week, demonstrating that Chekhov was right on the money in life as well as in art.

Which is more important, reputation or survival? Death obliterated the association between two boys and their assault and rape of a girl. Jacob Stiles and Philip Jensen instead were remembered as men who sacrificed their lives to keep America safe from fascism. Edmund Stiles had a small plaque made up. The memorial to his son can be found nailed to a hackberry tree in a corner of one of Liberal's pocket parks, the name of which I will not divulge.

3:48 P.M. Wednesday, April 2nd

Postscript from a Saturday, early June of 1942:

I woke to a quiet house, walked downstairs and found three plates on the kitchen table. Two had been scraped clean. Half a desiccated sunny-side-up egg yolk was stuck to the center of the third.

I opened the front door and saw no one, just grass, the road, and endless ripe wheat beyond. Where did they go? I ran back up to my room, looked out the window, and noticed three dark oblong smudges some four hundred yards distant. Immersed in a sea of tawny yellow under a pale blue sky, they rippled in the heat. Two stood together, the third a few feet away. I turned from the brightness for a few seconds, and when I looked back I saw two walking toward me, the third no longer in sight. Ma and Pa entered the house soon after, said nothing, didn't even look at each other. I asked, "How was breakfast?" Ma took the hint and cooked me up eggs and toast while I cleared the table.

Over supper that evening, Pa mumbled this pronouncement between soup slurps: "Year after next you go to college or into the army. One or the other."

Pa was a to-the-point guy. Superfluities such as those last four words were unusual. Maybe he expected me to say "Okay," nothing more. End of discussion, resumption of slurping.

College? Although we occupied a comfortable two-storey farmhouse, we were not rich. Socioeconomically, we resided in the upper middle class of the poor. We owned a few farm animals, a garden, and a wheat field that had recently, albeit incompletely, recovered from the dust storms. Although we never went hungry, my parents could afford to send me to college only if the chickens started laying golden eggs.

Ma looked at Pa, then at me. She smiled, and—oh, here's a thought—of the two figures standing next to each other in the field that morning, it's possible that only one lived in my house.

"I saw what you did at the trial," Ma said, "and as much as I didn't want you up there, well, you were smarter than I thought. You're my flesh and blood. I'm not a sharpie, didn't think you were either."

Ma and I waited for Pa's affirmation. It took him a few seconds to emerge from his bowl. "Yup. I thought you were as dull as Newton. Guess I was mistaken." Newton was our neighbor's bull.

"Thanks Ma, Pa. Appreciate the votes of confidence."

"I know it looks like we're just getting by—"

"I saw you out in the field this morning. Someone was with you. Does it have to do with me going to college? Because I won't take charity from a stranger."

"Let me finish," said Ma.

Pa interrupted before she had a chance: "That was just Farley. He stopped by, your mother fixed us some breakfast, and we walked him back to his farm. We small-talked about nothing of importance."

About nothing of importance—at least two more superfluities, possibly four.

Ma said, "We've managed to save up some money over the last little while, and seeing what you did at that trial—you know, with your memory and all—plus your good grades last year, well, it seems to us that maybe you're meant for something other than farming."

Much was left unsaid that evening. Pa expressed no bitterness over me getting a chance he never had, nor did he show disappointment over the likelihood that I would never take over the farm. Ma did not complain about the prospect of living out the rest of her life on a two-bit farm, with only a round-faced stone of a husband for company. No one talked about the war, nor whether my intention of enrolling in college instead of enlisting in the army was cowardly. Ma didn't tell me how difficult it was to wear Pa down, nor how fervently she hoped the war would end before I graduated. She didn't express her fear that I would return to Kansas on rare occasions and stay no longer than half a week when I did. (She was right about that). I held back as well, in fact behaved like a gangster's wife by not asking my parents about the money's origin. I didn't tell them that I was jumping up and down in my skin with excitement, nor that leaving Kansas for the first time in my life scared the hell out of me.

I've heard it said that families get along only when their members communicate effectively with each other. Right.

8:33 P.M. Thursday, April 10th

There is a brand new vacancy at the Manoir. Mrs. Ida Belkin suffered a heart attack over lunch. I experienced the event first-hand. The poor woman had been sitting at the table immediately to my right. The critical moment occurred as I was sampling my initial spoonful of split pea soup. In quick succession I heard the sharp clash of cutlery against dishware, a thud, and a scream. Mrs. Belkin fell facedown on the carpet, three yards from my right shoe. I got down on the floor, urged her to turn her face to the side so she could breathe.

"Are you okay?" Idiotic question.

Mrs. Belkin grabbed the fingers of my right hand with her left, held them so tightly I thought she might break them. Her sleeve slid away and I spotted numbers tattooed on her forearm's underside, along with a triangle etched into the skin below them. She looked at me hatefully, said something I couldn't understand, and followed it up with "How are you here?" After spitting blood on my hand, she released her grip. This from a woman with whom I had occasionally exchanged pleasantries.

The house nurse and two attendants rushed over, followed four minutes later by three husky ambulance guys. They huddled around Mrs. Belkin for the longest time, bound her tight to a stretcher, and carried her off, no oxygen mask deployed. I followed them into the lobby, did not return to the dining room. By the time I came down for supper, the notice had already been posted on the lobby corkboard:

Dear friends,

I regret to inform you of the passing of Mrs. Ida Belkin....

In its second paragraph it was stated that Mrs. Belkin had just turned ninety-four. As if that made it all right.

How ironic was her hallucination, given that I have lived my life in accordance with that most important tenet of the Hippocratic Oath: *Abstain from doing harm.* I completed my driving career without running over a cat, dog, squirrel, or any other animal. I never contracted nor transmitted a venereal disease, nor fathered illegitimate children, nor cheated on anything or anyone, rarely lied, yelled at people only under extreme provocation, and never ever touched one of my students inappropriately. Or appropriately, for that matter. To my credit, I was a cold fish. I've been a nonviolent soul, from childhood straight to the present. There are no black marks on my celestial scoreboard.

I'm getting nowhere. So I did something worthy sixty-odd years ago, big deal. The truth of the matter is that my little stroll down Memory Lane has uncovered no great insights. *Where have you been?* has not propelled me to *Where are you going?* Except—yes, except for that one clue, Ma's strange question: "But what if he finds out?" What if *who* finds out, and discovers exactly *what*? Was *he* me? If not, who the hell was she referring to?

Consider the improbability of my perfectly ticking heart. I'll be 83 in 11 days, so: Multiply 365.25 times 83. Multiply its product by 24 hours, that one by 60 minutes, and the whole mess by an average 70 beats per minute. The result totals up to more than 3 billion and 55 million beats, all of them synchronized to an electrical system that has yet to blow a fuse. Staggering, but really, how much longer can I expect such perfection to sustain itself?

Though my Manoir colleagues haven't been dropping like flies in a frost, they do pop off every now and then, in fact thrice since I joined the club. Each death freezes me for a couple of days, doom's inevitability having become inescapably salient. During these periods I sense that the tolling of my own bell is not far off. But then they bury the unfortunate schmuck, and the following day I've returned to my happy-go-lucky death-proof shell of illusion. Time's aplenty once more.

10:30 A.M. Monday, April 21st

I celebrated my farewell to 82 today by not being deterred. Instead of whiling away the morning reading some book, I worked on worming a path back to my early childhood. First I mucked around on the internet for ninety minutes, to no avail. Then I took a stroll in the park to clear my head. From the middle of a deserted soccer field I looked up and saw dark puffy clouds moving in rapidly from the west. Eureka.

On the morning of Monday, April 15th, 1935, a day after our worst dust storm ever, Pa and I dug out farm equipment from under drifts of sand, dust, and grit. He surveyed the land, which resembled the Sahara Desert more closely than Kansas, and said, bitterly, "Someday, sonny boy, someday all of this will be yours." Therein resides clue number two: Pa was not a renter. "All of this" was modest, but Pa owned it! His deed therefore must exist in a government office somewhere. Counties and states keep records of things like that, don't they? All I need is a scrap of information from the deed to get me started—an earlier address, a name, something I can use to trace my origins further back in time.

I'm going back to Liberal. I'll research my early childhood, and I'll look up Marcie Smith. If I find her above ground we'll share a couple of cupcakes for old time's sake. The trip should be short and sweet, two weeks' maximum duration including travel time.

Wait a sec. I'm going to need someone to drive me there. My kids won't do it, that's certain, and I will not travel with a stranger. None of my residence colleagues fits the bill, as they're too frail or too aggravating. Come to think of it, they're *all* too aggravating. But what about Shelley? Why not? She's an ideal choice, actually—competent, interesting, and pleasant. Easy on the eyes as well, but of course that's irrelevant. No doubt about it, she's the logical choice. No, not because I'm infatuated with her, which, incidentally, I most emphatically am not. She's too young and too brash and too—too strange, too goofy, too gothy. Moreover, I'm not that pathetic. Any male my age possessing even the smallest modicum of common sense does not entertain such idiocy. We have nothing in common. She smiles and I frown. She heehaws when I'm grim. She hauls around condoms and trash and pepper spray disguised as lipstick, while I jauntily tote nothing more than my wallet in my right pants pocket and a key in my left. I'll ask her to come because she's capable, period the end. She'd probably do it if I double her salary for the duration of the trip. If money doesn't sway her I'll come up with some initiative that will, like an all-expenses-paid trip to someplace marginally more interesting than Liberal, say Paris or Rome.

I'm getting ahead of myself. First off, I need to buy her something.

7:58 P.M. *Thursday, April 24th*

Mission partly accomplished. I approached the circulation desk this morning right after Shelley finished with the early birds, told her that while browsing around at Chapter's yesterday I came across a book she might appreciate: a collection of short stories by none other than Lyle Meblenny. Some doctoral student had pieced them together from scraps found in boxes. I read two of them on the bus. In one, a witch occupies the body of her lover's girlfriend, and in the other an emerald-throated hummingbird addresses two old women and tells them that death is not the end. Eat, drink, and be merry, because on the day after tomorrow we live. Ho hum.

I handed the book to her. "It was released four years ago. If you've read it, I'll give you the receipt so you can exchange it."

"Wow! Omigod I am so excited!" She kissed the fingertips on both of her hands, reached out over the desk, and touched my face with them.

"I remember when it came out. It was so expensive, sixty or seventy dollars. I totally forgot about it, so thank you super very much."

"You are most welcome. Oh, one more thing."

"Yes?"

"May I take you out to lunch? You can be my guest at the Manoir. There's an empty setting at my table."

"What fun!"

"May I interpret your response as a yes?"

"Hmm. Lunch with the old folks?"

"Uh huh."

"How's the food?"

"Killer stuff, prettied up just a touch for easy digestion. You'll love both it and the company. Prepare to be dazzled, because Mildred is a grand raconteur. If gossip about forty-year-old machinations in the Ladies Morning Musical Club is your cup of tea, you'll be entranced. Not to be outdone, Harold, her husband, well, wait till you hear him recount his old stationery customers. He tells a great story concerning a woman who couldn't decide between two types of birthday card."

"I don't know if I could take all that excitement, Carl. Besides, dazzling isn't good enough. On a drizzly day like today, I need scintillating. Tell you what. How about I drive us up to the Orange Julep and you pay for lunch? I'll be a cheap date."

"You own a car?"

"My boyfriend's. It's a Protegé, small and zippy."

"Great idea. I haven't eaten at a drive-in in decades, and I'll enjoy ogling those girls on roller skates."

"Yeah, and I'll get to flirt with the greasy ducktail guys."

Inside the Protegé, apperception of the Orange Julep's forty-foot globe did not approach high-definition. We had fogged over the windows so completely that the surrounding environment, a blur of orange and gray, was closer to a theoretical proposition than a collection of sharp-edged and discretely bounded buildings, roads, and automobiles. I sat sandwiched in the shotgun seat feeling contentedly cocooned, as if I had nested inside an egg with the intriguing creature sitting beside me. Around us, cars with dirt slathered on their flanks rumbled over slushy pavements. Distorted third-rate pop music from the 'Sixties and 'Seventies blared from speakers mounted on towers to our right and left. Enhancing the train-wreck aesthetic was a McDonald's to our left and one of the ugliest highways in existence directly behind us. Impressionist painters condemned to Hell paint scenes like this one over and over again until they get them right, which they never do.

"So, do you have a dark side?"

"Me?"

"There's no one else in here. Tell me yes or no, do you lust after pubescent girls?"

"Of course not."

"How about pubescent plus thirteen years?"

"I'm perfectly harmless."

"Then why did you go into university teaching?"

"Why not? It paid well and didn't require physical labor."

"I figured university profs were like priests, you know? Hang around young women, or boys in the case of priests, and you might just get some."

"I can't vouch for others of my former ilk, but I can for myself. I never came within a half-mile of temptation."

"And why was that?"

"Because—hmm. I don't know. Just never did."

Shelley snarfed down a handful of fries and took a couple of deep sips of the Julep, a concoction made from oranges, vanilla, and sugar. It's good for you, so I've been told. The Protegé's insides reeked of the fries, which was fine by me. My doc warned me off greasy foods, but when in Rome, allowances must be made. Does anyone order salad and a bottle of water at the Orange Julep?

"Nevertheless, I'm not all sweetness and light. In fact I might have been a demon back when I was an infant. A killer demon."

"No kidding! Please do tell."

I described my nightmare to Shelley, excluding her role in it.

"Granted, the dream implies violence on your part. No one else was in it to bludgeon your nonexistent brother, and your frantic attempts to shut his eyelids represents a need to blot out the evidence. But just because you had this horrible nightmare what, a grand total of twice, and they lasted a cumulative duration of maybe ten minutes, you deduce that you killed someone way back when you were a teeny tot? That's quite a stretch."

"Not just because. There are other factors as well."

"Such as?"

"Think of it as adding two plus two plus two. The first *two* is the nightmare. Here's the second: I've retained some faint recollections from way back, more like premonitions in reverse, actually, of a woman shrieking at me and of me falling backward and hitting the back of my head against something hard. My mother explained them away as sequelae from a childhood illness, something called encephalitis lethargica, but I think she made up the story, especially as I once overheard her saying to my father, behind closed doors, 'But what if he finds out?' Finally, there's the clincher *two*: other than the disturbing memories I just told you about, I can't recall anything before the age of six, nothing at all. I'm totally blocked. I feel kind of like Dorothy from *The Wizard of Oz* but in reverse, you know? As if somehow I got dropped *into* Kansas rather than out of it, and without knowing when, how, or why it happened. Add up all the *twos* and the resultant *six* is a deduction that's not so easy to dismiss."

"That deduction being exactly what?"

"That I was involved in something bloody violent, way back when. Something I even might have caused."

"Oh God, what baloney. Look, just because you possess a great memory for the here and now doesn't mean that you can dredge up real old stuff accurately, or even recall it at all. I don't remember much from that far back, and I'm way closer to age two than you are."

"But at least you remember a few things, right? Old images of your parents, or memories like burning your hand on a stove or getting a shot in the ass?"

"I remember running full speed ahead and stubbing my left big toe against a door. It hurts thinking about it."

"Exactly. But for me, it's like those years never were."

"Sorry, Carl, but you're sounding as crazy as a dozen loons. There's way too much inference involved for you to assume such a mantle of guilt. It's ridiculous. My advice is to forget about the whole thing before it becomes an obsession."

"It already is an obsession."

Shelley sucked up noise from the bottom of her cup, emitted a half-hearted "Fuck," and wiped off the inside of the windshield with the sleeve of her coat.

"Can we at least try looking at this logically?"

I could not help but smile. "Ah yes, logic. An old friend of mine from way back."

"Logic has its uses, though usually I'm a go-with-the-flow girl, you know? If I meet a boy I don't write out the positives and negatives. I simply confer with me and myself, and we decide, snap, just like that, whether to fuck him. I'm sorry, but in your case I was overruled. You would have been my first octogenarian, and only my third totally crazy lover."

"Shucks." I snapped my fingers in mock disappointment.

"No need to despair. I'll bet there are some pretty hot numbers at the Manoir who'd like a shot at you. I'm performing a public service by not doing you. Just how favorable is the female-to-male ratio anyway?"

"There are about a hundred single women and fifteen single guys."

"Guys? These beings, I presume, are the same as men?"

"Well yes. Fifteen of us men."

"Almost seven to one. Not bad. For you, that is."

"Right, Shelley. I live in a harem. Ten times a day I scout the hallways, my perpetual hard-on leading me on as I fantasize about luscious beauties lying in wait behind their doors, and of all the lasciviously oriented behaviors they can't wait to perform on my body."

She giggled. Good.

"Now may we return to the matter at hand?" I asked.

"Oh if you insist. The way I see it, the possibilities number three. Here's supposition number one: you hurt no one, and the nightmare is a figment of your overactive imagination."

Shelley wiped off the windshield once more and started the car. "Gotta get back by one." Vroom, sharp left turn out of the parking lot.

"That's the most likely outcome, and by far. It's almost certainly what happened, or rather, didn't. But how can you prove to yourself that you didn't do something, when you don't even know what that something is that you didn't do? Anyway, here's supposition number two: you did it. You really did do it! When you were a tyke you grabbed a rock or a hammer or a golf club and smashed it over your baby brother's head. Kaboom." Shelley vocalized a vile guttural explosion, then executed a multiple lane S-weave, doubly jolting my circulatory system.

"But if you had done him in, major shit would have hit the fan, no? They would have removed you from your family at the very least. Who knows, you might have ended up locked away in an asylum. What do they do with two-year-old killers anyway?"

"I don't know and I don't want to know. What's your third

hypothesis?"

"Someone else killed little Melvin. You don't mind me calling him Melvin, do you? It's a pet name of mine."

"Call him whatever you'd like."

"Okay. So someone does Melvin in. Could have been an intruder, a friend of the family, a deranged relative, maybe even your mom or dad. And you witness it. But because you are small and your brain isn't wired complete, you don't get it."

A short gap in the conversation ensued, after which Shelley turned to me while stopped at a light. "So you deduce that you must have done it. Ah guilt, such a wondrous invention."

"Great. Of your three explanations, two are terrible."

"But the other is by far the most likely. And here's the thing, Carl. Whatever did or did not happen eighty years ago is lost forever. You'll never know, never ever. And anyway, what difference would it make now? Should you find out that you knocked off your baby brother, what would you do about it? Whip yourself a hundred times, hand over your possessions to charity, and wander about the city in sackcloth and ashes?"

We pulled into the library parking lot, and a minute later she was back at her station, checking books in, checking books out. Damn, why didn't I have the nerve to ask her?

9:30 A.M. Saturday, May 3rd

I have an illness. It's the literary analogue of medical students' disease. Call it Captain Ahab Syndrome. I finished my second sojourn through *Moby-Dick* this morning. I had been forced to read it when a freshman at the University of Chicago. Hated it. True, I learned all about nineteenth-century whaling practices. And yes, on the day I finished it I was impressed, in the same manner I would have been impressed had I spent every day, from initial spadework to completion, watching the Empire State Building go up. I told my English professor that *Moby-Dick* would have made a fine short story, a novella even; it was a pity Melville didn't have a good editor to keep him in line.

This time through, I got it. I realized how fortunate Captain Ahab was. He is my new role model, and not because we are both ancient. Of course he wasn't quite eighty-three, but in those days fifty or sixty amounted to the same thing. I look up to Ahab because he had a purpose in life: kill the great white whale. No make-work or leisure time for him, lucky bastard.

Melville could have turned *Moby-Dick* into the blackest of tragedies by changing the ending:

After a fierce three-day battle with the malevolent and vicious whale, a battle in which Moby-Dick gains the upper hand after killing several sailors and severely damaging the Pequod, Ahab rushes to the front of the attack boat, putting himself in extreme peril. He furiously hurls his harpoon while bellowing those famous words:

"From hell's heart I stab at thee."

Ahab's weapon pierces Moby-Dick right between the eyes. The leviathan rears back, filled with fury. His final attempt to destroy his attackers fails, however, for he has been mortally wounded. Blood flows profusely, the sea turns red. Moby-Dick dies, the surviving sailors secure his carcass (Melville spends thirty pages describing precisely how they do it), everyone gets rich, and Ahab retires to live out his days in an old sailor's home off the coast of Maine. He plays shuffleboard and dominoes during the days, and tells sea stories and reads adventure books on cold, windy nights.

Alternatively, Melville could have introduced someone like

my Shelley into his book. She would ask of Ahab, "Why give a fuck
if the damned whale lives?" and he would reply, "True enough, my
dear, it matters not a fig."

Shelley was out sick last week. We celebrated her return by lunching at
the Patisserie de Gascogne, a French bakery-restaurant not far from the
library. If you enjoy your meal seated in a heavy cast-iron chair, set
before a circular cast-iron table painted dark green and not quite large
enough to support the totality of two sets of cups, cutlery, glasses, and
plates; and if you get a charge from eating adjacent to rumbling
refrigerated displays packed with containers of *blanquette de veau, lapin
a la moutarde, saumon aux agrumes,* and *coq au vin,* the Gascogne is right
up your alley. Unfortunately the food is too good, the pastries sublime.

"I could have returned to work last Thursday but my heart
wasn't in it. Ezekiel and I broke up."

"Ezekiel? That's the name of your boyfriend?"

"Ex-boyfriend, and yeah."

"Did you call him Zeke?"

"I tried that once. He threw off the blanket, stood on the bed,
raised his arms to the ceiling, and intoned emphatically, as if he were
Moses just come down from the mountain, 'Not Zeke! Call me Ezekiel.'
While he was naked. Cracked me up. He was cute, though not totally
sane."

"I'm sorry to hear it's over. I never met him, but I liked his
car."

My comments were followed by a half-minute silence, long
enough for me and twice as long as for a normal person to realize
that a more sincere expression of sympathy was required.

"Want to talk about it?"

"I'll only get bummed again." Ten seconds later: "I got his car
in an accident."

"Uh-oh."

"It wasn't my fault, really it wasn't. I was sitting still, stopped at a red light on Cote-St.-Luc Road. The car behind smashed into me. The woman driving it anticipated the light change a little too early. Boom, molecules collide. My car—Ezekiel's—it smacked the car in front on the rebound."

"No one was hurt?"

"Nah, and there was no question of fault. The woman who rammed me apologized. She was old, maybe fifty or sixty."

"That's *not* old. You know one of the things that bugged me about teaching?"

"Things?"

"Yeah, things. There were two—students who skipped class and asked whether they missed anything important, and nineteen-year-olds who employed the phrase, 'When I was young.'"

"Point taken. So this moderately aged person, she was all dressed up and had a badge pinned to her dress. She was on her way to some astronomy conference. Just a lady in her pre-golden years daydreaming about Betelgeuse or something."

"Ezekiel didn't believe you?"

"He believed me all right, but was pissed anyway. What ended it was his first question."

"Which was?"

"'How banged up is it?' Should have been something else. In fact, the right question never came, first or otherwise. He examined the rear bumper and the front grille and said he so hoped the steering, you know, the axle and the thingies attached to it, wasn't damaged or out of alignment. He could see I wasn't bleeding or limping, but I was shook up. Not one question did he have for me, not even a hug."

"What a jerk."

"Fuck him. Or rather, not. Too bad because we were a matched pair, the two of us being screwed up in exactly the same way and all."

"Huh? What do you mean?"

"Oh never mind. Maybe later. It's just that for a girl like me, suitable boyfriend material doesn't zip down the pike every day. What's up with you?" An obvious attempt to change the subject. I was happy to oblige.

"I'm planning a trip, now that spring has finally arrived. Feeling my oats. I need to expand, you know? So I'm going to hit the open road."

"Ooh, jailbreak. Escape from Manoir Zenda! Details, please."

"I'll be driving to Kansas."

"Triple woohoo! Who needs Florida when Kansas beckons?"

"My sentiments exactly."

"And why Kansas?"

"I'm going to tie up some loose ends. Find an old friend, visit family graves, that sort of thing. And I'll investigate my early years."

"Ah, to determine once and for all whether that nightmare of yours is based on anything real."

"Precisely."

"Good for you. It's a ridiculous windmill-tilting exercise, but what the hay, as they say out there, you've got the time and the money, so go for it. If you end up feeling exonerated in your own head, the trip will be worth it."

"That's my take. Given the alternative of spending an extra week or two here at the Manoir, it's a no-brainer decision. It's good to inject some variety in one's life, no?"

"Agreed. By the way, was the old friend a she?"

"Yes."

"And was she someone you should have married, way back when? Don't you love those stories that pop up in the news every now and then about some pair of long-lost lovers who find each other after sixty or seventy years? As teenagers they blew it, but finally, after several marriages, divorces, and maybe a spousal death or two along the way, the circle closes. True love blossoms, delayed but not denied."

"Not in this case, Shelley. Marcie Smith was a sweet girl, but there was no real attraction between us."

"Then why look her up?"

"I helped her get justice. Two guys raped her, and I got them convicted."

"Whoa! Really? I have the honor of conversing with the man who was once Carl Anderson, teenage vigilante?"

"You do."

"How exciting. Tell me all about it!"

I gave her the Readers Digest version, abridged to such an extent that my recollection took all of twenty-two minutes. It included an account of my imagery training, a description of how I memorized the Old Testament, and a partial narrative of the trial. Omitted were references to my two friends, Marcie's slowness, my parents, anything that might have reflected on my all-around social ineptitude, and a few additional details not worth mentioning.

"I'm impressed, Carl, really I am. Not many kids would have risked that."

"Thank you, my dear."

"So you're going to drive all the way to Kansas by yourself. Wow. You still hold a driver's license?"

"Of course. I'm an excellent driver."

"But when did you last drive a car?" Spoken with a harsh accent on the sentence's second word. "When *exactly* did you last turn the ignition key?"

"May 17th of last year, at 11:00 A.M. I leveled a hydrant while backing out of my driveway. Not so easy to do."

"Let me get this straight. You're planning to drive all the way to Kansas, and a year ago you couldn't make it out of your own driveway?"

"I never was much good in reverse. On a road trip to Kansas, though, I won't need reverse. I'll just keep moving forward."

"No need to parallel park?"

"None at all, because once you get out of the city and onto the high plains there's nothing but wide open space, even in parking lots. It's a simple matter of ignition on, shift from park to drive, and then onward, straight toward the horizon of the setting sun. Westward-ho!"

My brain commanded: *What the fuck, take the plunge.*

"Want to come?"

"What?"

"Want to come!"

"That's what I thought you said. Seriously?"

"Most definitely. I'll supply the car, or we'll rent a camper. I asked my children last Sunday, but the boy said he was busy for the next four months and the girl thinks I have incipient Alzheimer's. Do you have any idea how difficult it is to disabuse folks of that notion once they get it into their heads? Especially if you can't remember their names? Or their sexes?"

I could tell from the way Shelley squinted at me that her dubiety quotient was stratospheric. "Not that I approve of the venture. Oh it's so stupid!"

"It isn't stupid for me. Please come. I could really use your help."

"How long would we be gone for? And could we travel somewhere else a bit more interesting? Straight to Kansas and back doesn't exactly ignite the old wanderlust."

"Sure we could. We'll leave whenever you're ready. You name the vehicle and I'll rent it, even if it's a Cadillac. We'll be heading to the great metropolis of Liberal, Kansas, and maybe one or two locations afterwards."

"Liberal, Kansas. There's a place in Kansas that's liberal?"

"Nope. Liberal is in fact conservative. On the plus side, it's the home of Dorothy Gale."

"Who? I should know this woman?"

"Girl, and definitely. She's the one the cyclone transported to the Land of Oz."

"Oh of course, that Dorothy Gale. Hmm. What do you say we go to St. Petersburg instead and visit Raskolnikov's hovel?"

"Maybe next year. Come with me! You know, it would be good for you to get lost for a while. After a breakup you need a change of pace. Think of it: the open road ahead, adventure around the next bend. New locales every day, crossing paths with piquant characters. That sort of stuff."

"Piquant characters?" Shelley looked into my smiling eyes and burst out laughing.

"Not only that, I'll cover you salary and match it with an equal amount as a bonus. Double pay for as long as we are away, which I estimate at around two weeks. And I'll pay all of your expenses, including your own hotel room."

"Ooh! I *like* money. The conservative town of Liberal in the great state of Kansas, eh? Sounds ever so slightly more interesting than having lunch with your dashing companions at the Manoir. Give me a few of days to Google it and consult with myself and I, 'kay?"

"Sure."

She's going to say yes! How can she not?

9:00 P.M. Friday, May 23rd

A beautiful day. We took advantage by strolling through Westmount Park during Shelley's afternoon break. So much loveliness—a quiet stream to our right, newly mown grass ahead and off to the left, pale green lattices of leaf buds a couple of days prior to the bursting point above us. We stopped at a bench near the park's far end. She sat to my right, her red hair brightened to a golden auburn. Miracle of miracles, no one approached within a hundred yards for the entire duration of our conversation.

She extracted a joint from her left jeans pocket, matches from the right.

"Mind?"

"Nope."

She lit up, took a long drag. "Tick tock, take a toke?"

"No thanks."

"What's the matter, out of practice?"

"You might say."

"Wait, don't tell me. Your last time was forty-eight years, seven months, five days, and nineteen hours ago, right?"

"More or less." Actually it was at least two lives ago.

"Sure you don't want one? It's nice on a day like this."

I took the joint from her gingerly, careful not to burn my fingers.

"You're looking at it like it came from Saturn. Go ahead, enjoy!"

What the fuck, you only live once, right? I brought it to my lips, inhaled like my life depended on it, then coughed spasmodically for the following minute and a half. Shelley looked more bemused than alarmed.

"Thanks, but the rest is yours. No need to share."

"Okay. Now listen. I'll go to Kansas with you, but only if we agree on certain ground rules."

"Great!"

"Wait a minute, big boy. You might not be so happy with my conditions. There are three."

"Shoot."

"First, you pay me to do some research."

"On what?"

"'On what?' the professor inquires. I suppose you plan on riding into town, hitching your horse's reins to a rail, swaggering through the swinging doors of some saloon on Liberal's Main Street, walking up to the bar, placing your forty-gallon hat on it, and then, addressing the bartender and patrons, announce: 'Anybody around here seen Marcie Smith or my dad's deed?'"

"Not exactly. I figured we'd hit some government offices. An office of vital statistics and a deeds office in particular."

"Where?"

"I don't know, somewhere in Liberal."

"Carl, I'm a librarian. I'm trained to look up stuff, so you might as well let me do it. Government offices are probably the right places, but we need to know for sure. We'll have to find out where they're located, their hours, and their procedures. A case in point: vital statistics frequently aren't public. You only get the information if you're related, or if you can make a case. Would you know how to proceed if Marcie married and changed her name, or if she died, or moved away?"

"Nope. What do we do?"

"There are sources, all online. Places like Findagrave, Ancestry, and Familysearch for starters, state archives and more expensive and shadier sites if necessary. You'd be better off hiring a private eye, but I'll do. And I'm cheap, just twenty dollars an hour for eight hours max, though I may need up to a couple of hundred dollars for various memberships."

"No problem."

"Good. Now for my second condition—we set firm dates for leaving and returning. No Moses wandering around in the desert emulation for us."

"What do you have in mind?"

"I say we depart on Saturday, June 14th. I'll work the previous day and spend the evening packing. Gotta figure out how many outfits to take."

"Outfits? You won't need them in Liberal."

"You never know. I don't want to miss out on some gala square dance because I didn't bring the proper shoes."

She took another toke, closed her eyes.

"Anyway, we leave on that Saturday and come back on the Sunday night eight days after, no matter what. As per your offer, I get paid double salary for my week off, and also through to, and including, the following Monday, as I'll need it to recover—sleep in, wash clothes, buy groceries, that sort of stuff. I'll get a mini-vacation out of the deal as well, because the library will be closed on the Tuesday for St. Jean-Baptiste Day. So there you have it, a full week plus a few hours to uncover the mysteries of your life as a teeny tiny. If we can't figure it out by then, we never will. What do you say?"

"But it's going to take three days to drive each way."

"Which brings me to my third condition. We fly to Wichita and rent a car. No way I'm driving all the way from Montreal to Liberal and back."

"But you've got to. I'm afraid of flying." Terrified is more like it.

"No kidding. You, Carl Anderson, internationally renowned biblical scholar? How did you get around to conferences and all?"

"I flew but felt lucky after each landing, as if I had just won at Russian Roulette. I'd belt myself in, we'd take off, and I'd obsess about being trapped in a tube weighing so and so many tons, and with nothing underneath it except thirty-six thousand feet of air. Topping off the weltschmerz of my burgeoning phobia was one very long rough ride across the Pacific from Sydney. We hit a few air pockets and I was done in, white-knuckled from grasping the armrests for dear life. The other passengers looked relaxed, as if they were lying on chaises by a pool somewhere, but all I could think was *There's another big bump coming.* I gave up air travel completely after that trip. Drove, took the train, or stayed home."

"We need to get you over that." These were the very last words I wanted to hear. "The last time I flew I was seven, and I'm dying to try it again."

"You fly and I'll take the train."

"Train? You think there's a train connecting Montreal and

Liberal? No. I'll fly and you'll fly with me. Otherwise you go alone."

I tried every ploy within my bag of argumentative tricks to get her to change her mind: logic, humor, empathy and its poor relation, pity. I told her that I was bound to throw up on some innocent passenger after encountering even the lightest of bumps because my fright would immobilize and render me incapable of opening a barf bag at all, let alone quickly enough. Nothing worked. I never imagined she could be such a fucking little hardass.

She stopped by the Manoir a couple of hours later, alas not to give in.

"I got you a present." She handed me a small brown teddy bear. "Please take me for a plane ride, Carl. I came up with a plan and I know it will work. You won't be anxious at all. Well maybe a little, but just a tiny bit. Join me on the plane and I promise you'll be fine. I'll make sure of it. Please?"

She smiled and I was sunk. How stupid can I be?

8:30 P.M. Sunday, June 8th

Michael and Helen visited this morning, first time I had seen either of them in three weeks. As we sipped cappuccinos under floppy shade umbrellas out on the Manoir terrace, I informed them of my upcoming adventure. Their four eyes rolled in tandem. To their credit, my children refrained from verbalizing their conviction that I have become a foolish and infatuated old man. They worry too much I'm attached to her; or they worry I'm too much attached to her. Either way, their concern provides me with a modicum of satisfaction. Let them blame themselves, because I never would have met Shelley had they not urged me to move out of my house.

10:30 P.M. Friday, June 13th

Packed. I'm bringing sneakers, ear plugs, eye blind, melatonin, writing journal, enough clothes to avoid a laundry, my MacBook Pro (within which resides an electronic copy of *The Faerie Queene* for those nights when melatonin doesn't cut it), and my Lumix digital camera—an eightieth birthday present from Helen that I haven't used since the week after she gave it to me. I'll ask Shelley to head up the camera brigade. I don't require photos, but maybe she or my kids would appreciate a few visual mementos.

8:58 P.M. Saturday, June 14th

Anxiety is an onomatopoeticism. Its sound, both through the air and in the mind, sets my teeth on edge. That extra letter, the G, accounts for half the word's affect, the remaining half effected by the screechy zziiieye syllable following it. Yes, anxiety contains a G, and its X is nothing more than a stand-in for the more powerful Z. Anxiety's proper spelling is angzyety—scary looking and sounding, unlike its sister paranoia, which makes its living floating vowels into the air without visible means of support.

Last night anxiety gushed from a spout, the spigot having been jammed in the open position. I arose at 5:06 A.M., checked the flight to Chicago. Cancellation? No such luck. In the taxi I prayed for a crash limited enough to leave us unharmed, but extensive enough to total the vehicle, thus shaking us up sufficiently to postpone our departure. As Shelley and I were about pass through security, the idea of cracking a joke to the agent about nuclear suitcase bombs seemed a very fine initiative indeed. An incongruous sight removed the thought from my consciousness and simultaneously diminished my short-term discomfort.

A pair of flashy baby sneakers sat on an unmoving conveyor belt. Racing stripes jagged along its sides, the word *Puma* was printed on the vamps, and a sketch in red of a big cat decorated the toe boxes. Dad answered the agent's questions about sharp implements, aerosol sprays, and bottles of liquids while Mom held a shoeless, sockless, and bawling one-year-old in her arms. After witnessing this idiotic little tableau, I was loose as a goose for a good twenty minutes, until I spotted a group of rumpled passengers trudging into the terminal from the nether side of our departure gate. I might have congratulated them on once again cheating death, but my heart wasn't in it.

"Oh dear," said Shelley. "You're so very quiet. Feeling okay?"

I nodded, which she took for a no.

"I guaranteed you a stress-free flight, didn't I?"

"That you did."

"Then I'd better get to it, as they may be out of barf bags today."

She removed a black paperback from her backpack. "Ever see the film *La Lectrice*?"

"Can't say that I have."

"It's about a girl who makes her living reading to people, though in truth she ends up fucking one of them on the job. A fantasy of mine ever since I saw it."

"What, concurrent sex and reading?"

"No, silly, hiring myself out as a professional reader. I possess a very good sense of the dramatic, as I will now demonstrate."

Not a bad idea, thought I, *especially if she reads me something terrific or execrable*.

"And with what book do you intend to divert and delight me?"

"A wee little action-adventure book, with some sex thrown in from time to time. It's called *Story of O*."

I am no longer an ignorant Kansas hick. I know wherein the major concern of *Story of O* resides. I was too slow in protesting, however, for Shelley immediately had the book open and spread on her lap. As her right-hand index finger traced through each line of text, she floated her left arm gracefully through the air, its motions in precision alignment with the rhythm and music of the words:

It was the unknown friend who explained to the young woman that her lover had been entrusted with the task of getting her ready, that he was going to tie her hands behind her back, unfasten her stockings and roll them down, remove her garter belt, her panties, and her...

"Stop!"

Shelley raised her eyebrows, cocked her head. That's her faux innocent "Oh dear, what could the matter be?" look, identical to the expression Herman once gave me after gobbling up a piece of apple pie a house guest had left within striking distance.

"You know damn well *Story of O* is not an action-adventure book."

"Sure it is. It's got adventures galore and tons of action, depending on how you define the term. It will transport you!"

"Let the fucking plane transport me."

"Once you get by the story's, uh, touchy-feely aspects, the words flow gracefully, like a falcon riding a thermal, or a gazelle galloping across the Serengeti, or a squirrel climbing—"

"Touchy-feely, that's your phrase for it? Why don't you write to Air Canada? Request that they show the movie version on all its flights. Obsolete the airbags! What a fantastic cost cutting measure. Touchy-feely my ass."

"Why won't you just let me read it to you?"

"Please, *please* refrain. People will overhear you, especially with the fishwife presentation you're bringing to it."

"It's got to be recited with feeling, no?"

"Great. When we take off I'll be gripping both armrests. Half the passengers, myself included, will have the pleasure of hearing you recount a cozy little vignette concerning some woman being whipped and forced to give blowjobs to a conga line of strangers, her arms tied behind her and her back bound to a stiff wooden post.

Very relaxing indeed."

"Hey! You do know the book."

"A lucky guess. Don't you have anything less disturbing in your bag, like maybe *The Big Book of Aviation Disasters*?"

Shelley feigned a pout. "Okay, I give. We proceed to Plan B. You didn't think I would show up without a backup, did you?"

"Ladies and gentlemen: good morning and welcome to flight 517, to Chicago. In a few minutes we will be boarding passengers with young children and…"

"Sadomasochistic literature," I blurted, perhaps a tad too loudly. I rose from my chair. "Excuse me, bladder mollification break."

"Didn't you just take one a few minutes ago?"

"Don't worry, I'm not going to run screaming from the airport. My curiosity concerning your backup contingency is unbounded, so count on my return. Oh and by the way, don't bury that book too far down in your bag. Maybe I'll have a look at it later."

"Wait a sec." Shelley extracted the Lumix from her bag, snapped me before I had a chance to decline the opportunity.

"Wow, such a good looking guy! Have a peek." I looked like a vertical corpse magically propped up by an invisible meat hook.

"We'll initiate Plan B on the plane, okay? You're going to love it."

"Right. Not the slightest doubt about it."

"Nice to know you're not going to wimp out."

I had arranged aisle seats across from each other, Shelley to my right because it's easier to turn my head in that direction. After we settled in, she removed a large manila folder from her backpack.

"Here we go. Ta da, the vaunted Plan B!" Several sheets of glossy photographic paper edged out from the folder.

"One second." She frantically fished around inside her backpack.

"Oh no. I can't have forgotten it. Think they would mind if I dump the contents of my bag in the aisle?" Unfortunately, the seat next to her was occupied by a Sudoku-besotted granny.

"Yeah, they might get a tad upset."

"Fiddlesticks!" A few seconds later: "Aha!" Out came a beaten up tin plate. "Straight from a garage sale on Northcliff, manufactured before confederation. We'll have to manage without the marbles, though."

"How come?"

"I lost them. I lost my marbles!" I would have guffawed along with her, save for the adrenalin coursing through my bodily highways and byways.

"Okay, here we go. Do it!" She placed a photo on the plate and handed it to me.

"It's called *Composition With Red and Blue*. Worth a zillion dollars in person."

I stared at a reproduction of a Mondrian line painting. It consisted of a few black vertical and horizontal lines, the intersections of which generated a bunch of rectangles. The rectangles were shaded pale gray, except for a maroon one on the left and a blue one on the right a third the size of the maroon one. Mondrian spaced his lines irregularly. Some terminated at intersections, but three horizontal and three vertical ones bisected the entire painting. I examined the work for twenty seconds and then handed it back to Shelley. We were off the ground.

"Got it."

"Tell me."

"I'll do better than that." I removed a copy of *enRoute* from the seat pocket in front of me, tore out a page, and in its white space wrote:

twenty rectangles
all gray save two, maroon, blue,
crisscrossing black lines

"Nuts, too easy. Okay then, let's see how you do with this one."

She passed me another Mondrian, only this one was much more complex. It was a diamond made of many triangles, trapezoids, rectangles, and squares of different sizes and colors. I studied it for a couple of minutes, then closed my eyes.

"Wake up!"

"Prepare to have your mind blown."

"Second best but I'll take it. Shoot."

"There are sixty-three forms in the diamond. Eighteen triangles and four trapezoids border the edges. Its nineteen squares come in two sizes, nine small and ten larger, each about four times the area of the small ones. You'll also find twenty-two rectangles, of which two are much bigger than the rest. The big ones are colored yellow and blue, the yellow above the blue, and they're both close to the center of the painting. The remaining ones look like bricks. They're all the same size except for a tiny brown one over on the left. Other than yellow and blue, the shapes are colored pink, light gray and dark gray. The four triangles making up the diamond tips are gray, gray, blue, and yellow, that's clockwise starting from the top. Now as for the location of each...." I continued on for a few minutes while Shelley scoured the painting.

"Not bad, even fairly impressive. Now let's see if you can fill in the blanks. Courtesy of Photoshop, it's coloring book time."

Shelley handed me a monochrome version of *Composition in Diamond Shape* and five colored pencils. I filled in the colors, returned the sheet to her, and enjoyed watching her compare my version with the original. We were thirty-five thousand feet up and I didn't give a fuck, flying or otherwise.

"You know, you could run away and join the circus."

"Are you calling me a freak?"

"At a minimum. Maybe you're a total freakazoid. Let's find

out."

She removed two ten- by fifteen-inch pieces of cardboard from her backpack. They were bound together with masking tape, and sandwiched between them was a large glossy.

"I'll have you know I spent a whole five dollars to get this thing properly copied, all for the pleasure of watching you squirm." She handed me the photo.

"It's a Jackson Pollock. He named it *Croaking Movement*. Ribbit."

Broad swatches of red, orange, and yellow dominated the center of the painting. They were accompanied by intense dark green swirls, dispersed throughout the painting but prevalent in the upper center and down the right border of the canvas. Surrounded by the bright colors, they appeared darker than dark, as if they were black holes or empty space—nothingness lurking behind a universe on fire. Hundreds of thin white lines overlaid this mass of disturbance. Many were straight, but others formed circles, triangles, and ellipses. They encaged the angry colors, preventing them from bursting from the canvas and attacking the viewer.

"It's from a series of works he named *Sounds in the Grass*. The guy who put the book together wrote that this particular painting features 'restlessly vibrating nodes of color.' That should fix it in your mind, eh?"

I wasn't impressed. "You expect me to memorize this... this plate of decaying spaghetti?"

"Yup. And while you're at it, have a little respect for the dead."

How do you paint a sound? Could those "nodes" represent the expansion and contraction of a frog's body as air passes down its buccal cavity and through its larynx? I examined the painting more carefully. What nodes? My conclusion: no, not even in the most demented of minds.

I studied *Croaking Movement* for two hundred and fifty miles. At first, the painting's aggressive complexity disturbed me. But then

I saw it, or rather sensed it. *It* was the work's current, its attitude. The hidden face of God or of the devil glared at me from the work's underside.

I handed the photo back to Shelley.

"Question number one, mister hotshot fuddy-duddy genius: where's the signature?"

"Fuddy-duddy? I am outraged."

"Just answer the question."

"How decrepit do you think I am? It's in the lower left, J Pollock in heavy black letters. The J looks like a one. Now ask me something more worthy of consideration."

"Okay. There's a white triangle in the upper left quadrant."

"There certainly is."

"What's in it?"

"You'll find a circle in the upper part of the triangle, and it looks like an eye to me. An overripe banana is situated below. It's mainly brown but yellow near its left end, and it forms a frowning mouth."

"Anything else?"

"Much else! There's some orange underneath the mouth. Above and to the left of it, the color lightens to something more yellowish and diffuse. See the touch of darkness between the eye and the mouth? Monsieur has a moustache of sorts. You'll also find a small splash of orange and red to the left, plus a white line entering the triangle from the right, then turning sharply downward. A needle grazing the eye...."

Shelley grilled me at length on the painting, which was fine because I appreciated the distraction and enjoyed showing off. We paused when the flight attendant moved the drink dolly between us. He gave us each a shiny little silver packet. The granules, flakes, and additional miscellaneous particles within mine approximated the results from a project my clever daughter executed back in fourth grade. I remember the day well. She combined noodles from a dried chicken soup mix with ground-up potato chips, then microwaved the mess for ten minutes without covering the bowl. Tasty, salty, and burned to a crisp, mmm messy good.

The flight attendant rolled the dolly on to his next victims.

"Last one. Ready?"

"Bring it on."

Shelley handed me a letter-sized page, every square millimeter of which was covered by randomly angled prescriptions and health insurance statements. No drug names were shown, only anonymous numerical codes followed by information dealing with what was submitted and what was paid. I spotted a dozen illegible signatures, along with sixteen instances of "Manulife." The statements had been shrunk, causing the page to appear dense and heavy. "Shelley" was printed in the dead center, in Courier font, and a tombstone drawn near the bottom of the page was inscribed, "Randell."

She gave me an opening, as she did when she told me, fresh post-Ezekiel, that finding another boyfriend similar to her in some mysterious way would be challenging. I couldn't follow up, however, not across the aisle of a packed plane, and especially not because we had just hit a series of small bumps. Even though the captain didn't even bother to turn on the seatbelt lights, I couldn't have memorized even the first three lines of an eye chart at that moment.

"Later," I said, as I handed the sheet back to her. But when? Today I was a coward. I didn't bring it up on the Chicago-Wichita flight, nor on the ride from Wichita to here. And now, in this fourth-rate Liberal motel, she sleeps peacefully in her room across the hall while I ruminate about bad things.

11:32 p.m. Saturday, June 14th

What lunacy possessed me to take this trip? Had I stayed put in my own bed, some novel would have drowsed me by now. I would have placed it on my bedside table, switched off the lamp, and dozed off in three blinks of an eye. Instead, I anticipate unpleasant noises. The air conditioner bleats. Every few minutes its compressor kicks in, *crack*, as if someone hurled a rock at the window. Scarcely seventy feet distant, trucks, tankers, and tractors barrel up and down the road at irregular intervals. Groups of boisterous young men speaking rapidly in English and Spanish pass under my window. Their arguments increase in intensity, crest below me, then recede until the soup of unpleasant sounds drowns them out. When a freight train rumbles through town, my bedboard vibrates in sympathy with its unending bass tones.

I had last been in Liberal thirty-two years ago, for Ma's funeral. It was an unusually somber affair because only four people attended: me, Ma's longtime friend Francis Lautenbacher, with whom Ma lived for the last six years of her life, Francis's housekeeper Rosita, and some minister, an unremarkable man whose name I never learned and thus can't recall. Words flowed from his mouth like butterscotch. Despite perfect diction and a rich baritone voice, his sentences moved me about as much as if he had repeatedly intoned, "How now brown cow."

We buried Ma in a flatland cemetery, through a biting wind and under a slate-gray sky. After she was lowered into the ground, the minister recited one last prayer. I looked to my right and saw a stooped man watching us from just beyond the cemetery fence, some seventy yards away. Even from that distance and across so much time, I recognized him. He was the man who had attended the trial and sat at the extreme left end of the first-row pew—the man Ma avoided but told me she hadn't noticed. That's right, the guy I pretended to talk to while testifying in order to ease my discomfort because, after all, he was of no consequence.

Later that day I asked Francis about him. "Don't know him, except he shows up at the donut shop some mornings. Quiet man, decent manners." Damn, why didn't I ask what business he had with my mother?

While standing at Ma's gravesite so long ago, the thought came to me that in Kansas, flatness is oppression. The horizon is too straight. It surrounds, right, left, front, and back. There is no escape. "As far as the eye can see"—a cruel hoax of a saying, because in Kansas, expanse is prison. In Kansas, the earth asserts itself through the heaviness, density, and vastity of its flatness. Kansas is loaded with gravity.

Life is a temporary escape from the soil. It's a day pass, an act of grace on the earth's part. She allows a minute fraction of her being to reach upward and breathe free. Life is a loan, and it gets repaid soon enough. Every creature and every plant returns to the earth, because whatever grows up must come down. The pattern persists up the hierarchy: the sun permits the earth to scamper ellipses around it, but the day shall come when she will gather her children back to her. Galaxies will fold in their stars, drawing them to abodes of great denseness; and the universe itself, at a time so far into the future as to be unimaginable, will issue a command her trillions of galaxies will not resist: Return to me.

10:42 P.M. Sunday, June 15th

Shelley knocked not two minutes after I put down my pen last night. She slipped past me, crashed onto the spare bed, and pulled the couple of blankets she was carrying tight up to her chin.

"Just for a few minutes, okay?"

I touched her forehead. She was shivering, yet covered with sweat.

"What's the matter?"

"Nothing. My room's AC is less than optimal, that's all, so I woke up all hot and sticky. It was so bad I had to shower."

"But you're still sweating, and you're shaking too. Can I get you something?"

"Just let me be. Oh and give me your key."

"Why?"

"In case I need to return, so I won't wake you up."

"That's considerate, but wouldn't it be better to switch to another room?"

"Too late. No one's downstairs."

"You know, you really don't look too good."

"Please, not another word."

She fell asleep within ten minutes, and I followed suit soon after, in a chair with my legs resting on the foot of her bed. When I awoke ninety minutes later she was gone.

Fast-forward seven hours. My phone rang:

"Hello."

"Ah, my hero. You dressed yet?"

"Nope, just woke a little while ago. For some strange reason I didn't sleep all that well, though I racked up a few zzzs after sunrise. What about you?"

"I'm much better. In fact I'm feeling remarkably excellent. I guarantee it won't happen again."

"You sure?"

"Positive. It was one of those twelve-hour bugs, that's all. I probably caught it from that Christian music station. Remember, the one that tormented us between Greensburg and Meade? It's a good thing your hearing isn't as sharp as mine. Anyway, I've been busy—changed my room, walked over to Kansas Avenue, injected some coffee, and did a little shopping. Now I'm gung-ho for lunch. Might you be up for some Mexican?"

Shelley kept her sunglasses on all day, even inside a dimly lit restaurant burdened with the name, La Vida es un Taco. I would have been less concerned had her bloodshot eyes been the only sequela. A second one was mania. She fidgeted incessantly throughout lunch, talked a blue streak while simultaneously eating and showing off her purchases: a pair of soft amber slippers, two nail polishes, a navy blue sweatshirt with "Liberal Lady Redskins" inscribed in red letters on the front, and a bright yellow thong that she twirled in the air and accidentally dipped in her quesadilla sauce. After lunch she drove us around town faster than Roadrunner. Be beep.

She insisted we visit sites where my personal landmarks had been: the family house, long ago razed and replaced by a split level, now surrounded on all sides by identical split levels; the old Liberal High School, boarded up and pigeon-infested; the courthouse, torn down fifty years ago; and McGrady's wheat field. The first three amounted to cornhusks, but the McGrady sycamore was altogether another matter. Its topmost branches extended eighty feet into the air, and its trunk had broadened to such an extent that it was no longer climbable.

"Oh my goodness, what a prince of a tree it is!" Spoken by Shelley as we exited the Sonata.

"Yes. It's a majestic prince and it's lording over all this gold," I said, referring to the wheat surrounding us on all sides.

We sat, leaned back against its trunk. Shelley took in a few deep breaths, finally decompressed, thank goodness, and for the next couple of minutes I experienced an emotion sweeter than happiness. Temporal integration, that's what it was—living in the past, present, and future all at once. Unfortunately, such states don't last long.

"I've got some bad news."

"What?"

"It concerns Marcie Smith. She died four years ago."

"Oh no. Why didn't you tell me?"

"I only found out on Thursday, and it didn't feel right to tell you till now. Don't be mad, I'm just the messenger."

"I'm not. How could I be mad at you? But—but I'm, well, oh this is horrible. She's not supposed to be dead."

"Not supposed? According to who, you, God, or the coruscating effects of time? Marcie died at seventy-nine, Carl. How many of your classmates do you think made it that far?"

"I don't know. More than half? Don't women average about eighty-five these days?"

"For someone born today that might be right, but no, not for folks born eighty-three years ago. Many of your contemporaries smoked like chimneys, ate steaks on a daily basis, and chugged martinis. Their idea of exercise was getting up to go to the bathroom during a TV commercial. Marcie likely lasted longer than most. But for argument's sake, suppose she was still alive and living right here in Liberal, and you found her address, strode up to her front door, and knocked. What do you think you'd find?"

"I don't know. Of course she would have looked old. I could have dealt with that, but I wouldn't have wanted to see her afflicted with Alzheimer's."

"Because she wouldn't have remembered you?"

"No, just because it's awful to go out like that."

"You're disappointed not to have seen firsthand how your investment worked out?"

"My investment? What the fuck are you talking about?"

"Calm down. You know what I mean, how could you not? You risked a lot for Marcie back then, and now you'd like to know if it was worth it. Had she died within a few years after the trial, or if she had become a hooker or a criminal or a crack addict, or if you found her poor as a prairie dog, or married to some abusive guy, your investment—your involvement back then—it wouldn't have amounted to much. But if she lived long and happily, keeping in mind that such an outcome would have been less likely without your intervention, well then, that's quite the accomplishment, don't you think?"

"If I had found her alive but in a bad way, I might have been able to help."

"My Carl the altruist," Shelley countered. "I could ask why you didn't try to find her years earlier. Anyway, I learned a few things."

"Tell me."

"First relax, okay? You should, because there's nothing terrible to tell."

"I *am* relaxed."

"Good. Now listen. Marcie spent almost all of her adult life in Tucson. She married there in 1946, and had a son and a daughter who are both alive and remain in the Tucson area. The son's a doctor, family medicine, and the daughter directs bands in three high schools. You'll get a kick out of her name."

"Marcie had two kids?" One of my dumber contributions to the annals of verbal discourse.

"The son is Franklin, likely named after FDR, and the daughter is called—da da da dum da dum, wait for it—Carla."

"Carla. I suppose it's possible she was named after me. But what about her husband? Is he alive?"

"He died seventeen years ago. I couldn't find any record of her remarrying."

"That's way too young. What did he die of?"

"I don't know. In fact I found nothing on him at all other than his name, James Daniels."

"Wait a minute. Are you sure about that? James Daniels?"

"Yup. Like Jack Daniels, only James Daniels."

"Jimmy!"

"Who?"

"I never told you about Jimmy?"

"No."

"No? The short kid with a ton of attitude and blubber? He was one of my high school friends."

"You had friends back then?"

"I can't believe it! My friend the fat boy marries... marries the— marries somebody like her."

"Somebody like her? Don't you mean exactly like her?"

"Right. It's just that Jimmy and Marcie were opposites. Jimmy was a sarcastic son of a bitch. A really good friend, but boy he could be rough. And Marcie, well, she was sweet and quiet, a doll of a girl. I'm glad it worked out. Too bad he died, though, too bad they're both dead. Oh this is so sad."

"The fat boy marries the retarded girl." Yes, that's what I almost said.

10:11 P.M. Monday, June 16th

In an ideal world, today's events would have transpired just so:

With arms interlocked, Shelley and I skip up the stairs leading to the Seward County Courthouse entrance, singing, "We're off to see the Register, the wonderful Register of Lib." We knock on the Deeds Office door and are not told to come back tomorrow, because the Almighty Register, Mrs. Osita Zamorra, is eager to serve us with a smile. I hand Mrs. Zamorra a scrap of paper with my childhood address written on it. I inform her that by 1932 at the latest, my father had purchased a two-storey farmhouse and a few acres of land at the specified location, and that I wish to purchase a photocopy of the deed. The Register motions to an assistant, who takes down the relevant information and leaves the office. Ten minutes later she returns with the requested document, warm and snug inside a legal-size manila envelope. I pay a small fee, and there are smiles all around as we exchange *thank you*s and *you're welcome*s. Upon exiting the building I slide the deed out from its envelope. Shelley and I tap our heels together three times while repeatedly incanting, "There's no place like wherever." At the bottom of the page we find a date, Pa's signature, and the clue we were searching for: an unfamiliar address. We get in the Sonata, Shelley points it in the right direction, and vroom, off we go.

Events unfolded a smidge differently. The register's computer search this morning uncovered no real estate purchases in Liberal between 1925 and 1932 by anyone named Anderson. She then performed a "find" on the address of my old house. Up popped a February, 1929 sale. The buyer's signature was not Pa's, however, but that of Michael Bourgmeyer. Who the hell was Michael Bourgmeyer?

In addition to buyer and seller signatures, the deed included a description of the location, boundaries, and contents of the property. Other than a brief addendum concerning water rights, signed and notarized by one John Birtwistle, Attorney-at-Law, that was it. No birth dates were recorded, no previous addresses were given, and no driver's license information was shown. Michael Bourgmeyer might as well have lived on the moon.

The Register sent us on a trajectory that included the Seward County Tax Assessor's Office and the Liberal branch of Sunflower Bank. From the tax office we learned that Bourgmeyer paid property taxes on our house for almost fourteen years—from February, 1929 to the end of 1942. My mother, not my father, obtained title to the house on January 1, 1943.

The bank visit turned out to be even more fruitful, thanks to an accommodating manager and his heroic secretary, who spent forty-five minutes digging up Ma's account records from a wareroom in the back of the building. We learned that Michael Bourgmeyer took care of our monthly mortgage payments for the same fourteen-year period over which he paid our property taxes. In addition, he sent my mother a three-thousand-dollar check in March of 1929 and wrote out a series of sixteen checks in the amount of three hundred dollars each. They were deposited every six months for eight straight years beginning in 1935. Bourgmeyer's final gift was a solitary check, dated July 1, 1942—for ten thousand dollars!

By now it was 2:30 P.M. and hunger had overmatched our curiosity. We left the bank and walked across North Kansas Avenue to the nearest restaurant, a Wendy's. Perfect—air conditioning, salad bar, and the illusion that we could have been eating anywhere in

North America. We filled our plates, grabbed a booth, ate half of our lunches, then considered the possibilities.

"Looks like your mother was either one hell of a hooker or received alimony payments from Mr. Bourgmeyer. When were you born?"

"1925."

"Make that alimony plus child support. Now you know who put you through college."

"He might have been my biological father?"

"Might have been? More like definitely *was*. That's a shocker, eh? The guy you thought was your father turns out to be your step-father. Not only that, but for some inexplicable reason your mother and step-dad successfully deceived you for your entire life. Well, almost your entire life. Now you know."

"I'm flabbergasted."

"You should be, and you should be perplexed as well. Tell me, why do you think Mr. Bourgmeyer sent your mom three thousand dollars in 1929 but nothing for the next six years?"

"I don't know. Times were hard back then. Maybe he lost his job?"

"This is frustrating," said Shelley. "We can speculate to our hearts' content, but the bottom line is we know nothing about him—not where he came from, what he did for a living, nor why your folks split."

"Plus we have no way of finding out," I added, "though I have a very good idea of what he looked like."

"Let's have another look at that deed," said Shelley. She took it from me and stared at the addendum. "This guy's signature at the bottom, John Birtwistle. Of course he's dead, but I wonder..."

"What?"

"Yeah, he's dead but we're not, not yet. This Birtwistle guy, if he was the legal notary, which he was, he must have worked out of Liberal or somewhere nearby, right?"

"Seems likely."

"Well then, let's dig him up! Or rather, look him up. Jeez I hope he wasn't gay. We need him to have had kids. If no one threw out his records, we might be able to find out where Bourgmeyer came from."

"Shelley, we're talking about an eighty-year-old document that no one would have any reason to keep. It's as good as garbage to the rest of the world."

"True, but the world holds gigatons of old garbage. Granted it's a very long shot, but as we're already here we might as well go for it. It's either that or we return to Montreal with only half the story and our tails between our legs."

We found one Birtwistle listed in the phone directory, a George Birtwistle. Shelley made the call.

"May I speak to Mr. Birtwistle please... Oh hello!... My name is Sheila Rogers... No, you don't know me. I'm from Lawrence... Yes, that's right, the one in Kansas. Thank you for taking the time to talk with me... I understand... Okay then, I'll get right to the point. I'm studying legal history at KU, and my dissertation deals with contributions of western Kansas lawyers to the state's jurisprudence in the first half of the twentieth century. I came to Liberal hoping to research John Birtwistle, among others, as he was prominent around here between the wars. Might you be related to him?"

"Uh huh... Yes... Uh huh... I see." Repeat a dozen times.

"So you still have his records? Really? Oh that's so wonderful!... I see... Well yes, certainly... Uh, what?... *What?*... Twenty-six... Brownish with red tints... *Really?* Umm, medium to longish... Uh huh... I never measured. But why do you need to know?... Well yes, an impostor showing up on your doorstep would not be a good thing... Of course I'm not offended, but thank you for asking... Uh, thin to average. Is that precise enough?... Yes of course... That would be wonderful! Tomorrow at ten it is. How do I get there?... I see... Uh huh... Yes, right, got it! Should be easy. Thank you so very much, Mr. Birtwistle. I really appreciate your willingness to help me out. See you tomorrow!"

Shelley hung up, or rather disconnected. People don't hang up anymore.

"Creepometer's off the scale."

"What the hell was he asking you?"

"Just about everything but my favorite sex positions, and his voice pretty much drooled. But the good news is, he's kept everything! He plans on writing a family saga one day. Like he's ever going to do it."

"Sheila Rogers, nice alias. And 'How do *I* get there?' You didn't mention that I'm coming with you."

"That's because I'm a cagey bitch. Now let's go get me a dress, because I have to look like I'm not so cagey. With this guy, that should be a piece of cake. Think there's a Gap in town?"

Alas no Gap, but we outfitted Shelley admirably enough thanks to the combined resources of two North Kansas Avenue stores: light gray skirt extending all the way down to four inches above the knee, freshly pressed white cotton blouse buttoned all the way up to the bottom of the rose tattoo's stem, turquoise drop earrings framing her silver necklace (minus the bloodstone pendent), pale makeup, ruby-red lipstick, nose and eyebrow ringlets on vacation. Never have I seen a graduate student look so scholarly, so serious, so utterly professional. Mr. Birtwistle will be impressed.

10:38 P.M. Wednesday, June 18th

It was obvious from first glance yesterday morning that George Birtwistle had spent substantial amounts time, money, and effort to postdate himself. He wore two layers of makeup to our meeting—a damp floury base and a rouge topping designed to vitiate the pale-as-death impression. His interventions failed to shave off the years. Instead, he looked like the photonegative of some short frail guy wearing blackface. His eye bag job fell short because it created a split-level face—tight and firm above the nose, jowly and slack-jawed below it. Nor did his thinning hair, dyed blacker than an inkwell, contribute to the perception of vigorous manliness percolating from within his being. And let's not forget the betrayal of his voice. It was the opposite of firm and resonant—bassy and quavery, an imperfect imitation of a female impersonator's Katherine Hepburn.

Birtwistle acted respectably enough during the living room interview, which included an introductory apology for why his grandfather's papers were stored in the barn rather than in the house (they stunk) and a reminiscence of his Grandma Meg, the purpose of which was unclear to Shelley and me. A favorite game involved the old lady repeatedly beaning a four-year-old George with a volleyball from the top of a flight of stairs, all the while cackling, "I'll get you, my pretty." Then came a tedious exposition on the importance of his grandfather John's career, worth no commentary despite Shelley's copious note taking.

Decorum vanished by the wayside on the way across the road to the barn. Birtwistle walked next to Shelley, poked at her a few times. When they reached the road he grabbed onto her shoulders, feigning a loss of balance.

"What lovely earrings you have." He held her left ear in place by grasping it with his right thumb and forefinger, brought his eyes to an inch or two away from the object of his interest.

"Ha ha. Got to get close, you know. I see about as well as Mister Magoo."

"Who?"

"Never mind, you're too young. But oh my, your necklace is lovely too." Without releasing her ear, he stared into her bodice.

Shelley smiled uncomfortably. "Why thank you." She slowly swung both of her arms leftward, extricating herself from Birtwistle's proximity.

Upon entering the barn, Birtwistle pointed to the loft's ladder and suggested that Shelley climb it to find the cartons. As soon as she stepped on the first rung, he positioned himself right behind her. What a guy.

"Wow," Shelley said, upon reaching the loft. "There's lots of stuff up here."

"Unfortunately I haven't investigated it for quite some time, but if I remember correctly, my grandfather's boxes are labeled," Birtwistle replied.

"You've got dozens of cartons here, and so many big black garbage bags. There must be a hundred of them."

"Don't mind the bags, just find the boxes labeled 'Birtwistle, John.' They'll be together somewhere. Happy hunting!"

Fortunately I confronted the old goat after, rather than before Shelley located the boxes. I thought I was being discreet when I called him away, behind the barn and beyond Shelley's earshot. I informed him, very politely I might add, that I would not countenance further contact between his person and Shelley, as it was clear that she was finding his attentions unwarranted and unpleasant.

His response? "Sour grapes. Don't blame me that you're older than sin."

And mine, spoken while brandishing my cane: "I'm young enough to knock you flat on your ass before you can say Oz." Oh dear. My comment ended our visit. Boom just like that, he demanded we remove our own sorry posteriors from his property.

Shelley drove the curving two-lane country road back to town way too fast for my liking. After rattling my nerves for a couple of minutes, she braked sharply and pulled the car curbside.

"Great. Just what was needed, Sir Lancelot coming to my rescue. Thank you, kind sir." Steam emanated from her head. I might have imagined that bit, though I doubt it.

"You blew it! I had him wrapped around my pinkie, and what

do you do? Protect my honor. Ha! How could you be so thick?"

"I will not apologize, young lady. I thought you'd appreciate my intervention. He had his paws all over you."

"Young lady? How condescending! I'm not your child, I'm an adult! And it wasn't like he was molesting me. He had his hands on my shoulders, goddammit! Shoulders are not intimate, erogenous, sexual, or anything else. They're run-of-the-mill body parts, just plain ordinary fucking shoulders! And yeah, so he grabbed my ear. Ooh that *was* unpleasant, *so* creepy, but I handled it. It was no big deal. So what if he paid me a little unwanted attention? He was on the verge of letting us borrow those boxes, and then *you* had to screw everything up."

"Sorry. It's just that I didn't think you were—well, I didn't realize you found him quite so dashing." A non-sequitur with an unnecessary modifier, but what the heck, that's what came out.

Her mouth agape, eyes opened wide: "Quite so dashing? Are you mad? George Birtwistle, the poor man's von Aschenbach, quite so dashing?"

I shrugged, and we both started heaving with laughter. Tears streamed down her face. She looked up to the Sonata's ceiling as if it were the Sistine Chapel fresco. "God, how am I going to survive the week with this guy?" She turned to me, said, "So now what's the plan, mister doctor professor? How are we going to find your daddy's address?"

A moment of silence.

"You thinking what I'm thinking?"

"Great minds and all that." That's how I responded, though in truth I didn't get it until a couple of seconds after I saw her grin.

"Do we get to paint black marker stuff under our eyes, like swat teams and football players?"

"Sure. We'll find an Army-Navy store in town and buy fatigues, night goggles, soundless moccasins, the whole shebang." An Army-

Navy store in Liberal, Kansas? Absolutely, right between the Gap and the Starbucks.

And so it came to pass that I committed the only criminal act of my life early this morning, not counting book stealing and perjury. At half past midnight, equipped with crowbar and flashlight, we approached the Birtwistle homestead. The barn was bathed in the faint bluish-white light of a setting west Kansas full moon, and the wind was as calm as a Buddhist monk.

"Old people sleep lightly," I said.

Shelley cut the motor about a hundred yards before reaching the barn, and we glided in the rest of the way. We exited the car slowly and stealthily, taking care to leave the doors ajar. I raised the trunk an inch per second while Shelley approached the barn door, crowbar in hand.

"No need for this thing," she whispered. "The barn's unlocked. Return it to the store tomorrow and get a refund."

"Maybe not. We might still need it somewhere. But I won't bring it with us on the return flight," I whispered back.

"Smart thinking."

"Yeah. When we're over Toronto and you ask me 'How much further?' I won't be tempted to say, 'Three hundred twenty-five miles as the crowbar flies.'"

"If you make me laugh and he wakes up, you're to blame."

Shelley climbed up to the loft.

"You remember exactly where they are?"

"No problem."

She dropped the cartons over the railing, one at a time. Each produced a soft *mmmph* as it hit the straw-covered floor.

"Good thing there are no animals in here," Shelley said, *sotto voce.*

"Agreed. No chance of a cow alarm going off. Moo."

We stuffed nine of the cartons into the trunk and piled the

remaining thirteen, a collective acme of stench, onto the backseat.

"Disgusting," said Shelley. "What *is* that smell?"

"Reminds me of cow dung on a rainy day."

"Eew. Triple eew!"

Shelley started the car, and all four windows descended as fast as we could manage the buttons. After slinking away for a tenth of a mile, she gunned us back to the motel. Never have I been happier to exit an automobile.

We spent today rummaging through thousands of documents at a Blue Bonnet Park picnic table. Many pages were badly faded, which slowed our work and made it tiresome. The stink emanating from the cartons, barely diminished from last night's drive back to the motel, did not help matters.

We found no case notes, memoirs, address books, or diary entries, in fact nothing at all that would have interested a student working on her doctorate. Many of the cartons were filled with Birtwistle's bills, accumulated over the decades—heating, phone, electricity, travel, and so forth. We discovered what appeared to be a complete set of class and lecture notes, beginning with Birtwistle's elementary school days and continuing right through his final law seminars. One carton was taken up with the works of Shakespeare. Another three were crammed with random issues of the *Southwest Daily Times* and *National Geographic*. We came across hundreds of client invoices and receipts, but unfortunately none of them included the names of any Bourgmeyer or Anderson.

"Oh!"—Shelley's reaction upon discovering a mint-condition black girdle in the sixth carton. She unfolded it and out dropped a packet of letters. They were bound by blue, green, red, and yellow rubber bands.

"Love letters!" She opened one of them, quickly scanned it. It began with the salutation, "Dearest John," and concluded with "My Deepest Love, Your Margaret Always and Forever."

"Can we keep them?"

"Do you think John Birtwistle would have wanted that?"

"Who cares? Besides, he left nothing else worth anything. Better than being totally forgotten, no?"

"But what about Margaret?"

"Yeah, she probably wouldn't want us picking over her grammatical errors. On the other hand, she's well past blushing. One-hundred-year-old chick lit, should make for fun reading back at the motel, eh?" Shelley dropped the packet inside her bag. She returned the girdle to the carton, however, mint condition notwithstanding.

That smile again. Her t-shirt had become grimy and her face and arms were covered with sweat, but no matter, she looked absolutely great in the sunlight.

"Photo op," I said.

"What, now? We're all dirty."

"Come on, get the camera out." We shot each other. She wants me to delete them both, but that will not happen.

I found it at the bottom of the very last carton, inside a large brown envelope it shared with fifty or so similar documents: a carbon copy of the mortgage contract between Michael Bourgmeyer and Sunflower Bank, signed and stamped by John Birtwistle.

"Please let Mr. Bourgmeyer come from somewhere," I implored the document.

"There it is!" said Shelley. She pointed to the bottom of the second page, where below an illegible signature was written:

Robert Bennington, in trust for Michael Bourgmeyer, of
1201 Holiday Drive
Denver, Colorado

"I was born in Denver?"

"Likely," said Shelley. "But what does the *in trust* part signify?"

"I have no idea. What do you say we get ourselves and the car cleaned up, have a nice dinner, sleep on it, and consider our next step tomorrow?"

"I'm amenable," she replied. "But our first order of business is giving the Birtwistle Archive a proper sendoff."

"Amen."

We dumped the cartons and their contents, minus one envelope, one document, and a packet of thirteen letters, into one of Blue Bonnet Park's vomit-green dumpsters. John Birtwistle, thank you. May your soul, and Margaret's, rest in peace. Oh, and George? Forget writing the family history, and *please* forget young women. Treat yourself to a top-of-the-line sex doll.

2:14 P.M. Thursday, June 19th

I was asleep when she entered my room this morning, lay down next to me, and whispered seven words into my left ear:

"Vake up dahlink. I bring important news."

"Mm. Oh. It's you." I could barely see her, she was so close. Her forehead was almost touching mine, and my eyes, always misty in the morning, hadn't yet focused.

"Anyone else and you're in big trouble. Guess what! Your father was a criminal."

"Wonderful. Tell me the details over breakfast."

"No, now."

"Just grant me a brief trip to the bathroom."

"Okay but be fast about it."

She started in as soon as I closed the door: "Three cheers for the State of Colorado!"

"Three minutes, please!"

"Can't you pee faster than that?"

"Have a heart, will you?" I turned the faucets on all the way and sung "This Land is Your Land" at maximum volume until it was no longer necessary.

She started in half a second after I exited the bathroom: "I found some amazing historical records pages."

"Tell me."

"First off, was your mom's name Amanda?"

"Yes."

"Aha! In that case you'll be interested to know that Michael Bourgmeyer and Amanda Bourgmeyer, née Sterling, got married in 1921 and divorced in 1929. Halfway through their travail together they produced a certain Carl Bourgmeyer, who was born on April 21st, 1925. That your birthdate?"

"Yes again. What's this about Bourgmeyer being a criminal?"

"I found a Department of Corrections index on the site, so for the hell of it I entered "Bourgmeyer" into it. Bingo! The search yielded exactly one record, that of a certain Michael Bourgmeyer."

"What was his crime?"

"I don't know. The record was blank except for first name, last name, and a five-digit reference number. You can write to the Archives for more information, but I've got a better idea."

"Which is?"

"Given that we've got three days of muck-around time left before returning to Montreal, and also that you promised me a visit to someplace marginally more interesting than Liberal, let's kill the two birds with one stone. Take me to Denver! We'll figure out what to do at the Denver Public Library, and who knows, maybe you'll even get a peek inside the house at 1201 Holiday Drive."

"Assuming it hasn't been torn down and replaced by a parking lot," I said.

"Right. Though if they've replaced it with a Baskin-Robbins, don't expect me to grieve."

We departed Liberal three and a half hours ago, right after breakfast and an inside-and-out car wash. Shelley zooms us westward on Interstate 70 at eighty miles per hour, fast enough to arrive in the big city well before dark. I'm reclining against the Sonata's rear right door. My legs are stretched across the backseat, and I'm so relaxed, enjoying the sun, the landscape, and the rhythm of the road. Shelley announced "We're not in Kansas anymore" a couple of minutes ago, and now she's wailing along with some despondent soul on the radio:

> I've lost my treehouse lover,
> She's run off with some guy from the bar,
> Of her I'll never get over,
> Moaning skyward while cows mooed afar.
> Goodbye, my sweet treehouse lover...

She wears jean cutoffs and a tight green t-shirt, and her oversize black horn-rimmed sunglasses balance precariously on the bridge of her nose. Hair's flip-flopping as she bobs to the beat. How could I possibly be in better hands?

10:46 P.M. Thursday, June 19th

I write from our room in this hotel of elegant stripes. From my vantage point here in bed I see red stripes layering white pillow cases; red, black, and gold stripes streaking down the curtains; and yellow and white striped wallpaper brightening up all four of the room's corners. Every stripe runs vertical. Come to think of it, the woman who checked us in was thin as a rail and at least two inches taller than me. The bellboy was taller still and malnourished, a Giacometti figure come to life.

Our room. The *quid pro quo* sealing the deal was my willingness to put up with her snoring in return for her acquiescence in letting me keep my lamp lit late. I'm fond of her snores. They're soft steady swooshes, closer to genteel lakeside waves than grunting pigs. Moreover, I enjoy being awake when she isn't. It's a pleasant sentry duty.

This afternoon's debacle was entirely her fault. We were a hundred miles out when she suggested, so innocently, "How about we stop by it on the way? Or would you rather go straight to the hotel, change, and get on the treadmill?" Our original plan had been to proceed directly to the Monaco, check in, and have dinner. We would get a good night's sleep and save the research for tomorrow.

"My dear, can you see me on a treadmill?"

"Sure. You never saw a guy with a cane on a treadmill?"

"Can't say as I have."

"Step...step-TAP. Step...step-TAP. Best done to a calypso beat. Get an iPod, load it with 'Under the Sea,' and you're good to go."

"Okay, I give. Let's go see if the house stands. We're on the road anyway, and there's no rush to check in. If it didn't survive, we'll have saved ourselves a trip. But if we find it, we just look around on the outside, take a few photos, and head the other way. No knocking on or anywhere near the door."

"Check. But why?"

"It's better to call first and set up an appointment. If whoever lives inside has an unblocked landline we'll be able to phone, right?"

"Yup. Lots of websites supply phone numbers for addresses."

Shelley pulled off the road a few minutes later so I could move up to the death seat and reset Gustav Phineas Smyth, our pet name for the contraption. Against my better judgment, I had taken Shelley's advice and spent the extra eight dollars a day for it. She set it to Jack Bauer for the trip from Wichita to Liberal. When we missed our turn onto Kansas Avenue, Jack hissed, "Son of a bitch." Today we chose Gordon, an Englishman with a cockney accent. Shortly after we had driven halfway up Holiday Drive, a quiet street lined with evenly spaced majestic oak trees on both sides, he enthused, "Well done! You have reached your destination."

The address we were seeking matched a Victorian across from

where we parked.

"Hallelujah, it stands!" Shelley clapped her hands together and bounced her ass on the seat a couple of times.

"Dollars to doughnuts there's water back of it," I said.

"Dollars to doughnuts, eh? That's risking a bunch. Are you sure?"

"Maybe."

"Maybe you're sure? That's not logical. Either you are or you aren't."

"If you say so."

"Oh good. You know, some chicks dig strong decisive guys, but not me. As far as I'm concerned, there's nothing sexier than a guy unaware of his own cluelessness."

"What cluelessness?"

"Even better."

We exited the car, crossed the street. The house was positioned at the crest of a small hill, which afforded us a panoramic northern view. A block behind and below the house, two kids loitered near the backstop of a rundown baseball diamond. A small forest of pines, birches, oaks, and maples covered a strip of land past the diamond, and beyond the forest, as I had predicted, there it sparkled—a lake. It extended to our right and left for as far as we could see, and a superhighway hugged the horizon just past it.

As for the property immediately before us, *manicured* would not have been an apt descriptor. An unmowed weedy yard, an askew rusted front gate, and cracked wooden steps specked with gray paint contributed to the impression of entropy run amok. The condition of the house matched its surroundings. Myriad paint flakes dangled from its surfaces like pinioned hawkmoths, and a torn screen hung precariously off one of the upstairs windows. The roof's shingles looked like they had been replaced on a need-to-know basis. Seventy percent of them were black, the rest gray, white, or brown.

We approached to within forty feet of the front porch. Suddenly I knew: inside would be, had to be, a hallway extending all the way from the front door to the kitchen at the back of the house. A living room would be located off to the left of the hallway, and two smaller rooms would be found to the right—a sitting room and a dining room behind it. The kitchen would be spacious, and in its far right corner a monstrous beast of a black wood-burning stove—warmth—in all likelihood would be present no longer.

"What the fuck, Carl, let's knock."

"No!"

"But think of the time we'll save."

"Didn't you hear what I said?"

"Sure I did. I just don't buy it. Come on, let's take a chance."

"But we look like shit. Folks don't let strangers dressed like shit into their homes. We'll call in the morning. I'll make the appointment, and by then we'll be ready. You'll wear your killer grad student outfit and I'll have my good shirt and jeans on."

"Whoever's inside isn't going to mind what we look like. Besides, they probably look like shit too. If we come back all dolled up, they'll be intimidated."

"Can we continue this discussion away from the house?"

"And what if they don't have a landline?"

"Come." I retreated toward the street.

"Why are we leaving?"

"So whoever's inside won't phone the police."

We sat down on the curb.

"You're nervous, eh?"

"No, just feeling wrung out from the heat, that's all. Just give me a few minutes."

My discomfort diminished, supplanted by an acute impulse to caress Shelley's sunlit thighs, inches away. I let it pass, thank goodness, then closed my eyes. Only then did I process the fact that a couple of minutes ago I had smashed through the six-year barrier. I had recalled my house from when I was an infant.

"Take your time," Shelley said. "But once you're feeling a little better, let's do it."

"We should stick to the plan. And to be frank, I'm not prepared."

"Prepared? What's to prepare? We're here, right in front of the first house you ever lived in. Time to seize the day! Besides, what if they're not in when we come back? There's no guarantee someone's home now, but at least we double the probability if we give it the old college try."

"I'd rather not risk it."

"I know you're apprehensive, but you're going to feel the same way tomorrow."

"Shelley, we're going to blow it by forcing the issue."

"Oh for fuck's sake, don't be so timid!"

"It's a mistake."

"It is so *not* a mistake. Come on!"

Stubborn bitch. I could see that I wasn't going to win this argument, so I caved to save a little time: "Very well, then, but only for fuck's sake. And I told you so in advance."

We approached the house, me with justifiable trepidation and Shelley with unjustifiable confidence. She gave the knocker a good rap. Nothing. A second rap and a woman opened the door partway, just wide enough for us to see that she was thin, kind of mousy looking, and wore neither lipstick nor makeup. Her feet were encased in pink bunny slippers. A blond boy, six or seven years old, hid behind her and clutched at her worn gray housedress. And oh yes, the woman gripped a metal baseball bat in her left hand.

"What do you want? Are you Jehovah's Witnesses?" Sure, two Jehovah's Witnesses dressed like slobs, such clever disguises.

"Uh, no ma'am. We're here for a very different reason," Shelley said.

"Go away. I'm not buying anything, and I'm not giving money to any charity either." The woman started to close the door.

"I used to live here." She hesitated, giving me time to add, "Your house belonged to my family eighty years ago."

"Eighty? You lived here in, uh, 1928?"

"Yes, ma'am, born in 'twenty-five. My granddaughter and I are passing through Denver, and if you don't mind, I'd love to show her the house I grew up in."

"No kidding!" She smiled for a moment then scanned us again, the bum-like aspect inherent in our attire now registering on all the wrong brain cells of her frontal lobes, both hemispheres. Her smile slipped away like a last glug of bathwater dribbling down the drain.

"Sorry, but I'm not letting you in." She closed the door.

"I'm willing to pay you two hundred dollars for just twenty minutes."

She opened the door again, looked at both of us in alternation, thrice over.

"You got the money with you?"

I checked my wallet. Sure enough, it contained two fives and three ones. Improvisation sometimes has its downside.

"I'm afraid we'll have to come back. Would you know if there's an ATM nearby?"

The woman slammed the door shut. Shelley shouted, "We'll come back with cash!"

"You come back again and I'm calling the cops. Get the hell out of here."

From the house's interior boomed a one-word postscript: "Motherfuckers." I turned to Shelley, said, "The irony."

On the drive to the hotel, Shelley whistled "Treehouse Lover" under her breath, tapped her fingernails on the steering wheel, and smiled when a supermom in a silver Sienna cut her off. Throughout the interior of that magnificent head of hers she had been applying the finishing touches to plan B, Denver version. No doubt she started working on it before the air molecules displaced by our visitee's final word on the matter had settled back into their warm little nesting places.

The subject came up as we were walking down Champa Street this evening, on the prowl for a decent restaurant.

"Do you really need to go inside? It's just a big old creaky thing. We could find photos of a hundred houses just like it online."

"I recognized it. Not only that, it made me ill. I have to go back, no matter what we find at the library."

"But that bitch won't let you in."

"She will, once I show her some real money."

"How high are you willing to go?"

We had just passed a dusty gray Corolla with a 288 KLV license plate.

"Two hundred and eighty-eight dollars. Not a dollar more."

"No? Not a dollar? What if she says she'll let you in for two eighty-nine but not for two eighty-eight?"

"I'd hem and haw for a few seconds, make her think it's a tough choice. Then I'd give her the extra dollar."

"And after that, if she says two ninety or no deal?"

"I'd tell her to go fuck herself. Happy?"

"Yup. A little firmness in a clueless man is a good thing."

Tonight we scratched a minor fantasy itch: dinner together in an Indian restaurant. Despite prior discussions on the topic, we had never acted on this particular activity. The delay had become a running joke, especially after our lone Montreal attempt resulted in a visit to an establishment that had been shuttered for five months.

I should fast before going Indian. Shelley and I shared the butter chicken, just that one teeny entree. The dish must have had a false bottom. True, we also split pakoras, a veggie-stuffed nan, and a plate of basmati rice. I drank a beer, but only one. Oh, and how can I forget the vanilla ice cream with mango? A meal at an Indian restaurant without mango and ice cream for dessert is The Old Testament minus the Song of Songs. It's Beethoven's *Fifth* without the triumphant finale, *Ben Hur* with no chariot race.

As our steps back to the Monaco were no longer fueled by hunger, we took up a leisurely pace, stopping here and there to glance in store windows overlooked on the way down. One storefront was partly obscured by metal meshwork. Its sign, hung on high and engraved in big, bolded, and underlined black American Typewriter Font letters, proclaimed:

Ed's Guns

The display's foundation consisted of a six-foot-square platform covered by a purple velvet tablecloth. Six handguns, all silver-and-black six-shooters, rested on it. Four of the guns were aligned end-to-end vertically, muzzles aimed upward. The other two pointed at each other from opposite sides of the platform's midline, level with the second gun from the top and thus forming a cross. The guns glittered, courtesy of halogen beams illuminating their barrels. Four rifles suspended by ultra thin black wires floated about the peripheries, two on each side of the display.

"What a cute crucifix," Shelley said. "Do you own a gun?"

"I'm a pacifist. Wouldn't hurt a flea, and wouldn't be caught dead with one. A gun, that is. Or a flea."

"How about a spider? Would you let one live to a ripe old age if you found it in your room?"

"I make exceptions for spiders. I squash them with toilet paper and flush them into the St. Lawrence."

"But if you had one of those beauties you could blow them out of the water. If they were in the water, which of course they wouldn't be. Let's go in."

"Why? Are you in the market for a gun?"

"Yup. If I see a red machine gun I'll snap it up. But it's got to be red so it'll go with a certain pair of stilettos I own. No green or yellow machine guns for me."

"Geez Shelley, I get the pepper spray, but do you really need stilettos? It's not like we're living in fifteenth-century Venice."

"Stiletto heels, silly. Come."

"But it's a *gun* store. I hate guns."

"So do I."

"Then why?"

"I'm curious, George. It's not like we have pressing business back at the hotel. And who knows, maybe Ed's hot."

"What, you think you'll find a Clint Eastwood look-a-like inside and he's going to tell us to make his day by buying a six-shooter? And after, he'll ask you out on a date?"

"No offense, Carl, but Clint's ancient. I prefer a Matt Damonish kind of guy. Anyway, we'll find out soon enough."

The entrance to Ed's Guns was located at the end of a graffiti-laden corridor smelling faintly of urine. I pushed open a heavy steel door, and we were assaulted with a brightness that a more religious type might associate with the entrance to Heaven. A string of ceilinged fluorescents extended the length of the room, thirty feet to our right, thirty feet to our left, and the floor was made of imitation wood parquet, polished to such a high burnish that I had to shield my eyes. All that was missing was a chorus of a thousand angels intoning a *fortissimo* major triad.

Shelley's reaction: "Wow!"

Mine: "Where's my nictitating membrane now that I need it?"

An enormous gun rack supported by a chest-high faux mahogany base was mounted on the far wall. Hundreds of rifles stood at attention, each snug between notches protruding from the rack. Most of the rifles were amalgamations of brown and black, though the odd mother-of-pearl specimen was thrown in every now and then for good measure. Flimsy white strings connected triggers to dangling yellow price tags. Rows of shelves tucked underneath the gun rack were stacked with thousands of cute little boxes of bullets. They were shaped, colored, and sized differently from each other, a macabre inside-out take on the concept of biodiversity.

A succession of waist-high glass counters, positioned a yard in front of the far wall and running parallel to it, housed hundreds of handguns. Most were cowboy guns—inverted and upside down killer J's, their handles set back from the barrel so they could be inserted into holsters. Others were smaller and boxlike. These were the no-nonsense, unflashy, get-the-job-done guns. I spotted two or three snub-nosed tiny pistolets that could fit in the palm of a petite woman's hand. They were decorated with fake inlaid wood handles and stumpy silver barrels. Ah yes, the toy poodles of the gun world, adorable tempests in teacups.

Ed was not hot. He was a tree trunk of a man: short, stout, huge biceps, wide stomach, piercing brown eyes, cuff tattoo on his upper left arm, and a small silver sphere dangling from his right earlobe. He walked like a well-fed duck, and his t-shirt was stained sepia from too few or too many launderings. I found him disturbing. Perhaps I was thrown off keel because there was no *The customer is always right* sign in the store. Either that, or I was discomfited by being in close proximity to machines capable of immediately terminating animal and human life.

I intuited that Ed was going to be smarmy-friendly, and I've always associated smarminess with the potential for going postal. My prejudice. Thousands of perfectly innocuous smarmy people, spread out like coatings of spam across the continent, blithely go about their businesses without malicious thoughts running through their heads. Alas, it takes only one or two off-the-rails bad-apple ultraviolent smarm-balls to cast aspersions on the whole group.

"Can I be of service to you folks?" Ed smiled, revealing a gold upper right incisor.

"We're just looking," Shelley said. "I've never been in a gun store before. Cool place you got here."

"Thank you!" He flashed us another gold-tinted smile. "Take your time. Have a look around, and if there's anything I can help you with, just let me know." He turned away, then swiveled back. "We also sell toy guns. They make great presents. Want to see?"

"Peasants?" said I.

"Ignore him," said Shelley. "Sometimes his hearing is off. And yes, please, we'd love to see them."

"Really?" From me, not Ed.

"Patience, dear. Who knows, maybe we'll complete our Christmas shopping early."

We found pistols, rifles, and machine guns on the toy table. One of the pistols came with the following warning: "Not for children under eighteen." Shelley picked up a black metal handgun, only eleven ninety-nine. It looked real except for an orange stick protruding a quarter of an inch past its muzzle. Its packaging included the following text:

The outer casing and slide of this spring air gun are cast from solid metal alloy and frankly it looks pretty realistic. If it weren't for the blaze orange tip and the slightly smaller gun size we'd be concerned about our coworkers packing these at office meetings.

"That one's a best seller," Ed said. "A little more lifelike than the other toys, but you couldn't rob a bank with it. Ha-ha."

The thought of buying a dozen crossed my mind. I'd give them to the Manoir codgers and we'd tote them down to breakfast. Might improve the service. Shelley wanted one too, but I reminded her that passing such items through airport security might prove problematic. As we left the store, Ed flashed us one last golden smile and said, "Come back anytime, nice people!" Not bloody likely.

Unfortunately, our visit to Ed's was not the night's last notable event. Shelley got sick again, about a half-hour into her sleep. She hurried past my bed to the bathroom, snatched up fresh clothing along the way. Even in the dim light I could see her pajama bottoms and t-shirt sticking fast to her body, and a distressed look on her face. Door closed, shower on, twelve minutes, shower off. She returned dry, powdered, and wearing a fresh nightgown.

"Let me get you another blanket."

No response.

I found a spare in the closet, covered her with it.

"Want some tea?"

"Thanks. Actually, I'm feeling a little dehydrated. Bet that's why it happened."

"Baloney."

"No, really. To tell the truth I was feeling faint all day, especially after we encountered the bitch of Holiday Drive."

"Whatever. I'm staying up till you feel better or fall asleep."

"Suit yourself. How about we watch some TV? Maybe there's a liposuction operation on the Discovery Channel. Or is that on the Health one?"

"They only televise operations during dinnertime."

I made us the tea, then we settled in and watched *The Thirty-Nine Steps*. There was Mr. Memory, dolled up in a tuxedo and looking like a kinder, gentler Adolf Hitler as he performed for a raucous '30s British music hall crowd: "Am I right, am I right?" Shelley nodded off early on, right after the spy lady got knifed in the back. I watched the whole fucking thing.

Long day's journey from lightness to the brink of insanity: morning's sublimity outside the Denver Public Library succeeded by revelation inside, frustration at the ancestral residence, and trepidation following an unexpected return visit to Ed's Guns. Tonight is our last in Denver, barring the non-negligible possibility of imprisonment tomorrow.

The Denver Public Library keeps bankers' hours. Shelley and I, however, operate on Insomniac Nonstandard Time. We arrived forty-five minutes before the library opened, spent the interlude consuming croissants and caffeine-spiked beverages on the grass in front of a sculpture titled *The Yearling*. It's a life-size pinto standing on a 21-foot red chair. The pinto gazes outward, at a world full of possibility and traffic.

"Tell me why that thing makes me feel good," said Shelley.

"It just does."

"You can do better than that. You're versed in the explanatory, otherwise you'd never have gotten tenure, let alone had the big career. Come on, cough up something convincing."

"Because it's big and red? People like big red things, like fire engines, Santa Claus, and strawberry sundaes."

"That's hardly a satisfying explanation, and it doesn't factor in Seabiscuit up there."

"You want something a little deeper?"

"Yup. Expound a little. Snow me with pretentious bullshit. Or horseshit, rather, given the present context."

"Okay. It's all about juxtaposition."

"But isn't everything about juxtaposition?"

"I suppose, but in the present case we're dealing with a specific type. A statue of a horse all by its lonesome makes no particular impact, and a gigantic chair without some creature sitting or standing on it is a question mark. But if you place two such objects together—and by 'two such objects' I mean that one of them is an animal and the other is a blown up inorganic human product—position them in close proximity, arrange with a modicum of grace and taste, and voilà, you've created a surprise that's likely to charm."

"Such a cool analysis. And wow, think of the formulaic knockoff possibilities—a chimpanzee typing away at a twenty-foot computer keyboard, or a frog balancing on a gigantic skateboard, or, ha, how about a pig driving a limousine?"

"Sure, though there's some risk that the creation will suffer from insufferable cuteness. Concerning the artwork before us, however, let's be generous and characterize the attempt more positively. Think of it as playful fantasy, or a joke on reality, because in real life you'd never come across a horse on a chair. Anyway, that's my best guess as to why you like it."

"Hmm. No, I don't think so. Sorry to be contrary, Carl, but nope, definitely nope, that's not it at all. I just figured it out! I like it because it stimulates horse thought."

"Horse thought?"

"Yup. I stare at the horse and the chair and I'm not thinking, 'Oh how pretty!' or 'How exquisitely the artist combines forms to create a sensation of unity.' Even 'Isn't that sweet?' eludes me, because I'm in horse-think mode. What's going through my mind is 'How do I get down off this hard red thing without breaking my ass?'"

"So you find it amusing in a *Why did the chicken cross the road?* wiseass manner? If the horse could talk, you'd imagine it doing standup for an audience of horses, cows, and pigs?"

"Yeah, something like that." Shelley removed a small notebook from her bag and dashed off a few lines.

"I'm a poet!"

"Let's hear."

"Hold on… Okay, I've got it." She closed the notebook, looked right at me, and recited the following:

so much depends
upon

a red steel
chair-o

glazed with colt
urine

beside the big
building.

Fortunately, the library's opening bell rang before she could pen a sequel. Off we went to the Western History Department. Microfilm copies of the *Rocky Mountain News* and the *Denver Post* are stored there.

Shelley asked, "How's your sitzfleisch this morning?"

"Almost out. Shall I go to the store and buy some more?"

"It depends. What years do we need to check?"

"'Twenty-seven and 'Twenty-eight. Before Bourgmeyer's first payment on my parents' house, but not much before."

We stationed ourselves at adjacent microfilm readers. It took forty-five minutes for Shelley to get through January, 1927 of the *Post*, and for me to slog through three weeks' worth of the July, 1927 *News*. We had decided to stagger our search dates in order to increase the likelihood of quickly finding a mention of Bourgmeyer.

A coot seated at the station next to Shelley's intervened. He hadn't shaved recently, wore yellow running shorts and a plain gray t-shirt, and was disheveled at both ends: long, uncombed, white hair on top, sockless feet in beaten up sneakers at bottom. The guy's academic toolkit included a lined violet-tinted pad of paper, seven rainbow pencils, ruler, protractor, compass, topographic maps, and a MacBook stamped with a University of Denver imprint. Without these items in his possession he would have been indistinguishable from the half-dozen homeless men who entered the library with us.

He barked, "Try the General Index."

"The what?"

He pointed toward a massive bank of wooden card catalogs a couple of dozen feet from us. Each cabinet held sixty deep-dish drawers, and differed in color from its neighbors. The ones facing us were maroon, black, tan, and brown.

"What's in them?"

"About a million index cards. Within a minute you'll either find what you're looking for or know you're fucked."

Shelley pulled out the drawer labeled "Bou-Bue." She fingered through its cards and quickly found "Bourgmeyer, Michael." Yes! Three items were listed on the card, two from November, 1927 and one from the following April. From the microfilm reader we were able to print them out. Here is the November *Denver Post* story:

> *Two Dead, One Injured in Domestic Dispute*
> A Denver woman and her infant daughter died violently last night, and a two-year-old boy suffered a life-threatening head injury. The incident happened at the home of Michael Bourgmeyer, a Grand View lawyer. According to Mr. Bourgmeyer's deposition, the baby's mother, Pascuala Johnston, inflicted beatings on both children before committing suicide by drowning herself in Rocky Mountain Lake. The injured boy is Mr. Bourgmeyer's son. He has been moved to St. Anthony Central Hospital.

The Rocky Mountain News article from the same month presented no additional information. However, its April, 1928 story certainly did:

Bourgmeyer Convicted of Manslaughter by Jury

Grand View lawyer Michael Bourgmeyer was found guilty
yesterday of manslaughter in the death last November 19th
of Amy Mulligan. The verdict carries with it a sentence of
one to ten years, to be served in the state penitentiary.

The ill-fated infant fell from an unattended table while
Bourgmeyer was single-mindedly engaging in intimate
relations with the baby's mother, Pascuala Johnston, to
whom he was not married. The jury determined that
Bourgmeyer was negligent, thus responsible for little Amy's
death.

After finding her baby lifeless that fateful evening,
Johnston, stricken with grief, went berserk. She attacked
Bourgmeyer's young son, rendering him comatose for
several months, then drowned herself in Rocky Mountain
Lake.

Followers of the trial generally agreed that the verdict
was a just and fitting conclusion to the tragic events leading
up to it.

I asked Shelley if she thought it really happened that way—
that Amy's death resulted from carelessness.

"Seems so. Regardless, it sure as hell doesn't look like you killed
a brother. Or anyone else, for that matter."

"I don't fathom it. They left her alone on a table?"

"Probably a changing table. Safer than an ordinary table, but still,
you don't leave a baby unattended on one."

"Then why did they?"

"Passion of the flesh. Amazing how it obliterates common sense,
eh?"

"Let me get this straight. They were too busy fucking up a storm
to notice?"

"Apparently."

"But that's irrational, Shelley. It would have taken no more than a few seconds to put the baby back in her crib."

"Happens all the time, especially if alcohol is involved. I remember reading about a couple of drunken strangers who couldn't resist fucking each other on a jumbo jet, and not in one of those tiny bathrooms but right in the cabin, where they were sitting. Well, where one of them was sitting. A flight attendant had to douse them with cold water."

"Really?"

"Would I make that up?"

"Charming. But at least nobody died."

"Nearby passengers might have wished otherwise."

"So Amy falls off the table, cracks her head open, and kaputt, she's dead. Pascuala then goes bonkers, beating the crap out of the two-year-old me before plunging herself into the lake. Great. And my mother—where was she when all of this was happening?"

"Who knows? She might have been tending to an ill family member, visiting a friend, taking a vacation somewhere. Could have been anything. Maybe she had a lover too. What we do know is that when the cat was away, the rat's play resulted in two deaths, your injury, and the termination of your parents' marriage. Oh, and let's not forget the coma. You have no memories from when you were small. Maybe there were no memories."

"But according to the article my coma lasted a few months, not years."

"That doesn't mean that your brain sprung right back to tiptop shape as soon as you came out of it. You could have been subnormal for quite some time."

"Subnormal, eh?"

"Yeah."

"And Joseph Anderson? I guess we'll never know how he became part of my mother's life."

"He was your father?"

"Yeah. The real one, the guy who raised me."

"Once again, we can only guess. Nevertheless, appreciate your mom's solution. There she is in the middle of the big city. Her kid is critically hurt, she has no husband and probably no job, little money and no support as well, and she's got to make sure the two of you survive. So she marries this guy and off they go, far away from the ex, the house of death, Denver, the entire craziness of her former life. In return for accepting the slower pace of life on a farm in Kansas—"

"You mean its utter monotony?"

"Well yes. In exchange for putting up with that, she gets what she and you most desperately need—financial stability, peace, and quiet. Ee eye ee eye oh. Not a bad choice."

Ah yes, Liberal, Kansas circa the dawn of the dust bowl years— the perfect locale for settling down and fulfilling the American Dream.

We pulled up to the old Chez Bourgmeyer after lunch. Knock-knock, fee-fi-fo-fum. The specimen who opened the door towered over me by three-quarters of a foot. His vibe was menace, the consequence of a massive frown combined with the following outsize features: bulging forehead, heavy black eyebrows, broad nose, huge jaw, and a gappy row of stained upper front teeth. The intimidation factor was vitiated only slightly by the man's flowery muumuu. Four or five vines of intertwined yellow, pink, and blue flowers ran down its length. A small brass nameplate, centered right over his heart, was affixed to it: "Your server's name is PIKA."

"What do you want?"

Shelley stepped backward awkwardly, as if she couldn't decide whether to bow or curtsey. "We brought the money. Did your wife or whoever she is, did she speak to you about it?"

Just then the woman from yesterday showed up. She elbowed Pika out of the way. "You got it?"

"Yes," I said.

"How much?"

"Two hundred, just like I said I would."

"Not enough. Not close." Spoken by the big ugly surly guy. "Our price is five hundred, and that's for ten minutes. You'll see all the rooms but one."

"Why?" squeaked Shelley in a distressed tone.

"Take it or leave it."

"We'll leave it," I said. "Come on my dear, let's go." I tried taking Shelley's hand but she shook me off.

"No, we'll take it. Five hundred, but he gets to see everything. I can stay outside."

"Really?" I said to her. "Five hundred?"

"You have to do it!"

Pika laughed. "She likes spending her old man's money."

Turning to Pika I said, "I don't have that much cash with me, but I could write you a check."

"Cash only. Bring it tomorrow, because we're not ready now."

"Oh but please, we're on a timetable," Shelley said. "We're not looking to buy your house, just to look at it. We don't mind messiness. Heck, my grandpa here is one of the messiest guys you'd—"

"NOT TONIGHT." Pika slammed the door shut. Two visits, two slammed doors. Sheesh.

In retrospect, we behaved ridiculously. To spend so much money for a peek at the insides of any house made no sense. For what purpose? Not for personal gain, happiness, nor anything but knowledge, the same idiocy that got Adam and Eve into trouble.

Shelley and I reviewed the situation over the early bird special at Little India. Yes, we ate there two nights in a row. Bliss.

"What if we bring five hundred and then they want a thousand?" she asked."

"We'll turn them down."

She shook her head. "I can't accept that, not after coming this far. What do you say we pay a return visit to the gun store?"

"We are *not* buying a gun."

"Of course not, just a toy."

"But we could be arrested for breaking and entering, even with a toy gun."

"Nah, just for entering. We're not going to break anything."

"Home invasion is not a good thing, Shelley."

"True, but our intentions are noble. It's not as though we'd be robbing them."

"Oh that makes me feel a thousand times better," I said, laboring to make my sarcastic tone obvious. "Moreover there's a really good chance they won't be fooled. That Pika will laugh at us. He'll twist you arm, rip the toy from your grip, and crumple it up into little pieces with just one of his meatball hands. We'll be arrested and sentenced to ten years in jail, and I for one will die on the day preceding my release date."

"Jesus Christ, Carl, you've been reading too much Schopenhauer. These people aren't professional criminals, they're just folks. Greedy nasty folks, but folks nonetheless. I don't know about you, but if someone pulled one of those fakes on me and yelled 'A tour of your house or your life,' I wouldn't request an inspection of the thing to see if it was real. I'd opt for the grand tour and I'd give it in both official languages."

"Hold on a second. Do you realize what's happening here? You're becoming as obsessed as I am."

Shelley smiled, reached across the table, and placed her right hand on top of my left. "More so."

"You're willing to risk jail to find out something that's totally irrelevant to your life? It's not as if my history has any bearing on your well-being."

"We've already committed one crime, so yeah, let's go for the encore. It's the only logical continuation."

"You're quite nuts, you know that?"

"And you're quite dense not to have realized that before now."

A skinny Japanese-American kid overdressed in a gray suit and light pink dress shirt greeted us at Ed's. We showed him the toy gun we wanted. He looked at it disdainfully.

"If you want to scare shit out of someone, please consider one of these instead." He led us to a case at the other end of the store. It housed handguns.

"Oh we don't want a real gun," Shelley said.

He removed one of the beauties from its case. "This isn't a gun, miss. It just looks real except for the orange stick, which for a small fee I would be happy to remove. You can't tell anyone, though."

The gun's tag was marked WE 1911, and the company name was Airsoft, which I suppose is not the greatest choice for a *bona fide* gun manufacturer. Nor for a condom company, for that matter. The price: $99.99.

Our salesman opened up his laptop and showed us a YouTube video titled *WE 1911 Airsoft Review*. A chunky undergrad with a crewcut holds the pistol up to the camera. He rotates the gun so the viewer can observe it from different angles: "It is like the standard government issue gun. It is sly looking, it is looking good. It's one of those guns that you look at it and you say, that's a pretty gun." A demure brunette wearing a dark brown pinafore over a gray blouse then demonstrates the gun in action. She points it toward the ground, aims at a phantom rat, and fires ten times.

"Hey that's good enough," says the guy.

"Way beyond good enough," said Shelley. "She's cool. This one's on me."

After our salesman removed the orange tip with some heavy-duty pliers, Shelley placed the gun in her bag ever so gingerly, as if it were a Bichon Frisé favoring a tender front paw. She then asked the salesman to take a photo of the two of us together. It's a beauty. We're side by side and she's smiling, me not so much. I drape my left arm over her left shoulder. Her right arm is aloft, hand positioned six inches above my right shoulder. She holds one of those delightful teacup pistolets, and she's pointing it at my right temple.

4:13 P.M. Saturday, June 21st

I write from the backseat of the Sonata once again, but this time we head eastward. Our one remaining task before returning home tomorrow is to find Michael Bourgmeyer's gravesite. The Liberal Cemetery website lists him as "present," though without revealing the location of his plot.

Shelley and I keep complementary secrets. I know what happened on that dreadful night eighty years ago, and she knows what her illness is. I should have realized something was amiss from our first encounter, at the moment she dumped her armory of vials onto the Westmount Library reading room floor. She's got some serious autoimmune disease like lupus, Crohn's, cancer, or AIDS, and she's half afraid to tell me. AIDS. God please don't let it be that.

We invaded not quite four hours ago. I can't write about it just yet, not in the middle of this chaos. We've pulled over, onto the highway's shoulder. A prairie thunderstorm, replete with unceasing strikes of jagged lightning down to the horizon, engulfs us. Tumbleweeds bounce past like flubber, and a torrential rain shoots down hard; hundreds of clickety-clacks per second buffet our trusty Sonata. Visibility, even with the windshield wipers on high, is about a quarter of an inch. Time to put this journal away, sit still, enjoy the spectacle, and hope no asshole plows into us.

7:32 P.M. Saturday, June 21st

Still *en route*. We crossed into Kansas a little while ago, and now we're driving south toward Liberal. It's been a quiet few hours—no radio, little conversation.

Peaceable was not the appropriate descriptor for our third and final attempt to enter 1201 Holiday Drive this afternoon. Knock-knock. Pika and his woman opened the door, did not welcome us in.

Pika: "Show me."

I extracted twenty-five crisp twenty-dollar bills from my wallet, spread them out fanlike.

"Payment in advance."

I stepped back from the door. "No. Half now, half when we're finished."

"All now or fuck off."

I looked at Shelley, who had buried her right hand in her bag. "Yes?"

"Yes," she replied. "Let's get this over with."

I handed Pika the money.

"I count it." He brought the thumb and first two fingers of his left hand to his lips, wetted them, and fingered the bills slower than slow: "Twenty. Forty. Sixty. Eighty. Now!"

Damn, the fuckers slammed the door on us! There is a lesson to be learned from what followed, however, and it is this: it pays to maintain one's property. If you let your house go to seed it will bite you back, somehow, someway. Count on it.

The door's locking mechanism flew apart upon impact. Both knobs, escutcheon plates, and the latch crashed to the ground. The door itself bounced open on the rebound, and I made sure it stayed that way by ramming my left shoulder against it. Shelley unsheathed her mighty Airsoft WE 1711 and charged in. Holding the gun in both hands and at arm's length, she aimed it at the eyes of our two victims in rapid alternation, just as they do in the movies. Four hands reached for the sky. The thought does not reflect well on me, but seeing them scared shitless engendered—what's the exact noun I'm looking for? Oh yes: gratification. No one gets away with slamming three doors on Carl Anderson.

"Don't shoot," the woman pleaded. "Please don't shoot!"

Shelley took command, again as in the movies: "To the back of the house. Slowly, no fast moves." Once in the kitchen she took the money from Pika, placed it on a counter, and commanded the two of them to lie facedown on the floor. I counted out fifteen of the bills and stuffed them in my front right pants pocket.

"Listen carefully," I said, addressing our newly prostrate hosts. "I'm going upstairs. I'll look around, that's all. I'm not going to take anything, I'll be fast, and then we leave. No one gets hurt so long as you stay put. Surely you agree that's best, right? Especially as we're leaving you a couple of hundred dollars out of the kindness of our hearts."

"Please be quick," said the woman. "Donnie's uncle's bringing him back soon and I don't want him seeing no trouble."

A double negative. Was it a greater infraction than my imprecise use of the word *best*? I suppressed this train of thought as I reached the top of the stairs, at which point I found myself in the middle of a hallway extending the length of the house. I turned leftward, toward the two bedrooms furthest from the street.

The first was an epitome of blandness—beige walls, king bed, standing lamp, and a couple of small white plastic side tables, one occupied by a black desk lamp, the other adorned with six or seven crumpled tissues, a spent condom, and a depleted tube of Astroglide. The room's off-white wall-to-wall carpeting was dappled with a brown blanket, a pair of pajamas, a bra, some underwear, and three white socks.

The *pièce de nonrésistance* in the second bedroom was an ungainly and decrepit knubby yellow couch. It was far too large for the smallish room into which it had been stuffed, and its cushions, worn bare, were leaking their innards. The couch's arms were frayed almost to the vanishing point, as if a succession of hyperactive cats had used them as scratching posts. A wooden table with a massive ancient television on top of it was positioned scarcely seven feet in front of the couch—great viewing for the goggle-eyed. The room's final touch of class was provided courtesy of one of those old Macintosh computers, a bottom-heavy purple-and-white plastic blob. It straddled a couple of barstools, and its screen saver displayed fresh images of human genitalia every three or four seconds.

Next stop was a small utility area a few feet up the hallway. It housed a washer and dryer, an ironing board, bucket, mop, and red canister vacuum cleaner. Something about this space spooked me. I examined the floor and walls for clues, found none.

Two bedrooms to go, both at the other end of the hall. The one off to my right was Donnie's. Hundreds of Lego pieces and fifteen stuffed animals were strewn over its floor, the bed was unmade, and window shades had been pulled so far down that they looked broken.

No one could have slept in that last bedroom. It was bare, save for a stool, a couple of large rectangular tables iced with formica, black curtains covering the windows, a three-foot square panel filled with dozens of mini light bulbs, and two softly humming Ionic Pro air ionizers. One of the ionizers was positioned between the tables, and the other stood a foot from a closet at the back of the room. They were overmatched by the room's stench, which evoked a mix of incense and burnt popcorn.

The closet was a walk-in, and it was filled with potted plants— four on each of three shelves to the right, four on each of three shelves to the left. All of them sported green pointy rocket-ship leaves. I entered, closed the door, and, for some inexplicable reason, sat on the floor. Except for a sliver of light under the door, all was blackness. I drew my knees to my head and closed my eyes.

"Carl."

Shelley's voice sounded muffled, which wasn't surprising given that sixty feet and a closed door separated us. I didn't answer.

A minute later and a little louder: "Carl, you okay? Hurry up."

Still I did not respond. I couldn't. I shook, felt cold inside and out.

Thirty seconds more, this time shouted with maximum urgency: "Carl come on, let's get the fuck out of here!" Pika's booming voice then shocked me: "Come to me, little girl. Time to kneel before the mighty Pika and take your medicine." Walls thudded, footsteps reverberated.

So, how exactly does a panicked eighty-three-year-old professor emeritus rise from a closet floor as quickly as possible? Does he spring to his feet, lithe as a panther? Not exactly. His bones creak as he turns to his right. He plants both hands on the floor and elevates to his knees as vigorously as possible, banging his head against a shelf.

I demolished the shelf, toppling four plants and covering myself in soil. One of the pots hit my forehead hard enough to draw a little blood. On adrenergic autopilot, I shook the blow off, stood, and pushed open the closet door. I grabbed my cane tightly, expecting I would be swinging it at Pika within the next few seconds.

Shelley and I converged at the top of the stairs. "Let's go!" she yelled. Her face was red and the collar of her t-shirt had been ripped.

"What happened?"

"Come on." We hustled down the stairs.

Groans came from the kitchen. I looked in, saw Pika hunched over the sink. He was holding his hands up to his eyes. His woman was standing next to him, paper towels in both of her hands. She turned, spotted us, and yelled, "You blinded him! You're animals, you're fucking animals!"

Once outside I turned around for a last look at the house. Shelley grabbed my arm and gave it a yank.

"Come on, let's move it!"

"What did you do to him?"

"Let's go!"

At the moment Shelley turned the ignition, a black Mercedes pulled up opposite us. The driver, a heavyset bearded man, wore the biggest and darkest sunglasses I had ever seen. The boy sitting in the backseat nodded at us, as if to acknowledge that he both knew and approved of what Shelley and I had done to his parents.

Shelley raced the car up the street and turned right without paying heed to the stop sign at the corner. She drove like a maniac all the way to the highway, like they do in movie car chases. Seven long minutes, more harrowing than any plane ride I ever took.

"That was interesting," I said, once we were cruising on the highway.

"What an idiot. You know what he did? He decided there was no way I'd shoot him. He got up off the floor and laughed at me, looked at my gun and said it was a toy, and that even if it wasn't I didn't have the guts to shoot him. What were you doing up there anyway? You took forever."

"I moved as fast as I could."

"And then his wife, oh was she ever terrified. She told him to stay put, but no, he wouldn't listen. He went after me, said he was going to teach me a lesson, have fun with me. After, he'd take everything we had and kick us out of the house. So stupid! If I had a real gun I would have plugged him for sure."

"But you had nothing."

"Not nothing! He grabbed my arm up around my shoulder, tried to throw me against a wall, but I shook free. Then he got between me and the front door. He knew I couldn't escape, so he came at me slowly, laughing. Can you imagine? That was his way of scaring me, of letting me know he had all the time in the world. So I ran back into the kitchen, stuck my hand in my bag, and miracles of miracles, grabbed it on my first try. When he got within a few feet I charged him."

"*You* charged *him*?"

"Double bull's eye. Plastered him in both eyes with a couple of big strong orange squirts. And right after, my hero—that would be you—finally decided to show up. Hah!"

"You pepper sprayed him?"

"But good, Sherlock."

Aha. Chekhov smiles in his grave.

"So did you find anything interesting up on the second floor?"

"Wait a second. You brought pepper spray with you on the plane? You actually took it through Customs?"

"Hip hip hooray for Canadian security. Tell me what you found up there. Cathartic memory breakthroughs galore?"

"No."

"Really?"

"I'm sorry, Shelley. It was a waste of time, a total waste. I found nothing, absolutely nothing at all."

"You're kidding me, right? We nearly got beaten up, robbed, raped, and murdered, and it was all for nothing?"

"Correct. All for nothing."

"Fuck! Triple fuck!"

She doesn't need to know, and I'm not going to tell her.

11:32 P.M. Saturday, June 21st

Cemeteries are unsettling. They are parklike, but few people jog through them. You won't find playgrounds, ice cream vendors, snack bars, or swimming pools cohabiting with tombstones and underground dead people. It is impossible to avoid the Great Truism once past the cemetery gates—a real downer, so to speak—so the workers might as well make it explicit. Let them erect signs, Burma Shave style. Stroll past the first row of tombstones and read "Someday." At the second, "You won't be leaving." The third row: "So you might as well," and the fourth, "Make yourself at home."

The phrase "Rest in Peace" is a falsity. One cannot rest and be dead at the same time. Nevertheless, belief in eternal rest comforts the living. Martin Luther spends a lifetime producing religious doctrines, Bach composes tons of music, Balzac writes more novels than most people will read in a lifetime, and they all wind up getting exactly what they so richly deserve: rest. R.I.P. is the ultimate fantasy variant on stretching out on a couch and kicking back a cold one while watching the Yankees beat the shit out of the Red Sox. The *peace* part equates to the soul unwinding without having to think about bad stuff. It harbors no concern over inadequate achievements, no guilt for screwing someone over or something up, no crap of any sort. The need to get up and use the toilet or answer the phone is no more. No one changes the channel or asks you to set the table for dinner. Reserve "Rest in Peace" not for dead people, but for Mother's Day, Father's Day, and a day or two following a promotion or the reception of an award.

4:43 A.M. Sunday, June 22nd

In order to play Willow Tree, Liberal's municipal golf course, you drive west on Fifteenth Street past Liberal Cemetery. The cemetery is on your right. It extends a fifth of a mile, and stretches a quarter mile to the north. A black cast iron fence separates it from Fifteenth Street, and chain link fences delineate boundaries on its east, north and west sides.

Thirty-one spindly aluminum flagpoles line the Fifteenth Street border. They run flags up them once a year, on Memorial Day. Despite being unused the rest of the time, the flagpoles provide companionship of a sort, as it takes only a gentle breeze for their metal hooklets to clang. Sailboats. Close your eyes and you sit at a pier's edge, viewing the Caribbean Sea on a pleasant summer evening.

Liberal Cemetery was once set out in the middle of nowhere, but gradually people built toward it. A housing development borders its east. If you walk from the Fifteenth Street entrance to the cemetery's far end, however, past the tombstones and an empty lawn beyond them, you can look to the north and see nothing but a lone one-storey structure about a quarter of a mile away, a few barely visible telephone poles, and endless white-yellow prairie grass. Death behind, infinity ahead.

Last night's minor miracle: it took us only a few minutes to find Michael Bourgmeyer's tombstone. It is small and white, and his name and dates are inscribed on it, nothing else:

Michael Bourgmeyer
February 3, 1897—March 17, 1983

Shelley began tracing. "Think they'll lock us up for this?" The cemetery closed at 8 P.M. and it was exactly 9:02—a summer solstice Saturday night dusk—when she asked her question.

"For tracing, no. For trespassing, I doubt it. If someone in charge comes by, they'll just kick us out."

"I once did it in a cemetery."

"Did what?"

"What do you think?"

"Oh. That. Really? Over a grave or off to the side?"

"On it. There's nothing special about doing it anywhere else. That's barely different from park fucking."

"Which of course is no big deal."

"Hardly. You can't shock anyone with that. Anyway, I reached back and grabbed the tombstone. Kinda pretended I was chained to it."

"Was it anyone you knew?"

"Of course—boyfriend number six, a.k.a. crazy guy number two: Frederic Castillon d'Amboise."

"I meant the dead guy."

"Nope, just some stiff, though I made sure it was a guy stiff. Closest I've gotten to a three-way."

Shelley finished the tracing, then came over and sat down next to me. She spread the paper on the ground between us.

"Not bad."

"Thanks. Now tell me what got you so upset back at the house."

"Nothing got me upset."

"Bullshit. I had to call you three times, and when you finally made it downstairs you were white, except for the dirt and blood on your head. You looked like you'd come face to face with a ghost."

"I heard Sasquatch threatening you. I looked scared because I was scared."

"Okay, but you've said almost nothing since, not even when we stopped for lunch and gas. You were as talkative as old Mike down there. What got to you?"

"Are you going to tell me why you keep getting sick?" I picked up a pebble and threw it at the tombstone. Hit it right on the i.

"You first, then we'll see." She grabbed my hand. "Come on."

"No."

"Why not?"

"It's very disturbing."

"Well duh. We know two people die, plus you get your head split open."

"It's worse than that. I don't want to talk about it, ever."

"Well that's too damned bad, because after what you put me through this afternoon, you owe me. Besides, it's not like I'm going to tell anyone."

"Shelley, spare me. Please."

"No way. I'll badger the hell out of you until you give up the goods, no matter how long it takes, so you might as well begin. Now. Right now."

"There's no way I'm getting out of this?"

"No fucking way. Tell me!

"Alright, but don't say I didn't warn you."

"Fair enough. Now let's have it."

"Okay. Here we go." I cleared my voice, adjusted my shorts. Ineffective delaying tactics.

"Noise wakes the boy. He rubs his eyes, gets up, toddles down the hallway holding his teddy bear stiff to his heart. Teddy is gray and worn, lacking almost all of its fur. It's more of a puppet or a doll than a stuffed animal.

"The boy sees a lit candle resting on a wooden footstool close to the head of the stairs. A small wide glass diffracts its light so that the center of the flame glows orange and its periphery flickers green. The boy recognizes this glass immediately, because he's seen his father drinking from it many times.

"He passes by the candle, and sounds intensify. Finally he's at his father's bedroom door. It's ajar. He pushes it open a couple of inches, looks in, but can't make much out at first because it's too dark. He blinks a few times, notices blankets and clothing on the floor. Then he spots her back, her bare back. She's sitting on the bed, arms taut behind her, and she's pressing hard on his father's thighs. As she thrusts her body downward, her shoulder blades protrude from the shadows. She's hurting his father; the boy knows this because his father says nothing. She keeps attacking, up and down, up and down, over and over. Now she screams, and oh, what a scream it is! Even if the boy were to slam the door as hard as he could, she might not notice."

"Pretty intense."

"Yes, well you asked for it."

"So I did. Continue."

"A new thought dismays the boy—the woman will come for him. She will pin him to the floor, there will be no escape. The boy runs back up the hall, to her sleeping baby. It is swaddled tight in its wicker basket, which sits on a big table. The swaddling clothes are pink, but the boy doesn't know what that means. All he knows is that to stop the woman, he must hurt her baby. He notices a sadiron on a nearby ironing board, walks to it, drops his teddy, and picks up the iron with both hands. It's so heavy. He struggles, finally manages to hold it above his head. He moves toward the baby—"

"Stop."

I closed my eyes. A crow cawed faintly off to our right, and one of the flagpoles clanged softly.

"What happened after?"

"You want me to continue?"

"Afterward, yes. Not during."

A relief. I did not want to describe that sleeping face, creamy-smooth and unblemished. Nor did I wish to recount the blow, the single blow, and the blood—black in the dim light, flowing slowly from her tiny mouth like tree sap.

"The baby lies motionless, and suddenly the boy realizes he has broken it. Its fingers, barely extending beyond the swaddling clothes, twitch not at all. The boy must hide, so he runs to the bedroom opposite his own. Though it's dark, he quickly finds the room's closet, enters, closes the door behind him, and sits on the floor with his back against the far wall."

"Christ."

"Now can I stop?"

"No. Get it all out."

"You sure?"

"Yes goddammit! Don't ask me again."

"The boy waits, loses sense of time, feels he will live in blackness forever. He nods off but is woken by the woman's shrieks, in turn followed by calls from both her and his father. They shout his name repeatedly: 'Carl! Carl, where are you?' He covers his ears and draws his legs up to his chin as tightly as he can. Footsteps get louder, light suddenly fills the crack under the door. She opens the closet door, grabs him, yells something he can't understand, flings him hard. The back of his head cracks against the closet wall."

A minute passed without either of us speaking, moving, or looking at each other. Then Shelley exhaled, sighed, and said but one word: "Well."

She removed the following items from her backpack: a corkscrew, a small butter knife and plate, two orange plastic teacups, a striped hand towel from the Monaco Hotel, two foot-long baguettes, a chunk of Jarlsberg cheese tightly wrapped in saran, and a bottle of Witch in a Ditch—authentic Kansas red wine from Oz Winery, which according to the label is located in downtown Wamego. Got that? Downtown Wamego, not uptown nor midtown Wamego.

"Hungry? I sure as hell am," Shelley said. We had eaten a late lunch on the road after escaping Denver, but no dinner.

"What are you doing?"

"Time to celebrate."

"Celebrate? Just what the fuck are we celebrating?"

"You beating the rap, of course." She spread the towel over the grass, placed the cheese on it, cut baguettes into thirds, and piled them on the butter plate, which was black with orange stripes and also might have come from the Monaco.

"It's time for a picnic." She implanted the corkscrew into the Witch, had the wine breathing in three seconds flat.

"I don't get it. You're reacting as if I just told you that world peace and racial harmony are at hand."

"Well yes. I feel that good."

"Why?"

"Had you gone to jail, everything would have turned out differently."

"But I wasn't even three!"

"True, but it was the Roaring Twenties. The administration of justice was primitive back then. Some wacko wild-west judge might have labeled you a bad seed and concluded that society needed permanent protection. He could have sent you to an insane asylum, then had you transferred to a prison a few years later. If you had been given a life sentence, you'd be wrapping up eighty years right about now. That would be one for the record books, eh?"

Shelley handed me a teacup half filled with wine and offered the following toast: "To beating the rap. Now eat and drink up."

A cup of Kansas wine accompanied by processed Kansas wheat and topped with Kansas cheese. An intergenerational picnic conducted among the dead, not exactly the scenario envisioned by the great Omar Khayyam.

"You don't believe me?"

"That story? Nope, not for a zillionth of a second."

"How come?"

"There's a more likely explanation, Carl. A *much* more likely one."

"Which is?"

"It's the Medea myth. Man spurns woman, woman goes nuts and kills their children."

"You think Pascuala Johnston did it? That it wasn't an accident?"

"I'm positive. Look at the evidence."

It had turned dark and the air had become still. The flagpole clanging finally had ceased, and the crow had either gone to sleep or was off hunting.

"What evidence?"

"Her name, for starters. It's different from her daughter's."

"So? All that means is she was married and kept her maiden name. Or she married more than once."

"There's another possibility. Remember that Amy Mulligan was less than a year old when she died."

"So? What's the problem?"

"If Pascuala was fooling around with your papa, which she was, Mr. Johnston was no longer in the picture. He might have skipped out during her pregnancy, just after, or—"

"Or before that, possibly years before," I said. "Maybe there was no Mr. Mulligan at all! Mulligan could have been a name of convenience, taken to deflect suspicions of paternity away from my father. Amy might have been my sister."

"Half-sister."

"Great. I killed my sister. Not my brother, but my sister."

"You did no such thing. Pascuala did it, I'm sure of it. It's the only story that makes any sense."

Shelley stood, looked up. The sky had turned dark, and the Milky Way's band of stars shone sharp and bright straight across the sky, just like it did when I was a kid. She sat back down, now facing me. Our knees touched. Almost in a whisper she said, "Please understand, Carl. Pascuala was at the end of her rope. On that miserable night she endured a refusal from her lover to leave his wife, right after making love, no less. So she had a brain snap."

"Brain snap?"

"Yup. A few months ago I read about a woman in Australia who killed her boyfriend because he wouldn't let her listen to her favorite music. She ran to the kitchen, grabbed the biggest and sharpest knife she could find, charged back to the living room and stabbed him. Plunged that knife deep and true, right through the middle of his heart. Her lawyer called it a brain snap."

"No kidding."

"No kidding is right. Just like that, one dead boyfriend."

"But what about my experience this afternoon? Everything came together when I went upstairs. The images were so detailed they scared the hell out of me."

"All that detail is overrated. It's fallible, made up, not real. Had you told me that a pee stain in the shape of a parallelogram showed on the kid's pajamas, or that a miniature statue of Coronado at the far end of the hallway was missing half a nose, I still wouldn't have believed you. Sure, when you recall things on a plate or details from a photo, that's real. But what if there's no original experience? Minds abhor vacuums. They fill in the blanks, and often they come up with pure fiction. And don't forget, whatever did happen on that night eighty years ago got warped because it was filtered through the brain of a two-year-old."

"Shelley, I went into the closet. I sat down on the floor, grabbed my legs and closed my eyes, just like right after I—"

"Listen to me, will you? It didn't fucking happen that way. Please, let's not hear anything more of it. Or rather, let me rephrase my request more definitively. I don't want you to bring up the subject in my presence again, ever."

"But why?"

"Because life's a bitch as it is. There's no need to make it even harder."

I'll never know for sure if Shelley believed her own argument. Her vocal inflections sometimes were hard and sure: "Not for a zillionth of a second," "woman goes berserk," "I'm positive." She wavered only a couple of times, as when she said, "It's the Medea myth" and "Look at the evidence." She either believed her own scenario or intuited that my version was true, in which case she chose to perform an act of grace for me.

She removed the crowbar and the gun from her backpack and propped them up against Bourgmeyer's tombstone. I positioned the wine bottle between them, and she balanced a leftover third of a baguette plus some Jarlsburg on top of the tombstone.

"For the crow."

As we walked back to the car I said, "Please tell me why you get sick."

"Another time. We've had enough excitement for one day, don't you think?"

Our destiny today has been lounge king and queen at both the Wichita Mid-Continent Airport and Concourse E here at O'Hare. The flight to Chicago arrived three hours late, but fortunately for us, ha-ha, our flight to Montreal will be delayed by a duration at least as long. Thunderstorms. Weather generally moves from west to east, but today the storm decided to spend the afternoon and evening taxiing around the airport. At sunset we watched a plane get hit by lightning as it entered a bank of dark purple clouds. Shelley took it in as an aesthetic experience. She couldn't believe how lovely the plane looked for the split-second it was lit up all silvery. I didn't see it quite the same way.

The Wikipedia article on AIDS includes a graph that tracks two loop-de-loop lines, one blue and the other red. The blue one starts off high in the western sky and swoops halfway to the bottom before curving back up a little. It then slopes gently but inexorably downward, all the way to the eastern horizon. Picasso could have made a work of art out of this one line, say a small sketch titled *Reclining Woman*. The effort might have netted him a few thousand dollars. If he had titled it *CD4 T Lymphocyte Count (Cells/cubic mm)*, he wouldn't have been able to give it away.

The red line, labeled *HIV RNA Copies Per mL of Plasma*, explodes from the western horizon. It rockets from nothingness to the top of the graph before dipping back down on a trajectory as sharp as its ascension. The line does not return to the bottom, however. Its descent stops three-quarters of the way down and then turns to the right, initiating a long, slow ascent. When it reaches points east, it angles sharply upward. Just before this change in direction, the graph's maker inserted the following pointer: "constitutional symptoms." Halfway up the ascent he provided another one: "opportunistic diseases." The third and final marker, positioned to the far right and at the top of the mountain symbolically representing the triumph of billions of viral Sir Edmund Hillarys, required fewer letters: "death." For me, the two lines evoke a woman and a man in the bath. They face each other, she on the left, he on the right. She asks, "Why must you take me?" He replies, "We take each other."

Upon our return to the departure gate after grabbing dinner, Shelley started shivering. She put on her "Liberal Lady Redskins" sweatshirt and raised the hood. A family of four and their carryons had encamped opposite us. Judging from dad's Bermuda shorts and the children's Thing 1 and Thing 2 t-shirts—white circles with black lettering in front, a sea of red everywhere else—I astutely surmised that they were traveling home from Florida. Thing 1 was a blonde, about seven years old. Her eyes were half closed, and she leaned up against her mom. Thing 2 lay flat on his back on the carpet, in front of his dad. He was younger, four or five years old. Mouth open, eyes closed, temporarily dead to the world. Dad read a book while mom glared at Shelley and me.

"She thinks I'll infect the whole damn plane. Doesn't matter. What does is I need you to find me a couple of pills and water."

"No problem, but why not call it a night? Let me get us a room at the airport hotel and we'll fly tomorrow morning when you're feeling better and the skies are calmer."

"No. That's a waste of money and I want to get it over with. It's time to go home."

I grabbed her backpack and brought it to my seat. "My God, it's an apartment building. Tell me where to look, otherwise you'll recover before I can find it."

Shelley pointed at its right end.

"This one?"

"Yeah. It's called Paracetamol."

I unzipped the pouch. Found eleven containers inside, eight of them prescription. "Holy cow."

"I don't take them all anymore. I brought them along so I could practice, you know? When you stick your nose in that journal of yours, I put them on a plate."

I examined all eleven labels. "No Paracetamol."

"Shit. I should have put it in my bathroom bag."

"But you didn't, so now what do I do?"

"Check the pouch on the other side. If it's not there, I threw it in the sack."

"The bottomless pit in the middle of this thing? Heaven help us." I found seven more containers, all of them prescription except one—Paracetamol. "Got it."

She swallowed two of the pills and washed them down with half a bottle of water. "Thirty minutes and I'll be shipshape. You know, I really don't take all of those pills anymore."

"Then why carry them around?"

"I don't know, force of habit maybe. I never got around to cleaning them out. Honestly."

"Honestly? I counted eighteen vials, most of them prescription."

She ignored my comment, just went back to reading her book. But a couple of minutes later she said, "These days I take just one. You've figured it out, right?"

"AIDS?"

"Nope, HIV. I was born with it."

"Oh. Oh, I'm… I'm so sorry. I'm sorry and I'm speechless."

"But not scared?"

"For you I am, not for me. Now I understand why you didn't tell me."

"Yeah. Not only is it a great conversation stopper, it also ends friendships. All of the uninfected people I've told, without exception, talked a good short game before vanishing from my life."

"I'll be the exception. I'm going nowhere, absolutely no fucking where." She stared hard at me for a few seconds, grabbed my right hand and squeezed it.

We were quiet for a while. I stared ahead vacantly, unable to come up with more words, until: "Just don't die, okay? And deal with the chills and sweats as soon as we get back."

"Tomorrow. I've already made the appointment. That's why we need to get back tonight."

"Good, because I want to make absolutely sure you outlive me, and by a lot."

"Aw. That's the sweetest thing anyone's ever said to me. But don't fret about it, because the odds in fact do favor me. I may not make it to eighty-three, but it's far more likely that one day I'll be standing over your grave than *vice versa*. And when I do, I'll deliver a eulogy that will curdle the blood of your children."

"I can't wait to hear it. Just promise me one thing, okay? In case things don't turn out as they should."

"What?"

"Please don't pull a *Million Dollar Baby* on me."

"Huh? Oh. You think I might ask you to do me in?"

"Yes, if things got really bad. I couldn't do it."

"Relax. If I ever get to that stage, your help won't be needed. I'd prefer to do it myself, and believe me, I'll carry it out with elan and esprit, as they say in gay Paree. I won't be taking wishy-washy maybe-it-will-do-the-job sleeping pills. No cries for help from me. I'll choose an option like blowing my brains out with a Magnum .44, throwing myself in front of a train, or jumping off the Champlain Bridge head first. Maybe all three. And I won't wait till it's too late, so don't fret."

"Never have I been more perversely reassured."

Shelley turned ninety degrees away from me and stretched her legs. She leaned her back up against my shoulder and resumed reading, while I just sat there doing absolutely nothing.

"That reminds me of a story a friend of mine once told me about the great German theologist, Helmut Schlichter." Confucius say: when dealing with heavy stuff, tell joke.

"What reminds you?"

"Your phrase, 'I'd prefer to do it myself.'"

"Go on."

"Herr Doktor Schlichter— a very big deal between the wars, by the way—he taught at the University of Göttingen, and was quite the original thinker. He isn't remembered much nowadays, but his research, in which he challenged Wellhausen's documentary theory, was fifty years ahead of his time. I don't suppose you'd like to hear the details?"

"You got that right."

"Okay then, back to the story. At the conclusion of each semester, Doktor Schlichter threw elaborate parties for his students. *Jubilee* was his word for them. They amounted to intense mixtures of workshops and seminars during the day, always on a Saturday, followed by an evening soiree—again, his word—or to describe it another way, a typical "Wine, Women and Song" lawn party with orgiastic overtones. Quite a number of his students were women."

"I'll bet they were."

"Anyway, during one of the seminars a male student complained about having to take a bunch of classes at the university the following semester. Doktor Schlichter asked him what the problem was, and the student replied that he felt capable of learning the material on his own. In fact, he would *prefer* to do it that way because he could accomplish it more quickly and less expensively. So Schlichter told this joke."

"Oh good! Let's hear."

"A couple gets married. In the bridal suite that evening, they undress. But things don't progress according to plan, because the groom wanders off to a far corner of the bed, sits down with his back to his bride and, umm, manipulates himself. The bride approaches, quickly notices the blur of his hands as they move like synchronized pistons

over his most private part, and in a panicked voice asks, 'What's this?'
And he says—"

Shelley: "I'd prefer to do it myself!"

Glowering Mom looked away in disgust. Guess she won't be
passing that one on to hubby.

9:17 P.M. Monday, June 23rd

Last night's surprise: Helen waved at us from just outside the baggage
area. Not only that, she smiled. My daughter smiles as often as the
gargoyles of Notre Dame Cathedral. When I had phoned in our revised
and very late arrival information from Chicago, she had informed me
not to expect a pickup.

We dropped Shelley off at her apartment, a flat on Claremont
south of Sherbrooke Street. I walked her to the door.

"See you around," she said.

"Tomorrow. I'll call in the morning."

She gave me a hug. "Make it a little later, 'kay?"

"Later it is. Sleep well and long."

"For sure. Goodnight."

"'Night."

She turned the key, entered, and closed the door. I stayed put
for a few seconds then returned to the car, where I promptly lost it. I
rarely cry, and when I do it is a quiet event. This time I put my hand
over my face, tried to muffle it.

"What's the matter?"

I waved off Helen's question and turned to the window.

"I'm taking you to the house. The Manoir can wait one more
day for your return."

We stayed up until four. Over an English muffin and a cup of
tea, I gave Helen the *Cliff's Notes* version of the trip, omitting one, two,
or three insignificant events along the way, small items not worth
recounting.

She listened attentively, then asked, "So this Shelley—how did it go with her?"

"Just fine. She was very helpful."

"More than helpful, no? Otherwise you wouldn't have gotten so broken up when you guys said goodbye."

"She's got a serious illness. She told me about it for the first time earlier this evening."

"Oh."

"Helen, I'm fond of her but I'm not crazy."

"Have you shared life stories yet?"

"We were together for over a week, so yeah, we know something about each other."

"What about how you saved that girl back in high school? Did you tell her about that?"

"What? How do you know about it? I've never mentioned that story to anyone."

"Oh Dad, come on! Maybe not in the last twenty years, but you recounted the story to Michael and me on at least three different occasions. Granted, you may have drunk a bit too much eggnog on a couple of them."

Fuck, I remember none of it. How is that possible?

Helen smiled a second time—twice in the space of a couple of hours, a new world record. "Changing the subject— guess what?"

"Guess what, what?"

"You're going to be a grandpa."

"No kidding. Really?"

"Really!"

"Congratulations!" How about that. My DNA is a train and it's choo-chooing its way to the next station.

We hugged, following which I asked all the usual questions pregnant women expect to receive. I topped them off with one slightly unusual one:

"How's Frank taking it?" Helen's husband is the in-house expert on population control, two hundred pounds of inertia. He was upstairs snoring away, sounded like an accordion plugged into a washing machine.

"After the initial shock, very well. He doesn't know it yet, but he's going to make a wonderful househusband."

I slept till noon, might have gone even longer had it not been for their cat, a big tan-and-white tabby who prowls by the name of Elise. The fog of my slumber rolled out concurrently with a cat paw's repeated tap-tap on my nose. I opened an eye and saw two blue-gray eyes staring back at me, each with its own black vertical slit. I growled out a *rrrufff*, a soft one, but one conveying extreme annoyance.

"Elise! Get over here." Skitter skitter, door clicks shut.

From a Sealy commercial a few years back: A young woman awakens. She's attired in a newly pressed white cotton nightgown, her hair has been combed neatly, and her makeup has been applied with precision. No sex for her the night before, poor thing. Her arms unfold upward and forward as she simultaneously unclenches her fists and unsheathes a dazzling smile. Does anybody wake up like that? Other than me on this particular morning, that is. I had forgotten how good a full night's sleep feels.

I sat up, surprised by the brightness of the room. I had neglected to draw the curtains and was rewarded with a view of Helen's backyard flower garden. Against a yard-high stone wall she had planted rainbow flowers—irises and violets to the left, peonies, red roses, Indian paintbrushes next to them, then golden rods, black-eyed Susans, and bright green hydrangeas off to the right, near the wall's far end. Bees settled in on the red and yellow tones, and a dragonfly zipped back and forth. A lone cardinal hopped three times along the wall and flew off. Two squirrels entered the scene from the left, zipped over the wall and disappeared deep into the forest behind it. Eight hours of sleep. Recalibration, that's the word for it: the process by which rows and columns of neurons reset themselves, all nice and neat. Things are not so bad. People live with HIV these days, and Shelley will too.

Helen returned me to the Manoir a couple of hours later, and within a minute after entering my room I was ready to go back out. I called Shelley but there was no answer, so I set off in the direction of her apartment. So what if I couldn't get her on the line. Chances were good I'd find her. Carl Anderson, world's oldest stalker.

I was correct, spotted her walking toward me right after I turned south on Claremont. Despite the warm weather, she had on a heavy gray sweatshirt.

"On your way to rugby practice?"

She flashed me a quick tight smile. "That's tonight, but for now I'm off to visit my doctor."

"Are you up for a little company?"

"Sure."

Her doctor worked out of the Westmount Medical Centre, a block and a half from Shelley's apartment. In the waiting area, a sniffling blue-hair read the *National Enquirer*. Nearby, a heavyset man in a wheelchair sat motionless except for his right arm, which wavered slowly in a constricted arc. He was accompanied by his caretaker, a petite woman of Asian origin.

Shelley noticed me looking back a second time and whispered, "What did you expect, Brad and Angelina?"

"Is this guy your regular doctor?"

"Not a guy, and yes. She has a look at me, and if there are changes in my condition she refers me to a specialist or dispatches me off for tests. She's the general. I take the orders and she keeps me healthy."

"How often do you see her?"

"It averages out to once every two months. Shall we talk about something else? Anything else would suit me."

"Okay. How about we play Disease Geography?"

"What?"

"I say cold, you follow with diphtheria, I come back with amoebic dysentery, you say yellow fever—"

"And then you say Rocky Mountain spotted fever. Brilliant! So thoughtful of you to cheer me up by enumerating diseases I don't have."

"There is the possibility that one of yours might come into play."

"Not if we eliminate acronyms and three-word combinations, two rules that I insist we follow. And if we run out of maladies before I'm called, we'll move on to Life Problems Geography."

"Oh great. What have I spawned?"

"Yeah! I say dropout son and you retort with not enough food to eat. So I come back with teenage pregnancy and stick you with a Y."

"Youthful indiscretion."

"Save it for ice cream at the park. Warts. Your turn."

We ran through several dozen diseases. The last one before the receptionist called Shelley's name was tularemia. Twenty minutes later she emerged, waving two small slips of paper.

"Entrees to tests at the Royal Vic. She wants me to be evaluated."

"For what?"

"She doesn't like what's happening at night, says the sweating could be an infection but we both know it's sometimes a symptom of something bad."

All that optimism I felt this morning, gone. I had conveniently overlooked the night sweats. What an imbecile I am.

We walked up Claremont to escape the noise and traffic of Sherbrooke Street, then headed east. Within a few minutes we were wandering along Windsor Avenue. It's a quiet street. Poplars, maples, brick houses, and driveways fill up space on both of its sides.

"I've gone through this before."

"It's old hat?"

"Yeah. Twice, five and two years ago. The first time was a false alarm, and the second turned out to be a precancerous growth on the back of my neck. The doc removed it in twenty minutes."

"That's all?"

"Pretty much. They irradiated me a couple of times after, took another biopsy, gave me the all-clear. It was no big deal, just a scare."

"Quite a scare, I would think."

"I was shocked when she first told me, but she calmed me down, said everything was going to be okay. We would deal with it, and within a short period of time that would be that. And in truth, that *was* that."

"Both your parents had AIDS?"

"Yeah. My dad died when I was three, but Mom lasted another thirteen years."

"That must have been tough." *Tough?* I am the world's worst empathy projectionist.

"I don't recall my father at all, but I remember Mom going through hell those last few years. She came down with both cervical *and* skin cancer, and suffered through tons of chemo and radiation."

"How dreadful."

"That it was. The treatments gave her a few extra months, maybe a year or two, but at what a cost. What sticks in my mind more than anything is that from when I was twelve until she died, she lacked energy. Sometimes she was in pain, but always she was so very tired. In her last year the cancer spread to her brain. She became blind, then paralyzed, and finally had to be sedated all the time to avoid the agony, and, I think, awareness of the situation's awfulness. Definitely not a good way to die."

"I'm sorry she suffered so much, and that you had to witness it."

"I did learn from it."

"How so?"

"I'm an exemplary patient. I take my Atripla every night at

exactly 10:45, get plenty of exercise, am careful not to overstress myself, and I watch what I eat, despite what you may have noticed."

We meandered down Victoria Avenue. A few people with purpose were out and about. A bare-chested prematurely balding man in a black bathing suit was hosing down his Jetta, and a woman near the base of the street was scurrying two children into a house decorated with pastel helium-filled balloons tied to its front porch railings. Behind us, the sounds of two or three lawn mowers growled out of tandem. Was any of this necessary? A car stays dirty, two kids sit at home bored out of their skulls, yards remains unmowed, and the earth keeps turning. Big deal.

10:00 P.M. Thursday, June 26th

I visited Shelley's apartment for the first time this afternoon, after we returned from a jam-packed morning at the Royal Vic—eight till one with no break. Her use of the word "tests" the other day did not reflect the comprehensiveness of the experience, which included filling out forms and undergoing scans, bloodletting, and a needle biopsy. Three short procedures, three long waits.

Like me, Shelley lives in a one-roomer. Hers is half again bigger than mine, but its front door opens directly to the outside and is three steps down from ground level rather than three floors up. She doesn't own a bed, only a mattress that elevates her body a few inches off the floor. She's placed it in the room's darkest corner, likely to maximize warmth in winter. Her kitchen consists of a sink, a microwave oven, and an antiquated yellow refrigerator with a nail sticking out of its front panel where the handle once had been. Wall-to-wall lumpy gray carpeting covers the floor, and a small rectangular window, her only source of natural light, is encased too high up in the entrance door for her to have a view. She's living in a hole. It's bad enough in summer, but in winter it must be depressing as hell.

Her dining room set caught my eye. The table is made of walnut,

and stainless steel legs curve outward from a central point underneath
it. The walnut-steel combination inheres in the two chairs as well. I
found the set sharp, lovely, and completely out of place, given the
catastrophe of her living space.

"That's my baby, my pride and joy. My one big splurge, straight
from IKEA. It took me three hours to put it together."

I would guess that many modest homes harbor a special place or
two. Such a spot might be a den, an alcove, an attic, even a bathroom or
a closet. It's a sanctum—a setting for repose and escape, a space to
daydream. I would like to believe that when Shelley sits at her table,
she feels a comfort that nothing can erode.

A brown overstuffed couch and two beige recliners that long ago
belonged to a couple of mid-century psychiatrists, all worn past the
point of decrepitude, cluttered up the middle of the room. "I rescued
them from the trash, poor things. They deserved a home."

So does she.

7:15 P.M. Friday, June 27th

On my way back to the Manoir yesterday I stopped in at Westmount
Stationery, where I purchased two twenty-two- by twenty-eight-inch
white poster boards, a ruler, and markers in red, green, blue, brown,
and black ink. I finished the chart this morning, then memorized it.
Once the diagnosis comes in I'll rip it up and toss it in the trash.

Obtaining the information was easy. I didn't go to the library,
didn't even have to open a book. I typed "AIDS cancer" into Google
and up it popped: *AIDS-Related Lymphoma Treatment (PDQ®)*, patient
and health professional versions. After downloading and printing
out both documents, I gathered up the pages, stapled them together,
and repaired to my desk chair. I read the twenty-six pages of the
Patient Version straight through, from the opening definition of
AIDS-related lymphoma to the end of the glossary.

I titled my poster "To Be or Not to Be," then printed out my favorite photo of Shelley, the one with the big smile, sweat, and filthy t-shirt from Blue Bonnet Park. Glued it right under the title. Next I drew a box under the photo and labeled it, in green, *general physical examination*. I branched two lines downward from it, the one off to the right leading to a *no symptoms* box, and the one angled leftward pointing to *symptoms*.

I placed a blue *tests* box under *symptoms*. Below it: *complete blood count*, followed a little lower by *more tests*. Five lines extended down and away, leading to five more boxes: *lymph node biopsy* (four subtypes listed underneath), *bone marrow aspiration and biopsy, HIV test, Epstein-Barr virus test*, and *chest x-ray*.

I drew two boxes in brown another level down, and labeled them *positive* and *negative*. Under positive, *staging*. Three more lines down from *staging* led to *CT scan, PET scan*, and *MRI*. Below them, one big box marked *diagnosis*. Finally I drew four lines extending down from *diagnosis* to the bottom of the poster, where I wrote out the labels for the last four boxes, left to right: *stage I, stage II, stage III*, all in black ink, and *stage IV* in red.

The *AIDS-Related Lymphoma Treatment (PDQ®), Patient Version* describes options such as radiation, chemotherapy, high-dose chemo with stem cell transplant, and monoclonal antibody therapy. It concludes with the following sentence: *Patients may want to think about taking part in a clinical trial*. You don't include such a statement in your manual if existing treatments work.

I then took a look at the *Health Professional Version*. One particular sentence caught my attention: "At diagnosis, 66% of the patients have stage IV disease." Stage IV is defined as follows:

Disseminated (multifocal) involvement of one or more extralymphatic organs with or without associated lymph node involvement or isolated extralymphatic organ involvement with distant (nonregional) nodal involvement.

English translation: the disease is out of control, the prognosis is death.

I closed my eyes and let the poster slip from my hands. An image of roadkill, a dead squirrel I had seen in the street on my walk back from Westmount Stationery, intruded. The squirrel's tail and hind legs extended away from its body, and its furry white underside appeared undamaged. It could have been sleeping, except for the fact that its mouth was opened wide and there was dried red rot inside. Besides, when do you ever see a squirrel sleeping?

I left my room and did not stop walking until I reached one of the two hard stone park benches by the side of the library. I sat down and stared at the library's redbrick wall until the bright rays of the sun forced me away.

Given my age I'm supposed to be the infirm one, but apart from a little unsteadiness on my feet I'm doing fine, thank you very much. I should have chronic problems by now, and I should be suffering for killing that baby girl. I was only two and a half, but most other two-and-a-half-year-olds, all of them, in fact... Why couldn't I have slept through that night? So much would have turned out differently. I would have grown up with my real father. Amy would have lived, she might have had children, and who knows, one of them might have become a brilliant doctor.

11:22 A.M. Saturday, June 28th

I write from Starbucks. A young woman sits opposite me, one table down and about eleven feet away. She wears a full-length soft gray cotton sack dress, held in place by a bow fastened behind her neck. I noticed the backlit outline of her body when she walked in. Nice. Her shoulders and arms are bare, tanned light brown. Hair cut short, brown eyes, brown flip flops, soft feet, immaculately applied caramel toenail polish.

Nowadays I'm thinking that health should trump beauty. In a rational society, authors would describe their women according to hardiness rather than attractiveness:

> She was the personification of healthiness, and she had the numbers to back it up: a 55 bpm resting pulse rate, blood pressure of 110 over 70, straight-A negatives on all STDs, and a CD4 T lymphocyte count of 1100. Five foot two, 105 pounds, in the 99th percentile for lung capacity. Parents and grandparents alive and well, great grandparents lived to be centenarians. Fully vaccinated, sick an average two days a year, unblemished driving record. Goes to bed early, rises early. Vegetarian. Strong like bull.

Works for me.

1:22 P.M. Sunday, June 29th

Starbucks yet again. An unfortunate aspect of my current worldview is that I perceive battlegrounds between health and sickness everywhere. A fat guy on the other side of the room hunches over his laptop. A brownie and a Frappuccino topped with whipped cream adorn his table. I imagine dark damp morsels descending through his insides, emulsified into a swampy substance by the sticky liquid accompanying them. Globs of dirty gray gunk settle in his blood vessels, packed tight in the left carotid artery.

I write with a Pilot V5 Hi-Tecpoint pen. Its plastic tube is light blue and transparent, and there are fine hash marks on it. A pen to anyone else, it reminds me of a hypodermic needle.

The mural on the far wall is tinted in soft greens, oranges, blues, and grays. Though there are a few coffee cups dispersed throughout, it's mainly an abstract consisting of various geometric forms: an orange hambone resembling a grand piano as seen from above, tubular amorphous shapes lining the bottom, a blotch of yellow at the lower left looking like a humpbacked egg yolk. Leaves and flowers drawn in outline permeate the canvas, and myriads of small buds flutter in the background. I see capsules, microbes, and cancer cells invading lungs, stomachs, pancreases, hearts. Even the pad I write on is infected. Blue dots—tiny leaks from having written on the previous page—they're germs. My pages are filled with contagion.

	3:00 P.M. Friday, July 11th
"Give me an L."	"L!"
"Give me a Y."	"Y!"
"Give me an M."	"M!"
Etcetera…	
"Whaddya got?"	"LYMPHOMA!!!"

There are two sides to every story. From the disease's perspective, illness is an epic in the making, a brewing *How the West Was Won* in micro-miniature. It's a blockbuster, chocked with adventure, conquest, and colonization. The invading army, millions of suicidal soldiers, fight with the zeal of fanatics. There is deceit aplenty as well—mother and father cells, parent and child cells, formerly friendly neighbor cells, are at each other's throats.

In olden days doctors wouldn't call a shovel a spade. They disguised stomach cancer as an ulcer, lung cancer as pneumonia. Each cancer was matched with a shadow ailment, its own serious but curable malady. The denial approach ended when chemotherapy and radiation started to work, because it made no sense to deceive patients who might get better. Not that denial fooled anyone anyway.

Nowadays, denial is deferred. The oncologist opens your file and removes a piece of paper. He stares at it. From the frown on his face and because he does not look up at you, you conclude that the lab report is not good. In fact it is terrible. The doctor knows there is a one hundred percent probability you will die before the first flake of the first snowfall of the year brushes against the ground.

Does he tell you? Unequivocally, no. He defers. He informs you that you have stage IV AIDS-related non-Hodgkin lymphoma, and that it is not uncommon for death to follow within six months of diagnosis. But then he gives you an out: promising new treatments exist, and they have fancy names like post-chemotherapy stem cell transplant and monoclonal antibody infusion. Remission is unlikely but possible. Slim is better than none. Or he enthuses about some promising clinical trial in Toronto. Your consultation concludes and you trudge off to phone the trial's administrator.

I am getting ahead of myself. I pray that I catastrophize. Shelley's positive biopsy isn't a death sentence. You need one more test for that.

11:09 P.M. Wednesday, July 16th

A vial of blood. A few drops of lymph drained from her neck by a thin, silvery needle. A red fluid and a clear one, so insubstantial they could evaporate into the clouds. Ethereal substances, yet damning, heavier than the pounding gravity of the Kansas plains.

They put her in the tunnel. Gadolinium coursed through her veins, illuminating the tinged spots, the locales of betrayal. And now we wait.

10:12 P.M. Monday, July 21st

The magic number is not the dreaded four. My heart leapt when Shelley's oncologist, Doctor Vaincoeur, said, "Three." She has stage III disease plain and simple, just some tainted lymph nodes in the affected vicinity. There is no organ damage whatsoever. Not even the spleen was touched.

Shelley smiled at me weakly, then turned to the doctor and said, "No treatment."

I was flabbergasted. "Are you serious? You've got to be treated! You'll get cured, which is a hell of a lot better than the alternative.

Doctor, tell her."

Vaincoeur said nothing.

"Doctor Vaincoeur?"

He didn't even glance my way. "I understand, Miss Randell. Chemotherapy for your condition is often effective, but it lasts months, it's tiring, and you would find it unpleasant every now and then. Nevertheless, I hope you will reflect on your decision. Your life is at stake."

"Thank you."

"You are most welcome. Now if you will excuse me, I have patients waiting."

I exploded as soon as we left the office. A dozen people in the waiting room were sitting around reading magazines and books, talking, meditating, jerking off, whatever. They stared wide-eyed at me when I erupted almost at a shout.

"What the fuck is going on here? Don't you want to live?"

"No. Now leave me alone."

"I'll do no such thing."

"Oh yes you will. I'm taking a taxi, and you're not going to be in it. Call me later when you've calmed down."

"I'll never calm down!"

"Then goodbye forever." Off she went almost at a trot, and I couldn't keep up.

"Wait a second. Stop!" She didn't. Fuck.

Imagine a world without the automatic pilot. What if, upon waking each morning, you had to choose?

Good morning, mademoiselle, this is your wakeup inquiry. Do you wish to continue or would you prefer to give up the ghost?

It is curious that the death option is irreversible, unlike the life option. To be taken into a state of nonbeing for a day or two and then to be thrown back into the chaos of breathing, touching, pain, and pleasure—would the return be unbearable? I wish I knew. Humankind had exactly one opportunity to find out, but blew it. Christ died a tortuous death, but the real tragedy of those times lay elsewhere, in the failure to carry out a well-conceived qualitative research project focusing on Lazarus of Bethany's death experiences. What a fantastic case study he would have made! At the very least, someone should have interviewed the poor bastard, given that the option of putting him through a battery of psychological and physical tests was out of the question. What I wouldn't pay for the phenomenological narrative. Remember that Christ brought him back to life a full four days after he died. That's long enough for all the mortises—pallor, livor, algor, and rigor—to have come and gone, long enough to have detected a putrefying corpse at fifty paces, and certainly of sufficient duration to have yielded from Lazarus an exquisitely detailed first-hand report of what it felt like to be dead.

Shelley's autopilot is shot. She cannot continue by default, so she proceeds with conscious intent and selects the terrible option. Granted, she watched her mother suffer through chemo for no apparent benefit, but her own case is different. It's not anywhere close to hopeless! If I can just get her to push through, she'll emerge on the other side all fine and dandy. Sure, chemo is misery, or rather it holds that prospect. But wouldn't the suffering it entails, no matter how intense, amount to a minuscule hill of beans in the larger scheme of things?

11:30 P.M. Tuesday, July 22nd

I accosted her as she walked past the bus stop in front of the Manoir this morning, on her way to the library.

"Wait!"

She saw me, didn't slacken her pace.

"Please! I'm dreadfully sorry."

That stopped her, but she didn't exactly accept my apology with grace.

"You behaved like a total ass. How could you embarrass me so?"

"I regret it, sincerely I do. Listen, I made a mistake. But you have to understand—"

"No, *you* have to understand. Do you have any idea how awful you made me feel? We see the oncologist, he gives us the diagnosis, and I make my decision, which is final, by the way, absolutely final—and instead of getting support from you, the *one* person I trust, what do you do? You *yell* at me, and in front of all those people. They're quaking with fear from their own apprehensions, but do you give a fuck about them, or, for that matter, about me? No. All you can think of is getting your way."

"Okay, I admit to fucking up, but it was because—because—well, you know." *Because I love you.* Thought, not said.

"You could have asked me why. You might have said, 'I understand how upset you are, but please sleep on it before ruling anything out.' You could have shown concern and empathy, but no, you had to browbeat me instead. Don't you remember me telling you about my mom's chemo hell?"

"Of course I do, but every case is different. All I'm asking is that you take a longer view of things."

"There is no long view for me, Carl, any more than there is for a broken down, rusted out, junk heap of some twenty-six-year-old jalopy. Even if I were able to get through the chemo, which I serious doubt, something else would bring me down because my immune system's shot. Don't you get that?"

"No. I don't accept your conclusion, especially as medical research is always coming up with new possibilities. Please give yourself a chance, that's all I'm asking. Don't give up so easily."

Shelley resumed walking to the library. I trailed after her.

"At least let me investigate the problem before you pack it in completely, okay?"

"It's useless."

"No it isn't."

"All right," she said exasperatedly, "but under one condition. If you find some remedy that you think is magical, but I disagree—if I reject it and conclude that I'd rather take my chances doing nothing, will you support me? And can you assure me that never again will you explode like you did yesterday?"

"Yes, absolutely. I assure you of that, completely I do."

9:17 P.M. Monday, July 28th

Six days later, one assurance demolished. Everything is finished, and it's all my fault.

An irony: this morning's external trappings approached perfection. We had been sitting outside at Café Crème. It was uncrowded, a rarity on a warm summer day. The air was smokeless, the breeze gentle, and a diffuse light drained everything of its usual sharpness. The buildings of Victoria Avenue, which look so depressing on wet days, lost their edges. They were bathed in pastels—baby blues, pinks, yellows, and greens so fine that you could almost see through them. My cappuccino tasted smooth, bitter, and sweet in just the right proportions. A couple of tall dark women separated by ten minutes and fifteen years walked past us toward Sherbrooke Street, one accompanied by a giant white poodle with an intelligent gaze, the other by two intense schnauzers. But then I started in with my spiel and she went crazy. I made it worse because I was stubborn for one of the few times in my life. I did not stop, refused to shut up because everything depended on it, so she called me an idiot and left.

"Don't write, don't call, don't come to the desk when I'm working there. Don't say hello in passing, just get the fuck out of my life!"

She walked briskly up Victoria Avenue, turned around a few seconds later and yelled, "And no gifts, zero, none at all whatsoever. This is final, the end, never evermore!" She continued up the block to Sherbrooke Street, then vanished from sight with her first step to the right. I am stunned.

It's not as if she didn't know what I was up to. I saw her on three occasions over the past week, and each time I brought it up. I kept it brief, glossed over it because my preparation was not yet complete. By this morning, however, I had collected more than enough evidence to convince her that the probability of a long-term complete cure is very high indeed. I interviewed two oncologists and two general practitioners, plus I talked with a naturopath and four non-Hodgkin patients, two of whom are enjoying lengthy, perhaps permanent, remissions. I read up on the latest treatments, from both internet sources and journals in the Osler Library. I acquired the ideas, good ones, but she didn't want to listen. She's convinced herself that the whole mess of treatments—chemo, radiation, stem cell transplants, whatever—all would destroy her remaining pleasures in life. And for what? Zero to a few extra months from her point of view, fifty years and more from mine.

I recounted the three recovery stories I read online last night, and I shared with her the one piece of advice common to the survivors: be a strong advocate for your own survival. Be a fighter. If you agitate, stay on top of the latest research, and push for state-of-the-art treatment, you will get better. Chances are better than good. Chances are excellent.

Ah the academic mindset, the fucking academic mindset. If it were a place, it would be a beach on a foggy summer morning. Stretch out a towel over the sand, or on a big flat rock overlooking the water. It's a little cold, but no matter, for both the chill and the morning fog will dissipate, burned off by the sun's rays as they radiate through the pores of your skin. The fog will yield to a brilliant blue sky. Just lie on your stomach, turn your head to one side or another, shiver a little, and wait.

The fog is doubt. Doubt is necessary for people like me. A good academic instills doubt in his students. He kicks the stuffing out of the teddy bear of certainty, if I may be allowed a senior metaphoric moment. He implores his bright-eyed eager-beaver students to question everything, even himself. The only sacrosanct precept is the need to question, which must not be questioned. Nevertheless, despite and even in contradiction to throwing students off their keels (to haul around another unfortunate metaphor), most academics believe in the Better Day. No one speaks of it much except university PR officers, because it is the Lord Voldemort of higher education. Yes, that's it:

Optimism: the philosophy that must not be spoken of.

Though easy to ridicule, optimism thrives in the academy. That's a good thing, an excellent thing, if I may borrow a McGill University watchword. Long live optimism! Diseases will be conquered. Resources will be managed. Interventions will transform hatred to love between siblings, couples, and families, and between peoples of different religions, races, and ethnicities. Great artworks will be appreciated, nay cherished, by the masses. No one will go hungry, and everyone will dwell in warm and secure homes. Loved ones will abound, if not of the flesh and blood variety then of robotic imitations close enough to fool all but the most discriminating connoisseurs. Best of all, people and their pets will cease dying. Solutions to all problems are inevitable. Just do the research and watch the fog lift.

11:59 P.M. Friday, August 1st

Two men, a priest and a professor, sit at a bar. Neither has a banana in his ear. The prof turns to the priest and asks, "Father, what is the absolute worst sin a person can commit? Is it murder?"

"My son," the priest replies, "God forgives all sins of the repentant."

"Even the taking of another life?"

"Yes, if the murderer sincerely regrets his action."

"But what if the life taken is that of a child?"

"Child killing can be forgiven, my son, provided the murderer truly and deeply grieves the loss."

"How about fucking the kid beforehand?"

"My son," the priest says as he gives the professor a knowing glance followed by an almost imperceptible snigger, "a little Heavenly preparation never hurts."

Cynicism is adaptive. It obliterates blame and takes away hurt, because when everything appears ironic, stupid, and devoid of purpose, nothing matters. I'd adopt a cynical attitude about having bludgeoned little Amy Mulligan to death if I could. It's not an option, because *murderer* is an appellation that sticks. Categorize me as ex-husband, ex-professor, even ex-Kansan hick if you want, but no one can let me off the hook with the label *ex-murderer*. There are no ex-murderers.

It has been forty-one days since I learned of my role in Amy Mulligan's death. For a while I thought my concern might fade away. I had pushed the problem down, hid it deep inside and instead focused on Shelley and her illness. But now, in Shelley's absence, the Amy problem has resurfaced. The emptiness of my everyday existence has been displaced by something worse.

I charted out my options on the second of the poster boards I purchased a few weeks back. My charts usually flow downward, but this problem dictated a reversal of direction. Guilt is a hole and options are escapes, so I started at the bottom and drew lines upward. After positioning the poster in landscape mode on my desk, wider than tall, I inscribed the following near the bottom:

Amy dies.

I ruled in three lines, all emanating from a point halfway between the two words, and directed them northwest, north, and northeast. I labeled their endpoints *not responsible, seek advice,* and *responsible,* respectively.

I branched another two lines up from *not responsible*: to the left, *did not kill her*; to the right, *rationalizations*. I added a final branch above *rationalizations,* creating a fork leading to *spotless adult history* and *too young to be blamed*.

I briefly contemplated, then rejected, all of the *not responsible* options. To accept the innocuous—that I did not kill Amy Mulligan— is to defy my memory. To justify my actions by contending that in the following eighty years I did not commit violence upon anyone else is sophistry. A thief who steals a million dollars but abides by the law for the rest of his life remains a thief. Moreover, my mind is not a correctional facility; rehabilitation is not the issue here.

Finally, to accept the excuse of being only two and a half years old at the moment of my crime is abdication of responsibility. You ask, how could a mere toddler have known any better? I respond: What if *you* had done it? Could you have sloughed it off? According to law, responsibility for Amy's death rested with Pascuala Johnston and Michael Bourgmeyer. True enough, my father and his lover were negligent. Nevertheless, I was the instrument of death. A normal kid never would have left his bed, or he would have returned to it right after seeing some woman fucking his father, traumatized but still untainted by mortal sin. Or he might have screamed, ruining the evening for all parties and inducing a crying fit in little Amy. Upsetting to all, fatal to none. Unfortunately, however, my behavior extended miles beyond the normal range. I became a child murderer in both senses of the phrase.

I next considered the *responsible* branch of my chart. Above it I added a split: to the left, *penance and self-punishment,* to the right, *make amends.*

My penance and self-punishment role model is Oedipus. The gods really had it in for him, eh? During that first recorded instance in human history of road rage, Oedipus sworded his daddy. He solved the Sphinx's riddle, became king, married his mom, and raised four children, a.k.a. siblings. For fifteen years, life flowed on splendidly. But then Oedipus learned the truth, just as I did. In a fit of remorse he gouged his eyes out using his recently deceased mom-wife's jewelry.

I will not follow the oedipean path. I am too ordinary to cut it as the tragic figure blindly wandering around in exile, plus I can't imagine any kind of penance that would make me feel even the slightest bit better for having killed a defenseless infant. Self-mutilation is not a logical course of action.

I next considered the *make amends* option. This pathway might work well for quantitative crimes. Suppose you defraud Fred out of a thousand dollars. Proper restitution might consist of returning the thousand plus forking over another thousand as compensation for Fred's distress. With murder, however, the victim is the ultimate Humpty-Dumpty. Sure, pay the relatives off, but don't expect their delight upon receiving the unexpected windfall to salve your guilt. Or try saving others. Become a lifeguard, dietician, fireman, surgeon— another day, another life extended. That's the ticket! By lengthening the lives of the living, you make up for shortening the life of your murderee. You reestablish the net zero your conscience has been pining for. Really?

I see no solution other than by taking the middle path—*seek advice.* But what sort of advice, and from whom? No psychologists or psychiatrists, please, as I am allergic to professional help. An ethicist, perhaps? How about a criminal?

5:13 P.M. Friday, August 8th

No Shelley for eleven days now, and the slack in my schedule has not been filled by anything of interest. To the contrary, I've endured two run-ins. The first took place on Monday, over breakfast. As I was applying a coat of strawberry jam onto the thicker half of an English muffin, Mildred inquired, "So Carl dear, I haven't seen you with your little chippie recently. The two of you haven't broken up, have you?"

Unpleasantness sometimes arises between people because of differences in vocabulary. Leaving aside Mildred's imprecise application of the phrase, "broken up," my response was to ask whether she honestly did not know the definition of chippie. Had she assumed the unimaginable?

"Mildred, chippie means prostitute. You do know that, right?"

"Oh heavens, of course that's not what I intended! I meant it as a term of endearment. Isn't chippie defined that way too? And doesn't it also mean small, as in a chip off the old block?"

Mildred smiled at me insincerely. Harold, sitting to my left and directly opposite his wife, dropped his fork and looked under the table to see where it went.

A lesson learned from four-plus decades of university teaching is that if a student or colleague says something that is monumentally stupid, respond without derision, sarcasm, or any other indication that you think he or she is a moron. Always take the high road, whether you get paid for it or not, and that was the path I followed on this occasion.

"So you were saying, in effect, 'How's my little small one?' No, Mildred, chippie isn't a term of endearment. No man asks of his woman friend, 'And how's my little chippie today?' You might as well query, 'How's my cute little slut?' or 'How's my sweet little whore?'" Spoken with voice unraised, casually, offhandedly even, between muffin nibbles.

Mildred agreed that chippie was not the appropriate word,

then got to the point: "I was just asking about you and her, especially as you've been so out of sorts these past days."

To which I replied, "That's because the little fucker gave me the clap." Harold damn near choked on his food.

Run-in number two occurred the following afternoon. Michael came visiting. Usually he begs off with one or more of the following excuses: (1) schedule is hectic, (2) car is in the shop, (3) it's too cold, too snowy, or too cold and too snowy, and (4) he's caught some respiratory disease and does not want to kill off one or more of the residents by exposing his germs to them. The guiltier Michael feels, the more excuses he employs.

Michael attended McGill as a management student. He earned his B.A. and M.B.A., took a job as an assistant to some financial advisor working in one of the big downtown buildings overlooking the St. Lawrence, and two years ago became an advisor himself. These days he spends much time on the phone trying to assuage angry clients.

My son mellowed into adulthood too quickly. Watching him grow up was like watching a butterfly revert to a caterpillar. At six years of age he had me fasten a roll of ultra-light extra-strong taxicab-yellow adhesive tape to his bedroom ceiling. He needed to know how long it would take the tape to unwind and reach the floor seven and a half feet below (seventeen days, thirteen hours, four minutes, twenty-two seconds). At eleven, Michael was into Cabbage Patch Kids, doll houses, and Judy Blume books in a big way. I was concerned.

Five years later, he redeemed himself. One of his classmates, Eleanora Scarpettino, a tall girl with curly black hair, long eyelashes, and a well developed chest, came over to work on a presentation for the tolerance module of their moral instruction class. As no one else was home at the time, and as the topic of their project concerned LGBT and behavioral outliers such as transvestism and fetishism, my son's suggestion that the two of them exchange clothes might have been considered reasonable, almost rational, rather than off the charts.

Their enterprise would have remained secret had Michael not inscribed an epigram bordering on the obscene on the inside border of Eleanora's panties. Eleanora's mother called me the following evening, freaked by my son's imaginative but misguided attempt at courtship. She insisted I pay for replacement panties. Replacement panties, what a concept. But now, alas, at age thirty-six, my bachelor son Michael is a good dozen years past completion of his morph to Mr. Normal. Michael P. Normal, with the P standing for pleasant. He looks the part too, what with his round face, unthreatening height, slight build, lack of facial hair, and nifty patent leather shoes.

We sat on my favorite bench, the rickety one in front of the Manoir facing out toward Sherbrooke Street. It was no longer in need of a paint job because last spring someone decided it would look better stripped, sanded, and varnished. Too bad us residents can't be fixed up the same way. Stripped, sanded, and varnished sounds pretty good to me. Surely there's a spa for the elderly, a place people like me can go to be stripped, sanded, and varnished. We would return home after a week or two looking smooth, slick, and hard enough to be sat on.

After a few minutes of putter-putter talk, I provided Michael with the trip's blow-by-blow narrative, unexpurgated save for a few minor details. As he never met the man I used to call Pa, the revelation that Bourgmeyer was my biological father didn't faze him. I thought my infantile criminal past would shock him, but no. He smiled as I recounted the discovery, as if he had just learned something quaint about my character, equivalent in gravitas, say, to a predilection for orange cauliflower. But after I told him how I found the woman of my dream sitting at the Westmount Public Library circulation desk—no, I didn't put it quite that way. I told Michael that I liked being with her, nothing more—such an understatement that it amounted to a lie. His eyes darted away, then he started in with the *yes, but*s. When I expressed my distress over Shelley's illness, the rift between her and me, my need to do something to win her back, and, above all, the necessity of keeping her alive, he finally started talking in sentences.

"Dad, I think that maybe you ought to speak to someone."

"I did—doctors and patients."

"I mean someone to confide in, like a psychologist or a social worker. Helen could get you a referral. Lawyers know lots of people like that."

"What the hell for?"

"You're upset. Actually, you look depressed to me. It would be great if you would talk to someone about it, so you can move on."

"And what does *move on* mean?"

"You know."

"I do *not* know."

"Look Dad, I just want you to feel better. You can't do anything about... What's her name again?"

"Shelley."

"Right, Shelley. She told you not to meddle in her life, in fact to never show your face in her presence, right? So why beat your head against a wall?"

There are some things you refrain from telling your children. You don't admit to your son and daughter that you love a woman who is younger than they are, and who is more than two-thirds of a lifetime younger than yourself. You don't inform them that you fill up your hours obsessing over her. You don't mention that ever since you transited from wakefulness to sleep while reclining in a fourth-rate Liberal motel chair, she became your everything. And certainly you don't let them know that were she to die, you'd quickly put an end to yourself. No psychiatrist would get a shot at you. You'd take no antidepressants, and you wouldn't permit yourself to get caught up in any discussion concerning the irrationality of your thoughts. All thoughts are irrational. You'd end your life before anyone could electroshock, lobotomize, drug, or perform anything else of a therapeutic nature on your mind and your body, because there is not enough time left in the universe to reduce that particular darkness to a despair even a millionth of an inch lighter.

Instead, you answer by taking the offensive: "Michael, how does it feel to know that at sometime in the future, on an unknowable but inevitable day, every last bit of life will be squeezed out of your body and dispersed into nothingness? That you will cease to exist for all time."

"Dad—that's pretty morbid, especially the way you're putting it. But to answer your question, I don't think about it."

"Because you can't do anything about it?"

"Yes, damn it. It's unavoidable. I'd rather die later than sooner, but why think about something that can't be changed?"

"Because it's important. And it's fun to contemplate."

"Fun? Oh I don't think so."

"Sure it is. That's what's missing around here. I'm surrounded by old people. Most will pack it in within ten years, one or two likely within the next few weeks, and what the hell do we talk about? The weather. Last night's salad. How slow the elevator is. Anything but what it means to exist no longer. You'd think death would be Topic Number One around here, but it's nowhere on the radar."

"Of course it isn't. No one wants to talk about it because it's too threatening."

"Well damn it, Michael, I want to talk about it. Humor me."

"What's to consider? People get old, they get sick, and they die. You want to discuss what happens afterwards?"

"No, son. What I want to know is—" At that moment I spotted her, on her way to the library. Her hair was dyed blonde or she was wearing a wig. Blue cutoffs, yellow t-shirt, the stump of a mini-umbrella in her right hand. Excellent posture. She looked good, very fine in fact. Her body blinked in and out through the pines as she walked past, and then she was gone, off to my right and beyond my field of vision. She never glanced my way. I walked a few feet up the path to get a last glimpse.

"Dad?"

"Don't worry, son, I'm not losing it."

"What then?"

I sat back down on the bench. "Took care of a wedgie, that's all. Ever see the film by Kurasawa, the Japanese director—*Ikiru*?"

"You know I don't like foreign films. I can't abide the subtitles."

How the hell did he turn out so different from me? I would prefer *all* films to be subtitled, even ones spoken in English. Seeing the words adds a dimension to the experience. Besides, actors sometimes mumble or talk too fast.

"Here's the *Readers Digest* version: This man, his name is Watanabe—four syllables but as common as Smith here—he's been having persistent stomach pains, so he goes to a clinic, has an x-ray taken, and learns he's got stomach cancer. He's going to die within six months. Watanabe's been a do-nothing bureaucrat for years, decades even. He's accomplished zilch he's proud of, and his personal life is worse than zilch. His wife died long ago, and his family consists of an ungrateful son and a conniving daughter-in-law."

"Sounds like a real cheery film, Dad. Right up your alley."

"Right, very cheery."

"Connect the dots for me."

"Okay. After Watanabe leaves the clinic, one of the doctors asks a nurse: 'What would you do if you knew you were going to die within six months?'"

"And?"

"The rest of the movie reveals Watanabe's solution."

"Which is?"

"Go see the movie."

"Tell you what. I'll see the movie if you get professional help. Deal?"

"No deal."

Michael doesn't get it. He thinks I'm making a fool of myself, that I am destined to join the numberless legions of geezers who waste fortunes on young women. That is not it. That is definitely not it at all.

7:28 P.M. Thursday, August 11th

siblicide

- n

the killing of a child by its brother or sister.

I'm booked up on the topic. Siblicide is commonplace in the animal kingdom, particularly among birds, though it also has been found in wasps, salamanders, and hyenas. The eldest newborn kills the next to be hatched, or the first two out of their shells gang up and annihilate the third. The activity has survival value, except for the victim.

As in the animal world, human victims of siblicide often die before their first birthdays. The perpetrators, however, commit their homicides at a more advanced age. I read descriptions of several grisly cases on the internet this morning, and in all instances the killers were at least six years old. Why? Simple—society classifies younger murderers differently. We are the accidental causers of death. Or we didn't really mean it, or we were incapable of knowing right from wrong. Given that we mature with protectively distorted memories of the event, or with no memories of it at all—ah, in all cases but mine—what's the harm?

Madame Forget interrupted my bliss this afternoon. I was out sitting on my bench, reading the *Gazette*. She came over, plopped herself down next to me, and initiated a few putter-putter exchanges that caught us up on each other's recent trivialities. I tried short circuiting the intrusion by tipping over the gentilitial applecart.

"Mind if I ask you a personal question?"

"Well now, that would depend on what it is."

"You won't know until I ask it."

"True enough. Oh all right, go ahead. I'll take the chance."

Brave woman. She smiled as if I were about to pull a rabbit out of a hat, probably expected me to ask if she had a steady boyfriend.

"Have you ever killed anyone?"

"Why no, thank goodness. That's a very unusual question, Dr. Anderson. How come you're asking it?"

"Never? Not even accidentally, say, by running someone over?"

"No! Of course not."

"Well I have, and I don't know what to do about it."

I spent a few minutes providing her with the relevant background information, then said, "So here I am, eighty years later, and I don't know what to make of it all. I had always thought of myself as harmless, you know? Believed I'd traversed the years, if not in a sterling manner, then at least without causing grievous bodily harm. But I was wrong, in fact mistaken right from the get-go. It's upsetting, to put it mildly."

"But are you functioning within your regular limits?"

"What do you mean?"

"Are you getting enough sleep and eating well? And are you not feeling depressed or otherwise upset?"

"I'm okay physically. It's purely a psychological thing."

"Then your situation is perplexing, because viewed one way, there is no solution whatsoever. Dead is dead, after all. But looked at a little differently, you seek a solution when there is no problem."

"No problem?"

"None at all. Make an intellectual game of it if you want, but if you aren't affected, what's the concern?"

"I *am* affected. Thinking about having killed that baby is like having "White Christmas" play over and over in my head, only worse."

"My heavens, that does sound hideous. Nevertheless, your guilt will recede. Give it time."

"It's already been two months."

"That's not very long. Be patient. In the meantime, though, I'd advise you not to broach the topic to the residents."

"Why?"

"Your pursuit of that young girl is bad enough. You're making the women jealous and the men envious."

"What? My pursuit?" I was shocked that anyone would have noticed, let alone given a shit.

"Yes, your pursuit, that's what it is. Should you crown that particular perversion with wild stories of infanticide, the residents will think you are addled. I imagine they'd find you doubly disturbing, almost a pariah. So for your own good, keep it to yourself. Do you understand? And now you must excuse me, as I must shop before dinnertime."

Lickety split, off she went. Her backside receded from view with each dainty footstep, like a tugboat vanishing into the horizon as it chugs out to sea. Unfortunately, I didn't have the presence of mind to tell her that "young girl" wasted a word. Frumpy dumpy pain in the ass.

4:34 P.M. Thursday, August 14th

Upper floor of semi-detached cottage. Two bedrooms, furnished, prime location: quiet street bordering Westmount Park, steps from Metro, bus, shops, churches, synagogues, schools. Hardwood floors, newly installed quality Jeldwen doors/windows with electrically operated Kresta blinds. Yellow River granite counters in ultramodern and spacious kitchen. Elevator. October 1st occupancy.

Elevator! It's only $3,900 per month, which totals up to $46,800 a year excluding utilities. I can afford that, though in a few years I might have to whack the Manoir drug dealer and take over his business.

11:55 P.M. Saturday, August 16th

pariah

- n

    one who is shunned or made an outcast.

    a person eliciting revulsion in others.

Such a pretty word. Pariah Carey, the world-renowned leprous pop singer. Jeremiah, Delilah, and the Messiah shared jambalaya and papaya on the playa with a pariah named Zachariah.

For the price of an inexpensive meal I conversed with a pariah this afternoon. His name is Salvatore, he's homeless, and he has been a fixture at the local Starbucks for longer than I have been living at the Manoir.

Salvatore's face looks like it's been smeared in charcoal and patted down with rubbing alcohol. He wears the same dark green overcoat and black-and-white Converse All Star sneakers in summer as in the cooler seasons. Within a yard's radius he stinks, from whiskey if you face him and from a combination of whiskey and body odor otherwise. However, and unlike many of his persuasion, Salvatore is neither mentally ill nor devoid of social skills. He can smile, tell a story, and listen, which is more than I can say for some of my former students and colleagues. I have watched him successfully maintain extended conversations with coeds, though from the distance of a table or two.

He had settled into the room's only dark nook. Usually I sit as far from him as possible, but today I pulled up a chair at the table next to his, despite my favorite window table being unoccupied.

    "How's it going?"

My question elicited a brief startle response, followed by a smile and this verbiage: "Currently, my corporeal and cognitive realms are optimally equilibrated. All four of my limbs operate effectively to the limits of their normal kinesthetic ranges, and my sense organs admirably discriminate the subtleties inherent in the stimuli surrounding them. Yes, today has been a good day to sample the fruits of existence, excepting a few rumblings from below."

"Hungry?"

"Not to the nth degree. I consumed half a blueberry muffin three hours ago. The remainder is sequestered in the left front pocket of my outer-garment, and it shall satisfy my appetite at a more advanced hour of the day."

"That's all you've eaten?"

"Yes. On the positive side, I'm having no difficulty in maintaining my girlish figure."

"Tell you what. How about I trade you a meal for some conversation. We'll go to McDonald's and you'll order whatever you want, girlish figure be damned. I'll pay for it, and you'll tell me a little about yourself."

"Truly, I am astonished. May I inquire as to the motivation for my good fortune? Far be it for me to stare down the equine's throat. Nevertheless, I am curious if *you* are merely curious, or if you wish me to serve as a guinea pig for some form of academic investigation."

"The former. Had it been the latter, you'd be signing a confidentiality form right about now. I'm just a retired guy with a little extra time on his hands, and I'm feeling a little low. I'd appreciate some talk, so what do you say?"

"My good sir, you have yourself a bargain."

"As do you."

Over the succeeding twenty-five minutes Salvatore consumed a Big Mac, a supersized portion of French fries, a large diet Dr. Pepper, and most of a McFlurry chocked with M&M's. He ate his Big Mac slowly, fingers covered in mustard and catsup, relish dripping onto the table off the inner surfaces of his thumbs. He chews with his mouth open, lacks a couple of bottom front teeth.

"How long have you been underutilized?"

"An excellent euphemism, thank you. Two years and three months. I used to be a doorman at the Queen E—my second bout of long-term employment. I repeated my 'Good evening, ma'am's for eleven and one-half years. My current position as mendicant is an unfortunate temporary detour, an avocation in passing as it were. Soon I shall be earning well in excess of my keep, though not as much as in my initial profession."

"Which was?"

"Anesthesiologist."

"No kidding! What caused you to leave the profession?" Not that I believed him.

"My wife abruptly departed my abode, and her initiative in this respect impinged upon my job performance."

"Please talk plainly. I've heard enough verbal bullshit in my former profession to last two lifetimes."

"I thought you'd be impressed."

"Nope. You got plain food from me, so give me plain language in return. How did it happen?"

"She broke the news over a breakfast. Told me she'd been fucking some guy down the street for the previous four years, and that the guy's wife walked in on them unexpectedly the day before, just as my wife was wiping away residual semen from her lower lip. The bitch had to throw that in. Spiteful ultrabitch, that what she was. The guy's wife split immediately, and my soon-to-be ex back then, well, she informed me she was moving out, would be gone by the time I returned from work that evening. I felt trashed, but there were operations to attend to that morning. So I pushed her out of my psyche, figured I'd deal with that crap later. Unfortunately, I went three for five."

"Meaning what, exactly?"

"I ran five operations, three in general surgery, two obstetric situations. Lots of back-and-forth, checking readings, the usual routine, ordinarily no problem. But that morning I was fogged, couldn't think my way through an open door. I tallied three no-complications, one brand new mother permanently paralyzed from the waist down, and one triple-bypass stroke victim. Two monumental screwups, the worst one-day performance by an anesthesiologist anywhere, anytime. Until that morning my record had been unblemished, not one mistake in seventeen years. I had never even been sued. And then—well, between dismissal from my job, the lawsuits, and settling up accounts with the bitch, I was left with nothing. I went from one hundred and eighty thousand a year to zero a year, and it took just a few months to run through what was left, including the unemployment money. My whole goddamn life, gone in a flash."

"What a story. You really expect me to believe it?"

"As God is my witness, it's the truth. The whole truth I'm telling you, I swear it."

Such sincerity in his voice. Did he really think I'd sympathize with his behavior? Better if it was cock-and-bull.

"Do you feel any guilt?"

"About what?"

"About screwing up the lives of two people."

"Nope."

"Why not?"

"I'm too busy trying to survive. Guilt is a luxury of the fortunate."

"Busy? It looks to me like you spend your time sitting around Starbucks doing pretty much nothing."

"Not true. I may look tired, bored, or lost in thought, but I'm always on the prowl."

"For what?"

"Leftovers. Loose change, a fallen bill, someone to chat up. The

December before last, I spotted a wallet in the men's room. It was just sitting there under the sink. Pre-urination, it contained sixty-five dollars. Post, zero dollars. If I hadn't been sharp I would have missed it. It made a nice Christmas present to the self."

"Whoa. You didn't return it?"

"Shocked?"

"Truly I am. You're a petty thief."

"Gotta eat, right? It's that or die."

Or drink and die, I thought. "Ever get caught?"

"Never. I'm careful, and I stay away from big trouble."

"Like what?"

"Mugging and breaking into houses. I know guys who do that, but it's not my cup of tea. I hate violence, and jail freaks me out. I'd rather starve."

"Then I don't suppose you've ever killed someone."

Salvatore looked at me as if my coffee cup had transformed into a pitchfork, my head had sprouted horns, and my face had turned crimson.

"Forget it, man. I am not interested."

"What?"

"Thanks for the food, but I won't do that for any amount of money."

"Do what? Oh no, that's not what I meant."

"Now I get it! There really is no such thing as a free lunch, is there? Just stay away from me, far away, you got that?" Salvatore grabbed his McFlurry and hurried out the door.

I laughed my way back to the Manoir. An observer would have guessed that I was psychotic, in the throes of plotting the ultimate practical joke, or a village idiot, but in truth I was contemplating my new status as pariah's pariah. I derive comfort in knowing that from now on, making a total ass of myself is at worst a sideways move.

11:17 P.M. Saturday, August 23rd

This morning I successfully executed the first part of my plan, rapprochement, albeit with unexpected help. I took off for the library right after it opened. Shelley had explicitly forbidden me to approach her anywhere, anytime, but I was out of books. Even pariahs deserve to read a decent book or two every now and then, right? Librarians get that.

I entered, walked up the incline to and through the electronically monitored gate. Without looking to my left where the circulation desk was located, where she had to be sitting, I continued all the way to the library's far wall and then turned left into the fiction section. I selected eight of the fattest books I could find, working my way backward from the Z's to the M's: *The Yawning Heights, Infinite Jest, The Wandering Jew, Cryptonomicon, A Suitable Boy, Gravity's Rainbow,* and *The Man Without Qualities* in two volumes. Overkill. I could have knocked off eight residents by timing book drops from my windowsill just right.

With book bag filled to the brim I sauntered over to checkout, stopping on the way to examine the quick read and magazine shelves. I was as casual as a starched dinner jacket, as cool as a deep fried cucumber. Finally I arrived at my final destination, as they say on airplane flights. I huffed and puffed and hoisted the bag onto the countertop, all the while remaining as unflappable as a Japanese hand fan, as composed as Schubert's *Unfinished Symphony*. Out came the tomes one by one, and Shelley emitted an "ooh" after each.

"Quite a collection. Are they practice for your Evelyn Wood speed reading correspondence course?"

"How did you guess?" She half-smiled, so for some inexplicable reason I added, "I figured I'd be able to cut down on my trips here by taking out a lot of the big stuff all at once. That way you don't have to see me beyond the minimum." From the quickness with which her smile vanished it was apparent that my utterance did not create its intended effect.

"I see. One-stop shopping."

"Right. Even better would be a drive-in window, like at MacDonald's. If I owned a car I could drive up and ask for a Munro and a Murdoch to go, hold the Mailer, something like that." Why couldn't I have kept my mouth shut?

After she processed the books, she asked if I needed a taxi.

"No thanks. I'm not quite that feeble."

"Yet."

"Right."

"Okay then. Have a nice day."

Have a nice day? Granted, an improvement over "Fuck off, loser, I told you never to approach me again." Nevertheless the ice remained unbroken.

I hauled the books back to my room, took a nap, then had a quiet lunch with Harold and Mildred. Everything has returned to normal with Mildred. We established détente, thanks to a talk I had with Harold yesterday morning out on my bench. He came over and apologized for his wife's lack of tact.

"You know, she shouldn't have brought it up."

"I would have preferred that."

"But you know, she meant well. She wanted to show sympathy."

"What, by calling my friend a chippie?" My friend. Right.

"Yes that was bad. But you know, she didn't know what she was saying. She's not exactly a vocabularian."

I looked at Harold with mild disbelief and irritation—disbelief concerning the Mildred bit of information, irritation from all of his *you knows*.

"It's not the first time. She once dampened a dinner party by confusing expectorate with expound. She speaks French fluidly, by the way, that's how she describes it. Oh, and there was the time she accused my brother of being a master of oscillation."

"She meant obfuscation?"

"Either that or vacillation. Both would have worked."

After lunch I returned to my room, stuck my hand in the book bag, and blindly extracted one of the monstrosities. I walked out to my bench, sat down, and opened my hand's selection, which turned out to be *Cryptonomicon*. I had managed to read just a few pages, barely enough to go careening down Shanghai's Kiukiang Road on an out-of-control truck with Corporal Bobby Shaftoe and Private Wiley, when everything went black. A pair of soft hands shielded my eyes from the sun, and I felt fragrant and abundant hair against my left temple.

"Been faithful to me? Because if you've been fucking the residence chicks I'm gonna have to cut your dick off." Now *that* qualifies as breaking the ice.

Shelley sat down next to me. Her newly blonde hair fired up the blackest blouse I had ever seen. Silver earrings, tight jeans. How come I didn't notice those attributes this morning? Anyway, I wanted to kiss her. I did not, of course, but I really wanted to, very much I did.

She took the book from me, rifled through it and said, "I read it during a bathroom break two years ago."

"Anything you can read, I can read faster," I replied. "I'll have it done in the time it takes a slow chicken to cross the road. It's Zinoviev tonight as a chaser. And to what, incidentally, do I owe your presence?"

"I was noodged into coming. Bubba torture, as those of the Jewish persuasion say."

"Really? By who?"

"One of your residence chicks. A petite sparrow."

Mildred, no doubt, all one hundred seventy pounds of her.

"She droned on and on, said you were depressed, maybe borderline suicidal. She claimed your fate would be on her conscience for the rest of her days—"

"If you didn't finish me off yourself?"

"Precisely. In truth, your company ranks two or three notches above *meh*. I might even seek it out again sometime. That is, if."

"If I don't bring it up?"

"Exactly. But do feel free to make an ass of yourself in other manifold ways. I've always appreciated your inventiveness in that respect."

"But why give up when you still have a chance? You know that you do, don't you?"

She shrugged. "I don't want the struggle."

"But—" Shelley raised an upright left index finger to her lips.

"Okay." My shortest lie. "No need to pin me down and sit on my chest. I give."

"Just to let you know, I've taken steps to maximize my well-being."

"How so?"

"I'm following the alternative route. Number one, I'm a macro girl these days. It's barley, bulghur, brown rice, Brussels sprouts and beans for me. I feel brilliant except for when I'm farting, which happens maybe thirty-seven percent of the time."

"An alliterative diet. I approve absolutely."

"And second, I'm seeing Mr. Chong the acupuncturist."

"*The* Mr. Chong?" I said, with just the slightest hint of sarcasm in my voice.

"He works out of his apartment, a building down from mine. It's helping with the night sweats."

Isn't that sweet? Her cancer continues to degrade her body, but at least she'll sleep a little better at night. That's like filling a cavity right before getting your head chopped off. I need a plan, and I need it fast.

9:30 P.M. Thursday, August 28th

She came by unexpectedly this morning, with a book, a blanket, and two words by way of introduction: "Day off!" We went to the park for a morning's read.

Though the diagnosis came in thirty-eight days ago, the only change I've noticed is the color of her hair. I'm surprised. She knows that without treatment her yearly life expectancy is limited to single digits. Other than a few minor food and pincushion interventions, however, she hasn't broken from routine. She is either in denial or understands the truth of the matter more deeply than doomed bucket-listers who frantically spend their final months shoehorning in half a lifetime's worth of experiences.

Given impending death, would you opt for the inward or the outward path? Most people would choose outwardness if they could afford it. The outward man is a traveler, a risk taker, a devourer of people, food, money, and occasionally also of books, movies, and music. He strives for a full life, which by definition becomes the good life. "To hell with all of those ascetic Buddhist monks," he asserts. "What do they know? They accomplish nothing, other than making an art out of accomplishing nothing. Follow the maximalist path instead. Look back near the end and proudly reflect: I did it! It was worth it, because I'm full. I experienced, I learned, I disturbed people, shook things up. Maybe I'll even be remembered."

Shelley is no bucket-lister. She would rather read a book than go to Paris or experience the Milky Way on a moonless night from the Sahara. About an hour into our reads she interrupted, told me that her mother once scolded her for being more interested in books than in life.

"Reading is no substitution for living," her mother had said.

"Sounds like a decent tradeoff to me," Shelley had replied. I murmured my assent perfunctorily, as I was enmeshed in the intricacies of Van Eck phreaking as explicated in *Cryptonomicon*.

Just before we walked into town for lunch, she came up with an imaginative but ridiculous assertion. She told me that reading a good book is like having good sex.

"Isn't entering a book the same as entering a woman?" We were sitting on a bench bordering the children's playground. One bench over, an attentive new mother was nursing her baby.

"No. Not even for the ultra-literate."

"Sure it is."

"Sorry. I don't see it."

"In both cases, you immerse yourself. You go in. Your tunnel vision gets the best of you, and nothing else matters."

"I used to own a car. Was entering my garage the same as fucking?"

"That's different."

The mom next-bench-over giggled. Her baby, momentarily disengaged from mom's nipple, howled.

"So then, is the hallmark of great sex, and of great reading for that matter, the total obliteration of one's concern with dying?"

"Not a bad definition, unless you're reading something like *Death in Venice*. But you're missing an important connection, Carl."

"Which is?"

"Which is that books have souls, just as we do. When you're reading a book, you're not alone. It's unfortunate that books can't cry 'you're hurting me' when dumb-oxen read them the wrong way."

"Oh come on, Shelley. Books are nothing more than paper, glue, and bindings. They don't have souls."

"Then people are nothing more than water, organs, bones and toenails. People are things, just like books are things. And if people have souls, so do books."

Someone I knew long ago once volunteered the following advice: "Life is meant to be lived in the moment." By that criterion, this morning was about as good as it gets. But looking forward, it was a failure. Another day has passed and we're twenty-four hours closer to the moment when her disease takes irreversible hold. What must I do to get her into treatment, buy her a bookstore?

4:32 P.M. Tuesday, September 2nd

We lunched at the Gascogne today. The tables were all taken, so we sat at the counter facing Sherbrooke Street. Below us, on the other side of the window and under the Gascogne's big red awning, two elderly women enjoyed the great outdoors, Westmount style. They conversed, drank tea, and shared pastry morsels with a slobbery black Labrador retriever. Off to the right, a bum whose summer cottage is the bench down the block rifled through detritus abandoned by a family of five. Faster than a speeding bullet he whisked up a twoonie and a third of a dead sandwich. Yum.

As I was about to bite into my own baguetted *jambon et fromage*, Shelley said, "Do me a favor and tell me a little about your wife."

"Why?"

"Curious."

"There isn't much of a story. We met in the winter of 1965 and married three years and five months later. She died in 1982, struck by a snow plow while jogging. Freak accident was the *Gazette* reporter's term."

"Eew. Jesus, I'm sorry."

"It's okay. Happened a long time ago."

"Yeah, but still—"

"You know what sticks in my mind most?"

"What?"

"The policemen. Right before dinnertime on the evening of Thursday, January 14th, these two cops pulled up in front of the house. Laurel and Hardy in uniform. The thin one broke the news to me in what charitably might be described as broken English, and the other one, the one who looked like a Dunkin' Donuts test crash dummy, well, what an imbecile. He said that according to the snow plow operator, Renata didn't suffer. She died instantly, never knew what hit her. Her death was better than cancer, that's exactly how he phrased it. Imagine that. I can recite the whole conversation if you'd like."

"That's okay. I'm beginning to see the drawbacks of having a great memory. But why was your wife out jogging in a snowstorm?"

"Renata was the original fitness nut. She jogged everyday, in summer during thunderstorms and in winter through snow and over ice. She was more stubborn than anyone I ever knew."

"Was that part of the attraction?"

"Hell no. She claimed that the running kept her sane. The lie in that sentence is the word "sane." The truth of the matter is that exercise made her slightly less bananas. She was bipolar, but instead of zooming up and down the manic-depressive continuum, she fluctuated wildly between placidity and rage, never pausing for long anywhere close to the middle."

"A real loose cannon, eh?"

"Let me put it this way: in our idyllic nuclear family of one girl, one boy, a father, and a mother, the mother doubled as the warhead."

"Living with her must have been quite the challenge. Did you ever think of leaving?"

"The thought never entered my mind."

"Masochist."

"Maybe, maybe not. She had some positive aspects."

"Like?"

"Fierce loyalty to all of us, and warmth during her peaceful episodes. The sex was good, especially excellent when she was angry, though it was rarer then. And I appreciated how she ran the show with an iron fist."

"That's a positive?"

"Definitely. After she died, home life became unrelentingly exhausting, frustrating, and depressing. I battled with my kids over everything—homework, food, curfews, suitability of certain friends in the case of Helen, number of hours per day allotted to Michael's Nintendo addiction, ambient noise levels throughout the house, and so on. Had Renata lived, I would have accumulated a few hundred additional hours of sleep over the years."

"But everything eventually settled down, right?"

"Yeah, after five or six years of them running me ragged. They, I, or we matured. Now they're okay, except for occasionally erring on the self-important know-it-all side."

"Totally unlike their father."

"You got that right."

A couple of yellow jackets buzzed an abandoned Coke can left on one of the tables outside, sparking an outlandish idea—not ridiculous, mind you, just unexpected in the extreme. I'll give it some thought.

11:29 P.M. Thursday, September 11th

I despise the term "intergenerational." I associate it with tutoring, choir singing, and hootenannies held in church basements throughout mid-western states having names with three-to-one vowel-consonant ratios. "Intergenerational" is not sexy. Even worse is the phrase "intergenerational romance." Only a pedophile could appreciate it.

I am a hell of a lot less disgusting than most octogenarian males. I retain all but one of my teeth, not counting wisdoms, and the missing one used to be three-quarters of the way back on the right side of my mouth, where no one but my dentist could note its absence. No dentures for me. My breath is good, and I religiously use my Edge-Trimmer Super Pro Plus to clip away stray nose, ear, and eyebrow strands. I do not want to be mistaken for one of those ancient guys who sprout facial hairs in all the wrong places.

I stand straight up, and my thighs and legs are strong. Take a photo of my posterior from the waist down and there is no way I could be mistaken for anyone older than sixty. Make that fifty. No thin and flabby thighs on me, no matchstick legs either. I am toned for my age.

Who am I kidding? Woody Woodpecker I am not, and eighty-three minus twenty-six is way too big a number.

3:45 P.M. *Monday, September 15th*

For the hell of it I conducted a little internet research on erectile dysfunction remedies this morning. The first thing I learned is that they do not always work. Prospects are so-so for men over ninety. Second thing: one is more likely to go blind from them than from masturbation.

The drug names are a series of subliminal jokes. Levitra evokes levitate plus raise, though it also stands in for a girl's name, as in Levitra the gypsy sylph, or Levitra the Puerto Rican beauty: *Levitra...Levitra...I just met a pill named Levitra.* And let's not forget Levitra, irresistible jailbait: *Le-vi-tra: tap-tap-tap, past the palate and down the gullet you go. Fire up my loins.*

Viagra. The 'gr' combo confers the word with teeth. It elicits the word, "vigor." Add an E and you've got the anagram of "I ravage." Maybe Viagra appeals to the caveman mentality, whereas Cialis and Levitra cater to more sophisticated metrosexual types.

I've seen most of the commercials, and what irritates me is not that the men in them are young, nor that their women are hot, nor that there are no gay or transgendered ads, nor even that the advertising business model for these pills is based on the supposition that when a man observes his woman dancing on one foot, singing with headphones on, or cooking up a storm, the urge to fuck her rising from within his balls expands as rapidly and as assuredly as steam rushing from an overheated tea kettle. I'm not even upset by that idiotic phrase, "when the time is right," always timed right after the two of them smile goofily at each other.

No, what bothers me is that the drug companies engage in false advertising. On the surface, they sell dick levitation pills. Actually, however, they are in the insurance business. You see, it's not just a matter of blood flow. It's a matter of making sure you don't fuck up, ever. The pharmaceuticals know that at any age a guy can have an off-day. After, he worries about it. A second off-day follows, then a third. Pretty soon all of his days are off. Never fear, however, because now there's this little pill that takes care of the off-days. Swallow and you've got backup. You're insured, just like a good neighbor. Never fear, because your dick will automatically snap to attention faster than you can say Messalina three times running.

Here's what an impotence pill commercial should look like:

The camera pans across an upscale living room—wood paneled bookcases, stereo, fifty-inch digital television. Oriental carpets and a bear rug cover the floor, bottles filled with green, red, amber, and clear liquids glimmer off in the distance. There you have it, the entire upper middle class shtick effectively encapsulated in ten or fifteen seconds. Now throw in some smarm-laden saxophone music. A lot of people think that crap is sexy. I think "The Ride of the Valkyries" is sexy. I'm right.

Croaky moans and groans drown out the music as the camera zooms in on the high back of a dark leather couch. It hazes out momentarily, then hones in with the sharpness of a katakana. Aha! Now we see them plain as day, two horny octogenarians getting it on. The cameraman spares their nakedness, thank goodness, but not their ancientness—all those wrinkles, gray areas, bare patches where hair should be, sudden stiff joint movements. They writhe and sweat and pant like there's no tomorrow, and then she delivers the commercial's sole line of dialogue: "What the bejeezus Bertram, you're harder than buffed chromium." The narrator intones a deadeye imitation of Jimmy Stewart's creaky eighty-year-old voice: "Cialis. For when it's not too late."

My goodness, that would sell pills by the bucketful.

9:45 P.M. Tuesday, September 16th

We spent last night at the movies, saw a Hollywood romantic comedy called *It's All in Your Mind*. What a movie. What a plot. Tony and Doris live at opposite ends of Philadelphia. He's a radiologist working out of an inner city hospital, she's a beautician in a seniors residence. Both are timidly bi-curious. They do not act on their impulses, but because unfulfilled desires strengthen over time, at least they do in Hollywood movies, our hero and heroine are both driven to action.

Their solutions are identical. Both join the same online dating service, and both falsify their genders. Tony disguises himself as Maria, an unpublished romance novelist. Doris presents herself to the fictional Maria as Donald, a zoo keeper with affections for lions, tigers, and large birds. "Maria" and "Donald" progress from introductory emails to long tell-me-all-about-yourself messages, then on to pornographic story telling, and finally to out-and-not-so-out cybersex. Thanks to their fictional alter egos, Tony and Doris get their homoerotic rocks off night after night. There are some amusing moments in the cybersex scenes, including one in which Tony, typing excitedly at the speed of light with one hand, forgets that his penis is now a vagina. Fortunately, no harm comes of it.

All is fine within their insulated little worlds until, in a coincidence that could occur only in the movies, the lovers accompany their gay friends to the same gay bar on the same night and at the same hour. Through a series of tortuously contrived incidents that I will not recount, Tony and Doris stumble upon the truth. They are appalled. Their relationship shatters, thus establishing the conditions permitting the movie to adhere to the classic

Hollywood romantic comedy formula: boy must lose girl before regaining her, and both boy and girl must suffer and learn valuable lessons before achieving permanent bliss in each other's arms.

In the end, everything turns out hunky-dory. The couple's conniving friends successfully conspire to reunite them, and once back together, the two protagonists realize that they love each other as people even more than they lust after each other as bogus sex objects. They marry and drive off into the sunset. But in the movie's final moment, set in their house a few months later, they kiss goodnight before retiring to offices at opposite ends of the house. They then log on.

For ninety-five minutes we sat in the dark. Sometimes she rested her head on my shoulder, and once, for a minute, I considered stretching my arm over her chair, like you're supposed to do in a movie theater.

1:45 A.M. Thursday, September 18th

"Little did you suspect"—*thunderclapitus interruptus*—"that I'd put your life in danger today," Shelley shouted. We were sitting side by side, yet I could barely hear her through the racket.

Like many gazebos in the Chinese style, the roof of the Pavilion of Infinite Pleasantness was made of sharply descending curved pipes arranged in parallel strips. The pipes were coated with a metallic gray substance that amplified the hard rain striking it. Water racing through troughs between the pipes splayed out at the edges, creating curtains of droplets that melded light from dozens of lanterns into a haze of orange. A few minutes earlier hundreds of people had been wandering along the dirt and stone pathways of the Botanical Garden's Chinese Garden. At the first lightning-thunder salvo, however, they scattered like birds panicking from a gunshot blast. Some sought refuge in the big Friendship Hall, but most scurried to their cars or to public transport.

"I don't suppose there's a lightning rod up there," I shouted back.

"Doubt it. Humor me and close your eyes."

"Why?"

"Don't worry, I'm not going to do anything obscene."

I did as she wished. She then grasped my right hand with her left and yelled, "My eyes are shut too. It's just you and me, and we're in the middle of the Atlantic. We're rocking in the storm, and our little sailboat bounces around in the wind, struggling to stay upright." We locked arms and swayed back and forth slowly, at odds with being battered by a great storm.

It was Shelley's idea to flip the quarter: moose and we take the Sherbrooke Street bus west to God knows where; Queen Elizabeth and we head eastward. Queen Elizabeth it was. We got off at the Botanical Gardens and walked to the Chinese Lantern Festival, arriving at what would have been twilight on a normal day. On this day, however, heavy cloud cover had darkened the setting to midnight.

The storm subsided to a mist. The wind died,, and the lanterns, hanging from trees all around us and glowing like oversized irradiated tangerine lollipops, were as still as statues. The pond, glass. Even the few humans who stuck it out caught the feeling, for they moved slowly and hardly spoke. Neither did we on the bus ride back. Shelley looked out at the buildings, cars, cyclists, and people walking their dogs while I looked at her every now and then, wondering how she will react when I inform her of my morning's initiative. It was presumptuous, outlandish, impulsive, and possibly upsetting, but nevertheless logical. It had to be done. It's the only way forward, thus I took the only rational course of action. *Alea iacta est.*

8:42 P.M. Wednesday, September 24th

"Before I rise from my throne and relinquish authority as Librarian and Grand Poobah Dispenser of Books on this sixteenth hour of the twenty-fourth day of the ninth month of the year Two Thousand and Eight of our Savior—well, of your savior, maybe—in my official capacity, dear sir, how may I assist you? Might you have books to check out? Perhaps you have removed a volume or three from our pornography section and are hiding said volume or volumes in your briefcase to forestall shocking our staff? Never fear, for we librarians are made of stern stuff. We classify such items as erotica, and they have their own Dewey Decimal number: six nine dot oh six nine."

Shelley batted her eyelashes at me a couple of times, causing the adolescent girl seated next to her at the circulation desk, probably a staff member's bring-your-child-to-work victim, to roll her eyes.

"Dewey, eh?" I said. "How do you spell Dewey?"

"Why D-E-W-Y, sir. Or the alternate: D-O space W-E, question mark."

"Thank you for the suggestion, miss. I'll make sure to peruse the aforementioned section next time. But for now I'd like to show *you* something."

"Goodness, sir, not here! Please defer until we are amongst the bushes."

"Gag me." From the girl.

As we exited the library I said, "This way. I do indeed have something for you to see." We walked eastward across the park.

Fifty yards from Melville Avenue: "Seriously, Carl, where are you taking me?"

"Patience, we're almost there." I dug a key out from my shorts and pointed to the left half of a large semi-detached brick house across the street from us.

"We enter through the garage. I rented it. The top floor, that is."

"Ooh. Another escape from Manoir Zenda, this time for good!"

"You don't think I belong at the Manoir?"

"With those fogies? Hell no."

Shelley latched on my arm. "Take me in."

"That's the plan. Then you can tell me what a mistake I've made."

"Doubt it, except what the hell were you thinking when you rented the *top* half? You've got stairs to negotiate, and your clattering clankety cane is going to drive the people below batty."

I punched in the code on a keypad located to the right of the garage door. Once inside the hallway, I pointed to the elevator door a few feet away.

"Please press the button for me. I'm too feeble."

"What the hell did you pay for this place?" I said nothing, just smiled.

Shelley bapped the button with her closed fist, setting off a slowly expanding machine fart, a soft whoosh of air expelled with the utmost evenness of release. "Going up," proclaimed an officious female voice, to which Shelley responded, "Duh."

I like a hermetically sealed ambiance, and this place has it. The sensation captivated me the first time I felt it, right after the elevator door clicked shut. That toasty tucked-in feeling gets me every time. The real estate agent chattered on and on about the corridor's magical glow emanating from track lighting comprised of thirty-one blue crystal flowers. She pointed out the corridor's immaculate hardwood floor, asked me to consider the superb condition of a series of narrow red and black oriental carpet runners covering its midsection, raved about the kitchen's granitic countertops, praised the newly installed windows and their pale pink kimono motorized blinds, glorified the elegant furniture, and attested to the firmness of the king bed in the master bedroom. Nice, but what sold me was the elevator's click-and-whoosh. This house has deluxe soundproofing, at least as good as that of a coffin padded with layers of Corinthian leather. Do they really manufacture leather in Corinth?

The elevator door slid open and we were confronted with the

glowering visage of an oversized blue-point Siamese cat on the wall opposite us. It stared at us from behind its glass home with a wild pre-pounce expression. The cat's owner had affixed a brass plaque to the bottom of the frame: "Puffers, 1966-1979. RIP, you little devil." Who the hell names their cat Puffers?

Six more framed photos of felines lined the walls. They included such luminaries as Jimbo, an orange tabby with a sleepy look and overabundant whiskers ("1994-2007. RIP, sweet pussy"), Snort, a mean looking house cat with a white stripe down its tummy, kind of a skunk in reverse ("1980-1986. RIP you stupid car chaser"), and Puffers II, another blue-point who looked even fiercer than the original Puffers as it bit into the base of an unfortunate birch tree ("1986-2001. RIP sweetheart, love of my life").

"It's furnished."

"But no cats anymore, right?"

"Correct. I'm not a fan of kitty litter."

The corridor extended seventy feet—sixty to a closed door at the front of the house, ten to another one behind us. A third door was located halfway between them.

"Which door would you like to take me through first?"

I walked to the door at the back of the house and opened it. "This one. Come, have a look at the kitchen. It's modest, but adequate."

Her reaction upon entering the room: "Oh my God. Modest my ass! What do you have here?"

A stainless steel double sink built into a strip of countertop resembling an overexposed photographic concatenation of the Grand Canyon and pralines-and-cream ice cream. Above the sink, a large window overlooking the backyard. In the center of the kitchen, a fancy cooktop mounted on what decorators call an island. Directly to the right upon entering the room, gleamy stainless steel appliances and several banks of built-in wooden cabinets lining two walls. Shelley pressed a button to the right of one of the cabinets. Its front panel rotated, revealing pewter goblets on one shelf and eight dinner bells on the shelf above it. She rang them from biggest to smallest, producing an ascending minor scale.

"It's an impressive space. You could do some serious cooking here."

"Yup. I could nuke Kraft dinners to perfection."

The middle door opened to a windowless suite partitioned in quarters: bathroom and bedroom to the left, dining area and study to the right. The bathroom was outfitted in black marble and included toilet, sink, shower, whirlpool bath, and bidet. The rest of the suite was nondescript.

"I'm hungry," I said. "Let's grab a bite. We can see what's behind the remaining door some other time."

"No way! I'm opening the last door."

"Ah the last door!" I made threatening clawlike motions with both hands, as if executing a miser's dog paddle. In my snarliest voice I growled, "That's forbidden."

Shelley laughed and ran down the hall. I yelled, "Don't trip over the skeletons."

She flung the door open and sunlight illuminated the corridor, darkened only in the shadow of her silhouette.

"Jesus H!" She vanished into the room.

"It's the master bedroom," I said.

"As opposed to the tiny slave bedroom we just saw, no doubt about it."

The room was impressive enough, what with its large dimensions, huge bed, and bloodwood floor, not to mention a sitting area comprised of a square teak table and a couple of easy chairs. The four huge bay windows made it unique, however. They occupied eighty percent of the wall facing the park.

"Fabulous. No cats, right? That's what you said."

"No cats."

"But cats lived here for the last, what, thirty years?"

"Longer."

"Aw. You do know that this place is incomplete without a pussy in it, don't you?" She smiled and batted her eyelashes again.

"I'll disregard your essentialist construction of the female sex for the moment, my dear, just long enough to tell you that I am in complete agreement. This place is for you. Not for us and not for me. Just for you and only for you."

She stared at me, displayed four signs of astonishment simultaneously: mouth wide open, raised eyebrows, instantaneous flush of the cheeks, taut neck.

"Did I hear you right? I just want to know which of us is nuts."

"Speaking for myself, I'm perfectly sane."

"But how could I possibly...You're paying for the whole thing?"

"For as long as you want it. The first year's lease is already signed, so please take it. And don't fear for your privacy. I'll respect it, just as I always have. No sudden visits, nothing like that ever."

I walked to the window and looked into Westmount Park. To my right a dozen healthy children splashed around in the wading pool. On a nearby bench a healthy adolescent boy held hands with a healthy adolescent girl. To my left healthy men vied kicking a soccer ball.

"I figure if you insist on going out for good, you might as well do it in style. Please, pretty please, don't say no."

From behind, she embraced me. "Thank you," she whispered.

"Very welcome."

"When do I move in?"

"In a week. I've arranged for the movers to pack up your stuff next Tuesday. On Wednesday they'll move it over. Are you okay with that?"

She said nothing, just nodded and smiled a little.

Whew. I'm relieved.

10:50 P.M. Wednesday, October 1st

She cried when the movers took off. She had been fine, cheery even while they were hauling out the boxes, but when they drove off and the apartment was bare, she just sat on that raggedy old carpet, looked around at the emptiness, and bawled her eyes out.

"Why can't you be younger?"

I caught myself, didn't say what I was thinking: *Why can't you be healthier?* I sat down on the floor next to her, said, "I'd sell my soul to the devil to be your age again."

"The devil's a figment, Carl."

"I know. If I believed in him I wouldn't be an atheist." That comment yielded a smile from her.

"Seriously, there are fine younger fish in the sea."

"Most are rotten."

"But some aren't. Go find yourself a good one, and when you do, we'll rejoice together."

She hugged me, then cried another river. Damn, the house isn't enough. If I don't get her into treatment soon, it will become nothing more than a lovely hospice.

11:22 P.M. Friday, October 10th

I share my room here at the Trapp Family Lodge with Michael, who presently is absent. Helen and Frank reside next door, and Shelley has a room to herself, three doors down. I surmise she has company.

Leaf season is in full bloom. Why should she miss out, especially as she may not be around for another? I suggested the trip and she said yes. As neither she nor I own a car, we needed some unsuspecting stooge to transport us to and fro. That's when I came up with the brilliant idea. I asked Michael, told him I'd pay for everything. Wonder of wonders, he said yes. He even suggested that Helen and Frank join us. Wouldn't it be nice of me to offer them a mini-vacation in advance of the arrival of my granddaughter? Yes, a girl it is going to be.

After lunch the five of us went walking. We took the same trail I followed twelve springs ago, when I hiked with a woman whom I might have been courting. Back then, plant life expressed variations on life's color, green. The fern palms, shrubs, bushes, and leaves surrounding us ranged from the paleness of celadon, tea, and moss to the dark mysteries of viridian and myrtle. Today, however, the canopy was painted broader. Dead leaves blazed yellow, orange, red, amber, cyan, and shades in between and beyond. Do a color association with the word *death* and most folks respond with black. Incorrect. Death is gray skin. It is brown eyes turned blue, orange flames dancing through burning wood, puffs of superheated brown stardust framing the aquamarine core of a supernova.

Shelley and Michael walked faster than the rest of us, and after a short while they had moved beyond eavesdropping distance. Though I had no idea what they were talking about, I recognized an animation in Shelley that was beyond my power to provoke. Goth Girl and Mr. Normal may be hitting it off.

After half an hour, I had had enough. My left knee ached, and I wanted to return to the Stephenson book. I called to Shelley and Michael, told them I was heading back.

"Go on, have a great hike!"

Damned creaky voice. I sounded like a yodeler in an anechoic chamber. Helen and Frank turned back as well, but Michael and Shelley kept going. They didn't show up until just before dinner, ninety minutes later.

From my window I see a three-quarter moon hanging high and clear over a bank of clouds. The clouds hover over a ridge of hills on the other side of the road, far beyond any of the Trapp buildings. The gently undulating curves of the hills suggest the outline of a woman's body as she lies on her side, facing away from me. I will not be jealous. Too much is on the line for that kind of stupidity.

It is disrespectful to place the body inside a coffin face down, yet many people prefer to sleep that way. Why is that?

3:40 P.M. Saturday, October 11th

The Trapp is ideal for reading. A dozen Adirondack chairs, suitable for those of bookish persuasion, grace a tightly cropped lawn adjacent to the restaurant. I am sitting in one of them. Perfect. Courtesy of the sun and my sweatshirt, I feel neither too hot nor too cold. Should no one speak to me over the next hour and I feel no urge to urinate, my day will be made.

I am situated exactly where I should be situated. My certainty is a consequence of the Adirondack's largeness, its wide armrests, and the foreknowledge that rising from it would require appreciable effort. I sit in a chair that is good for my moral fiber, one that is the antithesis of plushness. I value the hardness of its wooden slats supporting my back. Adirondacks with cushions are abominations.

My beat-up hat rests on my head at a jaunty angle. How can an angle be jaunty? By not being parallel to the ground. I suppose the jaunty angle makes *me* jaunty. Ah yes, I am an eighty-three-year-old man sitting in a stiff wooden chair, a big book covers most of an armrest, and my hat says devil-may-care. This is the life.

9:12 P.M. Thursday, October 30th

We've settled into a routine. I walk Shelley home after work, or we go for coffee and pastries. On the way, she debriefs me. Today a prepubescent girl checked out *The Unbearable Lightness of Being*, a bum got kicked out even though he was perusing Renaissance art books discreetly, two setoffs were triggered by patrons who forgot to engage with circulation before leaving, and a false fire alarm briefly emptied the place.

Then comes my turn. Today's news: I got up, washed, dressed, had breakfast, went bowling with the prime minister, arbitraged Indian currency differentials in three markets to eke out a seven hundred thousand dollar profit, celebrated by having a smoked meat sandwich, fries, and sours at the Snowdon Deli, and took my usual power nap right after returning to the Manoir. I do not visit Shelley in the evenings, nor on weekends.

Renata would have screamed at me even more vociferously than the time I bought Michael a cap gun, a month into his Judy Blume phase. She handled that one with remarkable aplomb. Yep, with a suaveness befitting Cary Grant at his most charming she took a hammer to that poor little gun and smashed it into tiny little pieces while repeatedly yelling, "There will be no fucking guns in this house, not now and not ever," along with numerous additional utterances conveying the same idea. Good thing the kids were at school.

In the present circumstance, her tonsils would have quivered with indignation. She would have asked me how in God's name I could have come up with such an idiotic plan. Fix our son up with a woman who is HIV-positive? What the fuck was I thinking?

"How ever could you have imagined putting our son in such jeopardy? What if a condom breaks? And how can they have children without taking a chance on transmitting the HIV virus from her to him? Not to mention, did you ever stop to think about Michael's happiness? How is he going to feel after she pops off?"

Renata, shut up already. The truth is I gave no thought whatsoever to Michael's wellbeing. Deal with it.

11:59 P.M. Friday, October 31st

Trick or treat? At the Manoir tonight, Halloween was a nonevent. None of the ladies dressed up as witches for dinner, no geezers wore werewolf masks. No baskets of corn candy and Kit Kats and Glosettes were laid out on our tables, no orange and black streamers hung from ceilings, and no gap-toothed pumpkins, lit up orange from candles stuck in their innards, greeted visitors at the Manoir's entrance.

With proper notice we could have lured a hundred little brats here. They would have run up and down the halls, banged on doors, and shouted "Trick or treat?" The entertainment quotient would have totaled up to a big number here at the old folks home, because some scary characters inhabit the premises, characters that make Vincent Price look like the Buddha baby. We'd frighten the hell out of those kids, and they'd love it. Instead, the somnolence-inducing operations of our collective digestive systems remained unperturbed, permitting the usual post-supper sedateness to prevail. It's too fucking quiet around here. I am trapped in a communal sarcophagus.

I got my treat, though, and in spades. Michael stopped by on his way to pick up Shelley. I felt vaguely nauseous when he told me they would be visiting New York City for a few days, but then he added that she will be starting chemo sometime in the next two or three weeks.

HALLELUJAH!

11:12 P.M. Monday, November 17th

My existence has become little more than connective tissue linking Shelley's medical visits. Everything else drifts by unregistered. For the first time since I was a teenager, I've let my memory for the incidentals go to seed. I have no idea what I had for lunch as recently as three days ago. Egg salad sandwich? Sushi? Who cares?

I remember the appointments, though. There have been three: a PET/CT scan eleven days ago, a follow-up consultation with the oncologist five days after, and today's commencement of R-CHOP, Shelley's chemotherapy.

As Shelley's previous scan was taken over three months ago, Dr. Vaincoeur required another. I insisted on a private clinic, figuring she would find the experience less stressful than in a hospital and that we would get a quick appointment. Dr. Vaincoeur recommended a place on Guy Street, Michael cased it out, and I paid the bill. In the waiting room the two of them sat together on a couch opposite me. They whiled away the time playing a Shelley original, Fruits and Vegetables Geography. Whenever Michael got stumped he would kiss Shelley's neck, whisper endearments, hold her hands, and otherwise carry on with a fawning solicitousness that I approve of without reservation. Never before have I seen such warmth from my son. Incidentally, I'm reacting well, devoid of even the tiniest of jealousy twinges.

The oncology consultation involved just Shelley and me, as Michael had to work. Dr. Vaincoeur wasted no time in informing us that Shelley remains a straight-up stage III.

"Woohoo!" From me, not her. She flashed me a reproachful look, as if I had whooped my exclamation in a crowded movie theater at the exact moment Humphrey touches Ingrid's downcast cheek, she looks up, and he says, "Here's looking at you, kid." I shrugged and smiled in response, as if to let her know there was no way I could have restrained myself.

I've met Dr. Gilles Vaincoeur a few times now, and on every occasion he's emanated the same vibe: detachment. I thought oncologists would score high on the empathy dimension. Not him. He is a paragon of the dispassionate. Mind you, he is neither mean nor cruel. He is, simply, a black hole. Tall, thin, and sporting a neatly trimmed moustache and goatee, he reminds me of El Greco's portrait of St. James, who comports an expressionless expression conveying neither hope nor despair. I wonder if cancer doctors acquire the persona with experience. Maybe dispassion is the best way to present the R-CHOP regimen to a patient.

I knew about R-CHOP from my summer's research. It didn't sound so bad back then. True, the first day isn't a picnic. The patient sits patiently, oh so patiently, while four drugs, R-CHO, drip into her body through a cannula connected to the insides of one of her veins.

She washes it all down with a pill, a steroid called prednisone. On days two through five she swallows the pill. Sixteen days of recovery follow. Repeat six to eight times in succession and it's over with. Total treatment time thus varies from four to five and one-half months. Afterward, the patient undergoes a scan revealing that the disease has been obliterated. She is rewarded for her suffering with the promise of a life removed from imminent threat. It's as simple as that.

Shelley asked Dr. Vaincoeur about side effects. *Side effect*—a euphemism if there every was one. Side, as in less important. Side orders, sideshows. He was married and getting some on the side. Back in July, I looked up side effect on the internet. The technical term is adverse effect. There are two kinds, the adverse effect and the serious adverse effect. Death, permanent damage, and birth defects comprise the serious category. I should think so.

The R-CHOP run-of-the-mill side effect list is long. It includes infection, bruising, bleeding, nausea, vomiting, diarrhea, mouth and lip sores, pain in swallowing, rashes, blisters, and headache, not to mention darkening of the skin and of the fingernails. Many patients become anxious and depressed, and a chosen few come down with a condition called steroid psychosis.

Fortunately, Dr. Vaincoeur is not an insensitive man. Aware that Shelley might again refuse treatment were he to be brutally frank, he soft-pedaled it a little. He described the hair loss first, because it's universally expected. He then mentioned the symptoms that can be dealt with pharmacologically, such as constipation, headache, and nausea, without adding that sometimes the drugs either don't work or have side effects of their own. He refrained from bringing up a few of the more distasteful symptoms, ones that a woman would find particularly distressing because they degrade her desirability: facial sores, rashes, blisters, and skin discolorations. Finally, he withheld from Shelley his expectation that her first R-CHOP experience would be the easiest, and that later rounds would require her to contend with progressively greater amounts of discomfort, pain, and psychological displacement.

Today's visit spanned all of the daylight hours: check-in at the hospital early in the morning, a long wait, consultations with two nurses, a quick visit from Dr. Vaincoeur, forty minutes of prep and hookup, and the main course: an anti-nauseant appetizer in pill form followed by the gentle but ultraslow pumping of four drugs into a vein located on the underside of Shelley's right forearm. She spent the first part of the afternoon alternating between talking with us and reading a novel, *Malone Dies*. Dark as the title is, I've never seen Shelley laugh as hard as when she had her nose buried in that book.

As the sun lowered, so did her spirits. She complained of nausea and headache, especially during a rugged last half-hour. They gave her a couple of pills, but neither provided much relief, not even by the time we returned to the house.

"Jesus I feel so sick. This is going to be worth it, right?" Shelley asked her question in the taxi. The driver had just hit a pothole, and the bump nearly made her throw up.

"Piece of cake," I said.

"Given my current state, that's a hell of an analogy!"

"Oh, sorry, my dear. What I meant was this: try to look past the immediate present. Think ahead. In half a year you'll regard all of this crap as a blip."

"Exactly," Michael added.

I know, putter-putter stuff, but what else could we say? She asked for reassurance and we gave it.

Michael tends to Shelley tonight, and I take over in the morning. Doc says she stays home tomorrow, no matter how swell she feels. Good. I expect her to sleep well tonight and feel much better when she gets up. We'll have a fine time hanging out.

9:39 P.M. Tuesday, November 18th

When I arrived this morning, Michael told me that Shelley had crashed into sleep only a half-hour earlier. She had spent the night reading, watching TV, taking frequent trips to the bathroom, and, at 4:30 A.M., walking twice around the park with him. Despite having taken a sleeping pill and a melatonin wafer, her persistent headache delayed loss of consciousness. Michael looked pretty haggard himself, but he had to go to work. He'll be fine. He has a couch in his office.

Shelley slept straight through daylight while I alternated between reading, eating, and catnaps. The good news is that I finally polished off *Cryptonomicon*.

"Read to me." Her first words after waking up.

"Good evening, Sleeping Beauty. Would you'd like to eat a little something first?"

"Ugh no. In a couple of days, maybe, but not now. Just read, please."

"What? Anything in particular?"

"In the drawer. It's Margaret's last love letter to Johnny Birtwistle. That's what she called him, other than in the first two letters."

"Feeling any better?"

"Sure am. Like shit rather than like death."

"Wonderful."

I opened her bedside table's top drawer and removed the letter. It was dated May 28th, 1901. Its papers had yellowed, and the ink had faded almost to the point of invisibility. Margaret's handwriting was a model of legibility, however. Her words were all slanted slightly rightward, and she had spaced them with a precise evenness.

"Start on the second page, about eight lines down. Just the one paragraph."

Finally, we marry the Sunday after next! How perfect that the sanctity of our love can finally be validated in the eyes of our families and friends. I will forever regard our true wedding as having happened four days ago, however, when in the eyes of God we united for the very first time under His Realm. I lay beneath you, both of us shaded by the leaves of that tree, little more than a sapling, in our special meadow (how did you ever find such a heavenly place?). Endless prairie, the bluest of blue skies, the sun's warmth, you and me—the two of us become one with each other and with all of God's Creation. Surely our love was consecrated to the universe in that meadow.

"Once more."

When I finished, Shelley told me to go home; she would be fine by morning. She turned over and immediately fell back asleep. I stayed until Michael returned, then walked back to the Manoir. I'm shaken. Surely she'll improve as the drugs drain from her system?

7:58 P.M. Thursday, November 20th

She has not been behaving in her own best interest. I stopped by the library this morning, found her installed in the head honcha chair at circulation and carrying on an animated conversation with a nine-year-old boy about the literary merits of the Harry Potter books. The kid's mom stood no more than eighteen inches away. She repeatedly coughed and expelled mucus into and through a worn out tissue. Christ, what do I have to do to keep Shelley from getting sick?

We spoke about it on the way to lunch. "Okay, you need to get out of the house. I get that. But why go to work, where you are likely to come into contact with sick people? And if you must work, please wear a surgical mask."

For this I received one of her heehaw laughs and the following commentary: "How about they put me in a bubble, Carl? I'll be the bubble librarian. Who knows, maybe the oddity will attract business."

We had stopped at the corner of Sherbrooke and Lansdowne,

just after the traffic light turned against us. She stood erect in the sunlight, her smile shining through blonde hair brushing across her face. I thought, *How beautiful. How perfect you are.* It was just a moment, a blink, a break in the otherwise relentless progression of space-time. Not slow motion but absolute stillness, like the feeling I get when looking at Whistler's paintings of women in white and in blue, women too exquisite to have ever walked the earth. And the funny thing, the totally absurd proposition, is that I could tell she was regarding me, old me, in exactly the same way. The sublime and the ridiculous melded at the exact same non-moment out of time.

10:22 P.M. Monday, November 24th

Another weekend without her, and when she returned, calamity.

Ask me, mythical reader:

How did you spend your weekend? Did you let loose and drop ecstasy with a couple of blondes at some rave in a dark and echoey seafront warehouse while two dozen grimacing and twanging electric guitarists dressed in black from head to toe blasted the pulp out of your body?

I'm eighty-three. Of course not, you idiot.

Did you soar through the sky hundreds of feet up, paragliding from one Laurentian peak to another as eagles and hawks zoomed and cawed above and below you and the sun reflected its late afternoon light off the lakes below?

What do you think?

Maybe you read a novel? Half a novel? Patched holes in an odd number of socks?

Uh-uh.

Alright then. You tell me.

I moped. *Mope*, the action verb for inaction.

What exactly is *missing* someone? I did not misplace Shelley, nor did I fail to catch her. To miss is to feel pain in a loved one's absence, but what peculiar pain is that? Doesn't pain result from the presence of something noxious? I overeat, therefore I get indigestion. My stomach hurts because I've stressed it. Even hunger's pain is not caused by absence. It comes about because certain chemical processes take place in the stomach. But missing someone, that's phantom pain. It's antimatter of the heart.

I took action on Saturday afternoon, however. I bought a road map and a compass from Westmount Stationery. Upon returning to my room I cleared off my desk, opened the map, and placed it down flat. I pierced the compass spike straight through the heart of downtown Montreal, then adjusted the wing nut so that its extension traced a circle, the points on which represented a distance of one hundred and twenty miles. A trip of that distance makes a pleasant two-hour diversion for the minority of Montreal drivers who are sane.

I examined destinations falling on or near the circle. Of them all, the least desirable is Ottawa. If you fancy humdrum office buildings, nondescript apartment houses, stale museums, appalling weather, and a seat of government centered in a building that could double as the Addams Family abode, Ottawa is your cup of tea.

I went to the library after breakfast this morning, but Shelley had not shown up. I was told she had called in sick. I phoned, got her recorded message, so I left the library and walked over. The possibility that she and Michael might be indulging in a love-nest continuation to their weekend entered my consciousness. Walking in on them would not be good, so I called Michael's office just to be on the safe side. His secretary told me he could not take my call because he was in a meeting, which was enough verification for me. I continued on to Shelley's.

Imagine: your chemo consists of five drugs and four of them invade your body via needle, straight from an underinflated plastic bag hung on a rickety dolly to your insides. The fifth drug eschews the vein. It enters the old fashioned way. It is a pill, and you swallow it. A freaking little pill. Doesn't swallowing a pill and washing it down with a glass of water sound less threatening than allowing liquids to seep drop by drop directly into your circulatory system? Just how badly can one white pill screw you up? Prednisone. Change one of the N's to an S and you've got depression.

I arrived at her house, dialed her up once more before entering. Again, no answer. She didn't respond to my ring of the buzzer either. I took the elevator, called her name as soon as its door opened.

"Go away!"

I found her in the front bedroom, curled up in the fetal position. She was grasping her nightgown with both fists so tightly that she was close to choking herself.

"Don't hurt me! Don't touch me." She was shaking, and my god, what an awful look on her face. It reminded me of Mrs. Belkin's expression right before she died.

I sat down a few feet from her. "What the hell is going on?"

"I don't know. Everything."

"Did you sleep last night?"

"No. Get out of here. Leave!"

"I'm calling an ambulance."

"NO! No one sees me. They'll kill me."

"Then I'll phone Dr. Vaincoeur."

"Who?"

"Your oncologist. Don't worry, I'm not going to touch you." *Don't worry.* Another pathetic example of my non-empathetic floorside manner. At least I didn't say, "Don't worry, be happy."

Steroid psychosis. When I read about it last summer it was described as serious but rare. Vaincoeur mentioned it in passing. He had employed the phrase, "in a very small number of cases." What kind of fucking medicine is this? Hell strikes after taking it for only five days?

I was not surprised to learn later from Michael that the weekend had been a catastrophe. Thirty minutes from reaching

Ottawa, Shelley yelled for him to pull the car off the highway. She opened the door before he had stopped completely, ran down the embankment, and screamed at the top of her lungs for a minute before breaking into sobs. Michael wanted to turn back. Shelley's response: "Over my dead body." He volunteered no additional information, but it wouldn't have taken a genius to deduce that the trip must have devolved into a weekend of crying jags, manic visits to a dozen tourist attractions, interrupted sleep, arguments over little of substance, and maybe desperate lovemaking thrown in for good measure.

I called Vaincoeur's office, got a recorded message. Wonderful. Tried the emergency number, spoke to someone with a modicum of intelligence, and within twenty minutes a driver from Pharmaprix arrived with a bottle of risperidone. Damn anagram-happy drug companies—reduce the IR to an N and you've got prednisone all over again.

Shelley improved by the time I left earlier this evening. Michael's presence helped, and Vaincoeur's late-afternoon call, in which he told Shelley that he would adjust doses before the next round of chemo, calmed her down a little. Instead of being filled with panic, fear, and paranoia, she was merely disoriented and depressed. Merely? A week into chemo round one and already she's a mess. How the hell will she hold up over the next few months?

11:57 P.M. Thursday, November 27th

American Thanksgiving is superior to the Canadian version. You get a minimum of four days off instead of a maximum of three, and it comes around in the dark days at the end of November, when it is desperately needed. I attended many American Thanksgiving Day dinners in my early years here. I even hosted one. Before tonight, however, my most recent such celebration took place eight years ago. The ways of the old country erode with time's passage. That, and I get fewer invitations because my American colleagues have died off or retired to the great state of Florida.

Tonight's celebration was hosted by Helen and Frank. Being a loner, I appreciated how we were neatly paired off in couples. Michael and Shelley were inseparable, as were, of course, Helen and the creature inside her enlarged tummy. Frank coupled with the TV remote, treating the rest of us, whether we wanted it or not, to football before dinner and hockey afterward. I was matched up with Elise as soon as I sat down on the couch. She occupied my lap, became an immovable object. Despite her abortive attempt to eat me a few months earlier, her closed eyes, deep purrs, and wildly arcing tail discomforted me only mildly.

Sol and Marion, Frank's parents, drove up from Brooklyn for the long weekend. I find them tolerable, except when Marion asks stupid questions. Her choice this evening was, "So you guys, what's her name going to be?"

The question came at an unguarded moment after dinner. We had adjourned to the den in order to escape the ordeal of overeating in chairs. Instead, we consumed apple pie topped with vanilla ice cream as we sat on couches and loveseats.

In the history of the human race, has Marion's question ever been answered to everyone's satisfaction? How many times have prospective parents enthused, "Walter," followed by universal acclaim from friends and family? Very rarely, because Walter is an unusual choice for a girl's name, but you get the idea, right?

"Whoa," I said. "Unfair question."

"What?" Marion placed her cup on the coffee table, as if in order to do verbal battle she needed to have both hands free.

"It's a question with no good answer."

Frank was sitting to my immediate left. "But—"

I grabbed one of his arms before he could spill the beans. "Don't say anything, young man." I then turned to Marion.

"There are two conditions that must be fulfilled before your question can be answered satisfactorily."

Everyone looked at me, and I admit that I enjoyed the spotlight. There is a certain privilege conferred on a person of age, provided senility hasn't set in and no one else in the vicinity approaches him in elderliness. He becomes venerable. People attend to his every word.

"First, the prospective parents must have already chosen the name, and second, they must be willing to divulge it."

"But—" Frank again. This time I froze him in his tracks with a wave of my hand.

"Consider the condition of not having an answer. Outsiders— and by outsiders I mean persons other than the future mother and father—they have no knowledge of the causative factors. Perhaps the parents-to-be disagree, or maybe they are so carefree and happy-go-lucky that they haven't yet given their baby's name a moment's thought."

The room had become so quiet that I knew I could afford a dramatic pause without being interrupted. I took a sip from my coffee cup, put it back down with an elegant motion of my arm, and resumed my disquisition.

"Making the issue public would lead to a variety of outcomes, none of which are desirable."

"Carl, were aren't talking geopolitics here," Marion said. "I asked a very simple question. It's not a major issue, just an inquiry. What's my first granddaughter's name going to be?"

"A question requiring a short answer isn't necessarily a simple question, Marion. Consider the following examples, all of which can be answered very simply: How much money do you make, whom have you named as beneficiaries in your will, and how many times a week do you have sex?"

Shelley smiled. Good.

"I can see that I'm not going to get an answer tonight, at least not while you're hanging around," she responded.

"Oh come on, Marion, have a heart! Let's assume for a moment that Frank and Helen are determined to name their child Bertha, or maybe Gertrude, and that you can't abide either option. What are you going to do, stifle it?"

"Absolutely. I'd say nothing. I'd even smile and be gracious about it, unless they choose Salome or some other ridiculous name. Any name that doesn't disadvantage the child is fine by me."

"Then why do you want to know?"

"I'm curious! Isn't it natural for the future grandma to want to know?"

"What if Helen and Frank were to choose, oh—Estrellita."

"Why should I object?"

"You wouldn't say something like 'Oh, Estrellita! What a beautiful name,' followed by 'But dear, have you considered that kids may tease her?' in turn succeeded with 'I know that it's not my place to say, but please consider naming her Iris. Iris is such a nice name, so much better than Estrellita, which conjures up the image of some drug-addled Peruvian strumpet.'"

"Such words you put in my mouth! Okay, Carl, you win. I'll be patient until the moment of birth."

"Or until your son here spills the beans later tonight, after I'm safely sequestered back at the Manoir."

I don't care if Frank tells her or not. The purpose of my little intervention was to divert Shelley. Although she's improved since last Monday's trauma, she looked ill at ease all evening. She was subdued—hardly spoke a word, acted nothing like her usual ebullient self. Moreover, she ate like a bird. She even refrained from dessert, and she loves dessert. If someone were to serve her celery with vanilla ice cream and hot chocolate sauce on top, she would gobble it up and ask for seconds. Come to think of it, so would I.

Perhaps the chemo had her down, or maybe she felt awkward because other than Michael and me, she was with people she didn't know all that well. When Marion asked her unfortunate baby-name question, Shelley flinched. Though it was a momentary thing, just a quick glance away, instantly I knew that for her, an elephant was roaming the house: Helen was pregnant and she was not. Indeed, pregnancy will never be in her future.

10:13 P.M. Tuesday, December 9th

Energy equals mass times the speed of light squared makes sense to me, except for the speed of light squared part. No matter, because it's the fine-print aspect of the equation. Think of it as seasoning, like paprika for goulash. The meat of Einstein's invention is an elegant restatement of mind-body unity. The body is mass and the mind is energy. Mess around with one and you mess with both.

What a pity we can't share our bodies and mental powers for mutual benefit. If the theory of intelligent design had any validity, surely *homo sapiens* would have evolved into a life form having the capacity to permit the exchange of body parts between its members, à la Mr. Potato Head and Lego figurines. Our constituent parts would be interlockable, substitutable, even disposable. A midget and a giant might collaborate for mutual benefit. The eight-foot guy would simply donate two feet of his body to the four-foot guy. Symptoms of illness would be dissipated by dividing them up among the sick person and a bunch of her healthy friends.

Taking the rap for Shelley's hair loss would not have been a sacrifice for me, because absence of hair is not a hell of a lot worse than sparsely populated hair. Who knows, I might look even more dashing with the scrubbed-clean-absolutely-no-hair look than I do now, because impressing by design always trumps impressions of entropy.

The commencement of Shelley's second chemo cycle yesterday

must have set it off. My clock's readout glowed a bright red 5:38 A.M. when the phone rang.

"Mmmph. Hello?"

"I'm fucking shedding!"

"What?"

"Hair's all over the sheets. My pillow's covered with it."

"I'm sorry. Oh that's terrible."

"It's fallen out everywhere."

Curious, how the more devastating symptoms take a backseat to that first instance of chemo-induced hair loss. Strands slip effortlessly from the body like pine needles blown off a hardwood deck, and even though the loss is painless, it is sudden and unprecedented in the patient's life.

"My bed is a mess!"

"I'll come over. We'll clean the sheets and vacuum up every last hair."

"It's not just my head, Carl. I'm being deserted all over my body. I'm going bald everywhere!" She coughed a few times.

"You okay?" A dumb question, followed by a pause and then a giggle on her end.

"Oh. I just thought of a silver lining."

"What's that, my dear?"

"No need to shave the legs."

"There never was, as far as I'm concerned. I like women with hairy legs, especially in dark rooms."

"Ooh!"

"What? Did I say something lacking in sensitivity?"

"I just though of another advantage."

"Which is?"

"I'll be getting a free Brazilian, and without having to put up with the zing strips."

"Zing strips?"

"Don't you know anything?"

"Apparently not. What the fuck are you talking about?"

She laughed, which unfortunately triggered a fifteen-second coughing spasm. "Your homework assignment for the week is to Google Brazilian. And wax."

"I don't like that cough of yours. You should take it easy this week."

"Take me out for a wig first."

"Relax today, and if you're feeling better tomorrow we'll go then."

"But I need the wig today."

"Shelley, it's fucking freezing outside. Can't you wait a day?"

"No. And besides, we live in Montreal in case you haven't noticed. It will be just as fucking freezing tomorrow."

We took a taxi to the Decarie Square mall this afternoon. It houses a store specializing in wigs for women undergoing chemo. Shelley selected two wigs, which we took to a private fitting room. One matched her pre-chemo hair in color and thickness, and the second was long, curly, black, and all over the place. Cher's hair run wilder.

"My skank wig for extra hot dates. Here, give it a try."

"What?"

"Come on!"

"You want me to put that thing on top of my head?"

"My eyes are now closed, and will remain that way until you tell me it's in position."

I did as I was told. "You can look now."

"Ooh! I could have such fun transvesting you."

Shelley chose a hat in addition to the wigs. It was no more than an inverted floppy gray cup, and she looked chic in it, kind of Audrey Hepburn à la goth. I bought both wigs and the hat, but committed something of a *faux pas* on the way out when I asked the proprietress whether the wigs could be returned for a partial refund after Shelley's hair grew back. I still don't get it. Why should wigs differ from textbooks? Wouldn't it be ecologically sound to recycle them?

11:09 A.M. Sunday, December 14th

The history of any love relationship can be plotted. Begin by extracting a piece of graph paper from your desk drawer, then rule in the axes. Let the abscissa depict the passage of time, moving rightward. The ordinate represents feeling, along a negative-positive continuum. Zero on the x-axis signifies the instant the two lovers first meet, and zero on the y-axis indicates indifference. Feelings of negativity, ranging from mild disapproval all the way to hatred, fall below the y-axis's zero point, and the good feelings rise above it. The higher you go, the better it gets.

Let the y-axis have two discontinuities, one at its bottom and the other at its top. The lower break represents the chasm between dislike and hatred. Think of it as the emotional equivalent of a black hole's event horizon, except that once you enter a black hole there is no escape. Humans, on the other hand, occasionally emerge from hatred. The high-end discontinuity signifies the borderline between liking and love. In astronomical terms, moving from liking to love is like punching through the wall at the end of the universe. Yes Virginia, there is a wall all the way out there, it is a well kept scientific secret, and it is made of buffed chromium.

Each line depicts one person's feelings toward the other. You might color them pink and blue, but the graph works just as well with two pinks, two blues, and, in exceptional circumstances, two pinks and a blue. So, how would the ideal relationship pattern out on graph paper? If governed by rationality, I suspect it would trace two very slowly ascending lines. They would inch up together and at a tiny angle, say three or four degrees. Getting to know you, getting to know all about you.... A steeper inclination would signify rapid acceptance without verification. One should bond with another in accordance with acquisition of knowledge, correct? Or to put it another way: the appreciation of one's lover should grow in direct relation to the gradual apprehension over time of his or her sterling qualities, bearing in mind his or her deficiencies.

Unfortunately, relationships rarely follow such a pattern. Instead of the steady ascent, their patterns more often resemble the jagged lines of a polygraph as it tracks an arrhythmic heart. Complicating the picture is the fact that the materialism of love is multidimensional. Consider the following hypothetical example of how a woman might evaluate her lover. She ranks him high on attractiveness, generosity, healthiness, and sexual prowess, but finds him boorish thirty-eight percent of the time. Moreover, he is a borderline illiterate, having employed *u, lol,* and apostrophes before -s plurals in his emails. In addition, his sense of humor is worse than the Pope's, and he has not attended a concert or visited a museum in thirteen years. An accurate assessment of the woman's attachment to this guy would require tracking a dozen lines rather than just one. Yes, it's complicated. Data reduction based on a weighted average of factors is ineffective, because there are deal breakers in modern-life relationships, such as inattention in the bedroom or the employment of *alot* in written correspondence. Nevertheless, for the purpose of this exposition I'll pretend that data reduction reflects reality.

If the two lines cross the like/love discontinuity at the top of the y-axis, watch out. It is here that the trappings of materialism, those pesky plus-minus *Is it worth it?* considerations, lose importance. People abandon their critical faculties at such high altitudes. They mouth stupid words and phrases like *forever, soulmate,* and *the only one for me.* They get less upset than they would have been earlier in the relationship had their partners gained weight, lost money, or drank too much, because they have been snagged by the metaphysics of feeling. Jack *loves* Jill. So what if she no longer wants to go up the hill with him? He'll fetch the water anyway, willingly and without resentment. There you have it in all its glory: love. Unfortunately, the trip up the graph is not always one-way.

I'm more than a little concerned about the relationship arc traced out by Shelley and my son in recent days. I've sensed a downturn. The two of them usually bubble in my presence, but not yesterday. We ate at a local Chinese restaurant to celebrate the conclusion of chemo cycle number two on Friday night. Shelley and Michael never touched. In fact they barely looked at each other. Moreover, Shelley hardly said anything and ate very little food. The only other times I've seen her like that were at Thanksgiving dinner and when she sleeps.

9:22 P.M. Sunday, December 14th

My prescience was right on the mark, though I never expected the unravelment to come so quickly. Shelley called almost immediately after I finished writing my morning's entry. The first sentence out of her mouth was "Michael and I are history." The second: "By the way, I threw up into a bag of popcorn last night."

"Oh no on both counts. What the hell happened?"

"We went to the movies, saw *Slumdog Millionaire*, or rather its first few minutes. There's such a disgusting scene in it. A boy gets locked in an outhouse. He escapes by plunging through the floor into a pond or a lake, and winds up all covered in shit. It was so revolting."

Charming. Just what I needed to hear right before lunch.

"Not that I was feeling all that hot to begin with, so in combination with the piquant little scene that followed, in which the kid ran up a beach to get some famous actor's signature, mind you still covered in shit, well, that did me in."

"That's when you threw up?"

"You know that recording they play before beginning the

film? An announcer requests that members of the audience refrain from adding their own sound tracks to the movie?"

"Of course."

"I disobeyed it. I added both sound track *and* action. First I started retching. Loud retching. I rose from my seat, made it to the aisle and only then did I throw up, on the carpet right next to the wall, and let me tell you, waiting until I got there so I wouldn't vomit over three or four poor schmucks, that was hard. I fell to my knees and projectile-upchucked, first right into my popcorn bag, which for some reason I was still holding. The bag filled up and runover vomit besmirched the carpet. There was lots of it."

"Runover vomit? Besmirched? Jesus, Shelley, what century are you living in? Anyway, imagine the damage had you guys gone to some zombie movie instead."

"Yeah. Heads chopped off, blood and guts flying around. I'd be barfing into tomorrow."

"But what did this unfortunate incident have to do with breaking up with Michael?"

"Carl, your son is a wimp."

"What happened?"

"He's an imbecile. He has no idea what he is supposed to do. We had problems before, but this was the last straw."

"Come on, Shelley," I said in exasperation. "Get to the point."

"Okay. An usher came over and helped us out of the theater. Nice kid but probably some high school dropout because the first words out of his mouth did not portend genius. He wanted to know if I would like a complimentary Pepsi to wash the vomit aftertaste away, and a free bag of popcorn to go with it. Amazing how stupid considerate people can be. Anyway, I went to the girlie room, fixed myself up so I was more or less presentable, and was all set to go back and see the rest of the film. But the manager wouldn't let me."

"That was insensitive of him."

"I'll say. He claimed I might have the flu. He didn't want to risk the possibility that I'd vomit again and infect some of the patrons, which could lead to lawsuits."

"So nice of him to think of other people, eh? What did you tell him?"

"I'm afraid I lost it a little."

"A little?"

"I said I had no fucking flu, in fact I had nothing contagious at all except the HIV virus, but as none of his fucking patrons were going to fuck me during the film, and certainly not without wearing a condom, what's the problem? Then Michael told him that my retching was a side effect of the chemo I was on, as was my emotional state. The nerve! And when the manager, a big guy with receding hair dyed orange, when he insisted we leave and in exchange he would refund our money, Michael actually agreed! He fucking went along with it, and then he told me it would be for the best if I calmed down. Right in front of the manager he said that! We could see the movie some other time, that's how he put it. Yeah, sure. Right after he grows real balls!"

Rule One of relationship maintenance for the heterosexual male: if your girlfriend is a firecracker, back her up. Do it even if she isn't a firecracker. It is always good policy.

8:45 P.M. Tuesday, December 16th

Whiling away the afternoon at Mount Royal Park had been my brilliant idea. The sky was as clear as the tones of a silver-plated dinner bell when we got into the taxi. By the time we stepped out into the middle of a massive parking lot fifteen minutes later, however, heavy gray clouds, accompanied by a stiff north wind, had rolled in. We walked to the top of the sledding slope overlooking Beaver Lake, where I told Shelley that if some deity or scientist were to miraculously ratchet up the outdoor thermostat by two dozen degrees, I would be most grateful.

She looked me up and down and said, "That's pretty obvious. You're shivering like a hairless pussy. Shall we leave?"

"Of course not, we just arrived. Look at this place! Incredible, eh?"

I pointed to the lake, just past the bottom of the slope. Tentatively frozen, it emanated a flat peaceful gray. Snow, made glazy from yesterday's unusual winter rain, surrounded us. Hundreds of trees, leafless except for a few pines here and there, framed the scene, creating an amphitheatric effect.

"Seriously, why don't you fly the coop and spend the winter in Florida?"

"F-forget it," I shiver-stammered. "Florida is the epitome of deadness. You might as well dump me in a coffin."

"Oh come on, Carl, imagine the possibilities. You've got money. You could be the male version of Kathleen Turner at the end of *Body Heat.*"

"Now there's a mind-boggling thought."

Shelley stretched her arms forward and framed an imaginary vision by straightening her thumbs and aiming them at each other, fingers on both of her hands pointing upwards.

"Imagine. There you are by the pool, supine and sundrenched on your chaise. You're tensionless, just one big warm wet noodle. You hold a Mai Tai in your right hand and a fat Thomas Mann novel rests on one of those book reading trays people use in bed and poolside, patiently waiting for your undivided attention. Wouldn't that be the life?"

My feet were beginning to lose feeling, but there was no way I was going to admit defeat.

"I'd rather stay here. It's my home. And I enjoy winter."

"Like hell you do."

The sledding area was located a few feet off to our right. In order to prevent thrill seeking idiots from zipping across the hill and crashing into random men, women, and children, park workers had created lanes. Each was about ten feet across, and was separated from adjacent lanes by ribbons of snow about a foot high and eighteen inches wide. A sign informed us that sleds could be rented at the chalet down the hill, just past Beaver Lake.

"Tell you what, Shell. Let's rent a couple of sleds and race down the hill."

"Ha! That's all you need, isn't it? You could break your hip, or maybe sustain a sprained ass. And where would you put that cane of yours?"

"I'll sit on it, no problem. I'm not a delicate flower. Besides, look at that pathetic angle." I waved my right hand dismissively in the slope's general direction. "It's safe enough for babies. No one's going to get hurt."

Shelley looked me up and down again, and this time I did my best not to look cold.

"Okay. You stay here and I'll get the sleds." Fifteen minutes later she reappeared, trudging up the hill with a green tube under her right arm and a red one under her left. Her face was pink and she was sweating and breathing heavily.

"All righty," she cackled, as she handed me the green tube. "I'll see you at the bottom. Or rather I'm going to enjoy looking up from the finish line and watching your sorry ass descend at one mile per hour."

"Tires? There were no sleds available?"

"The guy said they're all being repaired. Seems there was a Weight Watchers convention in town over the weekend. Sorry, you'll have to be satisfied expressing your inner tube." Pointing to my cane once again, she added, "What *are* you going to do with that thing? It's way too long to shove up your—"

"Assuredly I will find a place for it," I said hurriedly.

Shelley hadn't noticed the new arrivals nearby, the only sentient beings on the hill other than the two of us—a man, woman, their preteen daughter, and their dog. Bundled in an oversized pink snowsuit, the girl was virtually invisible. Dad wore heavy brown mountain boots, snow pants, commissar's fur hat, ski mask, and one of those down-filled puffy coats that make the wearer resemble the Michelin Man. Cold he was not. Mom, on the other hand, continually huddled within herself. Her stylish but inadequate ensemble consisted of jeans, light boots, and a raincoat. She held a leash in her right hand, the far end of which had been clipped onto the collar of a miniature schnauzer who was doing his utmost to keep the line taut.

"I don't suppose you might be up for a small wager?" Shelley queried.

"What do you have in mind?"

"If I win, you take me back to the Orange Julep. You will hold your tongue while I order whatever I want. In fact you will compliment me on my excellent choice of cuisine. And, of course, you will pay for the taxi and my meal."

"You shouldn't be eating that stuff now."

"Why not? It's just a one-off. Would you believe I dreamt about their French fries last night?"

"No."

"Actually it was the night before."

"And what if I win?"

"That is so not going to happen. But pick something anyway."

"Okay. If I win, I speak to Michael—wait, don't interrupt. I'll apply all of my formidable skills of persuasion to get him to apologize to you for being such a fuckup."

"Save yourself the effort."

"Why?"

"I'm through with him."

"You don't miss him?"

"Nope. I'm over him completely. For me, a relationship is like a person. Kill it and it's dead forever. Nevertheless I accept your bet, but only because I want those fries. More than any man, for your information."

Doth the lady protest too much? I refrained from asking and chose a lane. Shelley picked the one to my left. We placed our tubes on the downslope's edge and got in. Shelley was able to tuck her legs inside, but because I was too damned tall I had to dangle my boots, as well as the cane, outside the tube.

"Ready?" she asked.

"As I'll ever be."

"Set..."

"The tension is unbearable," I replied.

"Go!" After only a few seconds, my tube started moving faster than I had anticipated. The additional speed must have been due to yesterday's rain, which had iced the run. Unfortunately, the tube rotated one hundred and eighty degrees so that I descended facing up the hill. I couldn't see Shelley, who was moving even faster than I was. What I did see, however, was the schnauzer, newly escaped from his mistress's grasp and charging toward me at the speed of light. When he was just a few feet away he growled, jumped, and sunk his teeth into my right boot. Mom, dad, and little girl, all still standing at the top of the hill, looked on in horror.

A half-minute later doggie and I arrived at the bottom. He clung to my boot while growling incessantly through his teeth, wiggling his torso from side to side, and wagging his tail furiously. Shelley was of no help in extricating me from the predicament. She just stood over me and the dog and laughed her ass off.

"Don't intervene," I said. "He'll bite you."

"I so wish I had a camera!"

Dad finally made it down. He grabbed the leash, pulled the dog from my boot, and apologized.

"You win," I said to Shelley.

"Don't I always?"

11:01 P.M. Saturday, December 20th

December is prime time for dying. Its days are short, frigid, and snowy, and its X-factor, the holiday season, is a risk multiplier for the old, weak, and lonely. Management has been doing its part to knock us off. Artificial wreaths adorn doors by the dozens. Christmas trees trimmed to the gills with lights, garlands, ornaments, birds, angels, and pounds of streaming tinsel stand in the main entryway, the lobby, and up against the wood paneling by the television in the East Room. The dining room tables are decorated with random bits of holly and mistletoe, though without candy canes so as to forestall dental emergencies. For the foreseeable future we will be using those annoyingly small stiff green and red napkins to wipe food from our faces.

"Season's Greetings" signs lettered in silver are as ubiquitous around here as rolling walkers. Come to think of it, what does "Season's Greetings" actually mean? Who is doing the greeting, and why must one be greeted repeatedly, day after day? And why are the more pleasant seasons less welcoming? Shouldn't they confront us with the same insane degree of persistence as winter does?

Shelley's perfect storm had been brewing for a week: breakup with the boyfriend, crummy weather, darkness, illness. Last Wednesday she contracted a painful sore throat, which was followed the next day by the full force of a cold. This morning she told me she's finished. She intends to refuse her next round of chemo, scheduled to begin on Monday.

"Take me to Texas and let me bake in the sun and eat steaks for a few months. Then bury me in the desert and mark my grave with one of those steer skulls."

By mid-afternoon she had had enough of me. She told me to leave, said she wanted time to herself. I got my things together, gave her a hug, and walked through the park back to the Manoir. It was not yet four-thirty, yet the lampposts glowed brightly. No one approached. I walked accompanied by the soft crunching sounds of my boots on snow and the silent song of the trees. Do trees suffer in winter? Of course they do.

It was not until I entered my room that I came up with a plan. It's little more than an elaboration on one of last spring's stratagems: *Buy her something*. If it works I'll be amazed.

8:14 P.M. Monday, December 22nd

Showdown yesterday at lunchtime. I arrived lugging three bags, each loaded with groceries from Atlantic Meat and Delicatessen. Shelley's reaction: "I sense bribery."

"There's not much point in denying the charge. Have a look."

"You're so predictable. As a matter of principle I should refuse whatever's in there and send you on your way."

"Feeling better than yesterday?"

She peeked in one of the bags. "Good thing you caught me hungry."

We unpacked a sirloin steak, a roasted chicken, a small bag of potatoes, green beans, a head of Boston lettuce, a cucumber, tomatoes, mushrooms, peppers, a sourdough rye, half a dozen small yogurts, two boxes of strawberries, four bananas, two sacher tortes, six bars of dark chocolate, and a couple of bottles of Rieslings.

"Yum! You're a conniver, but oh are you good at it."

"Then you'll come? I'll reserve the taxi tonight."

"No. I don't think so. I don't want to."

"Shelley, no one *wants* chemo. People say 'Let's go to the movies,' or 'How about some bowling tonight?' but never in the history of the human race has anyone declared, 'I'm in the mood for chemo, what do you say?'"

At least she smiled.

I added, "Let's deal with it later, okay? For now, how about some lunch?"

"Professor Carl Anderson, master of the soft sell. Yeah, lunch is an excellent idea. I'll order us up a pizza."

Pizza made no sense, given the food I had brought with me, but Shelley wasn't up to cooking and I am culinarily challenged away from microwave and tea kettle. Half an hour later we were dining on an all-dressed, accompanied by one of the Rieslings. Then we demolished the sacher tortes.

On my way out the door later that afternoon I told Shelley that I would stop by at 7:15 A.M. sharp. Either she'd come or she wouldn't, the choice was entirely up to her. No pressure, none at all, just don't refuse right now, okay? Sleep on it.

I should have been a used car salesman. My plan worked, which is not to say I endeared myself to her. She joined me in the taxi this morning but said nothing to me, absolutely nothing until they removed the iv drip six hours later.

10:48 P.M. Wednesday, December 24th

I write from Shelley's, where I have been ensconced since early this afternoon. I have two excuses for spending the day with her. First, it's Christmas Eve. No one, not even an atheist, voluntarily spends Christmas Eve alone. Second, she needs me.

Chemo round three has been so much rougher than the first two. Shelley remains congested and drippy from her cold. Half a dozen painful mouth sores materialized a couple of days ago. Tack on intermittent attacks of nausea and constipation, throw in insomnia, and it's easy to see why she's not a happy camper. Moreover, her face looks puffy, pasty, and gray. She won't stray from the house, says that even with the wig on she feels too ugly to be seen by people. Also, she insists that we refrain from exchanging Christmas presents. Later, she said, if and when the concept of *festive* approaches closer than the planet Neptune.

We spent the day reading, Shelley mostly in her big bed and me nearby in a chair. My concern about her choice of literature—*As I Lay Dying*—turned out to be unwarranted. She focused well, hated interruptions, found the book riveting. It is interesting how immersion in an imagined reality worse than her own permits her to sideslip the present, at least for a few hours.

Despite Shelley's various discomforts, the day progressed well until evening. She fell asleep at seven, awoke sobbing forty-five minutes later.

"What's the matter? Something hurt?"

She didn't speak, just shook as if chilled to the bone, cried, blew her nose, cried some more. Finally she stopped crying but still didn't move or say anything.

"Can I help? Get you something?"

She shook her head.

"Bad dream?"

She nodded.

"Tell me."

"Doesn't matter."

"I suppose not. I'm just glad it's over."

"It's the medication, or rather, medications. I'm taking so many I can't track them all. I have no idea which ones are doing what. I'm swallowing retros and chemos, anti-nauseants, pain killers, sleeping pills, laxatives. I'm a fucking pharmacy! One of those pills, or maybe a couple in combination just sent me ten thousand feet to the bottom of an ocean, all alone and struggling to breathe. I was locked in a cage, kept immobile by heavy chains wound about my neck, arms, and legs. Great. Carl, I really can't take this anymore. I tried, God knows, but enough's enough. From now on just let me be, okay? Promise me no more rounds of your goddamn chemo. Let's make tomorrow a truly merry Christmas. Yeah, let your Christmas present to me be an oath that never again will you remind me to take my pills. No more doctor visits, scans, none of that shit. Take all of it away somewhere and shove it up someone's ass."

I refrained from reminding Shelley that she was just two prednisone doses from finishing off round three, the likely midpoint of her entire course of treatment. I doubt she would have absorbed the information rationally.

"The whole thing requires what, another two to three months? Might as well be forever. And after—like magic I'll be all better? Really? Do you have any idea what I'm going through?" She almost shouted that last sentence, then broke into another round of sobs.

"I'm so sorry, my dear. All I wanted was to get you healthy again." Spoken in the most empathetic tone I could muster.

Her crying subsided, and then, after a few minutes of silence, came a surprising break:

"Tell you what. How about this? I'll finish off the round, but just this round. No more iv drips, ever. I'll take the two preds, but you have to help me get through tonight. It's Christmas Eve, Carl, fucking Christmas Eve. I used to love it. The quietness, the peacefulness, the total absence of conflict for a few precious hours, you know? But tonight Christmas Eve taunts me."

"We'll get through it together."

Another silence. What could I do to make time pass faster?

"Would you like me to read something to you?"

"No. My books are pretty heavy, and I'm not in the mood right now. How about you tell me a story instead?"

"About what?"

"Anything. Something interesting from your life, assuming you've got something interesting within those vast cerebral memory banks of yours to tell. How about one of your experiences with women? Not one with great sex in it, but a story about the one who got away. You know, a regretful lost opportunity. You must have a treasury of such vignettes to choose from, eh? Given that you were single for so long, I mean."

"I may have repressed those aspects of my experience."

"Then make something up, but don't tell me."

"Oh wait, I just remembered a real one! You're going to love it because I blew a great opportunity, and for the strangest of reasons. Not only that, the story's even got a moral."

"What, like haste makes waste?"

"Uh, not exactly."

"Hesitate and you are lost?"

"It's a bit more complicated than that."

"Whatever. Proceed please. You have my undivided attention." She wiped away moistness from her face, actually managed a smile.

"Many years ago I was invited by a very desirable woman to attend a concert with her, a piano recital. I was in Chicago at the time, and had just given a conference paper on the morning of April 24th, 1983, a Sunday. Its title was 'Symbolic Imagery in the Song of Songs.' Anyway, this woman came on to me after the session. On her badge was written Isabel La Paz-Zareza, and below that, The Ohio State University. An absolutely true story."

"But of course."

"Isabel was a little on the zaftig side, attractive beyond belief in that Rubenesque manner that goes so underappreciated these days. She was short, only five-two or five-three. Her straight blonde hair extended past her shoulders, and she wore a dark red lipstick that magically lightened whenever she smiled. What a smile. She might as well have told me to come and get it. And wow, did she knew how to dress. Her perfection of the art of feminine sartorial arrangements created a sort of oxymoronic impression, in that she came across as both scholarly and trashy. I won't go into the details, just take my word for it."

"Word not taken. Let's have the description."

"Oh if you insist. She wore this super-elegant ensemble—unbuttoned black jacket, black bra barely obscured by a frilly diaphanous white silk blouse covering it. Her black skirt terminated well above the knee line, and she wore black high heels. You'd probably call them stilettos. Simple but effective."

"Simple? She probably spent two hours getting it all together. Anyway now that I've got the picture, let's have the story."

"Isabel started up a conversation related to my talk. One thing led to another, and before I knew it we had ventured far from the Bible. We continued our conversation over coffee, and then, out of the blue, she invited me to join her for this recital. She had read a feature article in the Tribune the previous day. The writer raved about the music, describing it as incomparable, unique, magnificent, etcetera. He also touted the event as a once-in-a-lifetime experience because the music was so incredibly long and difficult that it was almost never performed. So I threw caution to the wind. I said yes without even asking Isabel who the composer was."

"That's really throwing caution to the wind, Carl. Such a dangerous thing to do. It ranks right up there with ordering off the menu and judging a book by its cover. I've always loved that breathtaking devil-may-care attitude of yours."

"Why thank you, my dear. But do keep in mind that I hate piano recitals. They put me to sleep."

"Oh the sacrifice you made in order to spend time with Miss Delectable. On with the story, please."

"The concert was held at Mandel Hall, on the University of Chicago's campus. It was an afternoon affair. Because of the favorable newspaper article I thought we might have trouble getting in. In fact I was counting on it. Instead, we found ourselves among two hundred oddball types ranging from mildly to severely nerdish. Some had even brought penlights and scores—compact tomes hundreds of pages long. As we were about to discover, all of their pages were filled with scads of tiny black notes."

"Sex and dense music, an unbeatable combination."

"Maybe for rock music, but not this time around. My date, the shapely and prodigiously intelligent Isabel, or the prodigiously shaped and intelligent Isabel, a.k.a. Dr. La Paz-Zareza, she and I were assaulted for five hours—correction, make that five insane hours for me but only two for her—by incomprehensible abstruse clusters of sounds. Tangles of chords clanged fast and furious through our ear canals. We suffered interminable fugues, gigantic monstrosities each lasting the better part of an hour. Passacaglias, variation sets, and random improvisations washed over us. Luscious Isabel gave me an ultimatum at the first intermission: it was her or the concert. Fool that I was, I chose the concert. Even though none of the music made any sense, I couldn't leave! I chose to hang out with the nerds and suffer three more hours of sonic misery rather than spend the rest of the afternoon, and probably the night as well, with one insanely gorgeous woman."

"But why? What made you behave so stupidly?"

"I couldn't tear myself away from the incredible artistic train wreck. I had to hear it through to the end, no matter what."

"Wow. I have to hand it to you, Carl. You certainly made the idiot's choice."

"Thank you again, my dear. Feeling any better?"

"Yeah. Hearing about your fuckups always cheers me up."

"I'll take that as a compliment, if you don't mind."

"Not at all. But you said your story had a moral. What was it? I'm puzzled because I don't see how you can possibly relate this episode of grand scale incompetence to anything instructive."

"Sure I can. The composer's name was Sorabji. Kaikhosru Shapurji Sorabji. He had modestly named his composition *Opus Clavicembalisticum*."

"What a mouthful."

"True enough. But here's the fascinating thing, Shelley: *OC*, as the cognoscenti call it, consists of twelve pieces. All of them are either highly structured, for example the fugues I just mentioned, or they come across as almost random. Though most of them sounded random to me because I'm not a musician, I was able to discern that the improvisatory sections were designed to be without structure, if that makes any sense. So, now do you get it?"

"Get what?"

"The story's meaning."

"What, that you can't tell a tale to save your ass? Nope. I got nothing, nada. I'm an obtuse bitch. Inform me, please."

"The only way *OC* makes any sense at all is if it is thought of as one man's representation of the universe as it traverses eternity. Both the music and the universe are knowable and unknowable. Hence they both have structure and chaos."

"Structure like solar systems?"

"And galaxies, with their exquisite pinwheels, or brilliant star clusters shaped like flawless spheres, or the whole thing together, expanding from one tiny point to an entity so vast we can't make out its shape, except we know it must be perfect."

"But you also mentioned chaos. What chaos?"

"Nebulas and shooting stars. Asteroids crashing into planets, exploding supernovae, quasars and pulsars. Catastrophes."

"Oh–kay. And the point of the story is exactly what?"

"Consider the universe as a work of art, Shelley. Think of it as an opera constructed on a cosmic scale, lasting an unfathomable duration, having a plot no one individual could ever follow, and leading to an uncertain outcome. It therefore follows that everything and everyone in the universe has a part to play. Your part, mine too, is as one note. We'll never know how this particular artwork began, nor how it will end, or even if it had a beginning or if it will have an ending, for that matter. Nevertheless, we have to play our notes. We can't cut them short. It's too important."

"Why? What happens if we skip out prematurely?"

"Nothing I'm capable of comprehending. I just know—I feel it intuitively. It is critically important not to exit before one's true time is up. There's your moral."

Looking back from a forty-minute vantage point, I see that my reasoning was not much different from telling a first-grader that his part in the school play, that of an immobile tree with no speaking part, is vital to the play's success. Nor does it differ from trying to convince Michael, so many years ago, that his role as perpetual substitute on a Westmount Mosquito softball summer league team made all the difference. He might as well have been the team mascot. He didn't even get to play until the fourth game of the season. With his team leading eight to nothing in the bottom of the third, the manager, a big guy with a pot belly, sort of a Canadian poor man's version of Antonio Porfiteza, called on Michael to pinch hit. Michael walked on four pitches, trotted down to first base, and was promptly removed for a pinch runner. There were tears in his eyes by the time he reached me behind the stands. Had I applied the same train of thought I had just foisted on Shelley, I would have told Michael that we should stick around: "Everybody has a part to play, no matter how big or small." Instead I gave him a hug and said, "Let's get the hell out of here." We buried his memory of the incident under a couple of McNugget six packs, fries, and Cokes.

Shelley could have demolished the validity of my argument easily, had she been so inclined. She could have cited any of the ubiquitous instances of cruelties, stupidities, and atrocities humans have committed over the ages, from animal torture all the way up, or down, to mass murder. "Try shoehorning that shit into your magnificent cosmic opera," she might have told me. But she did not fight back, and that worries me. She simply listened attentively to my explanation and then asked a question I had no answer for:

"So whatever happened to Isabel?"

3:01 P.M. Sunday, December 28th

I slept in the center suite's bedroom that evening, and for the first time since the previous winter my nightmare paid me a visit. It had mutated. Silver tinged every object, as if from a fine sleet—me, the rock I lay on, my dead brother. The woman's hair glistened from hundreds of silver granules latticed through it. I spotted evidence of an object under her robe's right sleeve, a tiny pinpoint of reflected light.

I awoke, heard the soft clanking of cutlery. *Get up Carl, get up now, right now.* I rose, walked to the kitchen door, opened it. I saw nothing at first because the kitchen lights were switched off. Only a weak glow from the hallway's pale blue track lighting kept the room from being totally immersed in darkness.

Shelley stood with her back to me, staring out the window. She was completely bald, which shocked me because she had always worn one of her wigs in my presence. I spotted the knife. It was small, sharp, and serrated, and she was grasping it in her right hand.

"What are you doing?"

She didn't move, just kept staring into the blackness.

"Go away." Spoken in a soft even tone.

"Put the knife down, Shelley. Please. I'll stay up with you, we'll work it out. It's Christmas, for God's sake." I took a step toward her. She turned, faced me, pressed the knifepoint firm to her nightgown right over her heart.

"Not another step." Again spoken with a voice already dead.

"Oh Shelley no, don't do it."

"Go back to bed and leave me be."

"Go back to bed? Then what, enjoy a pleasant sleep knowing you're about to plunge a knife through your heart?"

"I'll slit my wrists over the sink. It'll make less of a mess. Now go. Be grown up about this."

"Less of a mess? How considerate. What, you think the blood will miraculously fly into the sink after you collapse on the floor?"

"Go. Now."

"I should let you kill yourself because it's the mature thing to do? Tell me, how am I going to live with myself?"

I took another step toward her.

"Stay away!" Finally, some oomph in her words.

"Okay, okay. Just give me a second." I didn't know what to do. She would kill herself if I charged her, yet I couldn't leave the room.

"Get out of here. Now!"

"Okay, I'm going." But I didn't. I headed to the cutlery drawer twenty feet to my right. Damn, the one time in my life I needed my cane—halfway there I slipped, fell hard on my right kneecap. It hurt like hell. I looked at her, saw concern on her face but no movement, so I scraped my body across the floor until I reached the drawer. I raised my left arm, opened the drawer, and withdrew a knife identical to hers.

"What?" Alarm replaced concern.

"I'm going to die with you. Sticking around after you're gone would be agony, so we're going out together." Right, just like on a date.

"No, you can't!" She dropped her knife, rushed at me and gripped my forearms. The coldness from her fingers shot through my body like an electric shock. Instantly I wanted to die as badly as—as badly as one craves release in those impossible few seconds before climaxing. Suicide as escape from misery? Not this fucking time around! I was going to die in the best possible way, in a frenzy of exultation. We fought hard, me to consummate the deed, she to stop it. She held onto my arms, tried forcing the knife away and out of my grip, but I'm a man, I was the stronger. I shook her off, quickly plunged the knife—off the mark, goddamn it! It pierced the palm of my open left hand, sliced all the way down from the base of my middle finger to the underside of my forearm as effortlessly as if my flesh was as yielding as a tender chicken breast. The pain was searing but I didn't care.

Before I could make a second incision she leveled me with a head butt to the face. I fell flat on my back and she jumped on me, the full weight of her body leaving me gasping. She held me down, forced the knife from my hand. I uttered what I thought were to be my final words: "Too late, my love, too late." Success!—I hadn't missed after all. The cut had gone deep, blood spurted from an artery, a wet warmth covered my left arm. Shelley saw, screamed, screamed again. Her third scream faded from my consciousness and was replaced by nothing. No dream, no nightmare, no thought, just absolute nothingness, as pure and as quiet and as cold and as dead as the emptiness between galaxies.

10: 15 A.M., Sunday, December 29th
Upon emerging from unconsciousness three afternoons ago I felt pain centered deep within my left palm. I looked down and saw a tight beige cloth bandage wrapped around my hand, wrist, and three inches of my forearm. I have been told I must keep these areas protected for a month, and should I take up the piano it will be for the right hand only.

Fortunately, my right hand is functional. It had been immobilized by an elaborate intravenous drip entry system stretching from a pink syringe jutting into the back of my palm all the way up to the elbow. Two pieces of surgical tape, one wrapped around my wrist and the other fastened halfway up my forearm, held the system of needles, tubes, and valves tightly in place. They removed it yesterday morning, a couple of hours before Shelley and Michael showed up. Yes, they arrived together. At one point, however, Shelley asked

Michael to leave. After he was gone she closed the door and approached me. With her head no more than a foot from mine she said, "You fucker. You crazy fucker! You did the one thing, the only thing that could have stopped me from killing myself."

"I couldn't let you die, at least not alone."

"And I couldn't allow you to join me. I had to save your worthless ass instead. How could you do that to me?"

I shrugged. "Better late than whatever. Why didn't you do yourself in after the ambulance came?"

"I had to make sure you'd survive. It was close for a while because you lost a bucketful of blood. And after, I don't know. The time wasn't right anymore. To kill myself midmorning seemed kind of gauche. Anyway, I needed to tell you in person what a prick you were to do what you did. You're a fucking misogynist pig, that's exactly what you are, you know that?"

I smiled, she didn't. Surprise. I hadn't expected a third perfect moment in this life.

8:45 P.M. Thursday, January 15th, 2009

It's lockdown at the Manoir, on the night of what was the brightest of day of the year. The landscape glistened pure white from yesterday's snowfall. Not a cloud was to be seen. The mercury in my little window thermometer spent the day tracing tiny oscillations around the minus twenty-five mark. Minus twenty-five is no big deal. At that level, one adds a few layers. But the wind chill crashed the readings down to the point where Messieurs Fahrenheit and Celsius say hello to each other. Best to stay indoors.

Here's a phrase the late George Carlin might have had fun with: *in person*. Shelley and Michael were *in person* with me this morning, right after breakfast. They are back to holding hands, and she has progressed four days into chemo, round four. We talked for half an hour, then they both went to work. She should be at home resting, not out at the library.

I haven't yet met my granddaughter *in person*, although I did see her yesterday. She's four days old. I whispered a few stupid things into her right ear, thanks to the miracle that is the internet. Renee Michelle Carla Laredo. My second Carla, not bad. This morning I told Shelley that children should not be named after living persons.

"What's the difference?" she said. "You'll be dead soon enough."

Like all babies, Renee is ugly as sin. She has the typical newborn squashed face, and she cries much of the time, always with both fists clenched tightly.

"Beautiful kid," I informed her perpetually beaming mother.

5:24 P.M. Sunday, January 18th

I attended church today. The sortie was prompted by an illusion, or an hallucination, arising from my morning's visit to the library. As on many Sundays, I settled in at the Findlay Room's easternmost table. I intended to start *Remembrance of Things Past* for a second time. The attempt would require my undivided attention. The sustainment of such a concentrated state was compromised a quarter of an hour later, however, when a woman looking like a Julia Roberts-Diane Lane cross—impossibly lovely, and impossible to keep my eyes averted from for more than a few seconds—arrived. She wheeled in a red-and-white perambulator resembling a miniature Ford Fairlane convertible. Its tiny passenger was enclosed in one of those puffy coats that makes you think its wearer might float away, like a balloon filled with helium. The coat was pink.

Despite the distraction I soldiered on, making progress until I tangled with one of Proust's longer grammatical constructions, a fifty-line sentence choked with semicolons. It began as follows:

But I had seen first one and then another of the rooms in which I had slept during my life...

I attempted it four times without success. I'd get two-thirds of the way through, then glance at the woman with a lost-in-thought expression designed to camouflage the ogle. Simultaneous with the commencement of my fourth try, her baby began crying.

Breakfast. Mom vroomed the carriage to a previously unoccupied nook between two tall stacks of shelves. The maneuver made her less visible to others in the room, but quite frontally exposed to anyone who might have been sitting in my seat, had such a person been inclined to turn his head ninety degrees to his right. Making matters worse was her maternal inexperience; the bawler must have been her first kid, as her mom hadn't yet acquired the knack more experienced mothers have for covering a breast without smothering the child.

I figured I'd get no reading done under the prevailing conditions, so I relocated to the reference room down the hall, a good eighty feet and a couple of walls away. I sat down, opened the Proust, and rebooted to the novel's first sentence:

For a long time I would go to bed early.

Alas, the baby renewed crying as soon as I reached the following passage, about six pages in:

and when I awoke at midnight, not knowing where I was, I
could not be sure at first who I was; I had only the most
rudimentary sense of existence, such as may lurk and flicker in
the depths of an animal's consciousness;

How could I have heard her from such a distance? Babies are known for their powerful vocal cords, but really, *that* powerful? I moved again, this time to a reading room on the other side of the hallway. I shut the door behind me and once again set myself up for the read. Blessed silence! Soon I had made it all the way to this passage, on page thirteen:

And to see her look displeased destroyed all the sense of tranquility she had brought me a moment before, when she bent her loving face down over my bed, and held it out to me like a Host—

Aarrghh. The walls might as well have been made of parchment, for the baby's cry assaulted my eardrums even more intensely than before. I got up, walked back to the Findlay Room.

Relax. I had no intention of giving Beautiful Mom a piece of my mind, which I could have done politely yet phrased so witheringly that my words would have compelled her and her infernal daughter to leave the building. No, my curiosity was fuelled by something else—a sense of disconnection, or of events scheduled out of kilter, like a clock broken because time itself had become passé.

When I had approached to within fifteen feet of their hideaway nook, the crying ceased. I took a few more steps, peered in, and was beyond surprised to see some kid with buck teeth typing away on his Vaio. There was no baby, no mother, no perambulator.

I took a taxi to the St. Joseph Oratory. I'm not Catholic. In fact I'm not religious at all. In my working days I considered myself the Faculty's closet atheist. I classified myself as archaeologist, linguist, historian, and sociologist, not as a believer in the childish fairy tales beloved by some of my colleagues. But today was a Sunday, after all, and a cup of chamomile wouldn't cut through the gobsmackery that had just leveled me. I needed some serious despooking from a human, so I reasoned it out as follows: why not give a priest a shot? I'll confess, and who knows, maybe he'll sprinkle a little of that holy water my way. Guilt will exit my body wispwise, evaporating like steamy little beaver tails into the ether. Or he'll write me out a prescription: execute fifty Hail Marys, reflect seriously, vow never to bludgeon any more babies—and oh, leave a free will offering commensurate with the enormity of the benefit received. Give next month too. Congratulations! No longer will visions of little Amy screw up the old nervous system.

I climbed a hundred steps, entered, said aloud to myself, "Now what?" The Oratory has confessionals in most of its venues, but I doubted they'd all be staffed. Fortunately, I spotted a young man manning an information booth. He directed me to the Crypt Church, told me it's the place for confessing in English. I entered from the rear and immediately spotted two confessionals, snug up against opposite walls.

I walked toward the one to my left. It looked like a tripartite boxcar. Heavy dark doors encased in massive wooden frames defined both outer sections, the entryways for sinners. Its middle portion was obscured by a large pane of smoked glass. I couldn't see anything through it other than the yellow glow from a standing lamp.

The Crypt had been packed, as I had cleverly timed my arrival to coincide with the conclusion of the Mass in English. Droves of worshippers filed past me. Three sauntered over to the confessional. Two were unremarkable middle-aged men, and the third was a young woman wearing a full-length winter coat and white boots with high heels. They all carried shopping bags, two from Metro and one from a fruit and vegetable store. By the time the last of the three had been absolved of their sins, only seven or eight isolates remained in the Crypt. We were positioned as far apart from each other as possible, like a gathering of alleycats. I was beginning to feel self-conscious, even though I sat nowhere near the confessional. I wanted to leave.

So, how did I manage to work up the nerve to enter the confessional? Easy. I pretended I was going to the bathroom. A confessional is a spiritual bathroom, after all, and I needed to take a spiritual leak. I would piss away my big sin, then exit feeling so much more comfortable than before. I kept that goal in mind, not the process, which is exactly the attitude I had proposed Shelley adopt toward her chemotherapy.

I closed the door, knelt on the pad, and breathed in stale air. It took me a few seconds to adjust to the dimness, as the only source of light came heavily filtered through a grille separating me from the priestly chamber to my right.

We exchanged no words for half a minute, and then the priest cleared his throat.

"Hello," I said.

"My son, has it been so long since your last confession that you've forgotten how to begin?"

His voice surprised me. I was expecting Gregory Peck or James Earl Jones. Instead, I got Truman Capote. That's right, my priest possessed a high-pitched voice jam-packed with nasality. And yes, he even lisped a little.

"I've never gone to confession before."

"How old are you?" Jesus, he sounded like a girl.

"Eighty-three."

"Never?"

"Look Father, I know I'm laden with sins, but there's this one that's far worse than the others. It's definitely in the mortal category."

"Before you say anything more, my son, please repeat after me: In the name of the Father, and of the Son, and of the Holy Spirit, I confess for the first time."

I did as he asked.

"Now we may proceed. Let God hear your sin."

"I was responsible for the death of a child. A baby, actually. She was less than a year old."

"How long ago did this happen?"

"Very long ago, Father. Decades."

"How old were you?"

"What difference would it make? Had I never been born, this

baby would have lived."

"But why are you confessing your sin now?"

"I learned the truth of it only recently, and earlier today that truth caused me to hallucinate. I need to be absolved before my sin drives me crazy."

"It's not that easy. Are you prepared to consider your actions? To weigh its impact?"

"I've been doing that quite a bit already."

"But not sufficiently enough, it seems."

"Father, how should I proceed?"

"Set aside some time early in the morning and late at night for reflection."

"To do what, exactly?"

"To repent, and to determine your penance. As you focus ever more deeply on the consequences of your actions, you will come to realize what you must do. And as your repentance deepens, God will find you more and more worthy of absolution."

"Thank you, Father. But is there anything else I can do?"

"Yes. Pray to the Virgin for forgiveness every evening. And remember that God is merciful. He absolves you of this terrible sin."

The priest then recited the Rite of Penance. I thanked him for it.

"You are welcome. Oh, and I hope that you don't wait another eighty-four years for your next confession."

"Eighty-three."

"Yes of course, eighty-three."

"Father, am I allowed to make a suggestion?"

"Certainly."

"Thank you, and please understand—I offer it in sincerest humility."

"Go ahead."

"This confessional should be disinfected. The smell in here is pretty raw, and with people coming in all the time, some of whom may have colds or the flu, it seems like a good idea to me. It would be ironic if someone caught his death here, right after unloading his sins, eh?"

He actually laughed. Then he said, "Thank you, my son. I will consider your idea seriously."

Consider? Why the fuck couldn't he have said he would do it?

I exited the Oratory feeling no different from when I had entered. What had I expected? A little warmth? Understanding? Some empathy?

It was snowing heavily by the time I returned to the Manoir, frigidly cold as well. As I was about to enter the building, I noticed an unmoving figure sitting on my bench. He wore a heavy parka with a huge hood, big boots, and thick black gloves. Why would anyone sit out there in a snowstorm? I walked over to get a better look.

It was Ralph. Yes, Ralph Hendrickson, he of the drifting mind. I sat down next to him.

"Ralph, what in holy hell are you doing out here? It's minus ten, and with the breeze thrown in, minus twenty tops. You want to freeze to death?"

He looked at me, and that's when I saw that he had been crying. Imagine that, the big old geezer all swollen up and wet around the eyes.

He said nothing, just waved me off.

"Come on, buddy. What happened?"

Silence.

"I'm not leaving until you tell me."

"Go away."

"What's wrong?"

"Leave me alone."

"No way. Now tell me."

The fucker just sat there, didn't speak and didn't move for a solid minute, so I elbowed him in the ribs as hard as I could. Almost knocked him in the snow.

"Ow!"

"Say something, you cretin!"

Damn, he started sobbing. Ralph Hendrickson, king of Manoir Westmount, reduced to a blubbering mess.

"Sorry, I didn't mean that. It's just that whatever's bugging you can't be good." *Can't be good?* Good thing I never became a life counselor.

"You can't know."

"I can take that at least two ways. I choose the second. Now tell me. Come on, just a little."

He sniffled again.

"Ralph, what in holy hell is wrong with you?"

"The problem is you're right to call me a cretin. I am a cretin."

"What happened?"

"Just let me be."

"Nope. Count on the opposite. Now come on, let it go."

"Robbie…"

His son. "Robbie what?"

"He and the family came visiting."

"So?"

"First time in a month. Maybe longer, I don't know. Anyway, we had lunch. I asked my daughter-in-law a question about something or other, but I couldn't address her by name because I didn't remember it. She's been married to Robbie for a long time. Over twenty years, I think, though I could be wrong about that too."

"And then what?"

"Their kid told me her Mom's name, and immediately I forgot it. I stumbled and fumbled, made a fool of myself. And damn, I still can't recall it."

"Do you like her?"

"Never, not even from the beginning. She's a bitch, has been nothing but trouble, but my Robbie adores her."

"Then forget about it. You repressed rather than forgot it. And take heart that you remembered why you were embarrassed. That shows you've got some marbles remaining, right?"

"One day they'll all be gone."

At that instant it occurred to me that I might as well fess up to old Ralphie boy, right there on the bench with the snow vortexing around us. Ralph Hendrickson, Father Confessor *par excellence*. No way would he be able to breach my confidence.

"One day we'll all be dead. Hey I just came back from church."

"You? Really? I never thought of you as the religious type."

"I'm not. I'm not even Catholic. But I have an issue, and I wanted to work it out in Confession. Imagine that."

"What issue?"

"When I was two years old I killed a baby."

"No kidding. Really?"

"'No kidding.' What a response. You know, I'm beginning to think you're right. You really *are* a cretin. Would I make up something like that? It doesn't exactly put me in a flattering light."

"Was it accidental?"

"Nope. It wasn't premeditated, but I meant to do it, to the depths of my soul I did."

"But why? Why kill a defenseless baby?"

"Well now, that's the crazy part. I saw this woman humping my father, and I misinterpreted what was happening on a grand scale. I thought she was beating the shit out of him and that she was going to do me in similarly. The only way I could imagine stopping her was to hurt her baby as hard as she was hurting my pop."

"That's not logical."

"Not logical. Ha ha! Not logical, not fucking logical!"

I laughed, couldn't stop. Ralph looked at me in amazement, then shouted at the top of his lungs, "Not fucking logical!" Now we both couldn't stop. Yep, there we were, two old guys sitting on a rickety bench, laughing and shouting, "Not fucking logical!" over and over into a blinding snowstorm.

After a couple of minutes of this insanity I put my arm around Ralph and said, "Come on old buddy. Time to go inside lest we forget where the dining room is." And so we did.

6:27 A.M. Friday, January 23rd
Surely the most exquisite verse in the entire Old Testament, the deepest, the one that unlocks the mystery, is the second:

> Now the earth was unformed and void, and darkness was upon the face of the deep; and the spirit of God hovered over the face of the waters.

I would like to believe that Lyle Meblenny intuited its meaning as he plummeted from the Golden Gate Bridge. Let's give him the benefit of the doubt. Surely he figured it out during those last two or three seconds before his head exploded from its collision with water made hard as brick due to the speed of gravity. Meblenny of all people, the only writer on the planet with insight enough to animate the lowly prokaryote—he deserved to know.

Where is God? you ask. God is within you. No, you are not God. God cannot be prayed to, and it is nonsensical to imagine that God can help out at all. For God, the Prime Evolutionary Mover, the Divine Creator, the one and only Master Builder and the root cause of everything beautiful and ugly, amounts to nothing more nor less than the collective unconscious of bacteria, quadrillions of them raised to the quadrillionth power. For fifteen hundred million years microbes ruled the world; there were no others. And then something inevitable—not miraculous, just unstoppable and monumental beyond imagining—occurred. No sentient beings, no matter how intelligent, would have noticed. They would have overlooked the pale green foams permeating the oceans, the microscopic vibrations, the release of a few precious oxygen molecules into the atmosphere per second, every second, across the eons.

My fingers quiver.

Acknowledgments

I am indebted to Varley O'Connor, who read multiple versions of *The View North from Liberal Cemetery* and provided me with crucial advice, criticism, and support concerning all facets of novel writing.

Ted Thompson's input was critical, particularly with regard to character development and motivation. I am also grateful to Doug Kiklowicz for an extensive critique that included many helpful suggestions.

I attended the Squaw Valley Community of Writers Workshop in 2012, had a great time, and was the recipient of important criticism from my workshop leader, Max Byrd, and eleven very supportive and insightful group members. Thanks to you all. Thanks also to Glen David Gold for advising me on the opening of my novel, and for suggesting a number of instructive novels to read.

I am also very appreciative for the support, comments, and criticism from the following people, who graciously agreed to read all or part of my novel over the past seven years: Emanuel Chicoine, Peggy Codding, Alice-Ann Darrow, Rita Dolzan, Patricia Flowers, Lawren Freebody, Fern Lindzon, Roseanne Rosenthal, Peter Schubert, Wendy Sims, Emilie Wapnick, and Emely Weissman.

Thanks to Judy Brown and Jennifer Dewey, of the Denver Public Library, and to the late John Cook, also of Denver; to Lidia Hook-Gray, Liberal's most prominent amateur historian; Cynthia Sallaska, Seward County (Kansas) Register of Deeds at the time of my visit to Liberal in 2008; Gene Sharp, a 1947 graduate of Liberal High School and Liberal lawyer, who was kind enough to reminisce about the old Liberal courthouse; and Pastor Dave (sorry, I don't know your last name), who showed me around the abandoned and pigeon-infested old Liberal High School.

Thanks also to Tom Thompson, director of Manoir Westmount,

who took time out from his busy schedule to show me around the Manoir; and to Geoffrey Douglas Madge, who provided me with information concerning his performance of *Opus Clavicembalisticum* in Chicago back in 1983.

The beautiful book cover was designed by 2Faced Design. I am fortunate to have it gracing my novel.

Finally, thanks to Dr. Harshan Lamabadusuriya for medical information, and to my doctor, Dr. Celia Nattel, for additional information and for keeping me healthy.

Made in the USA
Middletown, DE
07 December 2014